THE TEMPTATION OF DESTINY

A "CALL OF DESTINY" NOVEL
BY

D.M. EARLEY

Editor: Lane Diamond
Cover Artist: Samuel Keiser
Interior Designer: Lane Diamond

EVOLVED PUBLISHING™

www.EvolvedPub.com
Evolved Publishing LLC
Butler, Wisconsin, USA

Printed in Book Antiqua font.

DEDICATION

To my wife Lorri, family, and friends that encouraged me to take an idea and run with it.

PART ONE

DAKOTA

CHAPTER 1
CROSSROADS

Dakota opened her eyes and looked around the familiar room. Indian dolls she'd played with as a young girl sat atop the dressers, and pictures from her birth to graduation from law school just one week earlier adorned three walls. The fourth wall displayed every fitness magazine cover she'd appeared on.

The room told the story of her twenty-six years of life.

She smiled as her eyes panned every nook and cranny, all of which contained some memento from one of the magical summers she spent here. She reminisced, as the collection captured her fondest memories of Wind River. She remembered rushing to bring her "treasures" home, knowing they would be displayed forever, as if in a museum dedicated to her.

She sighed contentedly at her special place, a comfortable place. She always thought if a room could hug her, this one would.

The smell of fresh coffee and bacon reached her from downstairs, pulling her from her reverie. She snuggled one last time with the thick old comforter that had kept her warm on so many crisp Wyoming nights. Today would mark the beginning of the next chapter of her life, one she had dreamed about for as long as she could remember.

She opened the door to her bedroom and looked out over the balcony. The log rafters, floors, and walls gave off a warm glow as the sun's rays washed over them.

"Lomasi, good morning," her grandmother said, looking up from the kitchen.

"Neiwoo!" Dakota offered a wide smile as she raced down the stairs.

The two women hugged.

As they pulled away, her grandmother reached out and stroked her hair. "My beautiful blossom, how did you sleep?"

"Like a log, Grandma. Where's Woo Woo?"

As a young girl, Dakota could not pronounce Nebesiiwoo, the Arapaho word for grandfather, and so she called him Woo Woo. It stuck to this day.

Her grandmother nodded toward the barn. "He is down tending to the horses. He wants to go for a ride up the canyon later today. There is a family of grizzlies he has been watching. He knows how much you love them."

"Oh, that's awesome. I can get pictures for my place when I find one."

"You know your grandfather and I would love it if you lived with us. He has counted the days for the past year, waiting for you."

"I know he has, Grandma. He told me every time I talked to him. I promise to stay at least for the summer. I've missed being here over the past four years. Between law school and my fitness modeling, I had no time for myself, but it was worth it. Now I'm back in Wind River, and here to stay."

Dakota hugged her grandmother and headed for the front door. "I'll run down to the barn to get Woo Woo. We can have breakfast together and get caught up. I arrived so late last night, we didn't have a chance to talk."

"He will love that, dear. He paced all morning but did not want to wake you."

Dakota stepped onto the front porch and looked out over the property. A brilliant carpet of summer wildflowers covered the rolling grasslands, which seemed to go on for miles. Where the fields ended, they give way to canyon walls painted with hues only nature could create. Beyond the canyons, the mountains rose, their faces painted by dark green alpine forests dotted with rushes of lighter green Aspens. The forests stopped abruptly, as if an invisible line existed. Rugged stone faces and snow-capped peaks touched the sky.

Dakota always said that a piece of Heaven had fallen to Earth here.

She looked towards the barn, where her grandfather led a horse into the corral, and promptly jumped off the porch and sprinted down the dirt road.

"Woo Woo," she yelled, closing the gap between the house and the barn.

Jim looked up, smiled, and headed for the road to meet her.

Dakota jumped up and hugged him, wrapping her legs around him the way she had as a little girl.

Jim stood firm against the impact. His imposing stature reinforced her dreams that he had been a great Arapaho warrior in past lives.

"Lomasi, the sun shines again on my life." His eyes welled up with tears of joy. "I have missed you so much. She represented everything good and innocent to him in a world he felt has lost its way.

"I have a special ride for us today, Lomasi."

"I know, Neiwoo told me."

He shook his head and laughed. "That old woman, she cannot keep a secret."

"Come, Woo Woo, let's eat and get caught up." She grabbed his hand and turned him towards the house, pulling him playfully, just as she did when she was young.

The three sat at the kitchen table for a couple hours catching up on the past four years. They talked about Dakota's parents, and the possibility of them moving back to Wind River after retirement. They discussed Dakota's new job on the legal team of the Tribal Council, and her position with Jim's law firm in Dubois.

A familiar sound from the living room interrupted their visit. "After all these years, I still love hearing that old cuckoo clock," Dakota said. "Woo Woo, what time do you want to ride today?"

"Whenever you are ready, Lomasi."

"Okay, I want to go for a run up to the Sacred Waterfall. It should only take around an hour and a half. I'll grab a quick shower and we can leave. How does noon sound?"

"Noon is perfect. Make sure you take bear spray," Jim cautioned. "The bears and wolves both have young with them,"

"Yes, sir, I will." She left the table.

Dakota came down stairs a few minutes later in her running gear. The spandex orange and black shorts, and matching bra top, complimented her sculpted body.

"Dakota Sky Reynolds, where are your clothes?" her grandma teased.

"Neiwoo, maybe the Sacred Falls will bless me with a great warrior husband. If I run into him on the trail, I want to impress him." She smiled and winked.

"The only great warriors you will see up there are the ones painted on the cave walls. Be careful. You have your spray and phone right?"

"Yes ma'am."

She hugged her grandparents and left.

Dakota ran along the edge of the grasslands and into the canyons, following an ancient trail that her ancestors had forged thousands of years ago. Despite its age, the path remained clear.

Her grandfather owned a good part of the lower canyon pass, and maintained the trail to host important clients on horseback riding trips.

She meandered through the canyons marveling at the majesty surrounding her. The sun-kissed tan rocks were painted with pastel colors alternating between shades of yellows, reds, whites, and pinks that no artist's brush strokes could ever capture. In spots, the canyon walls towered nearly 2000 feet. She imagined Arapaho braves standing on the canyon tops looking out over their land, guarding against other tribes, and watching for herds of Buffalo and Elk. Despite its seclusion, Dakota never felt afraid here. She believed the Spirits of her ancestors walked with her, protecting her in this magical place.

The pass made a sharp right turn, and she saw a familiar outcropping perched to the left, which marked the trailhead to the Sacred Waterfall. Arapaho called them Heetcenise' Beebeihit, Waterfall of Virgins. Her grandmother had told her the story of the falls when Dakota was young. Indian maidens traveled for miles to swim here, believing the Spirit of the Water would bless them with a strong warrior husband. Brides–to-be cleansed themselves in a final ceremonial bath on their wedding day. The ritual beckoned the Spirit to bless them with many healthy children, but once they gave their "special gift" to their husbands, they could never step foot in this sacred water again, as only virgins could swim here. Those no longer pure would suffer the curse of infertility by the Spirit.

The path to the waterfall winded along a cliff edge. In spots, a wrong move could lead to a shear drop to the canyon below. Given the state of the overgrown trail, it appeared she might have been the last person here, five summers ago. The grass growing across the trail covered loose rocks under foot, and the morning dew made the exposed smooth stones slippery. No matter, for Dakota knew the way to the waterfall like the back of her hand. With a little effort, and some precarious climbing, she soon heard the music of water splashing into the sacred pool.

The waterfall sat like an oasis in the middle of the woods. It cascaded ten feet over dark- green, moss-covered rocks, into the crystal-clear pool below. Tall ferns and leafy laurels outlined the water's edge at its widest and deepest parts. Where the pool emptied into the stream, large flat rocks lay strewn about. Dakota always felt the Spirit had provided them for the girls to lie on after swimming in the cool water, so they could bask in the warmth of the high-altitude sunlight.

She walked to the mouth of the pool and removed her clothes. Sweat glistened on her tanned body as the sun shined on her through the canopy, and her dark hair glowed with an incandescent hue. She stood natural in front of the pool, as many girls had over millenna, and after ambling waist-deep into the cool water, shivered. She dove forward and down into the depths of the pool, and swam to the waterfall. In the waist-deep water, she allowed the gentle cascade to fall on her from above, and felt the peace.

Her grandmother said the Spirit of the Water lives in the waterfall.

She leaned her head back, allowing the sacred water to hit her face and move down the front of her body. It flowed over her breasts and trickled down her pubic area, causing her to shudder as she became aroused. Her stomach tightened with each kiss of the water on her "special gift."

Dakota dove back into the clear pool and swam to the front. She stepped out of the stream and sat on one of the flat rocks. The sensation first of the cool water, and now the warmth from the stone, on her "special gift" overwhelmed her. She laid back and moved her hands in circles over her breasts and erect nipples, past her stomach, and between her legs. She closed her eyes and let the Spirit of the Water possess her, and arched her lower back. Her breathing quickened as she fantasized about the warrior husband that awaited her.

She stood up a few minutes later, her heart racing and body dripping with sweat, and dove back into the refreshing water. After cooling down, she swam to the front of the pool and stood knee deep in the water.

She looked upward, closed her eyes, raised her arms at her sides to shoulder level, and slowly spun to connect to everything that surrounded her.

"Hohou Hii3tone3en Cei3woono Neci," she whispered, thanking the Spirit of the Water.

Dakota left the Sacred Falls rejuvenated. Excited to go on the trail ride with her grandfather, she quickened her pace to reach the ranch sooner.

Anna sat on the front porch enjoying the warm summer sun. "Lomasi, how was your run?"

"It was great, Neiwoo."

"And did you swim?"

"Yes, the water felt awesome."

"Perhaps now you're here for good, the Spirit will bless you with a great warrior?"

"Sadly, I have had little success on the relationship side."

"Honey, you are beautiful inside and out. I do not know how any man would not want to be with you?"

"All the guys in college just wanted a party girl. The men in the fitness world just wanted sex to feed their egos. The few nice guys I dated for a while would break things off because I wanted to save my 'special gift' for my husband. I might be the only virgin over twenty years old in 2017!"

"Well, after looking at the guys in your photo shoots, that had to be hard," Anna said, fanning herself.

Dakota blushed. "Neiwoo?"

"Honey, I might be older, but I'm not dead."

The two shared a laugh only women could understand.

Dakota spun. "Here comes Woo Woo. Let me jump in the shower."

Jim walked up on the porch and sat down in the rocking chair next to his wife. She had a tall glass of ice tea and a sandwich waiting for him, as she did every day at noon.

"Lomasi is taking a quick shower," Anna said. "She should be down soon."

"Good, I have the horses ready." He looked at his watch. "She is so punctual—almost noon, as planned. Dakota will be a nice addition to the practice. It will need someone regimented like me to remain successful when I retire."

"Yes, she is just like you. Sometimes it drives me crazy." Anna smiled and patted the topside of his hand.

"Twenty years in the Army will do that, I guess."

She rubbed his shoulder. "That was thirty years ago, Old Man. I would have thought you would have mellowed by now."

"Woo Woo, are we ready?" Dakota said, opening the front door.

"Lomasi, do you want a sandwich before you leave?"

"No thanks, Neiwoo. I had a protein drink and will take granola bars with me." Dakota hurried to the hitching post to ready her horse.

"Regimented," Jim said, winking at Anna as he walked away to catch up with Dakota.

Jim and Dakota mounted their horses and headed to the trail behind the house. The first part of the path climbed steadily over a rush of loose rocks, where sparse, low-growing shrubs and pines created constant obstacles.

"Dakota, watch for rattlesnakes," her grandfather said. "They will be out sunning themselves. The sound of the horse's hooves on the rocks should scare them away, but as you know, they can be stubborn."

"I will, Woo Woo. What trail are we using on the ridge top?"

"We will follow the Dead Mountain trail, past the Noohoonxoehtiit Biito'owu, and then across the top of Eagle Canyon. I have seen the grizzlies up there."

"I never like passing the burial ground. I always feel like I'm being watched up there," Dakota whined.

Woo Woo looked over at her and chuckled. "Do not fear our dead ancestors. The live ones are our worries."

They continued the ride, talking about the history and ancient myths of areas they passed. Despite Dakota's having heard these stories many times, it never got old listening to her grandfather tell them. He was well spoken, with a distinctive American Indian accent. His deep voice and calm, steady tone made for the perfect storytelling voice.

As they reached the rim of Eagle Canyon, Woo Woo stopped his horse and dismounted. He grabbed his binoculars and panned ahead of them. "I do not see them yet, Lomasi, but I do not want to get up on them. An angry grizzly mom and her cubs is not something we want to encounter." He lowered his binoculars.

Dakota dismounted her horse and stood next to him, and they gazed out over the canyon valley. "It's so beautiful, Woo Woo. I'm so glad to be back here with Neiwoo and you."

"Dakota, I am glad you choose the path you did. I have had many good offers to sell the firm, but when you entered law school, I decided to hold on to it. When you are ready, I will pass it to you. I am tired. It is time for your grandmother and me to walk the final part of our journey."

"Grandfather, please, don't talk like that. You and Grandma will be around for a long time. I want one day for my children to know both of you, to learn from you as I did."

Dakota's eyes filled up with tears. Rarely did she call him "grandfather," and only in the most serious moments, or in social settings that required formal speech.

"Lomasi, do not get upset. We both plan on being around a long time." He pulled her close and hugged her.

They stood silent with their arms around each other's waists, gazing over the canyons. Dakota knew one day her fairytale here would end, but for now, she wanted to live in this magical land filled with romantic tales of beautiful Indian maidens and brave warriors.

"There they are," he whispered, breaking the silence.

"Where, Woo Woo?"

"Look at the small outcropping on the edge of the canyon, about one hundred yards out, just to the left. I saw the mother go up on her hind legs to survey the area. There she is again."

"I see her. Okay, let me grab my camera. I'll creep up the hillside and hopefully get a better shot."

Dakota moved into position and snapped picture after picture, capturing the mother and two cubs. The mother bear sprung up on her hind legs and lifted her nose into the wind.

"Dakota, let's get back on the horses. She either winded *us* or a male grizzly. She is in defense mode, and can close the gap on us quickly. I do not want to be forced to shoot her and leave the cubs orphaned. They would not live for more than a few days on their own."

The two mounted their horses and retreated, opening a distance between the bears and themselves. Her grandfather turned often, and looked with his binoculars to make sure the sow stayed with her cubs.

"Woo Woo, that was awesome!" Dakota said. "I got great shots of her and the cubs. I can't wait to show Neiwoo."

He smiled. "Just like when you were a little girl, always bringing home treasures from your adventures. I am sure she will have a collage of bear pictures on your wall by the end of the week."

He loved Dakota's child-like excitement. At the end of the summer, when she began her new career wading through the muck of humanity, he knew it would disappear forever. For the next two months, however, he would cherish every minute of it.

"Lomasi, I saw on the news this morning that the Aurora will be visible tonight."

"Our Ancestors' Spirits will dance in the sky tonight," she replied.

"You forget none of the ancient beliefs, do you?"

"Nope, I love them. Let's go watch the lights at Wolf Flats tonight, Woo Woo."

"I cannot this time, Lomasi. I have an early court date and need to be in the office at 7:00 tomorrow to meet my client. With the summer sun, it will be around 10:00 tonight before it's dark enough to watch the lights. I will be asleep by then."

"Okay, we'll watch them together the next time."

They traveled a different route home, arriving back at the west side of the ranch, riding leisurely through the sagebrush as they talked about the day's ride.

"Race you to the corral," Dakota challenged.

Jim looked at her and paused for a second.

"Getty up!" He closed his legs on his horse and slapped the reigns down on his back. The horse broke fast, jumping out ahead of her.

"Hey, no fair," Dakota yelled.

The two horses thundered across the fields. Anna must have heard from the kitchen, because she stepped out onto the front porch to watch the race finish at the entrance to the corral.

"You got me, cowgirl," Jim said.

"Yeah, and you tried to cheat, Woo Woo."

When Dakota was young, Jim would always let her win, but as she got older, he wanted her to know defeat. Now, Dakota's competitive nature had made her such a good rider, Jim couldn't beat her anymore.

Anna finished watching the race and returned to the kitchen. She smiled, knowing Jim was in a happy place. The sunshine of his life had returned for good. She knew that, with Dakota now living here, he would reduce his work at the firm and enjoy more of the life for which he and Anna had worked so long and hard for.

Dakota walked up to the front porch and opened the screen door. "Neiwoo, that smells awesome! What are you cooking?"

"Rattlesnake fritters and possum pie."

"*Yuk!*"

"I am kidding. It is chicken breasts with sage. Jalapeno cornbread is in the oven."

"Mmmm, I love your cornbread." She inhaled deeply. "Woo Woo said the Spirits will dance in the sky tonight. I'm going to Wolf Flats to watch them. Do you want to go?"

"I would love to, but I have to help your grandfather tonight with his case tomorrow. Your grandfather is so glad you are here,

Dakota. He has lost his zest for the legal world. It is time for him to walk away."

"I know, Neiwoo. We talked about it for a bit on the ride today. He said you guys are ready for the 'Final part of your journey.'" Dakota made air quotes.

Anna rolled her eyes. "God, he is soooo dramatic. But that is what makes him so dynamic in the court room."

Dakota's grandfather joined the two women for dinner. "Anna, once again you outdid yourself. That was delicious," he said, pushing away from the table.

Dakota smiled and nodded. "I agree, Neiwoo. I'm stuffed. I need a good run tonight."

"Dakota, two runs in one day?"

"Every day when I can, Neiwoo. The morning run is hard and fast, evening is slower but longer. It hits two different muscle fibers."

Woo Woo looked concerned. "Where are you running tonight? Remember, all the animals have young ones with them."

"I'll park at our gate and run the Hangman's Bridge loop. That should put me back at the ranch by dark. Then I'll hop in the car and head out to Wolf Flats for the lights."

Woo Woo nodded. "That's about six miles. You better get going if you are going to make it back to the gate by dark."

"Yep, I'll change and get going."

Dakota ran upstairs, changed in a flash, then hustled back downstairs and headed for the door.

"It's gonna get too chilly for those skimpy clothes," Neiwoo said.

"I know, Neiwoo. I have a set of sweats in my car for tonight on the Flats."

"Don't forget your bear spray," Woo Woo added.

"Got it!"

"Okay, be careful, and enjoy the lights," Neiwoo said.

"I will. See you around eleven. Love you both." Dakota closed the door behind her.

She drove to the gate and parked her car on the ranch side, so she could leave the gate locked. This time of the year, tourists sometimes made the wrong turn and drove onto the property, despite the many *No Trespassing* signs.

After the first mile, she came to Dingmans Crossroads. To the left or straight would be a five-mile circle. She paused for a second to choose which part of the loop she wanted to run. If she went straight, her run finished uphill; left, her run finished on a flatter incline. She chose the easier end of the run, and turned left.

She came to a right-hand turn to start her way back, looked down at her watch, and knew she was halfway through the five miles. She ran at a good pace and would hit the crossroads at dusk. She would run the final one mile to the gate under a closed canopy, it would be a dark but familiar run. She touched her bear spray for reassurance, though it had been years since she'd seen a grizzly on that road. When the Reservation opened more access to public travel, the bears moved farther back into the canyons. Still, the possibility existed of running into a stray wolf or mountain lion.

After about a quarter mile, she heard a car coming up behind her, and she moved to the right of the road to let it pass. A quick 'whoop' of a siren startled her.

"Ma'am, put some clothes on! You are distracting the drivers," came over a loud speaker.

She knew the voice, and stopped to turn around and look at the police cruiser.

A tall, good-looking officer got out of the car.

She ran and jumped in his arms, giving him a big hug. "Jimmy Red Cloud, you scared the shit out of me!" She lowered herself back down and punched him in the shoulder. "How are you?"

"I'm good, Dakota. Your grandfather said you were coming into town soon. When did you get here?"

"Late last night."

"Well, nice of you to call all of us. You didn't even post anything specific on your Facebook, just 'See you soon, Wind River.'"

"I know. I wanted to surprise you all tomorrow at the park. I knew everyone would be there for the concert."

"We will, but since you're gonna be my boss, I can't fraternize with you."

"Jimmy, I will only work with the Council on property law, not criminal."

"I know. I was just teasing you."

Dakota straightened Jimmy's badge. "Officer, what are you doing out in these neck of the woods, besides scaring me?"

"A camper up near Serenity Lake claims Bigfoot tore up their camp area and is circling them." Jimmy rolled his eyes. "You know it's a bear, so I'll make sure they have spray and give them my sermon on bear-proofing their camp area."

"It's that season. Well, you go save the day, and I'm gonna finish my run before it gets dark. And hey, tell no one you saw me. Let me surprise them tomorrow."

"Deal... and Dakota... welcome home."

"Thanks, Jimmy, it's good to be back. See you tomorrow night."

Dakota watched him pull away. Jimmy was the first boy she ever had a crush on. She believed that if she'd lived here, they would have been a couple. He was a football star in high school, earning a full scholarship to the University of Miami. It appeared he was heading to the pros, but in his final college game, he tore up his knee, and his career ended. Fortunately, her grandfather had counseled him on getting a disability insurance policy, protecting future pro earnings, and Jimmy left college with close to two million dollars. Not nearly what he could have earned in the NFL, but a nice way to start his adult life. From what her grandfather had told her, Jimmy had invested the money and was doing well. The police officer job allowed him to give back to the Reservation that supported him.

He'd remained single, a point Neiwoo mentioned every time his name came up in conversation. As Dakota thought about her quick visit with Jimmy, she was glad she chose the route she did. Had she gone the other direction, she may have missed him.

Perhaps the Spirit of the Water guided me?

A smile crossed her face.

She saw her next right turn coming up. From there it would be a straight level run to the crossroads and then the gate. She looked at her time. Her visit with Jimmy had put her behind schedule, so she picked up her pace.

As she approached the intersection, a silver pickup truck drifted towards the stop sign from the opposite direction. She turned right without stopping.

The truck pulled up alongside her and slowed to her pace. She heard the passenger window roll down.

"Excuse me, Ma'am," a deep voice with a heavy western accent called out.

Dakota looked over, quickly noticing the man had Hollywood good looks. His blond hair, piercing blue eyes and chiseled features caught her off guard.

"Hi, can I help you?" she said, still running.

"We seem to be lost."

Dakota stopped. She kept her distance, but could see three men in the truck. Glancing past the passenger for a second, she noticed the driver's dark hair, blue eyes, and handsome looks.

These guys could be brothers.

"Where are you trying to go?"

"Hangman's Bridge Campground," the passenger said, lifting a road map.

Dakota could not help notice the muscles in his shoulders and arms flex in his sleeveless shirt. "You're close. About two miles up the road will be an intersection. Turn left, and the bridge will be about a mile up the road. After that, you'll see signs for the campground."

"Might I be so lucky that you're staying there also?" He smiled.

She subconsciously brushed her hair away from her face. "No, I live right down the road."

"Well, I just moved here. I'm staying in the cabins till Monday, when my apartment is ready. I hear there's a concert tomorrow in town. Maybe we'll run into each other again?"

Between his good looks and western charm, Dakota found herself a bit interested, and smiled. "Perhaps we will."

"Thank you for stopping your run. Much obliged." The stranger tilted his cowboy hat at her, and rolled up the window as the truck pulled away.

Damn! First Jimmy, then Hollywood. I need to swim more often in the Sacred Falls.

She looked at her watch and up at the sky, and picked up her pace.

She reached Dingmans Crossing ten minutes behind schedule, as dusk gave way to the night, and started her last stretch. The canopy blocked the last bit of remaining light. In spots, she could catch the glow of her grandparents' home on top of the ridge, shining like a beacon in the night.

She started down the last dip in the road. After one small hill, she would be a couple hundred yards from her car. The muscles in her legs burned, as her body had not completely acclimated to the altitude yet. She slowed her pace, and suddenly, a set of car lights caught her in the eyes from the side of the road. She figured someone must have come up to her grandfather's gate and turned around.

The vehicle pulled out, stopped in the middle of the road, and two figures got out of the truck. The headlights blinded her, so she put her hand up to shield her eyes. As the figures continued walking towards her, she used her other hand to grip the bear spray.

She maintained her composure. "Can I help you?"

Dakota knew the woods well here. The river flowed beneath the concrete bridge she just crossed. To the right, just a few yards ahead, was the old logging road that connected to the Continental Divide Trail.

The strangers continued to move forward without saying a word.

She broke for the logging road, but a sharp tug on her hair stopped her dead, jerking her backwards.

A hand came up over her mouth. "Don't say a word, bitch, or I will cut you ear to ear," a voice whispered in her right ear as a knife waved in front of her face. The knife vanished as he reached down and pried the bear spray out of her hand.

She could now see one man as he walked out of the glare of the headlights. He wore a Lone Ranger style mask. He reached up and threw a hood over her head. The man in the back of her zip tied both her hands. They pushed her forward towards the vehicle, and finally into the back seat of the truck. She felt the truck pull forward and up an incline onto a rocky road. They were on her escape route.

What do they want? Am I being kidnapped? Is someone paying back my grandfather?

Her mind raced as she tried to maintain her composure. She knew this road like the back of her hand and, if given a chance, she would make a break for it. If they didn't hold her at gunpoint, she believed she could defend herself and outrun these men, escaping into the protection of the woods.

They drove for about ten minutes, and the truck came to a stop. She heard all three of the other doors open, and then hers. They yanked her from the truck and removed her hood. All three men wore Lone Ranger masks and cowboy hats. Despite the masks, she knew who they were. She recognized the truck. It was Hollywood.

"Number Two, set up the camera and light," Hollywood ordered.

They led her over to the lighted area and formed a circle around her.

"Turn on the camera, Number Two," Hollywood said.

"What do you want?" She tried to keep her tone even. "If it's money, my grandfather will pay you."

Hollywood snickered. "Trust me, Pocahontas, we will get money, but not from your grandfather." He scanned her up and down and said, "Take off your clothes."

"Fuck you!"

Hollywood walked towards her. "Hold her, Number Three."

He then pulled out a knife and drew the edge down her cheek. "If you scream, I'll slice that pretty little face of yours, understand? Now, we will not hurt you, if you do as we say. You see that camera? You'll be a star tonight. Our client will pay well for the movie you and the three of us are gonna shoot."

He moved the knife down her face to the top of her bra top and, with a quick flick of the blade, the spandex material separated, exposing her breasts. The knife continued past her stomach, stopping at the waistband of her shorts. He sliced it down to the top of her thigh, and the elastic material split and fell to the ground.

He then cut the tie wraps from around her wrists. "Move back, boys. Let the camera get a good shot of her."

Dakota stood naked in the camera light—exposed, violated. She'd seen no guns, and decided this was her chance to run. She looked at all three men, finding the one that looked the most out of shape, and made a dash past Number Two.

The three men gave chase, but the distance between her and the assailants widened in the darkness. She jumped over a small washout, but miscalculated her landing, and a sharp pain shot through her ankle as she crumbled to the ground.

The men caught up and huddled around her.

Hollywood backhanded her across the face. "I told you, bitch, do as we say!"

With a sharp sting in her top lip, Dakata leaned over and spit a mouthful of blood on the ground. She reached up to touch her split lip, pulled her hand away covered in blood, and realized that her best chance for survival now would be to follow their orders, no matter how repulsive.

Number Three reached down and yanked her up by the hair, and dragged her back to the camera.

"I fucking told you to do as we said," Hollywood growled. "If you weren't such a sweet piece of ass, which we'll get good money for, we'd finish up with you and throw you into the ravine for the bears to eat. *Now* do you understand we're not playing?"

She nodded her head, watching blood hit the ground below her.

"Now, get on your hands and knees," Hollywood barked, and pushed her forward. "Okay, boys, it's show time. Let's get Pocahontas's audition tape done and sent out to the client. There will be a bidding war over her."

"I bet she goes to Russia," Number Three said.

Number Two shook his head. "Nope, she's heading over to the Sand."

Dakota now realized this was not a simple rape tape, that they were human traffickers. She fell to her elbows, buried her face in her hands, and prayed in Arapaho.

"What the fuck is she saying?" Number Two said.

Number Three laughed. "I think she's praying to the Moon God or something."

Hollywood grabbed her by the hair and yanked her face towards the camera. The sandy Wyoming soil crusted in her blood and tear streaks. "That's a good look. The client will like this." He pushed her back down.

Dakota prayed between cries.

"Okay, Pocahontas," Hollwood said. "Enough praying. Time to fuck. Get up on your hands and knees, and look at the camera."

She heard his pants drop behind her, and lifted her head to look at the other two men. They stood naked, playing with themselves, getting ready to have their way with her. The sight of their vileness sickened her. Her head spun and stomach churned, and she lurched forward and dry-heaved.

Hollywood's hard dick sat at the top of her buttocks. He slid it down, stopping halfway. "Boys, this might be the prettiest ass I ever seen. I bet all that running makes it *so* tight. Maybe I'll fuck her in the ass first."

Dakota felt the head of his dick open her up.

Number Two laughed and took a swig from his whisky bottle. "Nah, I bet she's had more dicks in her than a urinal."

"Yep, like waving a stick in a cave," Number Three joked. "No, Number One, save that ass for me."

"Look at Number Three's big cock, Pocahontas." Hollywood laughed and twisted Dakota's head in Number Three's direction. "You think that tight ass can handle it?"

"Fuck all of you pieces of shit," Dakota growled, spitting blood out.

Hollywood laughed. "That's the plan."

"She has a dirty mouth," Number Two said. "She needs something to wash it out." He left the perimeter and walked towards her holding his dick. "Open up, bitch." He pressed his dick against her closed lips.

"No," Hollywood ordered. "We save that for the money shots for the client. Go back to your position."

Dakota spit the taste of him off her lips.

"Spitters are quitters," Hollywood joked.

The laughter of the men echoed in Dakota's head.

"Okay, enough foreplay," Hollywood said. "Let's shoot a movie."

As the head of his dick reached her "special gift," she looked up at the Spirits dancing in the sky and cried, "Why are you allowing this to happen?" Tears fell down her cheeks.

No longer would she be able to honor her husband with virginity. Profound sadness overwhelmed her. When they finished, they would kidnap her, and she would never see her family again. Tonight, her Camelot would crumble. Tonight, these vile men would steal her innocence, and her paradise would be lost.

She closed her eyes as he moved his dick between the lips of her special gift.

"Okay, Pocahontas," Hollywood said. "Tell me how much you want my cock."

"I want your big cock."

"Louder."

"I want your big cock," she said, louder and more convincingly.

"Leave her alone," a deep, non-familiar voice barked.

Suddenly, the truck lights shined on her and the three men. She could see no distinctive features of the man as he approached in the glare of the lights, other than he was tall and broad-shouldered.

"Number Two, shut off the camera," Hollywood said. "Get your phone out and film me while I fuck this guy up." He turned to the stranger. "Hey, man, she'll fuck you too. The more the merrier. Tell the stranger what you want, Pocahontas."

"I want him to fuck me hard."

"I said, leave her alone," the stranger ordered.

Hollywood pulled from behind Dakota. "Hey, asshole, once we get done fucking her, Number Three over there is gonna fuck you. He don't care much for girls anyway."

Hollywood walked towards the stranger naked. His dick remained hard, not bothered by the interruption.

The stranger walked towards the group with his head tilted down. "Nobody is fucking anyone tonight," he said calmly.

Dakota could now make out small details of the stranger. He wore a hooded poncho, from which long black hair fell. When he raised his head to make eye contact with Hollywood, his deep, dark eyes appeared soulless and angry.

Is this a Spirit that has come down from the sky to save me?

In a quick fluid motion, the stranger pulled a wooden walking stick from behind him and swung it in a downward motion, catching Hollywood's erect penis.

Hollywood fell to his knees, and then flopped onto his back, writhing in pain. His penis was bent sideways halfway up the shaft, and blood spurted from the tip.

She smiled and spit blood to the ground.

"You broke my dick, you motherfucker," Hollywood screamed. "My dick! My dick!"

Within seconds, the stranger moved to Number Two. He swung the walking stick high and caught him across the mouth.

Number Two's lower jaw shifted to the left in an unnatural motion. He fell to the ground spitting out blood and several teeth.

Number Three broke for the truck, went to the rear window, and reached into the gun rack hanging in back. The gun was missing.

The stranger walked towards him, stalking his prey.

Number Three pulled out a knife and took a wild swing at the stranger, catching him across the shoulder.

Without even flinching, the stranger brought the stick down on Number Three's arm. The loud sound of bone breaking echoed in the dark like a gunshot. He followed up with a second swing to Number Three's right leg, connecting at the knee, and the man's leg bent around the stick like rubber, knocking him to the ground.

All three men lay on the ground holding their respective injuries. Their cries echoed in the stillness of the night.

"You're a dead man, you cocksucker! You're a dead man," Hollywood yelled out, still holding his bleeding penis.

The stranger stood over him, pulled his stick up to make a final blow, and paused. He dropped to his knees behind Hollywood's head, and shoved the stick across his open mouth like a gag.

Hollywood struggled as the stranger pushed the stick deeper towards his ears.

The stranger leaned over to look into Hollywood's eyes, and in a slow, unwavering tone, said, "You cannot kill something that is already dead."

He then stood and pointed at the truck. "Now, all of you get in your truck and leave this place. If I ever see you again, they will never find your bodies."

The three men struggled back to the truck, and groaned as they struggled to climb in. As they pulled away, Hollywood, still defiant, yelled out, "We will be back to finish that cunt and you."

The stranger picked up the cell phone Number Two had used to film the events, and threw it over the cliff into the river below. Next, he smashed the camera and light to pieces and threw them into a deep ravine on the far side of the trail. He walked over to where the truck had been parked, and reached down into a group of bushes to recover the rifle he'd stolen from the pickup.

He then walked to Dakota.

Her body trembled from the shock of the attack and the chill of the night air. She sat with her knees against her chest, and arms wrapped around them trying to cover her nakedness. She looked up at him as the Northern Lights danced around his head like a halo.

He took his poncho off, used it to cover her, and reached his hand out to help her to stand.

She didn't know what to say. This stranger had saved her from being defiled by these disgusting men, and most likely had saved her life. She couldn't find the words of gratitude to properly express how she felt.

She extended her trembling hand to touch his shoulder. "You are bleeding."

The stranger's face softened with Dakota's act of compassion. "Are you from around here?"

She nodded and pointed to the glow of her grandparents' house. "My car is only about a hundred yards down the road."

He reached out and offered his hand. "I will take you home."

Dakota looked into his eyes; the storm had calmed, and his soul shined through.

Tonight, as the Spirits danced in the sky, Destiny brought five people together at a crossroad. It will surely change our lives forever.

PART TWO

JAKE

Chapter 2
Not Just Another Day (30 Years Ago)

The sun rose on Governors Island, NY, as Jake finished his run along the Island seawall. The horns from the Staten Island Ferry echoed through the still quiet of New York Harbor during this, his favorite time of the day. He leaned on the seawall fence and looked across the water to lower Manhattan. The city that never sleeps woke from its quiet slumber.

At the base gym, he ran into his roommate Sonny, a loud Italian guy from South Philly. Jake felt Sonny had missed his mark in the US NAVY and should work for an organized crime family, living the life of a *wiseguy*. Perhaps his path would lead him there after his military service. He often dropped names of known Mafia families in Philly. Maybe it was bullshit and an attempt to impress people, or maybe not. Regardless, Jake liked him.

"Yo, Jake," Sonny said, his thick Philly accent omnipresent. "What are you doing tonight?"

"I'm heading back to PA to hook up with some of my buddies from high school. They're coming in from college. Why?"

"Man, there's a new chick on base, and she is *hot*. She's here visiting her brother, who works at the Comms Center. I met her last night at the club. She's hanging out with my girl and some other Coastie dependents."

Jake shrugged. "So?"

"So... you should check her out. Most of the guys were scared to approach her last night — they just gawked — but you always find a way to get these girls to rap with you. It must be that *I-don't-give-a-fuck-if-you-like-me-or-not* attitude. I can't figure it out." Sonny shook his head and laughed. "In fact, I heard she got a job at the base sub shop. You should at least swing by and check her out before you head home. Go see if I'm not bullshitting you. Her name is Alexi."

Jake raised his eyebrows. "Sexy name. Sounds like a porn star."

Sonny winked. "Maybe she is, when you get her in bed."

"Okay, Sonny, I'll swing by and scope her out, but the last girl you talked like this about was married to an Ordinance Instructor. You had her story all fucked up. After I banged her, word got back to her husband, and I was checking my car for a fucking bomb for three months."

"Yeah, sorry about that, man. She should have told you she was married. But I told you: just give me the word, and I would have made one call home to my boys. That guy would have been crab food."

Jake made a masturbating motion. "Yeah, yeah, yeah. All right, it's time for you to get ready for work. I'll swing by before I leave for the mountains and tell you what I thought."

"You ain't going to the mountains, trust me."

Jake rolled his eyes and shook his head as he walked away. "Another Sonny, hot girl story," he muttered under his breath.

Jake had planned to work out, gather his stuff, and hit the road before 8:00 to escape the rush hour, but as he thought about Alexi more, perhaps it would be worth altering his plans.

He'd been in a two-year relationship while stationed in Petaluma, California, but when his girlfriend heard he was being moved to the East Coast for a tour, she ended it. He enjoyed the single life in Manhattan, where getting laid was easy in freewheeling 1987, but he also missed having a steady girl.

What the hell, why not?

He'd go check out the "hot chick" with the porn name around noon, then head home.

He finished his workout, grabbed a shower, packed his clothes for the weekend, and then made the short drive to the sub shop. He found himself excited to see this girl with the porn name, wondering if she was as hot as Sonny said, or if he'd had beer goggles on last night.

The lines at the sub shop were longer than he expected. He saw no new workers, and silently cursed Sonny as the lines tested his patience. The wiseguy wannabe had probably just messed up his plans, the thought of which pissed him off even more.

"Hey, Jake," the girl at the counter said.

"Hi, Linda, how are you?"

"I'm good," Linda replied in her deep southern drawl, something Jake always found attractive. She was a true southern belle, and the wife of one his friends. As was normal with most bases, the hottest girls were married.

Jake thought this every time he saw Linda. "Hey, I know you're busy, but can I ask you a question?"

"Sure, what's up?"

"Sonny tells me there's a new girl working here, named Alexi."

"Oh my God, you're probably the tenth guy that has asked about her. New meat on base." She rolled her eyes and shook her head. "Look, she's a sweetheart. She told me she won't date anyone on base. She likes to keep her stuff private, and we know how private you guys keep things here."

He looked at her, his wheels spinning, feeling more intrigued than ever, and now challenged. "Okay, say I was willing to waste my time and introduce myself.... When could I find her here?"

"She comes in at 2:00. The shop will be slow, so maybe you can waste your time then. Can I get you something to eat?"

"Oh yeah, guess that would be a good reason to hold up the line. A coffee and double egg sandwich. Thanks, Linda." He moved to the side.

"Hey, Jake."

"Yeah?"

"Honey, don't spin your wheels. She's only here till the fall."

He looked at her and smiled. "Thanks, girl, and tell your hubby I said hi."

After getting his order, he drove to the C school where Sonny taught advanced training in underwater demolition. It was lunchtime, and Sonny always ate on the bench next to the seawall.

Sonny saw Jake pull up, and walked over to the car. "Well, asshole, was I right?"

"Man, she wasn't on shift yet. I saw Linda, and it appears every swinging dick on base is trying to meet this girl. Linda said she's not interested in active duty guys, and is only here till fall. She said not to waste my time."

"What you gonna do?"

"Well fuck, I'm already past the time I was going to leave, so what's a couple hours? Honestly, dude, I'm curious to see what all the fuss is about. I'll head over to the gym for a couple games of hoops, stop by the deli afterwards, bang this chick in the parking lot, then head home and party my ass off."

"Okay, man, swing by and let me know how that goes. Also, bring me some of the shit you're smoking."

Jake laughed as he cranked up a heavy metal song on the radio, then flipped off Sonny and squealed the tires of his Camaro. In the rearview mirror, he saw Sonny shoot him a double bird.

Jake finished his last game of one-on-one, looked up at the clock, and headed to the shower. After dressing, he looked at himself in the mirror. "Okay, Sexy Lexi, your rules are out the window."

He walked into the sub shop to find things quiet, as Linda had said, and panned the store for the new girl. He saw no one, and became pissed-off again. He'd wasted his time on base today, and could have been in the mountains by now. As he walked out, though, a new voice came from the prep area behind the counter.

"Thank you so much for hiring me for the summer," she said. "I'm looking forward to working here." The voice was soft with a tone of sweetness, but no geographical accent as far as Jake could tell.

He could only see her from the back, until she turned and headed for her counter station.

Several guys immediately jumped in line, as did Jake. He caught glimpses of her as he moved up in line.

That asshole Sonny is right. Damn, this girl is hot!

He inched closer to on the counter, and went over his game plan.

Don't stare. Act like you don't give a shit.

His favorite guard against nervous approaches was something a friend once told him in a bar. "Just remember, man, no matter how hot she is, someone — somewhere — is sick of her shit. That's why she's in this bar by herself."

He chuckled to himself, ready for his initial approach. At the counter, he looked at her nametag, which said 'Alexi.'

"Hi, can I help you?"

In a split moment, Jake soaked in the beauty that stood before him. She looked up at him, her blue eyes dancing with the innocence of a child and the sultry gaze of a woman. He didn't know how long he stared, but it felt like an hour.

For the first time in his life, he was tongue-tied. "Ahh... uh... I would like... uh... a large Italian, double the meat, because you can never go wrong with twelve inches of meat." He'd tried to be funny, but had made a mess of it.

What the fuck did I say? Oh... my... God! She probably thinks I dance in the Village at gay clubs. That's the dumbest thing I've ever said to a girl in my life! What the hell just happened?

During the awkward moment of silence, which seemed to last forever, Jake wanted to crawl into a hole.

Alexi looked at him, smiled, and said, with humor in her voice, "Foot-long Italian, double the meat. Will that be all?"

Jake, hesitant to say anything, sheepishly replied, "No thanks."

"That will be $4.59 please. Your number is 27."

Jake fumbled with his money, his hands shaking as he gave her a $20-bill, and then walked away.

Alexi called out to him, "Excuse me, number 27, would you like your change?"

"Oh... yeah... sorry." He searched for something witty to say and try to save this disaster, but drew a blank. First, he told her he wanted twelve inches of meat. Then he walked away without getting his change. She must have seen his hands shaking as he reached for his money, too, and now probably thought of him with a single word: *Loser*.

He grabbed his change and the sandwich, and tried leaving the shop unnoticed, but on the way out, he passed Diane, who greeted him. Jake politely said hello without stopping.

He sat in his car and sighed. "Holy fuck, what was that?"

Every joke he'd ever made about guys stumbling over their words, while trying to pick up girls, had just returned on the Karma train and hit him head on. He shook his head, trying to clear the cobwebs of the last several minutes, and in his typical analytical way, tried to rationalize all of this. He was a highly trained spec ops soldier, with years of skills honed to not crack under the greatest duress, and... a girl at a sub shop shattered all of it.

Diane offered a simple greeting as she set her drawer up next to Alexi, then leaned over and said, "So how's your first week going?"

"It's good, Diane. Everyone is being really great."

"That's awesome. Most of the people are nice. You have your share of assholes, like anywhere, but... honey, with your looks, no one will give you a problem. Except a few jealous wives or girlfriends." Diane laughed.

Alexi politely laughed with her. She tried to be unassuming about her good looks, and comments like this always made her uneasy, despite knowing most were sincere compliments.

"Diane," she said, "who was that tall guy with the pretty blue eyes you said hello to as you walked in?"

"Oh, you mean Jake?"

"I guess. Cute, but kind of shy."

Diane's eyes shot opened wide. "Jake Michaels, shy? Girl, there's not a shy bone in that boy's body."

"Hmmm... he sure seemed nervous when he was ordering."

"Well, you must have rocked his world. Or maybe he was stoned."

Diane greeted her first customer, ending the conversation.

Jake drove back to see Sonny.

"Hey, dickhead," Sonny said, in his normal rapid-fire talk. "I thought you were leaving. Did you see Alexi? Was I kidding or what? Did you ask her out?"

"Dude, you were right, but man I fucked up."

Sonny laughed. "What did you come right out and ask her if she lived up to her name and banged like a porn star?"

Jake shook his head. "No, man, the exact opposite. I was tongue-tied like a fucking nerd. I have no idea what hit me. She looked up and our eyes met, and I froze like a deer in the headlights. *Never* has this happened."

"All-balls-Jake met his match," Sonny said.

"I need another shot at her. Do you know where she hangs out? I know your girl has been hanging with her."

"I know they're all getting together at the club tonight, but you're leaving."

"No, I'm staying. There's something about this one. Even if I don't hook up with her, at least I can take my shot. She can tell the rest of the girls I was a dick or something to keep my rep good." Jake laughed.

"I think Marcia said they're meeting at 9:00. You should get there at 7:00 and get a few drinks in you so your balls grow back." Sonny mocked by grabbing his crotch. He turned to walk back into the school, and yelled over his shoulder, "Good luck, Pussy."

Jake laughed and shook his head. Sonny might have had a good point—a little liquid courage never hurt.

At 7:45 PM, Jake took a slow walk to the club. He liked to walk along the sea wall, watching Manhattan shift from the chaos of the workday to a sea of lights. He looked at the skyline at night, imagining it as a giant, multi-colored beacon marking a path to a magical kingdom for adults. The City was wide open and uninhibited, embracing all the sex, drugs, and rock-and-roll attitude of the 80s. Despite loving the

freedom and solitude of the Poconos where he grew up, he was glad to be stationed here. He could never see himself living in the City for any length of time, but he believed destiny guided his life. This was where he was supposed to be right now.

The club filled up quickly once the band started playing. They did a great job covering all the popular rock and hair bands. Jake took a seat at the bar, providing a strategic view of the door to see when Alexi arrived. He ordered a shot and a beer and settled back to watch all the hairless rock Gods bang their heads as if they still had their hair Uncle Sam took. They played air guitar, trying to impress the girls as if in some weird mating ritual. The spectacle would provide entertainment as he anxiously awaited another opportunity to introduce himself to Alexi.

A few minutes past 9:00, the band took their first break, and people flocked to the bar from the dance floor. When a group of guys turned their heads in unison and nudged each other, Jake stood up to see what had caught their attention. Marcia, Sonny's girl, and Donna, Marcia's older sister, walked in with Alexi. Without gawking like all the other idiots, he found it hard to take his eyes off Alexi.

Her tight, black, off-the-shoulder shirt showed off her tan. The tight-fitting, faded jeans and high black heels she wore commanded attention. She passed a fan on the dance floor, and it blew her blonde hair backwards. The scene reminded him of an MTV video, and for a split second, Jake's world went into slow motion.

He muttered under his breath, "Holy fuck."

The anxiety that had gripped him at the sub shop returned.

What is wrong with you, dude? It's just another girl. Remember, someone — somewhere — is sick of her shit.

He turned to the bartender and ordered a double shot and another beer, and prayed Marcia didn't see him until he could down his liquid courage. Too late.

She strolled over and said with a big smile, "Hey, Jake, Sonny said you would be here tonight."

"What's up, Marcia?" Jake tried to fix his eyes on her, and not let them wander off in Alexi's direction.

"Jake, I'd like to introduce you to Alexi," Marcia said, with a matter-of-fact tone.

He knew Sonny told her of their earlier meeting at the sub shop, and that she was just going through the formalities.

Before Jake could respond, Alexi smiled and said, "We met earlier while I was at work."

Jake fidgeted, searching for something humorous to say.

Alexi didn't give him a chance. She asked, with a sexy overtone, "How was your twelve inches of meat?"

Marcia jumped in. "Jake, twelve inches.... Have you been hiding something from the girls on base?" She raised her eyebrows and smiled.

Jake shot back in his normal stride. "Well, Marcia, girls are not the only ones that keep secrets on base." He winked, raised his shot glass, and downed the liquor.

Alexi laughed.

Jake realized he'd broken the ice. Alexi was not only hot as hell, but also witty, a quality he found most attractive.

The band returned to the stage and opened with a Scorpions song.

Alexi started dancing and pulled at both of the girls' arms. "Oh my God, I love the Scorpions. Let's dance." She then looked at him. "You too, Jake. Keep me from getting hit with all that imaginary hair the guys are flipping around out there."

Jake laughed. "That's funny. I was just thinking the same thing. How about the air guitar mating ritual? Can you control yourself out there, Alexi?"

She grabbed his arm and pulled him toward the dance floor. "I don't know. It will be tough."

He normally didn't dance, but he couldn't resist the opportunity to bond with Alexi. He also loved the Scorpions. This gave them common ground he could pivot from when the music stopped, and that awkward moment of the first conversation came up.

As the night wore on, Jake devoured his time with Alexi. They danced, laughed, and talked nonstop. She was so vibrant and full of life. He'd seen something intoxicating in her eyes, and peeked into her soul, which was pure.

The lights came up in the bar to announce closing time.

"Oh my God, I didn't even hear them call last call," Alexi whined.

"Hey, Alexi, are you ready to go?" Marcia said.

"I guess, but I'm really not tired." She frowned, looking first at Marcia and then at Jake.

Jake jumped in. "Marcia, I'll take Alexi home if she'd like. We were just talking about a nightcap over at O'Learys. Alexi hasn't been to lower Manhattan yet. Do you and Donna want to go?" Jake already knew the answer.

Marcia winked at Alexi. "No, we're tired and both have to work tomorrow. You guys have fun."

CHAPTER 3
THE MORNING LIGHT

Jake woke to the chirping of the birds outside his window. He looked over at Alexi, who slept on her side facing away from him, her blond hair cascading off her shoulders to the pillow. The early morning light provided just enough illumination to see the curves of her naked back and the start of her hips. The sheets covered the rest of her.

He smiled, thinking about the dream he awoke from, in which he relived the first day they met almost thirty years ago, in 1987. He'd awoken from that dream hundreds of times over the years, and the memories had replayed in his mind thousands of times.

Destiny... never question it.

He rolled out of bed trying not to wake Alexi, and crept over to her side, laughing to himself as he positioned his dick an inch from her eyes. He then cleared his throat loudly to wake her.

She opened her eyes, pulled the sheets over her head and recoiled away.

"Hey, you're cockeyed," he said and laughed aloud.

"Oh my God, will you ever grow up?" She growled, "Can I *please* just wake up once without you assaulting me in the morning?"

"Well, if I ever stop, then you'll know something's wrong in our universe." He walked towards the master bath and closet area. "You'll miss me when I die," he joked.

Alexi sighed. "You'll outlive me."

"Jupiter's Cock," Jake yelled from the bathroom, quoting a line from one of their favorite Gladiator series.

"What now?" Alexi grumbled.

"It's cold in here."

Alexi shook her head, but couldn't help but smile a little. She should never have told Jake she hated the word "cock," because in true obnoxious fashion, he'd since used it more than he should, mocking her dislike for it.

As Jake did his routine, she lay in bed reflecting on this morning's rude awakening, just another in the long line of morning harassment she'd become used to. He'd added this new one to his arsenal recently. She recalled such common events as him standing in front of her with a cup of coffee and his dick side-by-side, asking, "Cock and coffee this morning?" She thought of his ripping her covers off and grabbing her tits like a schoolboy who just popped his first bra. The list went on and on.

Do other women have to deal with this same morning harassment?

She laughed to herself and thought she would never know, because she certainly wouldn't ask her co-workers if they ever woke up "cockeyed." Jake was right about one thing, though: if he ever stopped, she should worry. His playfulness was something she loved about him.

He came out of the bathroom with his workout clothes in hand, still naked, and sauntered over to his dresser loudly singing one of his favorite Meatloaf songs.

"God," she said. "It's like someone winds you up in the mornings. It's so obnoxious."

He looked over at her, and caught her looking at his dick.

She nonchalantly twirled her hair, trying to act innocent.

He donned a shit-eating grin. "Hey, you're a voyeur. I see you staring at me."

"I am not."

"Hey, my eyes are up *here*." He motioned upwards with his hands at his waist.

"You're so stupid."

Jake pulled his underwear up, but paused. "Okay, I'm putting this away, unless you want some?"

"No, I'm fine, thank you."

Jake laughed, knowing perfectly well that their schedule was too tight in the mornings for them to be fooling around.

"You'll miss me when I'm gone," he joked, leaving their bedroom.

Alexi yelled back, "You're not going anywhere. No one else would deal with you."

This was Alexi's typical morning. As obnoxious as it was, she would never change it.

They started their morning workout with a jog. The chilly late spring morning greeted them at the door, and Alexi shivered just a bit.

Jake looked up at the sunrise. "I love this time of the morning. It releases endorphins similar to the well-being effects of opiates."

Alexi sighed. "Great, just what you need in the morning—more happy juice."

As they jogged along, they passed a Gardenia tree with a new bloom. Jake stopped to smell it, insisting Alexi do the same.

"Smells great huh?" He inhaled deeply.

"Yep, like a Gardenia," she said with little enthusiasm, still trying to wake up.

"You know, this is the problem with the world now. No one stops to appreciate the small things around us and revel in the magnificence of God's creation."

Alexi agreed with him, and they resumed their jog. She'd seen him do and say this same thing many times when they hiked. He appreciated nature, finding true peace when in the woods—almost a religious experience to him. He often said his Cherokee Indian blood connected him to the earth. She never debated this, not knowing whether he really had a connection to the land, as American Indians believed they did. Maybe yes and maybe no, but *he* believed it, and that was good enough for her.

They finished their run and went down to their basement to workout.

They turned on their favorite classic rock station and started their routine. Jake loved to play trivia as songs popped up. Other than a few groups, Alexi never got the band right. He always laughed, teasing that they'd heard most of the songs over and over for thirty plus years, and over and over she would get the trivia wrong. He often accused her of doing it on purpose to see if he knew the answer.

As they moved through their workout, a song played that they both knew, from the Scorpions, the first band they ever danced to. It started with the most recognizable, haunting, whistled melody in rock history.

"God, I would love to see these guys again," Jake said.

Alexi nodded. "That would be awesome."

Jake positioned himself on the rings to do a set of dips. He knocked out ten and dismounted, yelling, "Burn, baby, burn." Then he walked over to Alexi, flexed his arms, and said, "Feel that. Go ahead, feel it. No soft girly-man arms here. You're a lucky woman."

Alexi grabbed his arm, offered a snippy, "Yep," and moved into the next room to work on abs. Once again, she thought: *Obnoxious, but he's mine.*

She finished her last exercise and went upstairs to shower, while Jake stayed behind to complete his workout.

After cleaning up, she started down the stairs and heard Jake talking in his office to someone on the phone. His tone was not pleasant. Whomever he spoke with had caught him early, which she knew pissed him off. He hadn't showered and finished his morning routine, and he hated his routine being interrupted.

"I don't give a fuck what the Contracting Officer wants," he said, "or the A/E, the pylon stairs will not work. They must find an alternative, and it will be a Change Order, period. Call me back in forty-five minutes. Let me finish getting ready for work." He slammed his phone down.

"Why the fuck is the world full of idiots?" he growled, not knowing Alexi stood behind him.

"Problems, Baby?" she said.

"No, just fucking idiots that need to be held by the fucking hand."

"Who were you talking to so early?"

Jake paused. "Ahhh... what's his name? You know... the Superintendent in Altoona."

"Jim," she said.

"No, not Jim," he said, still annoyed.

"Okay, Jake, you just hung the phone up, and you can't remember his name? Do you need Ginkgo or something? Are you getting goofy?"

"No, I'm just so pissed at that whole job. I'm ready for a vacation."

"Me too. One more week. Have a good day," she said, and walked out the door.

"Hey," Jake yelled.

She came back in. "What?"

"Nice ass, Sexy Lexi."

She shook her head and closed the door behind her.

She sat in her car and smiled. Jake was the only one that still called her Alexi. As she got older and started the mom and career part of her life, she introduced herself as Alexandra or Alex, depending on the situation. Jake had shared early in their relationship how he and Sonny kidded that she sounded like a porn star, and it occurred to her that if *they* thought that, other men may also and not take her seriously. Indeed, she insisted Jake call her Alex when they were not alone.

His recent temperament bothered her. She knew the stress of managing several jobs at one time was challenging. He'd set a deadline to have them under control by June 15, the day they would leave for vacation. He wanted to enjoy himself, and had promised her that the day they left, he'd turn his phone off for ten days. She also noticed he was more forgetful than usual. Everyone their age forgot names on occasion, or where their keys were—part of the aging process—but Jake had always enjoyed a steel trap for a memory. She'd never approached him seriously about it, but dropped little hints—like this morning, referring to the Ginkgo. She wanted to see what ten days of vacation did for his stress level, knowing that if camping in Yellowstone didn't clear his mind, nothing would.

Jake sat back in his office chair for a second and thought about Alexi's Ginkgo statement. He noticed a few months ago that he'd started forgetting things more often, and had frequent headaches. He researched the symptoms online and concluded that stress and normal aging were the culprits. Still, on his last annual physical a few weeks back, he'd mentioned it to Dr. Johns, who'd been Jake's doctor for the past twenty years. Jake trusted his medical opinions.

Dr. Johns also believed stress, combined with normal aging, was to blame—a relief to Jake, who'd started imagining worse. The doctor had asked him when he'd last taken a vacation. Jake said three years, but that he was leaving for one in about a month. Dr. Johns advised him to see how he felt during and after vacation, and said that if the symptoms persisted, they'd run a few tests to rule out anything more serious.

Jake had shared none of this with Alexi. He didn't want to worry her with their trip coming up.

Jake looked at the clock, then shut his computer down for the day and pushed away from his desk Just as Alexi walked in with two cups of coffee—part of their afternoon ritual.

"Hey, Baby, how was your day?" Jake said.

"Uneventful, but stress-free. I stayed busy, so it went by quick. Did your day get any better after this morning?"

"Yeah, it calmed down. I looked at two new projects and played a little hooky, checking out hiking trails in Grand Teton. God, you can hike for months out there and never finish all the trails. If a person wanted to go off the grid, that would be the place. That's what we should do: sell everything and move out there, live off the land like those people on TV do. Say *fuck* all this stress." He chuckled... towards the end.

"Yeah, really," Alexi said, no doubt just humoring him. "What's for dinner tonight?"

Jake paused. "Oh shit, I forgot about dinner. I was gonna cook Chicken Divan. I totally fucking forgot. Damn."

"I thought you said your day was calm?"

"It was. I guess I just got caught up in all the excitement researching the Tetons, and had a mind melt."

Alexi stared at him, a look of concern on her face.

He tried to brush it off as nothing. "No biggie. I'll whip up something else." He headed out for the kitchen.

The morning light shined through the sheer shades, waking Alexi. She found it strange Jake was not up ahead of her, plotting his morning assault. She looked over at him, still sound asleep.

She gently rubbed his shoulder. "Jake, are we not working out this morning?"

"What time is it?" He groggily rubbed his eyes.

"6:45. I slept through the alarm."

Jake forced his eyes open. "That's fine. It's leg day. We have time."

"Did you go to bed late last night?"

"No, but I had a dream about Kelsey. I dreamed she was in bed with us. It was so real that I could feel her fur and smell her breath as she mauled me, the way she always did in the mornings. I woke up, realized it was a dream, and then had a hard time getting back to sleep. God, I miss her."

"Yeah, me too."

Jake's eyes teared as he got out of bed and walked to the bathroom.

Alexi's heart had broken for Jake when Kelsey died unexpectedly six years ago. He'd loved that dog so much that it seemed a small part of him had died with her. She still remembered the look in his eyes when they lost her on the operating table—a look Alexi never wanted to see again. She'd never seen sorrow like that. His bloodshot eyes had floated in tears, and their deep blue color had lost several shades, as if something had been pulled out of him, a piece of his soul.

Even now, she had to fight back tears thinking about it, and cleared a lump in her throat.

Jake walked from the bathroom dressed, which surprised her.

Where is my morning harassment? No cock jokes or references?

"You know what, Baby? It's amazing how I dream of the dead, as if I'm in their world. It's always so vivid. All my senses are stimulated. I believe there's a thin line between their world and ours. It's reassuring. Honestly, that's why I've never been scared to die. I know the next step is there, after our brief trip in this world." His tone was solemn.

Alexi didn't like *this* "morning Jake." Despite how obnoxious the other Jake was, he was full of life and happy to start the adventure of a new day.

Her day had now started out sad, knowing Jake was upset from his visit with Kelsey in the "other world."

She went downstairs, and turned the corner looking over the bar-height counter into the kitchen.

Jake stood there with a strange expression on his face.

"What's wrong Jake?"

He looked down at the floor in front of the sink. "I don't know. Come look at this."

She walked around the counter.

Great. Now *what's wrong this morning?*

"Is there a plumbing problem?" She turned the corner and looked down.

Jake's shorts and underwear lay on the floor.

"Yes," he said, approaching her. "With *my* plumbing, and you need to fix it."

She laughed and ran, knowing he'd give chase. Their workout spun in a different direction this morning. Her normal "morning Jake" had returned, and her universe returned to normal.

CHAPTER 4
HEAVEN HAS FALLEN

The day had arrived: vacation was here. As Jake and Alexi finished their packing, she reviewed her checklist for what seemed like the hundredth time. "Jake, did we pack the hiking poles?"

Jake rolled his eyes and looked at his watch. "Baby, that's the second time in twenty minutes you've asked me that. We have everything, and we're running late. Your brother is waiting. If we forget something, we can buy it on the road. We have three days before we're in Yellowstone."

"Okay," she snapped back. "He's only five minutes away."

When they pulled into Paul and Lisa's driveway, Paul stood at the back of the RV pointing at his watch. "I thought we were leaving at 8 AM sharp?"

Jake motioned his head sideways at Alexi. "I was up and ready to go, but your sister was going over her list for the hundredth time."

"Oh, okay," Alexi said. "Who had to walk, workout, eat, and do all his morning stuff?"

"Hey, we have a long ride, and you all know how my back stiffens up if I don't work out."

Paul sighed. "Lisa was doing the same thing. We had three months to plan this, but at the last minute, she decided to rethink everything to pack."

Lisa walked onto the front porch. "Hey, are we ready to get this party started?"

"Heck yeah," Alexi answered.

The two couples finished packing the RV, and started their vacation. Jake and Paul had plotted the GPS course to avoid interstates. It would take longer, but it allowed them to see more of the country.

The first three days of the ride was pleasant. Alexi never heard Jake complain about his back. He turned off his phone as promised and appeared relaxed, and she saw as each day passed that the stress faded from his face. He seemed less forgetful in conversations, too.

It appeared this vacation was the answer.

The only thing that still stressed him out was the occasional poor driver. He would blurt out *"fucking idiot"* or something similar, and most of the time flipped them off as they passed. Even that subsided as they got closer to Yellowstone.

As day three drew to an end, the monotony of the flat Midwest geography had culled the excitement of the ride.

"I don't know about you all, but I'm ready to see the West," Jake announced.

Paul said, "I believe when we make the turn off I-70 onto I-25 towards Laramie, we should start seeing it."

"Hey," Alexi said, "let's stay in Laramie tonight, and eat our first western steak."

Lisa chimed in. "And a beer."

In unison, everyone laughed and agreed.

"Laramie makes me think of old the Old West," Jake said. "A steak in a dusty saloon sounds perfect."

Paul smiled and chuckled. "I don't know how dusty it will be, but sounds good."

They exited for Laramie, and the elevation increased along with everyone's excitement to visit this town with so much history.

"Wow, we're climbing," Paul said.

Jake nodded and donned a big smile. "I didn't know Laramie was on a mountaintop, but finally we're in the West I pictured."

Just as he finished, the next bend revealed something none of them expected: the Laramie Valley.

"Damn, was I wrong!" Jake whistled lightly. "It's not on a mountaintop." Excited, he turned to Alexi and Lisa. "Girls, can you see this?"

Laramie nestled in the valley below. The sun set behind the mountains, painting the landscape in an orange hue.

Alexi realized she'd been holding her breath. "That is beautiful." She looked over at Jake, who looked like a child opening a gift on Christmas morning.

"Oh my God," he said. "And to think we're *just* pulling into the West."

Lisa studied her phone, looking for a hotel and a good steakhouse. "I think I found a hotel, and a there's a saloon within walking distance. I looked at their menu. It said they specialize in western steaks."

"A saloon sounds good to me," Alexi said. "Maybe there will be real cowboys in there."

The girls chuckled.

The alarm rang at 6 AM, and Jake rolled over, gave Alexi a quick snuggle, and jumped out of bed. "C'mon, baby, let's get started."

He looked, and sounded, almost childlike to Alexi. She smiled and said, "Okay."

All stress had disappeared from his face. He looked rested, vibrant, and refreshed, and.... She couldn't help but notice that he was still sporting wood from the night before.

She pointed at his hard-on, raised her eyebrows, and said in a provocative tone, "What's going on there?"

In his best western accent, he said, "Well, darlin', that's what I use to poke cowgirls like you."

As he approached her, she threw the covers off. At that moment, a knock sounded at the door.

"Hey, you guys up?" Paul yelled.

"Yeah, be right there," she said. "Jake is in the shower."

She shooed Jake away, laughing, then jumped up, grabbed her robe, and opened the door.

"Good morning, sunshine," Paul said.

"Good morning, where's Lisa?"

"She just jumped in the shower."

"I took mine last night 'cause I knew we wanted to leave early. Jake will be finished in a bit. We'll meet you in twenty?"

"Sounds good. See you downstairs." Paul spun and walked away.

Alexi opened the bathroom door, laughing. "Bad timing!"

"Yeah, now I'll have blue balls all day."

"No, you won't." She dropped her robe and closed the bathroom door behind her.

They met Paul and Lisa at the coffee lounge in the hotel lobby.

"Six hours," Jake said, "and we're in Yellowstone. Everyone ready to start our vacation?"

"Hell yeah," Lisa answered.

"Let's roll," Paul added.

The drive from Laramie along I-80 highlighted the openness of the West. The prairies seemed endless as they passed ranches, wondering how many acres the landowners controlled. The properties stretched for miles.

"Man," Jake said, "I hope our next leg is slower so we can pull over. I would love to get some pics. It's kinda hard at 80 miles per hour."

"We'll be turning on 287, in fifteen miles," Paul said. "We'll be off the interstate and should be able to stop."

"That would be nice," Lisa said. "I'd like to send pictures to the kids."

Alexi turned to Jake. "Speaking of kids, have you been in touch with Johnny yet, Jake?"

"I lost service when we got off I-80. As soon as I have bars, I can call him or Andro."

John, or "Johnny" as Alexi called him, was Jake and Alexi's oldest son. He lived in Denver and was meeting them in Yellowstone today, traveling with Mike "Andro" Androleski and his girlfriend, Kelly. Jake and Johnny had met Andro eight years ago on Xbox, and had played almost every night together. They'd formed a friendship that Alexi thought was funny. This would be the first time they met in person, 1800 miles from home, but this was typical of both Jake's and Johnny's personalities, social butterflies who made friends easily.

Alexi often said to Jake, "You don't *really* know all these guys you play with. They could be serial killers or total idiots in real life."

Jake always answered, "Hey, we're friends on Facebook and have each other's phone numbers. People online date with less info and history than that! Besides, I've watched these guys go from high school to college and into their careers, so I think I have a good idea who they are."

He might have been right, but Alexi still liked to kid him about it.

As they traveled up US Route 287, the West manifested itself in more splendor than any of them could imagine. Miles and miles of vast open spaces stretched as far as the eye could see, showing little or no signs of population. Their heads moved as if on swivels.

In every direction, mesas and buttes dotted the plains. Multi-colored layers adorned them, as Jake said more than once, "In hues only God can create."

Alexi and Lisa took pictures nonstop, while Paul slowed the RV to take in the majesties that surrounded them.

Jake pointed to a spot ahead. "Hey, Paul, there's a point of interest up there. Let's pull over and take a group pic."

"Sounds good."

The point of interest looked over the badlands and massive outcroppings that marked a waypoint that Indians, settlers, and the Pony Express had used for navigation.

Jake walked off the paved area onto the Wyoming soil, crouched and scooped up a handful of the earth, and sieved it through his hands. He moved to a knee-high Sagebrush bush to pluck off a sprig and, taking a deep whiff, looked out across the plains as if surveying for something. He was connecting to the land.

"The soil is so fine and soft," he said. "It's like sand, and the Sage smells great." He walked with enthusiasm towards Alexi, as if presenting her with a gift.

She touched and inhaled the offering. "Wow, so soft, and the Sage smells like the stuff we cook with."

"Yep." Jake turned to gaze again at the outcroppings, and took a long, deep breath. "This *is* God's Country."

The group climbed back into the RV and continued the drive. They turned off the stale air conditioning and opened the windows to the crisp, refreshing, clean air, which enhanced the full experience of their drive.

Alexi watched Jake soak in the scenery, like a dog hanging his head out the window and enjoying the smorgasbord of smells. His eyes were wide, his face showed total contentment, and, for the first time in 1500 miles, he stopped talking.

His phone rang then, snapping everyone out of their sightseeing trance.

"Andro," Jake said. "What's up? Where are you guys?"

Andro's voice rang out on the speaker. "According to GPS, we're 500 miles out."

"Okay, man, tell John to drive safe. Service is bad once you get on 287. Text me every hour or so if you have service, and let us know how you guys are doing."

"How's the scenery?" Andro said.

"Dude, words can't describe it." Jake paused for some static, then added, "Hey, I'm losing you. Peace out."

He hung up the phone and turned to Alexi. "They're about two and a half hours behind us."

Alexi sighed.

"Don't worry, Momma Bear, you'll see your cub soon." Jake smiled.

"Actually," Paul said, "it's good that they're a little behind us. It'll give us time to check in and set the campsite up."

The trip continued, passing through Lander, Fort Washakie, and the Wind River Indian Reservation. Each town offered western-style architecture with American Indian influence. The two couples enjoyed this leg of the trip, often commenting on things each saw.

Paul pointed at a mileage sign. "Dubois is up ahead. Let's stop and fill up before we get into Yellowstone, probably a lot cheaper."

"How far is Dubois to the park?" Lisa said.

Jake answered. "I looked on my phone, and it looks like about eighty miles."

Alexi felt a little nervous again. "Cool. Try calling Johnny, Jake."

"I will when we get into town."

They pulled into Dubois. The downtown resembled a modern version of an old west town, with flat-front buildings, clapboard siding, and western colors, but retrofitted with modern architecture. Alexi wondered if any of the buildings had actually stood back in the Old West.

Everyone got out of the RV to stretch while Paul refueled.

Jake called John. "Hello, Son, Momma Bear wants to know where you guys are?"

They weren't on speaker this time, so Alexi waited through the pause.

"Oh cool," Jake said. "You guys made up time. We're a little over an hour out."

"Where are they?" she said. "How is their drive? Is Johnny driving?" She spoke in rapid fire.

"Hold on," Jake said into the phone. "I'm gonna pass the phone to your mom. Be safe."

Jake handed it over and whispered, *"Momma Bear."* He grinned and winked.

Jake listened as Alexi talked nonstop, probably not giving John a chance to answer. She was excited and naturally worried, having devoted most of her adult life to raising their three kids, John, Robert, and Danielle. They were grown now and living their lives, but it had taken a while for Alexi to settle into her empty nest. She often said she loved her life with Jake, now that they were once again just a couple, but she would always be Mom—not a mother—despite how old her kids.

Paul started the RV. "Okay, let's finish this up."

"Great job driving, man," Jake said as they pulled out. "Bet you're ready to take a break?"

"Yep, will be nice to take my hands off the wheel for a few days."

"One more hour, Honey," Lisa said.

As they continued on Route 26, the elevation continued to rise, and snow became increasingly prevalent on the side of the road. Paul and Jake watched the elevation on the dash GPS, and every time they climbed another hundred feet, they counted it out with excitement.

They crested the top of the Absaroka Mountains, and now sat on the Continental Divide. A sign on the side of the road caught everyone's attention.

Elevation: 9,659 Feet.

Jake grabbed the door handle. "We have to stop and take a pic here. Pull over, Paul." When they stopped, Jake jumped out and said, "Wow, I can't believe how much snowpack is still on the ground in June."

He couldn't help grinning from ear to ear ans he ran and jumped on top of a frozen snow mound.

Alexi smiled. "God, you're like a little kid."

Jake held out his hands. "C'mon, everyone, let's stand here with the elevation sign and snow, and take a pic to send to John."

After a quick picture, they resumed their drive. A short time later, when they navigated a sharp bend, the scene that unfolded in front of them took their collective breath away.

"Oh... my... God," Jake said.

On the horizon, the Teton Mountains commanded their attention, rugged, majestic peeks towering above the valley floor. Their tops looked jagged and sharp, as if designed to cut like a knife through the Earth's crust. Rays of sunshine pierced the clouds and glared off the snowcapped peaks.

"I... am... home," Jake announced.

Everyone passed right over Jake's comment, no doubt accustomed to him making wild statements.

Paul pulled the RV over and got out. Lisa sidled up next to him. "How would you describe that view?"

Paul shook his head and sighed. "No matter how many pictures you look at, until you're actually here, no words can describe it. In fact, now that we're actually here... no words can describe it."

Back in the RV and headed down the road, Paul said, "About fifteen more miles and we'll be at the campground."

Jake nodded. "I'm ready to sit around a campfire and drink a few beers."

"Hell yeah," Alexi agreed.

They pulled into the campground, checked in, and drove to their two adjoining sites, one for the RV, to be occupied by the ladies, and one for the tent Jake and Paul would sleep in. The men had decided months earlier that they wanted to sleep and wake in the crisp, clean air. The showers and bathroom building sat only fifty feet from their sites. All of them agreed they could not be happier with the setup.

"Jake," Alexi said. "Give Johnny a call and see how far out they are."

"Okay, I was gonna do that as soon as we finished setting up."

Jake and Paul set the fire pit up, and all the surrounding chairs, after which Paul plopped down, exhausted from the drive, and cracked open a well-deserved beer.

Jake joined him as he called John. "Hey, where are you guys?"

"We'll be there in twenty minutes," John replied.

"Oh, cool. I'm gonna tell your mom you guys are an hour out. You can surprise her."

"Okay, Father, sounds good." John called them Father and Mother when he was in a joking mood.

Jake found it funny.

Alexi and Lisa finished getting their things organized in the RV, and came out to join their husbands. "Did you talk to Johnny, Jake?" Alexi said.

"I just did. He's about an hour out."

Alexi beamed. "Cool."

Paul said, "Well, the sun is setting and it's getting chilly. Should we start a fire?"

Lisa and Alexi both answered in unison. "Sounds good."

The fire danced and illuminated the campsite, and the four road-weary travelers slipped into relaxation mode.

Alexi looked up, and sprung from her chair like a cat shot in the ass. She ran towards the tent area, to where John, Andro, and Kelly stood grinning. "There's my baby," she said as she gave him a big hug.

Jake walked over to the three, gave John a hug, and moved on to Andro, giving him a man hug as if he'd known him his entire life. He then extended his hand to Kelly and introduced himself.

Paul and Lisa greeted everyone from their seats, and Paul shouted, "Grab a drink, boys and girls, and have a seat at the fire. Dinner will be ready in about twenty minutes."

The first evening was perfect, as the group sat well into the night talking and planning their next four days. The fire was cozy and welcoming on their faces, as the nip of the Wyoming night bit at their backs.

Alexi commented how she found it so funny that Jake, Johnny, and Mike carried on as if they'd personally known each other for years.

They all answered, *"We have!"* and laughed.

Jake smiled and thought they'd all hold the fondest memories of this night.

Jake woke at first light, freezing in the tent, and looked over at Paul. "You awake?"

Paul laughed. "Yeah. How fucking cold are you?"

"Dude, I'm freezing. I have to piss, but I'm scared to walk outside. If it's this cold in here, under all these blankets and clothes, I can't imagine what it's like out there. I wish we would have remembered the tent heater."

"When you go piss, look at the thermometer they have hanging outside the shower area. I bet it's 20 degrees."

"Okay. Well, it's 6:30, and everyone is coming over for coffee and breakfast in an hour. I'll check on the girls first, and then go for a walk to loosen up... and hopefully warm up."

He walked into the toasty RV and sat on the couch.

Alexi had the coffee brewing and breakfast cooking. She smiled, but her eyes were fairly laughing. "How was the tent?"

"Well, it was so cold this morning, I may be a eunuch now."

She laughed amd handed him a cup of coffee and a breakfast bar.

His wife knew his morning routine well, and, despite being on vacation, he wouldn't deviate from it. He needed to do cardio in the morning to relieve his arthritis when he got out of bed.

She seemed to be reading his mind. "How did you sleep? How does your back feel?"

"Besides being cold," he said, "I slept great. The mattress is fine, and my back feels okay. I'm gonna take a walk along the Snake River, do a quick workout. Then I'll shower and be ready to eat a real breakfast, and to leave for Yellowstone. See you in forty-five minutes." He gave her a kiss and exited the RV.

"Hey, what about bear spray?" she yelled after him.

"Man, I'm not scared of bears around here," Jake yelled back as he jogged away.

He ran to the end of the paved road, which ended at a small knoll. He crested the hill, and stopped dead in his tracks. Below him lay a field riddled with early summer wildflowers. The Snake River meandered through it, and the backdrop of mountains, green with Alpine forests and snowcapped peaks, finished the postcard-perfect scene. He saw a well-worn single path and continued his run.

The trail traveled to the river and alongside it. He turned downstream just as a wake rippled in the middle of the water. The surface then erupted as a moose came up from its dive. He'd never seen a wild moose, and marveled at it for several seconds before continuing his run.

The path looped back through the field towards the campground, where ground squirrels popped up and down from their burrows as he passed. He noticed large hoof prints in the soft dirt, and large piles of scat, which he figured to be elk or moose that fed in the fields at night. At the end of the path, a pair of foxes, still in half their winter coats, hunted the meadows. He reached the blacktop, paused, and looked back just as a pair of eagles glided slowly down the Snake River, the sun rising over the mountains behind them.

He already looked forward to his morning run tomorrow, and wondered what gifts Yellowstone would give him. He couldn't wait to tell everyone at camp what he'd seen. The next day, he would get Alexi to join him, so they could reminisce for years about their morning runs in paradise.

The next three days were crammed with sightseeing, hiking, and wildlife viewing. Each day ended with a peaceful night at the campfire, discussing the once-in-a-lifetime marvels they'd seen that day.

Alexi noted that Jake had never seemed so relaxed. A peace had settled about him, as if he'd been searching for something his whole life, and had finally found it.

His universe was perfect.

"Well, boys and girls," Jake said. "Tomorrow is our last full day. I guess we tackle the Tetons? I was looking at this trail map...." He passed it around for everyone to examine. "I highlighted Paintbrush Canyon. We can take the trail there as high as we want to go."

"Sounds great," John said. "Then we can finish the day back close to camp, and explore down the road like the girl at the lodge told us. I want to check out the hot springs, and maybe get some wildlife viewing at dusk."

Everyone agreed, after which they finished their drinks and bid each other a good night.

The group stood at the trailhead for Paintbrush Canyon, staring at the snow-covered peaks in the distance.

Jake took a deep breath and looked at the others. "Well, boys and girls, are we ready to tackle this? We should be used to the altitude by now."

John nodded. "Let's see how high we can get."

"We'll take it slow and steady," Paul added. "We have all day."

The hikers made the steady ascent, passing pristine alpine lakes and crystal-clear streams. The path meandered through lush green forests of pine and towering hardwoods.

Jake and John had taken the lead, and when they come around a switchback, they stopped suddenly.

Jake put his hand up, signaling the group to pause, ad pointed towards a meadow. "Grizzly," he whispered, and held his finger to his lips.

They paused to see which way the bear was walking. It stood on its hind legs, looking in the opposite direction intently. After a moment, the young grizzly dropped to all fours and ran into the cover of the woods.

"He must have heard hikers up ahead," Jake said.

"That was fucking awesome," Andro said.

"I got some pictures," Lisa said. "I hope they came out good."

The group gathered around her to look at the photos on her phone.

"Good job, Lisa." Paul kissed her on the cheek. "They're great."

The hikers passed the meadow and made a hard right turn. The path narrowed and became rocky, and water trickled under their feet.

"Are we on a creek bed?" Alexi said.

Jake shook his head. "I wouldn't think so. It's probably runoff from the snow."

As the path continued a sharp climb, the running water and slippery rocks challenged the group. They came to a trail marker and stopped.

Jake caught his breath. "Well, we're at 10,400 feet. How is everyone doing?"

"I'm good," Paul said.

"Me too," John said.

Alexi, Lisa, Andro, and Kelly all agreed.

Jake motioned forward. "Okay, let's press on."

The trail made a sharp switchback through a dark pine forest. Jake stopped and looked back at the group.

"What do you see, Dad?" John said.

Jake pointed up the trail. "Is everyone ready to walk in the snow at 70 degrees?"

"Man, we hit the snowpack," Paul said.

Jake smiled. "There's something surreal about walking in the snow when it's this warm."

"Hell," Alexi said. "My shoes are already wet, so let's keep going."

The group trudged through the snow in the shaded parts of the trail.

Jake paused and said, "It looks like the snow has melted up ahead in the sun. Hopefully, we'll have a clear path from here. I don't know about anyone else, but that was a bitch to walk through. My legs are burning."

"You need more cardio, Father. Mine feel fine." John laughed.

"No, *Son*, I need to be thirty years younger. Smart ass."

The group reached another alpine meadow, where wildflowers carpeted the ground. The clearing allowed them to look out over the Teton Valley.

Alexi paused mid-breath. "My God, this is beautiful up here."

"We're getting closer to Heaven." Jake smiled and nodded towards the area behind her. "Look over the tree tops behind you."

"Wow," John Said. "We're almost at the base of the peaks."

Jake grew more serious. "Yeah, but I'm afraid we may be as far as we can go. Look how dark and angry the sky is. Those are snow squalls, and we're not prepared to get caught in them. I suggest we head back down."

John shrugged his acceptance. "Man, I think we accomplished our goal today. We stood at the base of the Tetons. Next time, we'll plan for the weather."

Jake stood silent for a moment, then bent down and scooped some of the runoff water into his hands. "You will never drink purer water."

That afternoon, the group ate an early dinner and left for their last adventure, going off the beaten path behind the campground. One of the girls at the lodge had told them about the *"where the locals go during tourist season"* areas, complete with hot springs and waterfalls higher than the ones at the Grand Canyon of Yellowstone. They didn't have time to make the eighteen-mile hike to the waterfalls, but they could check out the hot springs and ride around the back roads, exploring the less traveled parts of the park.

As the sun started setting, it bathed the landscape in an orange hue. They drove slowly along the dirt roads, looking for wildlife.

"Stop the van," Jake yelled.

"What did you see?" Paul said.

"Check out those weird birds out on the edge of the field, just left of that knoll." Jake pointed as he jumped out.

He and John walked into the large, marshy field.

"Are you all coming?" Jake said.

"No, we're fine," Paul said. "The mosquitoes are terrible."

Jake smiled and winked. "Sounds like the hike up Paintbrush kicked some asses."

Jake and John were still high on adrenaline, fed by their love of all they'd found in the parks. They moved quickly, but quietly, sneaking up on the birds.

Jake looked back at the van, and paused. He looked in all directions, and the vastness they stood in the middle of hit him. He raised his arms from the side to shoulder height, closed his eyes, and spun slowly around several times. In a whisper, he said, "Thank you."

He caught up to his son, who was still trying to get close to the skittish birds. "John, the sun is dropping behind the mountains. Let's go back to the van. We'll never get close enough to these birds for a good pic."

When they reached the van, everyone was laughing.

"Jake, what was that spin all about out there?" Alexi said.

"Man, you can't fully appreciate how vast this place is until you stand in the middle of it and do a Sound of Music spin." He laughed, downplaying his actions.

If he told them the truth, they would never understand. Jake had reached out to connect to the Earth in all directions, to say thank you and goodbye to this *"piece of Heaven that had fallen to Earth."*

Chapter 5
Goodbye to Eden

The last night in camp was reflective and more solemn than the previous nights, as realization had set in. This wonderful vacation, in one of the most beautiful places in the world, had reached its end. That night, family would say goodbye to each other, and friendships consummated by physical interaction would move back to voices and texts over media. Early tomorrow morning, they would start their journey back to reality.

"Well, Mother and Father," John said. "We're leaving at zero dark thirty, so we should get to bed."

As the fire died down, they all knew that when the last of the wood burnt out, so would their time together. Everyone stood up to hug and say goodbye to each other.

Jake saw Alexi was holding back tears as she embraced Johnny, and he fought back his own emotions as he then hugged John.

"Be safe tomorrow, Son," he said. "We need to come back here and spend more time in paradise."

"I agree, Dad. Honestly, we should move out here."

"I would sell the house tomorrow and come back, but your Momma may have something to say about that." Jake smiled and pointed his head at Alexi.

John turned to her. "Mother, could you live out here?"

"It's beautiful, and this is a hard place to say goodbye to.... We'll see."

Jake knew Alexi was humoring them, as it wasn't the first time either of them had visited a new place and wanted to live there. Once they got back to their everyday lives, they'd bounce back to reality, and this would be a fleeting thought.

Andro and Kelly walked up to Jake and Alexi to say goodbye. When they'd first met Kelly, they greeted her with a handshake. Now they hugged, having established a mutual comfort zone.

"Jake, this was awesome, man," Andro said. "You know I spent more time on vacation with my Xbox Dad as I did my real Dad. Thank you for inviting us on your family vacation." He pulled away from a man-hug with Jake.

Jake laughed as the two separated. "It was great, man. Funny we both traveled 1800 miles to meet each other in person, finally."

Alexi added, "We should all get together next summer somewhere."

Kelly smiled and said, "That would be great."

Jake nodded and offered his own smile. "Andro and I will talk about it over the next several months."

John, Andro, and Kelly finished their goodbyes and left for their campsite.

As Jake watched them fade into the night, he wondered where Destiny would take them next year, or if there would even be a next year. Maybe this was just departing conversation with good intentions.

Alex got an early start on packing, taking advantage of the fact that Jake had woken early to take his last run in paradise.

Paul walked into the RV to grab coffee. "Did you talk to Jake before he left?"

"Yes," she said. "He had his coffee and said he'd be back in twenty minutes to help break down camp."

Paul sighed. "Yeah, that's what he said to me, but that was almost forty-five minutes ago."

Alex said, "I was packing and didn't pay attention to the time. I'll go down to the trail and get him. He's probably shooting pics or watching some animal. I know the route he takes."

She grabbed the bear spray and exited the RV, more alarmed than she'd let Paul know. Jake was *very* punctual and knew they had a schedule to keep this morning. It would be unlike him to deviate from plans.

She crested the hill at the end of the campground, looked towards the river, and spotted Jake standing motionless on the bank. Just as she'd figured, he was watching something in the river, and either lost track of time or didn't care, this being his final morning in Yellowstone.

She approached from his left side and looked in the direction Jake stared. Nothing appeared out of the ordinary, but he didn't break his gaze.

"Jake?" She walked towards him and paused, waiting for him to look over at her. Now only ten feet from him, she said louder and with more authority, "Jake!"

He still didn't respond.

She stood next to him, still unacknowledged, and looked at his cell phone lying at his feet. She walked directly in front of him, and saw a blank stare in his eyes. "Jake," she said firmly, reaching out and touching his shoulder.

Startled, he snapped out of his trance. "Damn, Alexi, you scared the shit out of me."

"You didn't hear me calling your name?"

"No, I was watching a grizzly and her cubs on the other side of the river. I must have zoned out. I was trying to get a picture for our bookcase. It would have been perfect," he said in a matter-of-fact tone.

Alex bent over to pick up Jake's phone. "Your phone is on email, not photo. I thought you wouldn't do any work until we got home?"

"I know, but our vacation is over. I fired it up this morning in the tent, and had over a hundred fucking emails, twenty voicemails, and so many texts that I stopped fucking reading. I realized reality was back."

His voice was angry, and his face once again showed the stress that she hadn't seen the entire vacation. It occurred to her that all the therapy the last eight days provided had been erased in seconds.

"Why did you come down to the river?" Jake said.

"Because you've been gone for forty-five minutes."

"Damn, I knew I was gonna exercise a bit longer this morning, because we're driving. I guess the work shit pissed me off, and I ran longer than I thought. Then I saw the bears."

Alex thought now was not the time to bring up his faraway stare, given that he'd already grown agitated by work stuff.

They walked briskly back to camp

"You know," he said, "I was thinking about what John said last night, about moving out here. I'm so fucking tired of work, traffic, crowds, and the hot weather. I could easily sell everything tomorrow and call it quits. I've been working since I was sixteen. I'm tired. This is the most relaxed I've been in my life. I felt connected to this place in some familiar way. I couldn't put my finger on it, and then it hit me. Do you remember my dream of running with my mom in heaven when we were still dating? I knew you were the one, but I was scared about commitment."

"Yeah, I remember."

"Remember how I described endless rolling hills surrounded by majestic mountains? As I jogged with my mom, a long-haired girl passed us, and Mom said, 'Catch her, Jake! She's your future.' I ran out ahead to catch the girl, and when I looked back at Mom, she faded away into the horizon. That horizon was the view we saw from the road in Canyon Country. I've been here in my dreams. This is where we're supposed to be, where we finish the last chapter of our lives."

She heard the conviction in his voice. She knew he often dreamed of deceased people, and firmly believed they were visiting him. He put reverence in those dreams and felt they were a snapshot of his Destiny. He felt the Spirit World, the earth and the universe were all connected. He read too much Native American lore, but if it gave him faith, so be it.

Alex didn't know how to respond. He was dead serious, but she was more concerned about the state she found him in than moving to Wyoming.

"Jake, we'll look at this when we get home. We'll do some research."

The next four days traveling home were uneventful, the mood subdued. The trip seemed to drag, as everyone knew it was time to go back to work. Jake was quiet and distant at times, and Alex knew he hated leaving Yellowstone, but there was something more. It showed in his eyes, something he chose not to share. Was it his dream? Had he seen something in that dream, long ago, that was unearthed out there? He would eventually share his thoughts, but for now, best to let him work things out in his mind.

Monday morning, the alarm rang at 5 AM as normal. Jake and Alex settled back into their routine.

"Oh my God, I hate that noise," Alex said, groggy and agitated.

"Not me," Jake said. He sprung up, ripped the covers off her, and quickly rolled over and straddled her. "I think you need some C and C to start your week back after vacation." He moved his hips further up her body, stopping at her chest. His dick pointed straight at her.

"Stop," she said playfully, grabbing a pillow and covering her face. "We need to work out. You know we have no time in the morning." She lifted the pillow up just enough, to talk.

Jake dismounted her. "I know."

She was glad to see him wake up in a good mood, after he'd been so quiet on the ride home. He must have worked out in his head what had distracted him the last morning in Yellowstone. They'd need to discuss what happened that morning, but she didn't know when the right time would be. She decided to address it tonight after dinner.

Jake always told her, *"Procrastination is the thief of our tomorrows."* Alex wouldn't allow her tomorrows to be taken from her. If something was wrong with Jake, she'd make sure they addressed it quickly.

They had a great workout, and moved on with their morning routine.

Alex got out of the shower and saw she missed a call from Johnny. She found it strange he would call at 5:30 AM Denver time, and worried it might be something serious.

"Johnny is everything all right?" she said, as soon as he answered.

"Mom, I'm fine, I just wanted to ask you a question about Dad."

"Okay, good. What about Dad? And *no*, we didn't discuss moving to Wyoming yet."

He chuckled. "No, not about moving to Wyoming. Have you noticed anything strange about Dad?"

"Like what?" Alex almost knew the answer already, but was scared to hear someone else say it.

"I saw him staring into space several times while we were out there, almost like he wasn't there. It was brief, and when he got back to normal, he didn't even acknowledge it—just moved forward without skipping a beat."

"I didn't see that, Johnny."

"Honestly, Mom, you wouldn't have because of where you were sitting in the van. I figured he was just mesmerized by all the scenery, but then, the last morning, I walked into the bathhouse and saw him staring into the mirror. He stood motionless, and I called out to him twice before he snapped out of it."

"Did he say anything?"

"Nope, just like nothing happened. I asked him why he was in there so early. It was like 4:00 AM. He said he couldn't sleep, so figured he'd start his day early. He hugged me and told me to have a safe ride, and left. But there was just something off about the whole thing."

Alex had two choices: share what she witnessed before vacation and the last morning at the river; or, in order not to worry Johnny any more than he was, cover for Jake at this point.

"Hmm, that *is* strange, Johnny. I know he was upset about leaving there, and the last morning, he was looking at work stuff in his tent that pissed him off. You know how your dad gets when his wheels are turning, like he tunes the world out."

"Okay, maybe that was it, but just watch him, Mom."

"I will, Son. I have to get ready for work. Love you, and don't worry about your dad."

"Okay, Mom. Love you too. Bye."

Alex put the phone down on the sink, her hands shaking tears filling her eyes.

Is this more than just stress? Is my beloved Jake being pulled away from me by some insidious disease? Was what I saw at the river a telltale of our future?

"Stop!" she said to herself. "Calm down, take this one step at a time, and first talk to Jake tonight."

Jake sat at his desk with his back to the entrance to his office. He heard Alexi come downstairs and walk up behind him.

She turned his chair around, got down on her knees in front of him, and pulled his shorts down without a word.

He lifted himself off the chair to assist her. "What's this all about, Sexy Lexi?"

She looked up at him with her sultry blue eyes and, in a provocative tone, said, "Didn't you say C and C this morning? Well, I had my coffee, so now I'll have the second C."

Jake closed his eyes and melted back in his chair, enjoying the morning gift from his girl with the porn name.

Alexi finished, stood up, and looked Jake in the eyes. "I want you to know how much I enjoyed our vacation, and that I love you."

"Well, if I'd known you would like Yellowstone *so much*, I would have taken you there much sooner... and every year. Hell, every month!" He laughed and pulled his shorts up.

"You're so stupid. I have to leave for work. Have a good day. Love you." Alexi left his office.

Well, that was out of nowhere, but I ain't complaining.

His phone rang, ending the morning bliss, and the workday from hell had begun. After two weeks away, the stress would probably make his head explode, but the little surprise from Alexi a few minutes ago had him calmer than he would have been to start the barrage.

Alex started her drive to the office happy she'd taken the time to satisfy Jake this morning. The call from Johnny had her emotions churning, and if something were wrong with her husband, she'd cherish every moment she had with him. She never wanted to forget his gaze, his voice, his laugh, his touch, his smell, his taste. She would make sure the love of her life was fine, and then they'd explore moving west for the "final chapter" in their wonderful life.

The late afternoon was typical in all aspects, as Alex came through the front door and was met by the fragrant smell of curry.

Jake sat at his desk, and turned his chair to greet her. "Hello, Baby."

"Hi, it smells great in here. Whatcha you cooking?"

"Curried chicken with a heavy accent of coconut, and jasmine rice."

"Yummy! Let me grab some coffee, and I'll be back."

She joined him in his office, and they breezed through a brief conversation about their uneventful workday. Jake looked relaxed, which made this as good a time as any to bring up the "conversation."

"Jake," she said. "Before we went on vacation, I was getting a little worried. You seemed to get agitated easily, and you'd become more forgetful. I figured you were just stressed out and needed a vacation."

Jake cocked his head and raised his brow. "Okay, and...?"

"Well, when we were on vacation, you looked like you were back to your old self. I figured, okay, you just needed a break. But the last day at the river really worried me."

"Because I was late? Or because you scared the shit out of me? I don't understand, Alexi."

"I called your name three times, and had to touch you before you even knew I was there. You were motionless, and looked like you were a million miles away, like you were in a trance."

He paused for a second, keeping his expression even. "Baby, I was just overwhelmed by leaving there, and all the work bullshit that was on my phone. I guess I was in deep contemplation."

She sighed. "Johnny called me this morning concerned about you." Her eyes filled with tears.

"Concerned about what?"

She relayed what Johnny had said.

He put his head down, and remained in that position long enough for Alex to grow impatient. "Jake," Alexi barked.

He lifted his head, and his eyes said, even before his words, that what he was about to tell her was not something she'd want to hear.

Instantly, a tear rolled down her cheek.

"Alexi," he said. "I talked to Dr. Johns before we left on vacation. I was becoming a bit forgetful, and was having headaches. He said it was most likely stress-induced, and some common aging issues, and told me to see how I felt on vacation. What I didn't tell him was the short-circuit feeling I get, as if my mind just takes a break from reality. I called him today to make an appointment."

"How long has this been going on? And why have you not told me about this?"

"Several months." He sighed. "I didn't want to worry you about what is probably nothing."

"Nothing, Jake? You stare into fucking space, you have headaches, and that's nothing?" Her lips quivered, and tears trickled down both cheeks. "Your mom died of brain cancer. Did that ever cross your mind?"

"I guess I forgot." He laughed, an unsuccessful attempt to ease the tension.

"This is not a joking matter. I can't *believe* you would keep this from me."

"Alexi, calm down. I'm fine. It's just stress."

"When is your appointment? I *am* going."

"Tomorrow."

"Tomorrow? Does that not make you think Dr. Johns is concerned?"

"No, he happened to have a cancelation," he answered in a matter-of-fact tone. "And then we made plans to go golfing."

"What time? I'll rearrange my schedule?"

"11:15 tee time."

"Not your damn tee time! Your appointment," she growled.

"Easy, easy... I was just kidding. It's at 9:45."

She sprung from her chair and stormed from his office. "Let's eat. I'm hungry."

Alex had sat silent as they ate dinner, and now stood up from the table. "Are you playing Xbox tonight?"

"Yes, at 7:00. Why?"

"I'm going upstairs to get caught up on my shows. I'll talk to you in the morning."

"Hey, don't worry. We'll be fine."

She looked back, forcing a weak smile. "I know. I'm just a bit more worried than you, I guess."

She went up and watched her shows, merely going through the motions. Her concentration remained locked on the events of today. Jake was clearly more concerned than he led on, and it terrified her.

Could tomorrow bring news that will alter our lives? Am I facing the loss of my Eden?

CHAPTER 6
SEASONS

The alarm rang at the usual time, and Jake jumped out of bed with his usual enthusiasm. "Sexy Lexi, let's have a good workout, go talk to Scott so he can put our minds to rest, and move on with a better day than yesterday."

"Okay, I'll be right down," she said between yawns. "I need a cup of coffee before we get started."

"Did you not sleep well, baby?"

"No, my mind raced to exhaustion. The last time I looked at the clock it was 1:15."

"Relax, Alexi, it will be fine."

The drive to Dr. Johns took only twenty minutes, during which time the couple avoided conversation about the upcoming visit. They both knew that speculation would only lead to anxiety.

Jake's mood had lifted Alex's spirits. He knew his body better than anyone, and didn't appear overly concerned, so that helped to relax Alex.

Jake checked in at the front desk, and a nurse escorted Alex and him to an exam room, where she took his vitals and told them the doctor would be in shortly.

After several minutes, there was a tap at the door, and the nurse re-entered. "Mr. and Mrs. Michaels, the doctor would like to see you in his office versus this exam room. Follow me, please."

Jake's look of concern, which he immediately tried to hide, resonated with Alexi.

He donned a smile and said, "He probably wants to show me a new golf club, gun, or some toy he bought. It's not out of the ordinary for me to go to his office. We've been friends for years."

She nodded. "Okay."

"Come in," Dr. Johns replied to the knock on his door.

"Mr. and Mrs. Michaels, Doctor," the nurse announced.

"Yes, have them come in. Thank you, Sherri."

Jake and Alex walked in to find Scott and another gentleman. Jake approached the two men and extending his hand. "Scott, if you're busy, we'll step out."

Scott shook Jake's hand and said, "No, it's fine." He moved over and hugged Alex. "After all these years, I still don't know what you see in him?" He chuckled as he pulled away from her.

She smiled graciously. "Me either, Scott. How is Mary?"

"Patient as ever to put up with me, just like you with that joker." He motioned toward the other man. "Jake and Alex, this is Dr. David Abrams. He's a neuropsychologist and a trusted friend of mine."

"Dave Abrams," the scholarly-looking doctor said, holding his hand out to greet Jake and Alex.

"That's a golfer grip if I ever felt one," Jake said. "Are you joining us this afternoon?"

Scott answered for him. "No, Jake, Dave his here because I asked him to join us. Please, everyone sit down."

Alex raised her eyebrows and glanced at Jake and Scott. "Did Jake's blood work show something you did't pick up on before vacation?"

"No, Alex, his blood work was perfect. In fact, all his tests were good. I'm not concerned about his body. I'm concerned about his temperament, headaches, and forgetfulness. Instead of putting you guys through weeks of waiting for specialist appointments and fearing the worst, I wanted to have Dave do an exam now and get his opinion. He may conclude it's just stress and normal aging, as I did." Scott maintained a comforting tone throughout.

"First and foremost," he continued, "please do not race to conclusions. The questions and exam Dave will do is to determine if there are any early signs of degenerative brain disease. While rare at Jake's age, dementia can begin to manifest itself. Early onset of Alzheimer's is being diagnosed with a bit more frequency. I want to rule that out."

His tone then turned more professional. "I need both of you to be completely honest with Dave. He'll ask some personal questions. Please answer them candidly."

Jake and Alex stared at each other, then back at Scott, and simultaneously said, "*Okay.*"

Doctor Abrams positioned his notepad on his lap. "Jake, Scott told me you spoke with him before and after your vacation regarding some forgetfulness and headaches. Are there any other symptoms you've not spoken to him about yet, either physical or mental?"

Jake shrugged. "Physically, I have no real complaints, just some pain in my joints, neck, and back from Degenerative Joint Disease. That's all in my records, which I'm sure Scott shared with you. Besides the forgetfulness, I've been experiencing a *short-circuit* feeling in my head for the past several months. I didn't tell Scott about them, figured it was just spasms from the DJD in my neck. The headaches only seem to happen when I've been working long hours on the computer, or had a very stressful day."

Doctor Abrams peered over his bifocals. "Explain to me the episodes of forgetfulness and the short-circuit feeling. What do you feel during these periods? Are you aware of your surroundings while these are happening? If you are aware, how long would you say they last? Are they concurrent with each other? How often do they occur?"

Jake nodded. "When these short-circuit feelings happen, I see a flash of light, not through my eyes but in my brain. Then I'll get a brief episode of brain fog and confusion, and remember nothing. They're brief, maybe thirty seconds, and they happen maybe 2-3 times per month. As for the forgetfulness, it seems like every day I forget such things as where my keys are, sometimes small tasks that I've planned, but nothing extraordinary like names, faces, etc. That's about it."

"And he stares into space," Alex quickly interjected.

"Oh yea, that's what I'm told," Jake said, rolling his eyes.

Dr. Abrams put his pen down and shot a glance at Scott. "Alex, please tell me more about the staring?"

Alex recounted the morning at the river, and what Johnny had told her.

"Jake," Dr. Abrams said, "do you recall these episodes? Did you experience the short-circuit feeling at the river or other times on vacation?"

"I don't remember staring. I had a short-circuit at the river, but no other time on vacation."

"Alex said that you were agitated the last day of your vacation. Explain why, please."

"I'd turned my phone on to find over 100 emails, numerous texts and phone messages. I'd been so relaxed in Yellowstone, and realized after I hit that button that I was going back into the shit."

"How would you rate your ability to handle work stress in your life?"

"I do very well with it, but I find myself growing impatient with work. I'm getting to the point where I'd like to start winding down."

"How would you say you handle everyday stress? Does it impact your relationship with Alex or your sex life?"

"No issues on either." Jake shot a wink at Alex.

Her cheeks burned hot as she smiled and looked down.

"Okay, is there anything else we need to discuss before we move on to some testing?"

Jake and Alex both shook their heads and replied, "No."

Dr. Abrams handed Jake a small booklet and a pen. "In here, you will find two tests. They're designed to identify Mild Cognitive Impairment, or MCI, and early Dementia. I want you to take both of these. Please hand me your phone. Combined, they should only take 25-30 minutes, and maybe much less. Any questions?"

"No, Doc, but I have to admit you're throwing around some scary words right now. Is there something Alex and I should know?"

"Jake, I don't want to scare either of you. I'm just trying to eliminate possible causes of your symptoms."

Jake started the first test, which was pretty basic—demographics, today's date, some picture identifications, a memory question, a few number calculations, some basic drawing, and a verbal question that Dr. Abrams asked at the end.

The second test was similar except for a short story Dr. Abrams verbalized. He asked Jake several recall questions at the end.

"Well," Jake said. "How did I do?"

"Jake, on both tests you missed the recall on verbal portion, and your answers were partially correct. The test is designed for 100 percent accurate answers. On the whole, you scored in the normal range on both, so that's a positive note. These tests have roughly an 80 percent success rate in identifying cognitive issues early."

Alexi smiled at Jake and clutched his hand. "Dr. Abrams, does this help you with identifying Jake's symptoms?"

"It helps me *eliminate* things. It doesn't give me answers to his symptoms, but I know what testing to do next. Cognitive issues are a process of elimination, except, of course, from acute injuries, congenital disabilities, etc."

"What's next, Doc?" Jake said.

"I would like to have an EEG, MRI, and CT scan done on your brain and brain stem. These tests will help me further eliminate possible causes. I have the equipment in my facilities, so we don't have to wait for an appointment at the hospital. How's your schedule this week?"

"I'm flexible, and the sooner, the better."

"Okay, let me call my office. Please give me a second." Dr. Abrams stood and walked to the corner of Scott's office.

"Scott, what do you think of all this?" Jake said.

"I think you're just getting old, and we both need to retire and worry about hunting and golf only."

"No, seriously, Scott," Alexi snapped.

"Alex, honestly, this is not my expertise, which is why Dr. Abrams is here. We'll let him direct everything. If there's required treatment after his diagnosis, I'll handle that."

Alexi nodded.

"Jake, is Thursday at 8:45 a.m. okay?" Dr. Abrams asked from across the room, holding his hand over his phone.

"Yes sir, that's fine."

Dr. Abrams confirmed with his office, then rejoined them by Scott's desk. "Jake and Alex, it was a pleasure meeting both of you. I'll see you on Thursday."

Jake and Alexi stood up, both surprised the meeting ended so abruptly. They reached out one at a time to shake his hand and return pleasantries.

"Dr. Abrams, is there nothing else to discuss today?" Alexi said.

"Today was a good first step. Until I look at imaging, I really can't speculate at this point. Again, this is a process of elimination. I'll have a much clearer picture by week's end. I know it's frustrating not having answers, so Scott and I will do our best to come up with a diagnosis after we do the tests on Thursday."

Dave said goodbye to Scott and exited the office.

Jake shook his head and sighed. "Scott, what the hell is this all about?"

Scott looked sober. "The tests you took are a good sign that there's a problem. It's not acute right now, and it's in the very early stages. The tests you'll do on Thursday will help Dave rule out a good deal of conditions, such as Epilepsy, and biological issues. I'm not a specialist, so let's let him handle that."

"Epilepsy?" Jake said, raising his voice. "Would I not know by this age if I had *fucking* Epilepsy?"

"Not necessarily. It develops as we grow older more often than most people realize. In fact, your staring episodes, and short-circuit feeling, can point to Epilepsy. The EEG will tell us that."

"Okay," Jake barked. "I've had enough with this brain shit! Let's go golfing."

"Sounds good," Scott replied.

"Great, I'll drive. Alex rode with me, so we'll drop her off at work on our way to the course."

"Jake, I'll follow you. I need to leave the course and meet with my better half at our accountant's."

Jake and Alexi prepared for a short five-minute drive to her work. They got in the car and sat in silence. Each tried to find the right words to open the conversation once they started rolling.

"Well...." Jake waited for Alexi to comment.

"Well what?"

"I don't know. I forgot what I was going to say." He let loose a hearty laugh.

"Jake, this is not fucking funny! Are you not concerned about anything that just happened in there?"

"No, not really."

"I am. Do you realize they're testing you for Alzheimer's, or Dementia, or who knows what? Do you realize how serious this could be? How our lives could change drastically?"

Jake heard the fear in her voice and saw her eyes well up. He needed to find the words to diffuse the situation. The humor hadn't worked, nor did his matter-of-fact attitude.

"Alexi," he said calmly, " Scott has always been over-reactive to things. Remember when I had that pain in my side, and he sent me to the hospital, thinking I might have had a heart attack? It was just a disc issue in my back. He always jumps to the worst-case scenario to eliminate dread."

"I remember."

"Relax, baby, let's see how the tests go on Thursday. If there *is* an issue, we'll address it. You know me. I'll have a plan and a backup plan for whatever."

"This is not a plumbing problem or something. There's no cure for this shit. The medical community has no answers. The richest, most powerful people in the world die from Alzheimer's. What makes you think you can have a plan?" She emphasized *plan* with air quotations.

"Take a deep breath and exhale. Again, you know how Scott is. Besides, I haven't had any issues since the last day at the river. It's probably just stress related."

Jake placed his hand on hers and smiled. "Stay positive, and have a good day. I'll talk to Scott while we're golfing. If there's anything else we need to worry about, I'll text you. Okay?"

"Okay, have a good game," she said, forcing a smile as she stepped from the car.

Jake met up with Scott at the country club's pro shop.

"Holy fuck me, Batman!" Jake almost yelled. "I wish you would have told me Dr. Abrams was gonna be there, so I'd have time to prepare Alexi. You know how freaked out she gets. She thinks I have some old age disease and will be in a diaper next week."

"You know I like to work backward, eliminating the worst-case diagnosis first. But, honestly, I don't like the short-circuit feeling and staring episodes. I spoke with Dave after you left, and he thinks it's a classic sign of focal Epilepsy. Now, the good news is we can treat this with medication, and then life will be pretty normal for you. A much worse scenario would be a degenerative brain disease like Alzheimer's, Lewy Body Dementia, Picks Disease, and the list goes on. The tests on Thursday will help us diagnose this."

Jake heard the seriousness in Scott's tone, and paused for a second. "Well, hell, let's hit some balls before I forget how to keep score."

When the two golfers made the turn after the 9th hole, Jake figured this was a good time to text Alexi and let her know Scott was just being himself and testing for the worst scenario first. This would calm her down.

She responded as expected.

OK. Smiley Face. I feel a little better. See you this afternoon. Luv you."

The men finished their round and sat at the country club bar.

Jake decided to press it a little. "Well, Scott, you just spent four hours with me. Did you see me do anything crazy other than throwing my putter into the woods on the 16th?"

Scott raised his beer to cheer. "No, my friend, you were your normal poor sport and piss-poor golfer." As they lowered their beers, he added, "What did you think about the new cart girl? Nice ass or what?"

Jake smiled. "Too bad we're not thirty years younger. She would have been in the woods with me by the 14th hole." He raised his beer for another cheer.

"What.. helping you find one of the fifteen balls you lost today?" Scott countered.

Jake winked. "She would have found two."

Scott smiled as they lowered their mugs. "Ah, the fantasies of old men."

After another round of drinks, they walked to their cars, put their clubs away, shook hands, and agreed they'd see each other at Dr. Abrams on Thursday.

The next day and a half was pretty normal for Jake and Alex. They decided to not dwell on *what ifs* and wait for the tests on Thursday. Jake shared with her the possibilities of Epilepsy and assured her medication would control it. They spent a few hours on the computer researching Jake's symptoms, educating themselves for the next visit with Dr. Abrams.

Thursday morning arrived, and as usual, they began their day with exercise. Jake harassed her a little, as normal, and showed little concern about the upcoming tests. They discussed where they would have lunch afterward.

Alex found his attitude reassuring.

They arrived at Dr. Abrams at 8:15 a.m. and filled out what seemed like a short novel of paperwork. Shortly after returning the paperwork, they called Jake back for his tests.

Alex picked up some informational pamphlets on aging and brain-related diseases, to pass the time. She recognized a good deal of the terms from their research, so the disorders felt less intimidating despite the gloom that surrounded each of them.

Jake returned to the waiting area an hour later, sat down next to Alex, and described the tests.

As the minutes passed, his impatience mounted, and he stood up to stretch just as Dr. Abrams and Dr. Johns enterded the lobby.

Doctor Abrams extended his hand. "Hello, Mr. and Mrs. Michaels, how are you this morning?"

"We're good, I guess," Jake said. "We'll be much better when we know the results of the tests."

"The radiologist is looking at the images as we speak. I'll call you back in a few minutes." He smiled, nodded, and departed.

Scott turned to her. "Alex, how are you?"

"Nervous."

"I understand. These tests can conjure up some damn scary possibilities. Hopefully, in a few minutes, we'll get good news and move forward in the right direction, treating Jake's symptoms. I'm going back with Dave to review the results. I'll see you guys in a few."

"Thanks, Scott," Jake said.

Jake stared at the clock. "I hate waiting. It's been almost forty-five minutes."

"Relax, Jake, I'm sure it takes time to read the results."

A nurse approached the couple. "Mr. and Mrs. Michaels, Dr. Abrams is ready to see you. Follow me, please."

They followed the nurse through what seemed like a never-ending labyrinth of turns. Jake could feel Alexi's anxiety grow with each step.

He was ready to dismiss all of this and get back to his normal routine. "Are you okay, Alexi? You look scared, baby."

She sighed. "I'm mentally exhausted. I want to get this over with, get good news, and relax."

He nodded and squeezed her hand as the nurse opened the door.

"Jake and Alex, please have a seat," Dr. Abrams said.

Scott sat behind the desk with Dr. Abrams. Paperwork was strewn in front of both of them.

The doctor said, "We have all of the imaging reports in front of us. I was anxious to review the EEG, which we use to identify abnormalities in the brain's electricity. It's a good indicator of seizures and Epilepsy. That report showed no abnormal activity, so I'm confident we can rule out Epilepsy."

Jake and Alexi glanced at each other and smiled, squeezing each other's hands.

"The next two tests Scott and I looked at were the MRI and PET. The MRI showed slight cerebral atrophy. Now, it is common for our brains to shrink as we age. Your atrophy is more in line with someone in their late 60's, so a bit more advanced. The PET shows elevated plaque and tangles, again more indicative of someone 10-15 years older."

Jake looked at Alexi, watching as she teared up.

He then glared at the doctors. "Guys, I have no fucking idea what this means. Am I going to be wearing a diaper and walking around pissing on my neighbors' lawns in two months? Please speak English."

Alexi grabbed his hand. "Calm down, Jake." Even as she said this, tears poured down her cheeks. She turned to their longtime friend. "Scott, I read that brain atrophy is common in Alzheimer's. Does Jake have Alzheimer's?"

Dr. Abrams responded for him. "Alex, Cerebral Atrophy is a common symptom of many diseases that affect the brain. Right now, we just don't know. There's no sign of tumors or suspicious growth, which is great news. Examination of certain parts of the brain ruled out diseases such as Parkinson's. The memory issues and staring would point towards early signs of Dementia."

"If this is Dementia or Alzheimer's, how many years of quality life would I have?" Jake said calmly, looking at the floor.

"It's hard to tell—could be four years or twenty. Every person is different."

Jake lifted his head and looked squarely at Dr. Abrams. "What's next?"

"If these are early signs of Dementia, it's very early," Dr. Abrams said. "We've caught this in preliminary stages. I want to retest in six months and see if there's any advancement. I need both of you to keep detailed notes of any changes in mood, memory, concentration, or problem solving, and the number of times the short-circuit feeling and staring occurs."

Scott added, "You know I'm always available if something is just not right. We'll spend plenty of time together golfing and hunting over the next six months, so we can discuss any changes. I want you to realize—both of you—that it's entirely possible these abnormalities are *all* we'll see for years. Please do not overreact to this."

Jake and Alex shook their heads, stood up, and said nothing. They were in a place neither had been before. They said goodbye to both of the doctors, then stopped at the front desk to schedule the follow-up appointment, and walked speechless to their car.

Jake opened the car door for Alexi, walked slowly around to his side, got in, and looked at his girl, whose tears fell and dotted the collar of her shirt. Holding back his own emotions, he searched for words to comfort her.

He turned his body to look her in the eyes. "Hey, Alexi, we'll be all right, okay?"

She stared at him, her lower lip quivering, and forced out a weak, "Okay."

"Trust me, you taking care of me while I slowly lose grip with this world is *not* our Destiny."

She nodded and said nothing.

They drove for several miles in complete silence, occasionally broken by Alexi's sniffling.

"You know," she said. "People always wish they could see what the future holds. Then, once you get a glimpse of the future, you realize it's best to leave it unknown."

He reached over and clutched her hand. At this point, he could offer no words to comfort her; she would have to deal with this in her own way.

"Are you hungry, baby?"

Alexi stared forward, answering without emotion. "I am, but I just want to go home right now."

As they finished the ride home in silence, Jake reflected on the past thirty years. The seasons of their lives had been full of sunshine, warm blue skies and brilliant colors. Now the winds of change had blown in, and a dark, cold, foreboding winter approached.

Chapter 7
Fail to Plan, Plan to Fail

Today's visit had overwhelmed Alex with a torrent of emotions and thoughts. Her perfect Universe faced its mortality.

Will my coming years be filled with watching Jake's soul be slowly sucked from him? Is the man who is so strong, vibrant, and full of life going to morph into a fragile, depressed shell of himself? How will I cope with the decline in his cognitive skills? Will I be forced to put Jake into a home, each visit hoping that he might remember a sliver of our life? Is it too early to talk to the kids? How will they be able to cope financially with Jake's inability to work? As the disease progresses, will my memories of the man I spent the last thirty years with only be ghosts of the past, cruelly haunting me, taunting me to the brink of insanity? Jake's physical abilities will eventually leave him. He'll become increasingly dependent on others. His pride and dignity will be lost. He'll live in a world that, if he could understand it, he would never tolerate.

She buried her head in a pillow and sobbed, knowing her cries would be reserved for alone times. She would have to be strong in front of Jake, and find the strength to handle this. He was always the pillar, but now she would have to take on that role as the disease progressed.

Stop! she told herself. *In six months, they may find there's no progression. It may be Jake's aging process is just a bit more advanced than it should be. I must be positive. Since the last day at the river, Jake has been okay. Maybe stress is a trigger to his staring episodes. Perhaps his memory loss is just his brain getting overloaded and tired. Maybe I need to insist he scale back his workload. Is it time I agree to sell our house and move to the West, and a less hectic lifestyle?*

Whatever path this takes, Alexi would have to fight to preserve her Universe—*their* Universe.

Jake sat in his office staring at his computer screen, deep in thought.

Is my life going to be a slow, cruel decline into hell for Alexi and the kids? Will I become a burden to her? Will I regress to where she has to watch over me like a child? Is her identity going to be lost? Will it morph into his fleeing identity, as she grasps to hold onto both, creating one sad identity? How will I provide financially for her? How will I protect her? How will I return the love it takes to care for me? Will I one day look at her and the kids, only remembering glimpses of our life, if I'm lucky? Will my world become an abyss of darkness and isolation as my brain slowly erases all that is sacred to me? Will my body eventually fail, making all essential human function reliant on others? Will I end this life feeble, with no dignity?

"*Fuck this!*" he said aloud, snapping out of the grave, depressive thoughts that clouded him. If this would be the new path of his life, he would find a way to make Alexi's years as pleasant as possible. He'd analyze the situation, educate himself, and create a plan. He would not allow this to erase all memories of their life, replacing them with years of sadness, grief, and hard work for her.

He recited to himself the words by which he lived his life: "Fail to Plan, Plan to Fail."

The alarm rang at the usual time, and Alex watched as Jake jumped out of bed and went directly to the bathroom. A good night's sleep seemed to have energized him after yesterday's exhausting events.

They walked out on the front porch, under a crystal clear early morning sky, and Jake looked up as he did every morning. "All the stars look in place. I'm happy to report the Solar System is in order today."

Alex shook her head. She believed Jake sometimes said things just to hear himself talk.

They jogged for a few minutes, making small talk, both trying to resist the elephant in the room... and failing.

Alex broached the subject. "Jake, about yesterday... what are you thinking?"

"I need time to wrap my head around the whole thing. I want to hop on my bike and do an Easy Rider thing, travel across the country — wind in my face, long black hair blowing behind me like a mane, beard wrapping around the side of my face."

Alex smiled in spite of herself. "First, you have no hair, and it's gray. Second, your beard is at best an inch long." She sighed. "I'm serious. This is not a joking matter."

"Alexi, I'm dead serious... minus the hair thing. You know this is something I always wanted to do. I don't know what the future holds, so I want to do things while I still have my wits."

Alex paused for a second. "Will you do this alone or with some of your friends?"

"I thought about meeting Mike, Dave, and Burt in Sturgis. That would be a good meeting point for them coming from the West Coast. Then we can cruise down through the Rockies into the Southwest. If they can't make it, then I'll do it myself."

"You're serious, aren't you? When would you make this ride?"

"Before the summer is over, maybe the middle of July."

"That's two weeks from now. Don't you need time to plan this out?"

"Nope, and that's the point: I don't want to plan, I just wanna go. Be free from the stress of organizing things and clear my head. Then, when I come back, I'll tackle this shit head on."

"What about rooms? It's summer, and people are on vacation."

"No rooms—sleep under the stars in a tent, just like in Easy Rider."

"Have you talked to them yet?"

"No, I was going to call them after you and I talked. I just thought about this last night."

"How long would you be gone? What about work?"

"I figured two weeks, and all my projects are close to being finished. I have a break until mid-August, when the next one kicks off."

"Well, if that's what you want to do, I say go for it. I know you've talked about this since we met, but... I'm worried about you having one of those staring spells on your bike."

"Honestly, Alexi, I think they were stress related. I've been fine since vacation. If I have another one or two in the next couple weeks, I'll rethink it."

As Alexi got ready for work in the bathroom, she thought about Jake's trip. Her emotions were divided. On the one hand, she wanted Jake to go; on the other hand, she was scared to death he would have a spell and crash. But... Jake had been riding a long time, and she remembered in their wilder days how they would party all day and night. Both of them could barely walk straight, and they would ride home. If Jake could do that, he could probably handle a little spell.

Besides, he knew they were preceded by the "short circuit" feeling, so he could pull over in time. Knowing Jake, he would take all secondary roads and travel at slower speeds.

She came out and headed downsatairs. "Have a good day, Jake," she said as she passed his office.

"You too, baby." As she approached the front door, he added, "Hey!"

"What?"

"Thanks for supporting me on this trip."

"Okay, Easy Rider, I have to go. Luv you."

Jake opened maps on the computer and planned his route. He plotted his course on secondary roads, setting up stopping points at campgrounds along the way. He estimated 400 miles a day would be comfortable and have him in Sturgis in three, maybe four days, depending on the weather. Happy with his route, he printed everything out and made careful notes. He didn't want to forget any details.

He sent a text message to Mike, Dave, and Burt. Each responded positively but needed to look at their schedule, and said they'd let him know by the end of the day. Content with the morning progress, he dove into his work day.

Deep in thought on a set of construction plans, his text message alert went off, scaring the shit out of him.

Why the hell did I have the volume so high?

He chuckled and looked at his phone, and realized it was 4 p.m. His workday had flown by. The text had come from Mike, who said he was in.

Jake typed in his reply.

> *Awesome. I'll call you tonight when I hear from Dave and Burt.*

He walked into the kitchen to start dinner, and thought, in the Western spirit of the day, Bison burgers with smoked Gruyere and caramelized onions would be perfect. While he kneaded the meat, two texts alerts went off, causing him to shake his head.

It never fails! Every time I prep food, the damn phone goes off.

He walked over and looked down. Texts from both Dave and Burt regretfully declined the ride. Both offered other dates, and Jake thought about it, but stuck to his guns. He wouldn't spend days trying to organize this trip.

He sent his reply to both.

> *That sucks, guys, but my schedule is tight after August 15th. We'll get together around the holidays.*

The next couple weeks carried forward the status quo with Jake and Alexi. They took some weekend trips, spending quality time with each other in the mountains and at Hilton Head.

Alexi had seen no symptoms in Jake, who seemed completely relaxed. The shock of the doctor's visit had worn off a bit. It still lied heavy in the back of her mind, but was slowly being replaced by the possibility of a more favorable prognosis.

Jake focused on his trip and buttoning up work related stuff. He spoke several times of the doctor visits, always confident and telling Alex everything will be fine.

CHAPTER 8
IN THE WIND

The day Jake had dreamed about since he first saw Easy Rider finally arrived. The alarm rang at the usual time, and he remained in bed for a few minutes looking at Alexi, playing back in his mind the first time they woke up together. She was as beautiful today as she was so many years ago. He soaked up the moment as if burning her image into his brain. He felt confident in his riding skills, but the possibility existed this could be the last time he'd wake up next to her. He leaned over, kissed her cheek, and got out of bed.

Alexi opened her eyes with the kiss. "Good Morning," she whispered.

"Good morning, baby."

"How excited are you?"

"I feel like a kid on Christmas morning."

Alexi's eyes twinkled as she pulled her covers down. "Why don't you come back to bed for a bit?"

"I won't argue with that. The road can wait a little longer."

They lay in bed afterwards, talking about the trip, and Alexi, as usual, went over a checklist for him. Normally, he would grow impatient with her, but given the circumstances, he obliged.

"Are you running with me this morning?" he said.

She moved her head off his chest and looked up at him. "Yeah, but we'll have to make it a bit shorter since we deviated from our schedule."

"Okay, see you downstairs."

The couple finished their run and prepared for their day. Jake loaded his bike up in the garage, prepping for the trip. He checked and double-checked his list to make sure everything was packed.

Alexi walked out to say goodbye. "Well, Easy Rider, are you ready?"

"I am. Give me a hug."

They embraced each other, holding the hug longer than normal. When they pulled away, Jake could see Alexi's eyes well.

"Hey, I'll be fine," he said.

"I know. Just make sure you text me when you stop for gas, and call me every night."

"Baby, you know I will."

They kissed one last time, and Jake straddled his bike. A moment later, the sound of thunder filled the garage.

He pulled into the driveway and looked back at Alexi. "I love you."

"I love you too. Be careful."

He nodded and pulled away, watching Alexi shrink in the mirror, as she stood motionless trying to catch every second of Jake she could. She waved one last time to him before he went out of sight, and he returned the wave.

Jake's GPS had his first stop at 515 miles, entering Indiana. Now refreshed, he leaned against his backrest, kicked his legs out on the highway pegs, and settled in. Traffic was light, allowing him to travel a bit above the speed limit. Based on his calculations, he should be close to the Tennessee border when he made his next gas stop.

The gas light came on just as he'd calculated, about twelve miles from Tennessee. He pushed forward and stopped just over the border in a small, sleepy country town.

He walked into a gas station to grab a bottle of water after filling up.

"Good Morning." A female voice with a thick southern accent greeted him as he entered.

He looked over to see a cute blonde girl behind the counter.

God, I love southern accents.

"Good Morning." He walked up to the counter to pay.

The clerk looked out the window and back at Jake. She twirled her hair as she straightened her posture, pushing her chest out.

"That's a pretty bike. Where are you heading?"

"Out west."

"All by yourself?"

"Yep."

"That's a long, lonely ride."

Visions of all the biker movies Jake had watched ran through his mind. In another life, he probably could have put her on the back and had some "road comfort" along the way.

"It is, but I'm meeting a friend out there, so it won't be bad. Have a nice day."

"Byeeee," she said, with a twinkle in her eye.

Jake drank his water, stretched, and texted Alexi.

Hey, baby, in Tennessee filling up. Nice ride so far.

Alexi texted back.

Cool. Be safe. Luv you.

He looked at his GPS, and figured the next gas stop would put him in Kentucky.

The next 300 hundred miles went by quickly. As promised, he texted Alexi when he stopped again, keeping her up to date on his progress. His GPS showed he was 135 miles from Marengo, Indiana, his first overnight stop.

He pulled up to the front office at the campgrounds, and got off his bike slowly, his muscles tightening up from the ride. He stretched and walked into the office.

"Good Afternoon," the gentleman at the front desk greeted him.

"Hello, checking in under Jake Michaels."

"Yes sir. One second, please, let me pull up your reservations." After a short pause, he said, "All right, Mr. Michaels, here we go. Here's a map of the campgrounds. Make a right on the road after the office. Follow it for about a hundred yards and your tent site will be on the left. It's number 128."

"Thank you, sir. It looks like you're pretty crowded today."

"We are. By the way, the site next to you has a group of girls from Miami. They're partying hard. If they get too loud tonight, let us know. Quiet time is at 10 p.m. Heck, they may be passed out by then."

Jake smiled and winked. "I should be fine, but thank you for the warning." He took a slow ride through the lively park, taking in the party vibe at each site.

As he passed the party girls, one of them yelled, "Woooo, nice bike!" She lifted her shirt and flashed her tits.

He smiled and couldn't help notice how firm they were. He knew she had no idea he would be camping next to her, and laughed. He parked his bike twenty feet from the girls.

When the one that flashed realized where he was staying, she looked at the other girls and buried her head in her hands. The group laughed at her embarrassment.

Jake unloaded his gear and set up his camp. As the night started to fall, he built a fire and prepped his dinner, then figured it would be a good time to call Alexi.

"Hey baby," he said.

"Hey, where are you?"

"At Marengo campground, just built a fire and gonna eat."

"How was your ride? How do you feel?"

"The ride was good. The weather was perfect. I'm stiff as hell, but other than that I feel great. I wish you were here."

"No you don't. Then all the wild biker chics you'll meet would ignore you," she joked.

"Yeah, they are everywhere." He looked over at the party girls and chuckled to himself.

"Where do you stop tomorrow night?"

"I'm gonna try to make the Iowa border. As long as the weather is good, it shouldn't be a problem."

"How far from Sturgis will you be from there?"

"About 600 miles."

"Cool, maybe you can make it in three days?"

"I'll try, but not gonna push it."

"Okay. Well, I'll let you eat and get some sleep. I bet you're tired."

"I'm exhausted. I love you. Good night."

"Good night, Easy Rider. Love you too."

Jake finished cooking his burger and relaxed in his camp chair.

One of the party girls walked over to him. "Excuse me, sir, can you help us?"

He looked up from the fire and smiled. "Please don't call me sir. It makes me feel old. My name is Jake."

"Okay, Jake. My name is Stephanie."

"Nice to meet you, Stephanie. What do you need help with?"

"We can't keep our fire going. Can you look at it?"

"Sure."

Jake walked over to the girl's site. Empty wine bottles, beer bottles, and liquor bottles covered their picnic table. "You girls are partying, aren't you?"

They all raised their drinks and laughed proudly, as a group of twenty-somethings would.

Now that Jake was close up, he could see how pretty the girls were. *Boy, if I was twenty years younger and single....*

"Hey, everyone, this is Jake," Stephanie announced.

"Hi Jake," the three other girls said in unison.

The girl that had flashed him earlier said, "Jake, would you like a beer?"

"That would be great. It's been a long ride." He knelt down next to their fire, and lifted the logs to allow air to flow better. With a few fans, the flames jumped to life.

"Yayyyyy." The girls bounced and clapped.

"Here you go, Jake, a beer well earned. My name is Jill," the flasher said.

"Thank you, Jill."

"So, Jake, where are you going?" Stephanie said.

"I'm heading out to Sturgis." He rolled his head to loosen his neck.

"Wow, cool ride," one of the other girls said.

"Where are you coming from?" Jill said.

"North Carolina." He again rolled his head around.

"Is your neck bothering you?" Jill said.

"Just stiff from the ride."

She moved behind him. "Well, you're in luck. I'm a massage therapist."

She began to rub his neck and the top of his shoulders, her touch soft but with a firm massage movement. He pictured her perfect tits from earlier, and felt himself getting a little aroused.

Okay, enough of this.

Her hands felt so good, and his neck loosened up so nicely, he decided to give it just a few more minutes.

"You're really tight." She moved her hands to the top of his shoulders and then his upper arms. "Jake, you've been working out," she added in a provocative tone.

"I try to stay in shape." He felt his dick stir more.

Okay, time to get out of here.

"Thank you, Jill, that helped."

"Are you sure, Jake? I can go longer if you like. You built a nice warm fire for us. That's the *least* I can do." She slid her hands from Jake's shoulders to his chest.

He stood up. "I appreciate that, Jill, but I'm leaving early tomorrow." He looked around the campfire. "Thank you, for the beer, ladies."

"Thank you, for lighting our fire," Stephanie said, winking.

He walked into the darkness to his camp, and muttered under his breath, "Add alcohol, get girls gone wild."

His alarm went off before dawn. He walked out of his tent into the still campground, the early morning silence broken only by the songbirds. He planned on a good run, and hit the road before 8 a.m. While circling the campground, he spotted empty alcohol bottles of all types on picnic tables, from one campsite to the next, and could only imagine the stories behind those empties.

He finished his run, packed up his campsite, checked out, and sent a quick text to Alexi to let her know he was on the road.

The first 120 miles passed peacefully, with almost no traffic. He pulled in for his first gas stop, and sent a text to Alexi. After wishing her a good morning and telling her his location, he continued his trip.

The road flew by quickly under his tires, the Saturday traffic still light. He relaxed and took in the sights, but suddenly he felt odd. He recognized this and pulled over. The short-circuit feeling preceded a spell. When his head cleared, he looked down at his watch: this one had lasted about forty-five seconds. It was his first since starting the trip, the last one coming the week before he left. He'd learned how to identify them, and more importantly, how to hide them from Alexi for the past eight months. Had she not caught him at the River in Yellowstone, the doctors and she still wouldn't know about them.

This was his second spell in the past ten days, which meant the frequency was increasing, along with the duration.

He gathered himself, stretched, and continued his ride. After two hours, the light came on warning of low gas. After filling up, he ate lunch and checked in with Alexi, then returned quickly to the road. The GPS showed him arriving in Burlington, Iowa in 290 miles, which would be his next overnight stay.

He rode across the Mississippi River with some anxiety. Bridges were the only place he worried about having a spell — they offered no place for him to pull over and let it pass — but he reached the other side without incident.

A 'Welcome to Iowa' sign, followed by a Burlington sign, sat on the right side of the road. GPS directed him to his hotel.

He checked in at the front desk, went to his room and plopped on the bed, exhausted from the ride. He texted Alexi to update her, and let her know he'd talk to her tonight before going to sleep, he took a quick shower, dressed and walked downstairs, and asked the front desk clerk where he could find a good steak.

The brunette embodied all the stereotypical looks and mannerisms he expected from a Midwestern woman. "I like the Creekside Café. They serve a good T-Bone, are reasonably priced, and after dinner, they turn into a good local bar. They have a great southern rock band playing tonight, if you like that kind of music."

"I do like southern rock, but have to get on the road early. A T-Bone sounds great, though. How far is it from here?"

"You can walk to it. Make a right when you leave the hotel and then the first left. You can't miss it. Better hurry, 'cus they stop dinner service at 7 p.m."

"Looks like I have a half hour, so better get going. Thank you."

He walked into the saloon-style restaurant, which had Western décor, maybe a bit overdone, but it still looked comfortable.

"Hello, how many?" the hostess asked.

"Just one, please."

"Would you like a table, booth, or a seat at the bar?"

He looked around the restaurant. The bar was crowded, and besides, he was tired and didn't feel like making idle talk with strangers tonight. "A booth would be great."

He sat down and looked over the menu. The girl at the hotel was right; prices were more than fair. He ordered a cold beer and a 16-ounce T-Bone.

After dinner, he ordered another beer. The dinner crowd had mostly left and the nighttime crowd was filtering in as the band was setting up on stage. He looked at his watch: 8:30. The band started at 9:00, so he'd finish his beer and leave before the music started.

He paid his bill and walked towards the front door, passing a group of girls. They all had cowboy hats on, western style shirts, and tight jeans. He looked back at their asses as they passed.

Ain't nothing better than a pair of tight jeans on a nice ass.

"Hey, asshole, you looking at something?" a voice rang out.

Jake ignored it, thinking the comment had been directed to someone at the bar, but then a hand touched his shoulder from behind.

"Old man, I'm talking to you."

Jake turned to a tall skinny man looking him in the eyes. "Did I do something to piss you off man?"

"I don't like the way you looked at my girl's ass," the cowboy said.

Jake smelled booze on his breath.

"Leave him alone, Jimbo," a girl from the group said, walking back towards Jake and the cowboy.

"Honestly, man, I meant no harm. I'm sorry," Jake said.

A small crowd gathered.

The cowboy poked Jake in the chest. "That's my girl, fucker."

Jake took a deep breath and glanced at the men with the cowboy. "Again, I apologize. I meant no harm."

He turned to walk away, surprised to see no bouncers or management coming to break this up. In fact, it appeared most people would be happy to watch the altercation.

"I don't accept your apology, Mister," the cowboy said. He grabbed Jake's shoulder again.

"Jimbo, for God's sake, let him alone," the girl urged.

Jake paused for a few seconds with the cowboy's hand on his shoulder, then spun quickly, grabbed the Cowboy's arm and twisted it downward. The Cowboy's body followed his arm as he fell to the ground. Jake held onto his arm and twisted harder, then put his boot across the man's face and pushed his head towards the ground with the heel. He kept twisting pressure on his arm as a couple more cowboys approached.

"Now you listen, Mother Fucker, I apologized *twice*. You tell your buddies to back off. If they don't, I will break your fucking arm!"

The cowboy's girl looked in Jakes' eyes, and the rage she saw clearly frightened her.

The cowboy cried in pain as Jake exerted more pressure.

"Mister," the girl pleaded. "Let him go, please. He's been drinking too much."

Jake glared at her, still pushing his boot into the cowboy's face and twisting his arm to the point it bent grotesquely, then released his grip, said nothing, turned and walked out the door.

"Let him be," the girl said behind him, likely holding back some of her boyfriend's buddies.

He walked calmly back to the hotel and couldn't help but chuckle.

Hell, that felt good. It's been a while since I had to throw down. I guess I'm not that old.

"How was your dinner, Mr. Michaels?" the front desk clerk said, as Jake passed her.

"T-Bone was excellent. Thank you. Have a good night."

He sat on his bed, fell backwards, and dialed Alexi. "Hey baby."

"Hey, biker boy, how are you?"

"Good, I just ate a delicious steak, drank a couple of beers, and got into a little scuffle."

"A scuffle, where?"

"At the restaurant. Some cowboy had a bit too much liquid courage. He ran his mouth to the wrong guy, and ended up on the floor with a boot in his face."

"Jake, you are not twenty-five. These young boys don't fight nice anymore. You're lucky he didn't pull a knife or gun on you."

He laughed. "No, Alexi, he's lucky. I may be older, but I didn't forget my training. One guy, one gun, I like my chances."

"Jake, I'm worried enough. I don't need you playing Rambo out there."

"Calm down, Sexy Lexi. I promise... no more fights. This is the only stop I have in a town. I'll be under the stars the rest of the trip."

"Okay, promise?"

"I promise. What's going on at home?"

"Nothing. It's pretty boring without you around."

"Do you like your peaceful mornings with no one harassing you?"

"I love them."

"Whaaaaat?"

"Just kidding. I miss you. I'm crossing off the days on the calendar till you come home. How are you feeling?"

"I'm fine, just tired and sore at the end of the day. No other issues."

"I *bet* you're sore."

"Okay, Sexy Lexi, I'm leaving at first light. I'm gonna try to push into Crow Creek, South Dakota tomorrow. I'll finally be out of the Midwest. The ride is boring, as you remember, and I'm ready to see God's country again."

"How far is Crow Creek?"

"About five hundred miles or so. If the weather is good, it'll be an easy ride."

"Okay, be careful and send me some pics of South Dakota."

"I will. I love you. Goodnight."

"Love you too. Talk to you tomorrow. Goodnight."

The alarm rang at 5:00 a.m. Jake went for a quick run, ate breakfast, and checked out.

The perfect weather and non-existent traffic allowed him to average eighty miles per hour, meaning he'd be in South Dakota around noon.

Jake made his first gas stop, and texted Alexi.

200 more miles to South Dakota.

She responded.

Awesome, send pics.

When he approached the "Welcome to South Dakota" sign, he pulled over next to it, snapped a selfie, and sent it to Alexi.

She responded.

Yayyyyy.

He felt good, the weather perfect for ridin, and made good time through South Dakota. After a quick lunch, he set his GPS for Sturgis. If he could average seventy miles per hour, he would arrive in Sturgis around dinnertime.

He texted Alexi again.

Sturgis or bust.

She responded with a smiley face.

The ride through South Dakota was flatter than he'd imagined, but once he hit Crow Creek, elevations started to vary. He stopped several times to send Alexi pictures and gas up. The last stop was twenty miles outside Sturgis. He looked to the horizon, where mountains rose.

Finally! The West I saw on vacation.

He rolled into Sturgis, and it was everything he'd pictured. He sent Alexi several photos, then saw a sign that changed his plans.

Deadwood: 13 miles.

He rode through Sturgis and continued onto Deadwood, and called the Deadwood/Black Hills KOA to make reservations for a tent site.

"Wild Bill Hickok, here I come," he said, then jumped on his throttle and thundered out of Sturgis.

He pulled into the KOA, checked in, and rode to his campsite, ready to relax. Eight hundred plus miles had his body aching.

Where are the party girls at now?

The sun dropped along with the temperatures. He barbequed chicken, drank a Guinness, and settled in for the night at his campfire.

He picked up his phone, dialed, and said "Hey, baby," when Alexi picked up.

"Hey, cowboy, how's Sturgis?"

"Don't know. I'm in Deadwood."

"Deadwood? What's in Deadwood?"

"Wild Bill Hickok's Grave and a ton of Western history."

"Okay, does Mike know you switched gears?"

"Unfortunately, Mike can't come. His work load won't allow it."

"Well, shit. You rode all that way and now have to be by yourself?"

"Yeah, I was looking forward to spending time with him. Honestly, though, I'm fine just moving at my own pace."

"I know, but I would have felt better if you were with someone."

"Well, in a few days I'll be in Denver with Johnny."

"That's true. How was your ride today?"

"It was a long eight hundred miles, but that's the last day I push my schedule. I'm a day ahead, so now I can relax and take a nice slow ride into paradise."

"You sound tired."

"I am. I'm gonna drink my beer, hit the tent, and pass out."

"Okay, well, I love you. Call me before you start your ride to Yellowstone."

"I will. I love you too. Goodnight baby."

He opened the overhead flap on his tent and gazed up. The South Dakota night sky rivaled any planetarium. He stared at the Milky Way, wishing Alexi could share this with him as he drifted off to sleep.

Nature's alarm clocks woke Jake up. Their early morning songs echoed through the quiet campground, and a profound calm fell over him. Today, he was going back to *Heaven on Earth.*

He started his early morning run, and quickly felt the effects of the elevation. Deadwood sat at around 4500 feet. It would take him a few days to acclimate to running in the elevation.

After a brisk run, he sat at his campfire and made his first batch of "cowboy coffee," which smelled great as it percolated over the open flame. He moved it off to the side of the fire ring to cook eggs, and after eating, he took his first sip of the aromatic brew.

"Jupiter's cock!"

He looked around to make sure no one had heard him. This was the strongest coffee he'd ever had. "No wonder the cowboy's shot each other. They were jacked up all the time." He laughed.

He then dialed Alexi. "Good morning, Sunshine."

"Good morning, Easy Rider."

"Baby, the stars were awesome last night. I wish you could have been here."

"Really, that would have been nice. We got ripped off last time we out there. Too many clouds."

"I know, and this morning I made my first cowboy coffee."

"How was that?"

"The strongest shit I ever had in my life. I need to practice a bit with it."

Alexi laughed. "Well in nine days you will be drinking my coffee again."

In mid-sentence, their conversation had ended, so he redialed her.

"Hey, baby, my damn phone just lost service for no reason. Sorry about that. What were we talking about?"

"The coffee, Jake. Are you okay?"

"I'm great, why?"

"Because you forgot what we were talking about."

"Just a senior moment. No worries."

"Okay, what time are you leaving for Yellowstone?"

"As soon as I pack up. I'd say in about thirty minutes."

"How far of a ride is it?"

"It's about four hundred miles to the West Gate. I'm planning on taking my time. I want to enjoy the scenery and take tons of pictures."

"Well, enjoy yourself, and please send me pics. Love you."

"I will. Talk to you later. Love you too."

The ride from the Black Hills of South Dakota into Wyoming was nothing less than amazing. Jake stopped to take picture after picture, and forwarded half of them to Alexi. At 4:00 p.m., he stopped for gas, anxious to talk to her regarding the pictures. She would be on her way home from work about now.

"Hey," he said. "Did I send you enough pictures?"

"Oh my God, I finally had to put my phone on vibrate. Did you get very far? It seems like you were taking more pictures than riding."

Jake chuckled. "Actually, not really. I'm gonna stay in Basin tonight. I'm about sixty miles from there. Hey, check out the last picture I sent you."

"Hold on. I'm coming to a light. Does that say Hazleton, just like your hometown?"

"Yep. I didn't know there was a Hazleton, Wyoming. I need to post that on Facebook. All my old friends will enjoy it." He glanced up and around. "Okay, baby, let me get going. I'll call you when I get camp set up."

"Okay, talk to you tonight."

The ride to Basin mesmerized Jake, as he wound his way through canyons, along mountain passes, and badlands. The road bordered the Bighorn River. He glanced at it often, picturing himself fishing the deep holes and long rifts. He was at the gateway to paradise.

The road started a steady climb up one of the passes, and a sign announced a scenic overlook in two miles. As the sun was setting behind the mountains, he looked at his watch and figured one more picture before pulling over for the night. Another sign for the overlook had an arrow directing him off the main road. The sign had two points of interest on it: the top point highlighted the town of Sulphur Springs in two miles; the second one the scenic overlook in a half mile.

Jake followed the narrow road, which offered no room for error as it snaked along the spine of a ridge, with sharp drop-offs on either side. He was surprised at the amount of traffic on this small road, and the speed at which they traveled.

His worst fear hit him, as he felt a spell coming on. In a split second, he analyzed everything. He was moving at forty-five miles per hour, and traffic was on his ass pushing him. A line of oncoming traffic worsened the situation, and the road had no berm for him to pull over. He saw a dirt road turnoff about twenty feet in front of him, and had no time to control this situation before the spell would take over. Visions of his life and Alexi flashed before him. He was helpless. In his last act before slipping away, he put his right-hand turn signal on, down shifted, and leaned to make the right turn onto the dirt road.

Now, only Destiny could steer his wheels in the wind.

Chapter 9
Miracles

Jake sat on his bike with the kickstand down and bike turned off. He was on the dirt road he'd aimed for during his last effort to escape the traffic, before slipping into darkness. After eight months of spells, it had become clear that he had cognitive control during the episodes, but he remembered nothing. He shook the cobwebs loose and stepped off the bike. The dirt road was not the scenic overlook, but the view was spectacular. He meandered down the road about fifty yards, where it ended with a sheer drop to the river below.

He surveyed the area, decided it would be a good place to camp for the night, and grabbed his phone. "Hey baby."

"Heyyyy, East Rider."

"You should see where I'm camping tonight. I was on my way to a scenic overlook, but found a random dirt road and went down it. The view is unreal. I'll send you a picture in the morning."

"Where are you?"

"Near Sulphur Springs."

"Never heard of it."

"Me either."

"So, I take it you're not at a campground?"

"Nope, I'm under the stars all by myself, just like I pictured this ride forty years ago."

"Aren't you scared of bears or wolves or mountain lions?"

Jake chuckled. "Sexy Lexi, after what I lived through in Somalia, not much walking this earth scares me."

"Yeah, but you had a gun."

"Good point. But honestly, they're more scared of us than we are of them. I have no food to lure them in tonight, only dehydrated shit. Trust me. The hungriest animal might turn their nose up at this."

"Okay. What's your plan tomorrow?"

"I'll be in Yellowstone by lunchtime."

"Cool. I bet you're excited?"

"Yeah, I can't wait to ride through the parks."

"All right, I'm beat. Work was rough today. I'll let you get to bed with all the wild animals. Talk to you in the morning. Love you."

"Love you too. Goodnight."

He woke to the sounds of the woods coming to life. He unzipped the tent, walked into the crisp morning, and inhaled the mountain air deeply.

"Good morning for cowboy coffee," he said, exhaling.

After eating two breakfast bars and drinking a cup of liquid speed, he stretched and did a few sets of pull-ups on a limb, then grabbed his phone.

"Good morning, Love of My Life."

"Good morning, Mountain Man. I see you didn't get eaten."

"Nope. Wait till you see this place. I'm gonna ride down to the cliff's edge and shoot a picture before I leave."

"Cool, I can't wait. The pictures you've been sending are awesome."

"Now remember, as I get closer to the park, my cell service will be sporadic. I should be at the campground a little past noon, where the service is good. So don't get worried if you don't hear from me until then. Did you get the photo I sent last night of the stars?"

"Yes, at like 2 a.m. It woke me up. You stayed up late last night."

"No, actually I sent it at 9:30 my time, 11:30 your time. Service is brutal out here. Okay, I guess you'll see this morning's picture sometime today."

"Yeah, I remember how bad service is there. Will you be at the campground noon your time or my time?"

"Your time."

"Okay, I'll talk to you at lunch. Be careful and enjoy your ride. I have to get ready for work."

"Okay, baby, love you. Oh, hey, before you go, you'll be getting a pic to brighten your day." He laughed.

"Oh boy, I can only think what that can be? Love you too. Bye."

Jake packed up camp and fired up his bike.

Alex hung up. She knew that after Jake's trip, the reality was that they'd be moving out West. She remembered how depressed he was after their vacation. After this trip, his heart would stay there, and that he'd only be going through the motions at home. He sounded so happy, so peaceful.

She took her 10:00 a.m. break when her text message notification sounded. The picture from Jake was exactly what she'd expected, with him naked, posing with the mountains in the background. She raisesd her eyebrows, and had to admit it was actually a good dick pic. Normally, they were just close-ups. He would use a photo editor and put hats on the head of his penis, smiley faces, etc. They were totally juvenile, but she gave him credit for creativity. The more she thought about it, Jake had not sent her one in a long time. She remembered a hilarious one she'd saved and pulled it up, noting it was dated over a year ago. Clearly, Jake was in his happy place now.

It was 2:00 p.m. and no text from Jake. She knew the service was bad in the parks, but the picture of his campground he promised had never reached her. She sent a text thinking maybe he'd lost track of time.

Hey, where are you?

After thirty minutes without an answer, she though the charger on his bike may have stopped working. Even if that were so, though, she knew Jake would find a way to charge his phone. He'd never travel without it, and never allow contact to be lost with her.

Her workday ended, and she was concerned that Jake hadn't texted her. He should be in his camp by now. She texted Johnny asking if he'd heard from Jake, and he said not since last night, but he reminded her of the service issues. She didn't want to worry him at this point, and agreed.

She tried another number, and a friendly voice answered, "Good afternoon, Flagg Ranch."

"Good afternoon, my name is Alex Michaels. I'm checking to see if my husband Jake Michaels has checked in yet?"

"One second please, let me look."

"No, Mrs. Michaels, I do not see that he's registered yet."

"Hmmm, okay, thank you."

"Mrs. Michaels, do you know what gate he's coming through?"

"West Gate, I believe."

"Okay, I know traffic is terrible coming from the North and West gates today."

"Okay, thank you." She hung up and lowered her phone slowly.

Her text message notification chimed. It was Johnny.

Any word from Dad?

No.

Her phone rang instantly. "Hey, Mom, did you call Flagg Ranch?"

"I just hung the phone up with them, Johhny. They said traffic in the park is really heavy."

"Okay, yeah, it's the busiest time of the year there. When was the last time you talked to Dad?"

"This morning, before he left for Yellowstone. That was around 8:00 a.m. his time. He said he would be in Yellowstone shortly past noon, and checked-in around 1:00 his time."

"It's 3:00 out here now."

"I know. I'm gonna call them back at 5:00 your time."

"Okay, Mom, let me know. This isn't like Dad."

Alex paced, watching the clock and her phone. Every time her text alert sounded, she hoped it was Jake. He'd printed out his route for her before leaving, so she checked on the computer for any reported accidents from Sulphur Springs to Yellowstone. There were a few minor incidents reported, but nothing involving a motorcycle.

It was 5:00 p.m. in Yellowstone, time to call again.

"Flagg Ranch, can I help you?"

"Yes, I'm checking to see if my husband Jake Michaels has checked in yet?"

"No, ma'am, he has not. I know he's past check-in time. I tried to call him to verify he's coming, because we're booked and have a standby list. He didn't answer."

Alex fell silent for a few seconds. "Okay, please keep his reservation. I spoke with him this morning, and I know he's heading your way. He's on a motorcycle, and may have broken down in an area cell service isn't available."

"Yes, ma'am, we won't cancel unless we're directed. He's paid in full."

"Thank you. I'll call back in a few hours to check again."

"That's fine. If he checks in, I will ask him to call you."

"Thank you."

Almost eight hours had passed since she heard from Jake. She would call the campground before dark, knowing Jake would not ride at night.

Her phone rang, and it was Johnny. "Any word, Mom?"

"No. I called the campground, and they said they tried to call him after he failed to check in at 2:00. They didn't reach him, just his voicemail."

"Hmmm, this is not like Dad."

"No, he's called or texted every time he stopped for gas the entire trip, and he's been sending pictures nonstop since he got into Wyoming, but I've received nothing from him for hours. In fact, the last thing he said was he would send a pic of where he stayed last night. That never reached me. I'm worried, Johnny."

"Should we call the police?"

"I thought about it. I've checked the route he was taking for accident reports, but there's nothing. Your dad will not ride at night, so I'm gonna call the campground at dark. If he hasn't checked in, I'll call the police in Sulphur Springs."

"Okay, let me know. And Mom... he'll be fine. Maybe he diverted off track for a picture, and his bike broke down. He's probably cursing up a storm because he has no cell service." Johnny laughed nervously.

"I'll call you after I talk to the campground. Love you."

Alex watched the clock tick, minute by minute, until 11 p.m. east coast time, and still no word from Jake. Twelve hours had passed with no contact from him.

"Hello, Flagg Ranch. Can I help you?"

"Hello, my name is Alex Michaels. I'm seeing if my husband checked in yet."

"Yes, Mrs. Michaels, we spoke earlier. No, ma'am, he hasn't checked in yet."

Alex's hands trembled as she thanked the desk clerk and hung up. She stared into space as dreaded visions raced through her mind. Her phone snapped her back to reality. She took a deep breath and regained her composure.

"Hey, Mom, anything?"

"No, Johnny, I'm calling the police. Can you please call Robert and Danielle? I haven't told them yet. I wanted to stay off the phone in case your dad called. I didn't want to worry the whole family."

"I will, Mom. Call me after you talk to the police."

"I will."

She took another deep breath and dialed.

"Good evening, Sulphur Springs Police Dept, Officer Gray Cloud speaking. Is this an emergency?"

"No, ma'am, at least I hope not. I haven't heard from my husband in over twelve hours. He was heading to Yellowstone on a motorcycle, and last time I—"

"One second, ma'am, let's slow down," the officer said calmly. "First, let me ask you a few questions. What is your name and your husband's name?"

"Sorry, my name is Alex Michaels, and my husband's name is Jacob Michaels. He goes by Jake."

"Okay, where are you calling from?"

"Ashville, North Carolina."

"Okay, you said your husband was on his way to Yellowstone. When was the last time you heard from him? Why have you called Sulphur Springs Police Department?"

"Yes, officer, he was traveling to Yellowstone. I spoke with him this morning, a little over twelve hours ago. He said he camped overnight on a dirt road near Sulphur Springs."

"Well, there are a lot of dirt roads around here. Did he give any description?"

"He said it was a beautiful overlook of the Bighorn River. That was it."

"That describes one of probably thirty roads around here. Mrs. Michaels, I have to ask this. Are you and your husband having any relationship issues? Does he have any issues with drugs or alcohol? Has he ever disappeared before?

"No ma'am."

Alex told Officer Gray Cloud how Jake had stayed in contact with her nonstop the entire trip. They were happily married for twenty-eight years, and he had no substance abuse issues. She told her he sent a picture of himself this morning. He was also sending a picture of the overlook before he left camp. That picture never arrived.

"Mrs. Michaels, can you send me the last picture your husband sent this morning? It's possible there is something that can help me identify where he was."

Alex paused. *Of the hundreds of pictures Jake sent, the most relevant would be a nude picture. And to make it worse, I have to send it to a female.*

"Officer Grey Cloud, I'm a bit embarrassed by that picture."

The officer chuckled to herself, clearly having a good idea what's in the picture. She had seen dozens like it in her career and personal life. "I assume it's compromising, Mrs. Michaels?"

"Yes." Alex's voice wavered.

"Well, I promise that *few* people will see it. Please send me a normal photo also, one that I can distribute. What's your husband's cell phone number? I can have the police in Cody run a location check on it."

Alex's voice raised. "Will that show where he is now?"

"If it's on, we can track the pings to the towers. If for some reason the phone is off, it will give us the last known position."

"Oh, that would be great. How soon will we know?"

"It won't be until tomorrow morning. The Cyber unit is off at nighttime. Even if they were working, a nighttime search in the mountains and canyons is near impossible without a good starting point."

Alex's voice flattened. "I see." She'd read enough about missing person cases in the backcountry. Usually, they didn't end well. This wilderness was unforgiving.

Officer Gray Cloud said, "Mrs. Michaels, it sounds like Jake has the gear to spend the night. I'll send a message to Cody as soon as we hang up. Tomorrow morning, I'll speak with the oncoming officers. We'll find him. Please send me both pictures and his cell phone number. Also, if you send a picture and the VIN of his motorcycle, that would be helpful."

"Yes, I'll send everything as soon as we hang up. Thank you for your help."

Alex looked at the nude picture of Jake, and tears rolled down her face. She kissed her fingers and placed them on her phone. Her world was unraveling.

She thought about trying to block out his private parts on the photo, but worried she would ruin the picture, or worse, erase it. This could be the only clue as to where Jake was, if the phone tracking failed. She hit 'Send.' In seconds, another woman would have a private picture of her Jake. They wouldn't know the man he is, just as some nude guy on a mountaintop.

She lowered her head, and the tears fell freely to Jake's desk. She settled back in his chair, imagining the bolsters where his arms wrapped around her. She wanted to hear his voice, assuring her everything would be fine. Silence filled the same office that had once been so alive with their conversation.

A notification on her phone snapped her back to reality. She had three missed calls and several texts from her kids, so she set up a group call to explain everything. One by one, each child joined.

"Mom, what's happening?" Danielle said.

"Do John and I need to go out there?" Robert said.

"What do the cops think?" Johnny said.

The volley of questions made her head spin. She recounted every detail, from this morning to the phone call with Officer Gray Cloud, excluding the nude photo part. The phone call ended with more questions than answers.

The last call Alex made was to Paul and Lisa. She told them everything she knew.

"Alex, do you want me to come over and spend the night with you?" Lisa said.

"Thank you so much, Lisa. I'll be fine. I need to sort all of this out. I'll call you guys in the morning, once I hear from the officer in Sulphur Springs."

She lay in bed and sent another text to Jake, hoping this one would reach him. She prayed for a response. The bedroom seemed suddenly empty, the darkness that usually helped her move into a peaceful slumber now surrounding her with dread. She rolled over to Jake's side of the bed, and could smell him. She pulled his pillow towards her and slid it under her head.

The alarm rang at 6:30 a.m. The last time Alex had looked at the clock, it was 1:15. She was still clutching her phone, which had no messages from Jake. She stared at the room as the early morning sunlight filtered through the shades. Normally, she opened her eyes with the expectation of the day. This morning was different. Something was wrong. Jake would never do this to her.

She started the coffee and went for a run. Jake had taught her how exercise helped the thought process, and she needed to be clear. There would be time for emotions, but now she needed to be focused.

Jake and she never ran with their phones. Today would be an exception. The three kids, Paul, and Lisa all texted her. She responded briefly—*no news*—so they didn't worry about her. She would talk to them once she spoke with the police in Sulphur Springs.

Her phone rang at 8:30. Caller ID read Sulphur Springs Police Department. "Mrs. Michaels, this is Officer Gray Cloud."

"Good morning, officer. Do you have news?"

"I showed the picture of your husband to one of our officers, and he recognized the area. It's an old scenic overlook. He's waiting for first light to go there."

"Okay, good, how will that help?"

"We can make sure he left the area. Hopefully, there will be a clear tire track in the dirt showing us which way he traveled. I also have confirmation from Cody PD that they'll start tracking first thing this morning."

"Okay, great. I appreciate how quickly you're working on this."

"Yes, ma'am, the first twenty-four hours are the most important. Fortunately, it's summer, so we don't have to worry about hypothermia in the event he's injured. Survival rates are much higher now than in the winter."

"Officer Gray Cloud, something you should know. Jake is prior Special Forces. He's well trained in survival. That's not my concern."

"That's good to know. Our officer will be on site in about thirty minutes. I'll call you once he reports back."

"Thank you. When will we know about the tracking of his phone?"

"Wyoming has no privacy rules regarding tracking. There's no red tape to deal with. The Cyber unit comes in at 8:00 a.m., so I expect to hear from them sometime before 10:00 a.m."

"Okay, I'll wait for your call. Again, thank you so much for your attention to this."

She blasted a text to everyone with the update, and asked that they limit conversation for a few hours so she didn't miss any calls from the Sulphur Springs.

She paced the floor, and every minute felt like an hour. Anxiety, the likes of which she'd never experienced, flooded over her. She needed to stay positive. Jake was a survivor.

At 9:40 a.m., her phone rang. "Mrs. Michaels, this is Officer Gray Cloud."

"Please tell me good news, officer."

"The officer on scene confirmed a fresh campsite and motorcycle tracks. There's a track down to the old lookout. The track turned and headed to the exit. It appears he traveled west from the dirt road. This would be the direction one would take to Yellowstone."

Alex breathed a small sigh of relief. "Okay, that follows what Jake told me. He said he would drive down to the cliff and take a picture for me. Then he was leaving for the Park."

"And that is the picture you still have not received, correct?"

"Yes, that's correct."

"The officer on the scene is traveling up Route 20 as we speak, to see if his motorcycle is along the road."

"Okay, I'll wait for you to call me with any news. And again, you said we should hear something from Cody around noon my time, right?"

"Yes ma'am."

She again updated everyone. Each member of the family had stopped their daily lives, hanging on every word she told them. John,

Robert, and Danielle had spoken amongst themselves, and had cleared their schedules in preparation to be at their Mom's side, if bad news prevailed. They knew her as a strong woman, but they also knew Jake was her life.

At 11:45 a.m., her phone rang. "Mrs. Michaels, this is Officer Hal Jones. I've relieved Officer Gray Cloud. She's updated me on everything. I wanted to call and introduce myself and give you an update." His voice was deep and authoritative with a thick Western accent.

"Yes, sir, please give me good news."

"The Officer that was at the campsite reported no motorcycles along Route 20. Cody PD said they're having some technical issues, but they expect to have a full report shortly."

"Okay." Alex's voice deflated.

"Mrs. Michaels, Officer Gray Cloud said your husband is ex-Special Forces?"

Alex heard a curious tone in the Officer Jones's voice.

"Yes, sir, he is."

"Did he see battle time?"

"Yes, several times. Why do you ask?"

"Does he have PTSD?"

"No, not that I know of. The VA and his primary civilian doctor never diagnosed him with it."

"Okay, PTSD is strange. It can manifest itself years after events. You've seen no changes in him, correct?"

Alex paused, thinking it was time to come clean with Jake's condition. Maybe it could save his life. Maybe they would search differently.

She took a deep breath. "Before Jake left, his doctors diagnosed him with slightly advanced brain atrophy. They said his brain resembled shrinkage more normal of someone 10 to 15 years his senior."

"Does he have dementia?"

"They don't believe so, and if he does, it's in the very early stages, nothing that will alter his life right now."

"Okay," he said. "I'll call you when I hear from Cody PD. It should be soon."

Alex hung up. Officer Jones's questions made her think. When they talked again, she would ask him. His mentioning of PTSD was a new revelation.

Is it possible that's what Jake has, and not the death sentence of Dementia?

She needed him back. He needed to be retested.

Her phone rang twenty minutes later. "Mrs. Michaels, Officer Jones."

"Yes sir."

"We have the report back from Cody. It shows Jake traveled North towards Yellowstone. It showed in the first half hour when he left the campsite that he traveled around forty-five miles an hour. Then something strange happened. For the next thirteen hours, his travel slowed to around two miles per hour. That's walking speed. At that point, the signal died."

"I don't understand. What does this mean?"

"Just looking at the tracking, it would appear he left his bike and started walking. Based on the location of the pings, he was moving north along the Bighorn River. We're sending a helicopter out to travel this route."

"Okay, so that means he's alive?"

"It would appear he is. Why he has elected to stay in the canyons along the river, and not go on the road to flag someone down, confuses me. He's covered roughly twenty miles."

"Officer Jones, I don't know, but Please, I beg you to bring him home to me." She broke down sobbing.

"Mrs. Michaels, we'll do our best to find him."

She regained her composure. "Officer Jones, why did you ask about PTSD?"

"I'm prior Military. I don't have PTSD, but have friends that do. I've seen them do some bizarre things. I've worked two missing person cases in which PTSD appeared to be the underlying issue."

"The PTSD cases... did you find them alive?"

"One we did, one we did not. The one who did not make it had a severe case. He wondered off naked at night in the middle of the winter. He stood no chance. It would appear your husband has all his faculties."

"Yes, sir, he does."

"I'm going with the chopper crew on the river search, and I'll call you as soon as we know something."

"How long will it take?"

"Considering we have a clear tracking signal, we can cover the area quickly. I would assume several hours."

"Okay, thank you."

She called everyone with updates, but they had more questions than she could answer. She felt so helpless and out of control.

Paul and Lisa, after hearing the tone of her voice, felt it best to be with her, and said they were on their way.

The flight crew walked around the small helicopter doing their pre-flight inspection. Officer Jones greeted them, and handed the pilot the tracking report to enter into the navigation system.

"Hey, Hal, how are you?" the pilot said as they shook hands.

"I'm good, Dave, how are you?"

"Doing good, man, six more months and retired. So what do we have here? I'm told another missing person case."

"Yea, this one is a bit strange. The missing person is an ex-Special Forces guy on a motorcycle trip to Yellowstone from the East Coast. He left the old scenic overlook on Burning Bush road yesterday morning, where he camped the night before, and traveled on his bike for about a half hour to the Pintail Canyon area. It looks like he parked his bike there and walked along the river for close to twenty miles. At that point, he goes dark."

"PTSD?"

"His wife said no."

"When was the last time she heard from him?"

"6:30 a.m. yesterday. He sent her this picture and broke camp."

Dave looked at the picture and laughed. "And my wife thinks I'm the only old man sending dick pics."

Hal laughed and patted Dave on the shoulder. "Well, let's go find this guy."

The flight to the search area took only ten minutes. They flew low over the Bighorn, following the meandering river through canyons and over flats. The first waypoint sat two miles ahead, which was where tracking showed the bike had parked. The helicopter slowed to a hover, then Dave dropped lower and inched northbound.

"I don't see anything," Hal said over the headset.

"Me either. I'll creep along the river for the next forty miles. We'll pass the waypoint where his phone went dark. I'll fly further downriver in case our boy is still walking."

"If he is walking, why the fuck not simply go on the road and get help?" Hal said.

"Maybe he doesn't want help. Maybe he's going off the grid."

Hal cocked his head and raised his eyebrows. "I thought about that."

The two men continued to move downriver to the next waypoint.

"Hal, at the bend is where tracking shows our guy went dark?"

Hal gave a thumbs-up. "Damn, the river is high for this time of the year."

Dave made a casting motion. "Yeah, all the rain is fucking up my fishing." He pulled the chopper into a hover, dropped it down, and drifted back and forth.

"Nothing. No campfires or anything," Hal said.

"Let's head downstream for another ten miles or so," Dave said. "He couldn't have gone much farther than that. The fishing trails along the river end, so unless he has a raft, he's not going past there."

The two men flew to the northernmost part of the river that one could walk. The rapids were fierce, and they agreed there was no need to go any farther.

"We'll do the same search on the way back," Dave said. "The sun will be at our back, so maybe we'll see something we missed flying into the sun."

Hal nodded his head, not taking his eyes off the river.

The return search was uneventful. They passed where the signal stopped, and continued upstream towards the area where tracking showed the bike had stopped.

"Man, I don't know," Dave said.

Hal shook his head. "Me either. How much fuel do we have?"

"Plenty, why?"

"Let's take another shot to the last known ping."

Dave spun the chopper around and started downstream.

"Hold on, Dave. I saw a shiny spot in the woods, next to the pull-off where tracking said the bike stopped moving."

Dave turned the chopper as Hal guided him over the canopy.

"One o'clock, Dave."

"I see it. The sun is catching whatever it is now. We wouldn't have seen that earlier. I'll lower us down as close to the treetops as possible."

Hal gave him a thumbs-up.

"Fucking canopy is thick," Hal said. "That ravine is steep. Can you put me down in the clearing? I'll get out and look into the ravine."

"If that is his bike, why the fuck would he stop here?" Dave said.

"His wife said he's a picture nut. Maybe he wanted a shot of the canyon walls across the river. Remember, what we take for granted, other folks don't."

Dave lowered Hal onto the pull-off.

Hal looked up at the dirt road heading to the highway. It was a decent incline but drivable. He walked towards the river overlook, and noticed something odd. There appeared to be blood in the dirt, and slide marks too. The bloodstain had formed a small puddle. A spotty blood trail led to the edge of the overlook. The twenty-foot drop to the rocks below was steep, but traversable.

He pulled out his binoculars and saw what appeared to be a larger puddle of blood on the rocks next to the river's edge. He walked back to the slide marks, which made a short trail to the right side of the lookout, then over the edge. He drew his binoculars up, spotted a motorcycle in the ravine, and immediately drew a picture in his mind of what had happened to Jake Michaels.

Hal radioed Dave to tell him what he'd found, and directed the pilot to return to the station. He was calling a search crew to the scene.

Dave gave him a thumbs-up and flew off.

Hal walked cautiously around the area, surveying the ground for more clues. He wanted to reach the bike to verify the VIN. Though certain it must be Jake Michael's, he had to follow protocol. He could do little else until the search crew arrived with ropes, so he walked out to the overlook, pulled out his binoculars again, and looked down the riverbank, where he saw nothing out of the ordinary.

The sound of a vehicle finally coming down the rocky road behind him drew Hal's attention. It was the mountain search and rescue team.

"Hey, Hal, what do we have?" Officer Wilson said.

"Mike, walk this way, please."

Hal pointed to the slide marks and possible bloodstain, then showed him the bike in the ravine, and what appeared to be blood on the river's edge. "Let's spray the stains to confirm blood, and grab some ropes to get down to the bike. I'm interested in seeing what, if any, gear is with the bike. Tracking showed his GPS moved at walking speed downstream for close to thirteen hours."

Mike nodded. "If this is blood, there's a decent amount, but probably not enough to render him unconscious. I'm anxious to see if there's any trace moving along the river."

"If this is our guy," Hal said, "he's ex-Special Forces with combat experience. He would know how to dress a wound, but what puzzles me is why he would go along the river and not to the road."

Dave shrugged. "It could be a head wound. He could have been confused and stumbled to the river. Maybe he lay down there for a bit, gathered his senses, and started walking. A head trauma could have him confused. I don't know, man."

Officer Bill Drake called out from the first puddle. "Mike, Hal, this is blood."

Hal acknowledged it with a nod. "Just as we suspected. Let's get down to the bike."

"Thanks, Bill," Mike said. "Please spray the area leading down to the blood puddle at the river. Hal and I are going into the ravine."

The two men reached the bike, and found a considerable amount of gear still attached to the backrest. His helmet lay a few feet from it.

Hal sighed. "Well, he left with no gear. The helmet was on the bike, so a head injury is possible." He confirmed the VIN, leaving no more doubt that it was Jake Michael's motorcycle.

The two men stood still for a moment, silently trying to piece together the events.

Mike broke the ice. "Hal, I think we have head trauma and a confused guy out there."

"I agree. Let's go see what Bill is coming up with."

Back with Bill, Mike said, "What do you have?"

Bill took a deep breath. "We have blood drops coming down the rocks from the lookout. From this puddle, there are drops right to the river's edge. I found this piece of cloth near the river. It has blood on it. I sprayed the area, twenty feet upstream and downstream, and found no sign of blood."

After a few moments of silence, Hal walked over to the blood drops at the river. He looked at the roaring water and the piece of cloth in his hand. He reached into his pocket and grabbed the picture of Jake. The fabric matched the pattern of Jake's flannel shirt.

He turned at the search team. "I think our guy washed his wound, and bandaged it with a piece of his shirt. Confused, he started walking downstream. Let's get the dogs out here. We have a good scent for them, and we know where his phone died, so we can start our search there. We have plenty of light. Let's bring this guy home."

Hal knew the next part of his task would be the hardest. He'd have to call the family and update them. As in cases past, he wouldn't build false hope, but only report the facts. They would likely ask him dozens of questions, and for his opinions, and he'd be honest. No other way to do it.

He walked back to the search cruiser to connect to a landline through the station. "Mrs. Michaels, this is Officer Jones. Can you hear me Okay?"

"Yes, sir, I can."

"Okay, we flew a search based on the tracking of Jake's phone, and found his motorcycle. It appears he had a low-speed accident on a dirt road."

Her voice crackled. "Is he okay?"

"He wasn't at the scene of the accident. We found some blood but nothing that would be fatal at the time of the accident. It appears he bandaged his wound with a piece of his shirt, left the scene, and possibly walked downstream all night. *Now,* please understand... this is only based on his phone tracking. We have no proof yet that this is what he did."

Alex fell silent as her hands trembled. She had a difficult time holding her phone.

Paul came to her side and braced her. With a blank stare, she handed the phone to him, then walked to her couch and sat down, staring forward.

Lisa quickly moved next to her.

"Mrs. Michaels, are you there?"

"Officer, this is her brother, Paul. Can you fill me in, please?"

Paul got the full update.

"Officer Jones, how far off the road was Jake's bike? Was he deep in the woods, such that no one would see him?"

"That's the part that has us confused. He was only twenty yards from the main road. *Now,* we have no proof of what I'm going to say—it's only a theory—but he may have suffered head trauma, become confused, and started walking. He took none of the gear from his motorcycle. This makes us believe even more that he's dazed."

"Okay, what's next?"

"We're sending a search team with dogs to the last known location of his cell phone. They're being deployed as we speak. I'll join them as soon as I hang up, and call with any updates."

"Thank you, officer. Please find him."

"We'll do our best, sir. We have a highly trained crew and the best gear for search and rescue in these canyons."

Paul ended the call and walked over to Alex, who was regaining her composure.

"Alex, they think Jake is alive but may have a head injury. He may be confused and possibly wandering. They're sending dogs and a search crew to the last place his phone pinged the tower. They'll find him."

Alex stared forward and muttered, "I should have gone with him."

Lisa placed her hand on Alex's knee. "They'll find him."

"I need to call the kids and let them know. I may be all they have now." She again broke down, sobbing uncontrollably.

Paul and Lisa looked at each other, speechless.

Hal arrived at the search area ten minutes after the search specialists. He briefed them in more detail than the station officer, as the tracking hounds yelped, ready to go. Hal walked over and gave their handler the piece of cloth with Jake's blood on it.

The dogs grew more anxious with the scent on the cloth, and their noses shot directly to the ground. Hal instructed the handler to search downstream one mile from the last ping, while he and two officers would walk upstream looking for any clues. The two groups synched their handhelds.

"Gary, over," Hal called out on his walkie-talkie.

"Yes, Hal. Over."

"How are the dogs acting? Over."

"No trail yet. Over."

"10-4, same here. Over."

The two groups continued their search track for another hour.

"Hal, over."

"Go, Gary. Over."

"I'll work my way back closer to the road. The dogs are finding no scent along the river. Over."

"10-4, that's a good idea. We'll do the same. Over."

Hal's group turned and headed back to the original search area.

"Hal," Jay Storm Walker said. "Hold on for a second. I caught a flash of something bright on the other side of that eddy." Jay was a native Shoshone, and one of most revered trackers in the country, his skills handed down through generations. He'd worked on some of the highest profile missing person cases over the past twenty years. Every police department and Federal Agency had tried to hire him, but after serving twenty-five years in the military, he retired, choosing to do contract work only.

Hal looked. "Where, Jay?"

Jay pointed. "Look at that flat rock. Watch as the water rises and falls with the current. Something is hung up in the brush."

"Damn, Jay, how the fuck did you see that without binoculars?" Hal laughed and lowered his binoculars.

Jay smiled and winked. "Know *where* to look in the river, because most of it will give you no clues."

Hal raised his binoculars again. "It looks like a square or rectangle, hard to tell because of the brush holding it under the water."

"Could be fishing clutter?" Jay said.

"Most likely, Jay, but we need to check it out. Normally, we could cross around here, but this bastard is roaring right now."

Jay nodded. "About a quarter mile upstream is a slow rift area. Even with the water high, we should be able to get across. It will be about chest deep, but the water is pretty warm right now."

"All right, you stay here, and I'll go up. If you see me come floating by, throw me a rope."

Jay laughed. "Lassos are for white men. Hope you can swim."

Hal reached the rift area, looked at the water, and shook his head. As a safety precaution, he tied a rope off to a tree and his waist, so that if he lost his footing, the river could only take him thirty feet or so.

He walked into the water. "Holy fuck! Warm, my ass!"

He cautiously walked across the slippery rocks as the current pushed against him, but he reached the other side and walked downstream.

"How was the water?" Jay yelled over the sounds of the river.

"Warm as bath water. You should hop in," Hal hollered back, and threw up his middle finger.

He moved along the rocky shoreline to the object, bent down, reached around the brush, and retrieved it. He looked at the item and lowered his head. It was a cell phone in a floating case.

"What is it?" Jay yelled.

"It's a cell phone in a floating case."

"Hey, some fisherman will thank you."

"I hope it belongs to a fisherman." He shook his head and yelled, "Meet me back where I crossed."

Jay gave him a thumbs-up.

A bleaker picture of Jake's misfortune formed in Hal's mind.

If this phone was Jake's, it's possible he never walked from the accident. He might have moved to the river's edge, as the blood drops show, lost his balance, and fell into the raging river. His phone floated downstream until it ran out of a charge. This would explain why the hounds have found no scent yet.

They met at the crossing area, and Hal shared his thoughts and asked Jay's opinion.

Jay agreed his theory was possible, adding that with the river this high and fast, if Jake fell in and was injured, his chances of survival were not good.

Hal nodded. "Let's get back to the trucks. I'm calling Gary."

"Gary, over."

"Yes, Hal. Over."

"Do you have any tracks? Over."

"No sir, nothing. Over."

"Okay, bring it in. We found a phone. Meet you at the trucks. Over."

"10-4. Over."

The search crew reached the trucks, and Hal removed the phone from the case. It had a universal charging port, which he plugged into his car charger.

The android took a few minutes before springing to life. Hal looked at the screen and needed to go no further. Twenty-one new messages showed "Alexi" — that would be Mrs. Michaels — was the sender.

Hal lowered his head. "Jay, please call this number: 555-223-2269."

A few seconds passed, and the phone in Hal's hand rang.

Jay and Hal looked at each other. The rest of the search crew lowered their heads.

Hal looked at the river. "We'll search till dark, and again at first light." He walked over to Jay and looked him in the eyes. "You're the most experienced here. What do you think?"

Jay paused, gazed up the river and then down, and looked at the blood puddle where Jake's bike had fallen.

"I think it will be a miracle if we find him."

PART THREE

CONVERGENCE

CHAPTER 10
VISIONS

Samuel Red Hawk woke suddenly, shaken by his dream. He sat up in bed, grabbed his glasses and phone from the bedside table, and called his daughter. "Anna."

"Father, it is after 11:00. Are you okay?"

"Yes, I am fine. Is Lomasi home?"

"No, she is watching the Spirits dance at Wolf Flats. Why do you ask?"

"I have had a dream. The Spirits spoke to me. They said she is in danger. They showed me evil white men and a warrior."

She rolled her eyes and shook her head. "Father, I am sure she is fine."

Her father was 89 years old. He held the ceremonial title of Medicine Man on the reservation. Older generations believed in his powers, and Anna respected her father, but felt the only gift he had was the wisdom that comes with age.

She looked towards the front window and saw headlights coming up the drive. "Father, in fact, I see Dakota driving up our road as we speak. Jim and I will be over tomorrow to pick you up as planned. Lomasi cannot wait to see you. Now you go back to bed. Lomasi is fine. Love you."

Sam tilted his head up and closed his eyes. "Hohou Hii3tone3en Cei3woono," he whispered, thanking the Spirits. "I will see you tomorrow, Anna. Please hug Lomasi for me."

Sam hung the phone up. He believed in what the Spirits showed him, but perhaps, tonight, they had provided him a look into the future. Tomorrow, when he would see Dakota and Jim, he would warn them. He knew Anna did not believe in the ancient ways—to her, they were myths—but Dakota and Jim believed.

Anna looked out the window. As Dakota's car came closer, she saw two people and laughed to herself.

Dakota must have run into one of her childhood friends at Wolf Flats.

Jim slept on his recliner in front of the television.

"Jim, wake up. Lomasi is home, and she has a guest with her."

He chuckled. "Just like when she was young, always bringing home friends unannounced." He opened his eyes wide and shook his head, forcing himself to wake quickly.

Anna watched the car park. Dakota wasn't driving, and Anna didn't recognize the driver. The stranger walked to the passanger side and opened the door for Dakota, then helped her out and wrapped his arm around her. She wore an oversized poncho, and her head hung down, fixed on the ground.

"Jim, hurry, something is wrong." Anna raced to the front porch.

The stranger walked Dakota towards the house, bracing her from an obvious limp.

They rushed to their granddaughter. "Dakota, what is wrong? Are you okay?" Anna cried out.

Dakota looked up, her eyes filled with tears, her mouth and chin covered in dried blood crusted with dirt, and a little fresh blood. She was silent.

The stranger looked up at Jim and Anna, his steady gaze showing no emotion. "She was attacked."

"*Oh my God!* Anna, get her inside," Jim barked.

They took Dakota and led her to the house, and Jim looked back from the front porch at the stranger. "Please, come in."

Anna helped Dakota upstairs to the bathroom, and grabbed a washcloth to clean the blood from her face. The split in her lower lip continued to ooze. "Honey, take off this dusty poncho." She helped pull it over Dakota's head.

Dakota pulled the poncho back down quickly. "No, grandma."

Anna saw she was naked under the poncho. The two women looked into each other's eyes, and that moment of silence told the story.

Anna's eyes welled. "Oh my God, Lomasi." She hugged her sobbing granddaughter, trying to comfort her.

"He... saved me, Neiwoo. He saved... me," Dakota struggled to say between sobs.

Jim stood with the stranger in the living room. "What happened out there?"

The stranger shook his head. "Do you have a cloth and some water? Can we sit down?"

"Sure, please come in the kitchen."

The two men sat at the kitchen table.

The stranger removed his shirt, reached over to his shoulder, and pulled off a blood- soaked cloth.

Jim saw the stranger had tied the cloth into a make shift field dressing, and knew instantly the stranger had been trained in first aid. He also noticed a tattoo on his forearm, and it was unmistakable—he had seen this before.

"You are cut," he said. "That will need stitches."

"I have butterfly stitches in my first aid kit. They'll help." The stranger looked down at his shoulder. "Your granddaughter was attacked by three men tonight. She's fortunate." His eyes stayed fixed on the wound as he wrapped a new field dressing around it.

"Attacked?"

The stranger looked up and told Jim what had happened, but Jim couldn't help think the man was telling less than the whole story, based on his demeanor. Perhaps the stranger left out the most graphic details in order to spare Jim from having that terrible picture of his granddaughter etched in his mind forever.

Jim fell silent as tears rolled down his face. In an unsteady voice, with his head lowered, he asked, "Was she raped?"

"No."

Jim rasied his head and made eye contact with the stranger. "Thank you, soldier."

The stranger raised his eyebrow. "How do you know I was a soldier?"

"Your tattoo... only a few men have it. The blood tear skull with the Somalia flag on the forehead."

The stranger nodded his head. "I assume, then, that you served?"

"Yes, twenty years Green Berets." He extended his hand out to the stranger. "Jim White Feather."

The stranger shook his hand. "Colonel, I've heard of you. Your reputation is well known in the Special Force's ranks. Pleasure to meet you."

"What is your name, son?"

The stranger paused. "Sonny Telesco."

"Sonny, I thank you for bringing my Dakota home." Jim released his handshake. "Excuse me for a second, Sonny. I need to call the police, and then we need to get you stitched up."

"Colonel, no police, please."

Jim's brow furrowed. "These men need to be caught."

"Their injuries will require medical attention. I ask you as a favor: please give me some time to move on. Tomorrow morning you can report this. The police will be able to apprehend them based on their reported injuries. I also have the license plate number of their truck."

Jim leaned forward, his eyes narrowed. "What or who are you running from, soldier?"

Sonny's eyes did not waver from Jim's glare. "Not running from, Colonel, running to."

The bathroom door opened, and the two men looked up to see Dakota and Anna coming downstairs.

Jim sprung up to hug her. "Lomasi, how are you feeling?"

"Grandfather, I'm okay," Dakota said, calmly.

She walked over to Sonny and reached her hand out. "Thank you, sir, for being there." She paused, then hugged him.

He remained motionless during the hug.

"Anna, Dakota," Jim said. "This is Sonny Telesco. He is prior 75th Ranger Regiment. We are all fortunate the Spirits guided him to us tonight."

Anna followed Dakota with a hug, expressing her gratitude.

The echoes of multiple sirens interrupted the moment, their wail bouncing through the canyons and carried in the crisp night air. Jim's phone then rang. It was the Sheriff's Department. He declined the call.

"Who was that, Jim, so late at night?" Anna said.

"I did not recognize the number."

"Colonel," Sonny said. "Do you have a place I can camp tonight. It's time for me to go."

"You can stay here tonight," Dakota blurted.

"Colonel, please," Sonny said, with an increased pitch.

"Do you have your gear?"

"Yes, sir, it's in the car."

"Come, grab your gear." Jim led Sonny towards the front door.

"Jim, let him stay with us," Anna insisted.

Sonny turned to her and bowed his head. "Ma'am, I appreciate that, but I don't want to impose."

Jim squinted and nodded slightly. "Anna, let it be."

Dakota raised her eyebrows, looking at her grandmother, but Anna shrugged back as the two men left.

Once outside, Jim said, "Sonny, that was the Sheriff's Department."

"Colonel, hard to believe those pieces of shit would be so brazen as to call the police."

Jim sighed. "Indian girls are thought of by many as disposable, an unrecognized demographic. Those men could have been questioned in the hospital, and they might have fabricated a story along the lines they were partying with a girl when a man attacked them out of nowhere. It would cover their tracks, and no one would give it a second thought. They were most likely calling to ask for permission to search the property, or warn Anna and me."

As the sirens drew closer, Jim saw the distress in Sonny's eyes. He pointed in the darkness, tracing a path in the air. "Go behind the house, and walk up the hill. There is a small cave about forty yards up and to the left. It will be a good place to spend the night."

Sonny grabbed his gear and a rifle.

Jim noted the weapon. "Nice rifle, soldier."

Sonny held the gun out. "I took it from those bastards."

Jim noticed engraved letters on the gold receiver. "I do not have my glasses. What do those letters say?"

"R.B.D.—I guess those are one of the asshole's initials." Sonny started into the darkness, then looked back at Jim. "Thank you, Colonel."

"Soldier, tomorrow we will get that shoulder stitched, and we will talk."

"Yes sir."

Sonny reached the small cave, and looked over the moonlit land below. The sirens grew louder as flashes of their lights illuminated the canyon walls in the distance. He hoped the colonel would keep his word, and suspected he would, but still his anxiety built as the sirens and lights drew closer. When they reached directly in front of the ranch, his heart raced. The group of emergency vehicles passed by the lane to the ranch and attack site, and he listened and watched as they disappeared into the night, after which he released a pent-up sigh.

His shoulder throbbed as, exhausted, he laid his head on his camp pillow.

"Jim, we need to call the police and report this," Anna said.

"I know. Sonny asked that we wait until tomorrow. He said the three men were injured, and would need to go to the hospital. He also has the truck's license plate number, so it should be easy enough for the police to apprehend them."

"I *don't want* to wait till tomorrow, Jim. Why does he want us to wait?"

"He wants time to move on."

"Jim, I don't care what he wants. Those men attacked Lomasi. *I want them caught.*"

"*No!*" Dakota blurted, with authority.

Jim and Anna looked at her.

Dakota locked her eyes on the floor. "That man saved my life. Besides a busted lip and a twisted ankle, I'm fine. And I'm alive. He stopped them from raping me, and probably kidnapping me, or worse. I owe it to him to keep whatever secret he is hiding." She looked up at her grandparents. "I don't want my name dragged into this when I'm starting a life out here."

Jim straightened up. "Honey, the cops are coming. Those guys probably made up a story in the hospital about being attacked out here by a man. You know the cops will believe them, but you can put them behind bars if you identify them. Your wounds will tell the truth."

"No. Those pieces of shit do not know who I am. I'm not getting involved. We owe it to Sonny. Let the cops chase a ghost." Her voice was steady and settled.

As the sirens drew closer, the three of them fell silent and darted glances at each other. Each, no doubt, rehearsed in their heads what they would say to the Sheriff's Department if they came to the ranch.

The Emergency vehicles approached, but when they reached the turn to the ranch, they continued on their previous path.

Dakota stood up from the table. "I'm going to bed."

Jim watched her walk away. *The muck of humanity has caught her. She will no longer be the same whimsical girl.* He lowered his head.

Anna pulled him back from his sadness. "Jim, what do you think?"

"I think we honor Dakota's wishes. I think I need to have a talk with Sonny tomorrow. I think the Spirits have sent a dark cloud, and a storm is coming to our lives."

Anna paused for a few seconds. "My father called right before Dakota got home. He said he had a vision, in which Lomasi was in trouble, and that he saw three white men and a warrior. I didn't pay attention to him." She dropped her head and wept. "I thought it was his dementia talking."

He walked over and comforted her with a hug. "Shhhhh.... He always talks about evil white men and warriors. Besides, we could have done nothing. The attack had already happened by the time he called."

She dried her eyes and nodded her head. "You're right, but my heart breaks for her. She told me bits and pieces. She said those men filmed her. They joked about what country would bid the most for her. What type of men would do this?"

He shook his head and dried a tear from his eye. "I do not know. I do not know."

The two sat for a few minutes in silence, staring at the kitchen table.

"It has been a long night," he said. "Why don't you go to bed and try to get some sleep?"

"Aren't you joining me?"

"In a few minutes."

Anna nodded and headed to their room.

Jim walked into his office, sat at the computer, and pulled up an Army website that connected soldiers to each other. He navigated to 75th Ranger Regiment, and typed in *Sonny Telesco*. The website brought up service-related information confirming Sonny had served honorably for twelve years.

He stared at the computer for a few more seconds, squinted, and shut it off.

CHAPTER 11
THE RIVER

Hal walked from the river to his cruiser. "Mrs. Michaels, this is Officer Jones. Can you hear me all right?"

"Yes sir, Officer."

Hal told Alexi they'd found Jake's phone floating in the water. She remained silent while he updated her.

"Officer, how long will you search for?"

"Given the fact that it's summer, and Jake does have survival training, we'll search actively for two weeks on the scene. We'll wire pictures and descriptions to the surrounding Police Departments, and hang posters up. Our search really never stops."

"I understand. I'll fly out there tomorrow."

"Yes ma'am. If we turn up anything, I'll call you. If not, I'll meet with you tomorrow."

"Thank you, Officer." Alex hung up. Calm and composed, she gave Paul and Lisa the update, and then called each of the kids.

Johnny, Robert, and Danielle each told her they would meet her in Jackson Hole tomorrow.

Paul and Lisa agreed to fly with her in the morning.

Alex, Paul, and Lisa arrived in Jackson Hole at 12:55 PM. Each of the kid's flights arrived within the next two hours.

"Paul, our rental car is over in town," Alex said. "Do you and Lisa want to take the shuttle over and get it? I'll wait for the kids."

"Okay, Alex, same place as vacation, correct?"

"Yes."

Alex walked over to the windows looking out at the mountain

ranges. She remembered how excited they all were the first time they'd seen them, and Jake's amazement—like a little kid—and tears filled her eyes. She fought them back, trying to maintain her composure.

She told herself, *Jake and I* will *once again share time here.*

The last few weeks had made her realize how short and precious life really was. There was no time for procrastination.

She moved to the arrival area to greet Danielle.

Danielle made eye contact, rushed through the line of passengers to her, and buried her head on her mom's shoulder.

Alex knew she now needed to be the rock, just as Jake was in difficult times. Her kids needed her.

"Shhhhh, baby, it will be okay. Your dad is a survivor."

Danielle wiped her eyes and sniffled. "I know, Mom. How are you doing?"

"I'm all cried out, Danni. Now it's time to be positive and bring your dad home."

"Where are Uncle Paul and Aunt Lisa?"

"They went to get the rental. Let's grab your bags. Johnny's and Bobby's flights will be here soon."

Paul and Lisa rejoined them at the airport as the two boys' flights arrived. They all loaded their luggage in the van and left for Sulphur Springs.

"Mom," Bobby said. "How far of a ride is it to Sulphur Springs?"

Paul answered as he set the GPS. "About three and a half hours. We should be there around six or so."

Alex said, "I'm calling Officer Jones to let him know we're on our way. I spoke with him earlier to see who we should contact when we arrive. He gave me his cellphone number."

"I take it there were no updates?" Johnny said.

"No, they were organizing four search parties and a raft crew. That was it." Alex didn't mean for her tone to sound so flat—almost hopeless.

As the family continued their trip, they rehashed the known events, each of them theorizing where Jake was.

They were about a half hour from Sulphur Springs when Johnny shouted, "Slow down, Uncle Paul." He pointed to a light pole with a missing person poster on it and a picture of Jake.

The family parked and rushed to the sign. Alex recognized the picture as the last photo she received from Jake—they'd cropped his face from it. The description was perfect: six-foot- four, approximately 225 pounds, short gray hair and full gray beard, blue eyes, multiple tattoos on both arms.

The surreal moment silenced the family. As reality set in, tears flowed down Alex's cheeks. She walked to the poster, sobbing loudly, and kissed it. "Where are you, Jake? Where are you?"

Johnny put his hands on her shoulders and gently pulled her back from the poster. "Come on, Mom."

The family returned to the vehicle.

Only sounds of sniffling broke the silence in the van for miles, until Alex's phone rang. "Yes, Officer Jones."

"Mrs. Michaels, one of our search crews found a campfire about ten miles from Jake's bike. It appears to be from last night. Do you know if your husband has a fishing pole with him?"

"I know he said he would buy one when he got closer to Yellowstone. He planned to buy a three-day fishing pass for Wyoming, but he didn't say if he'd bought a pole yet or not. Why do you ask?"

"There were fish bones in the embers."

"Well, that's a good sign, right?"

"It could be. There's no proof it's Jake's, but it's encouraging. How close are you to Sulphur Springs?"

"Paul, how close to Sulphur Springs are we?"

"Three miles."

"Three miles, Officer Jones," she reported.

"Okay, and you're staying at the Red Feather Inn, correct?"

"Yes sir."

"I'll meet you at 7:00 PM, if that's fine with you?"

"Seven o'clock sounds good. See you then." She hung up.

She smiled, clasped her hands, and looked up. "They found a fresh campfire from last night, about ten miles from Jake's bike."

Everyone reacted positively to the news. After the poster, they all needed a lift.

Hal arrived at the Red Feather at 7:05, and walked to room 269 to meet the Michaels family.

THE TEMPTATION OF DESTINY

Mrs. Michaels opened the door. "Officer Jones, Alex Michaels... pleased to meet you." She reached out her hand.

"Mrs. Michaels, nice to meet you."

"Officer, please call me Alex."

He smiled. "Okay, Alex."

Hal introduced himself to the rest of the family, and they reciprocated. He knew the next part of this visit would bring a barage of questions. He'd updated Alex on every development, and wasn't a patient man, and hated repeating himself, but given the situation, he understood and obliged them.

"Okay," John said. "Officer Jones, what's next?"

"Tonight, we're flying a ten-mile square search grid from the campfire we found. The area around the campfire is densely wooded and the terrain is rocky, so even the most experienced hiker couldn't go over ten miles in a day. Hopefully, from the air, we can see another fire."

John nodded. "10-4."

"In the morning," he continues, "we're putting a search crew on the river. The water is dropping now that we've had three days without rain, so the boats will be able to navigate the water."

Paul jumped in. "*On the water?* Are you looking for a body?"

Hal knew the answer to this, of course, but elected to sidestep the truth. It was too early to worry the family more than they already were. "No, the water search will allow us to see areas that are hidden from the crews on the ground and in the air. We're not ruling out that Jake may have fallen in the water, and possibly got to shore in a remote area. Given his military training, he would know how to survive a water emergency."

"Okay, I understand. Thank you."

"Officer Jones," Robert said. "John and I are former Rangers, like our Dad. Can we join the search?"

Hal paused for a moment. "Normally, I don't allow family members to join a search crew. Emotions can cloud judgment, but if both of you want to search the area upstream from your Dad's bike, that would be fine. We've focused most of our search downstream."

Hal and Jay both firmly believed Jake had fallen in the water, and thus their concentration on downstream. Perhaps the boys would find evidence Jake went upstream. He doubted it, but figured it would help the family to contribute to the search.

"Okay, great. What time should we be on site?"

"I'll swing by at 6:30 AM, and you can follow me to the search area. I'll do the morning brief, and we'll start at first light. In the meantime, let's all get a good night's sleep." Hal excused himself.

The search party met at 6:45 AM where they'd found Jake's bike. Hal updated everyone, including news that the night search had produced nothing. They would fly both day and night searches in a new grid today. He introduced John and Robert to the rest of them, and assigned a new search area to each group.

"Okay, men, let's get started," he said.

Several hours later, they'd received no reports from the four search crews. Hal and Jay stood on a small ridge looking over the river.

"What do you think, Jay?"

"Three days now... an injured person... I think we are chasing a ghost."

"We've both seen amazing rescues, but in this case, I agree."

Hal looked at a watermark on the canyon wall across the river. "The water is dropping. What do you think about recovery?"

Jay said, "There are some deep areas in the river. With it as high as it was, the body could have gotten caught up on the bottom. There are numerous small caves under water. If it went into one of them, we might never retrieve it."

Hal nodded. "Yeah, as fast as it was moving, the body could be miles from where we think he fell in."

Jay nodded. "Also, he was bleeding. If the body washed up on shore, a grizzly could have dragged it away. This time of the year, they're eating as much as they can."

Hal's radio broke their conversation. "Search Team Water to Hal. Come in, Hal."

"Yeah Bill."

"Hal, we've found a flannel shirt one mile down from the crash site. It's tangled up in some brush under the water. It matches the shirt in the picture. Over."

Hal and Jay dropped their heads.

"Bill, what does the river look like where you found it? Over."

"I found it at the front of a pool, after a long area of rocky rapids. The shirt is pretty beat up. Over."

"10- 4. Meet me back at the crash area. Over."

Bobby and Johnny heard the transmission over the dedicated search band, and looked at each other. Their mutual gaze told everything. They walked over to each other and hugged, as reality was setting in. Their dad may not have survived.

Hal, Bill, and Jay stood at the crash area.

Bill handed over the shirt and a compromising photo of Mrs. Michaels in a plastic bag. "Looks like our guy is an ass man," he said.

When they heard John and Robert coming up from the river, Hal put the photo in his pocket. "Boys," he said.

"Officer Jones," John said, looking down at his dad's shirt.

"This is not a good sign," Robert said.

Jay shook his head. "No, it's not."

"What's your plan, Officer Jones?" John said.

"We'll continue the search today and tonight, as planned. Tomorrow we'll continue to search, but also look at recovery. The water will be lower and calmer. We'll put dive teams in the river."

John dropped his head. "Understood, sir. We're going back to the hotel. We should be with our mom now." He walked from the group.

"Thank you all for your help," Robert said, then turned to join his brother.

The officers remained silent while watching the boys walk away. They knew what would follow. They'd watched this scene play out too many times over the years.

Johnny and Bobby pulled up to the hotel room, and sat silently for a few seconds in the car.

"I'll tell Mom," Johnny said.

Bobby nodded his head and choked out a simple, "Okay."

The twenty steps to the room felt like an eternity, as if time moved in slow motion. John stopped to take a deep breath, and opened the door.

Their mom jumped up from the couch, saw the boy's faces, and reacted as a mother would who knew her children's expressions so well.

"No, no, no!" Her voice grew louder with each word. She shook her head as tears welled up in her eyes. Then her knees buckled and she dropped to the ground.

Bobby raced to comfort her.

John said calmly, "They found Dad's shirt submerged under the water. They're still searching. Tomorrow they're putting divers in the water."

His mom's sobs were deafening, but not much they could say, really.

She looked up at them. "Take me to the crash site. Take me to the last place my Jake was."

John shook his head. "Mom, that's not a good idea right now."

"Take me!" she shouted. Then, more quietly and between sobs, she said, "Take me, please."

John said, "I'll call Officer Jones."

He walked outside to the hotel lot and dialed.

The officer answered. "Yes, Mrs. Michaels."

"Officer Jones, this is John."

"Yes, John. How is your mom?"

"She's not good. She wants to come to the crash site."

"John, I don't think that's a good idea. We're pulling your dad's bike from the ravine now. The blood is still visible in the dirt. It would be hard for her, for any wife."

"I know, but you don't know my mom. She *will not* take no for an answer. Perhaps you can move dirt over the blood?"

Jones paused for several seconds. "We've collected all the samples we need, and all the photos are done, so I can clean the blood up. Give me an hour to get the bike up and clear the wrecker out. I'll need someone to collect Jake's gear."

"Thank you, sir. See you in an hour."

He walked back into the hotel.

His mom had calmed down, but her eyes were frozen in a distant stare. "What did he say, Johnny?" Her voice was emotionless.

"We can go there in an hour."

She dropped her head and nodded.

The family approached the crash area as the helicopter slowly hovered several hundred yards up the river. Hal and Jay stood next to Jake's bike, which was up on its kickstand.

Mrs. Michaels walked out in front of the family, and Hal greeted her.

"Officer Jones," she said. "Thank you for letting me come. I want to look at Jake's bike first, please."

"Yes ma'am."

She walked up to the bike, slid her hands over first the handgrips and then the seat, as if trying to feel Jake. She then moved to the side of the bike, asked Officer Jones for the keys, and upon receiving them opened a side panel. She pulled out Jake's wallet and held it to her heart.

Officer Jones looked away, shocked to have to fight off his own tears. He'd been with many families in the past, in just this situation, but today was different. A quiet but true love shined in Mrs. Michael's eyes and in her every move.

She opened the wallet and searched through it. "Officer Jones, has anyone searched the bike?"

"Only the pack, to see if Jake took his gear, but I've had the keys the whole time. Why do you ask?"

"All of Jake's cash is gone. More important, an old, very private photo I gave him when we were young is missing. He carried it with him for almost thirty years."

Hal looked at Jay.

"Perhaps he spent his cash and didn't have time to go to an ATM before the accident," Jay offered.

"I could see that, but the picture... he would never lose that."

"Maybe he took it with him, Alex," Hal said.

"But why not his whole wallet?"

"I don't know. We believe he had a head injury. He may not have been thinking clearly."

Hal felt she was going through enough, and didn't need the embarrassment of knowing strange men have seen everything she has in the photo.

"Please take me to the river," she said.

The two moved down the rocky bank.

"Where do you think he went in, Officer Jones?"

Hal pointed to where the blood puddle was.

Alex dropped down to her knees, rubbed her hands over the cleaned area, and began to sob.

Hal knew this was a bad idea. He bent down to lift her up.

She looked up with a sad smile. "My tears that fall in the river will find my Jake."

CHAPTER 12
GOODBYE JAKE

Four weeks had passed since Jake disappeared, and they'd found no clues hinting at the possibility of survival. The dive team had found his watch in week two, and shortly thereafter his dog tags, which he never removed.

This beautiful, brutal wilderness had claimed another victim.

Officer Jones had to make the call he so dreaded, to inform the family they were ending the search. It would begin the process of finality, but without a body, they'd never truly experience closure. That might have been the hardest part. There was always a thread of hope without a body, which some would hold onto—a thread that bound them to the past, never allowing a future.

He took a deep breath and dialed the number.

"Hello, Hal," Alex said, with less formality. They'd spoken so often, they'd collectively moved to first names.

"Alex, four weeks have passed, and we've exhausted all avenues. We held the active search two weeks longer than protocol dictates, but we must terminate it now. The posters will remain in place, and all police departments will monitor John Does, but there's nothing else we can do on our end. *I am sorry.*"

"I understand. My family could not have asked more of you and your department."

"I wish this would have turned out differently, Alex. My department will request a death certificate be issued, which will declare Death in Absentia. I know this is hard to hear, but you need to know the process."

"I understand. I've been preparing for this after Jake's dog tags were found."

"If Jake had life insurance and they give you a problem, please call me."

"Thank you, Hal. I don't believe there will be a problem. Last week, I spoke with our attorney, and he said something about the element of peril—legal mumbo-jumbo."

"Element of Peril accelerates the presumption of death," Hal said.

"Yes, I guess. Again, thank you for everything."

Her calm demeanor did not surprise him. She *was* holding on to a thread.

Alex hung up the phone. When they'd found Jake's dog tags, she knew their universe had changed. Now was the time for formalities. She would make final arrangements once the death certificate arrived. She would appease the rest of the world, which would move on without Jake, but her world would pause.

She sat down at Jake's desk. His high-back leather chair hugged her almost as he'd done. She spent hours, everyday, sitting there. She drank her coffee every afternoon in his office, as they always had together. She left everything on his desk precisely as it had been when he left—Jake hated when she moved things.

It was the morning of Jake's funeral. Alexi had chosen not to have a wake for him, given they had no body. There was no sense in having friends and family pay respects to an empty casket. The funeral would provide the formality of saying goodbye.

She watched the church fill up. Among attendees were friends and family she'd not seen in years. She kept her composure as familiar and unfamiliar faces expressed their condolences before the service.

"Alexi," a familiar but long-forgotten voice called from behind her.

She looked back to the owner of the one voice that could break her composure, and tears rolled down her cheeks. As her eyes met the tall, dark, longhaired man, the gravity of today overwhelmed her. The reality of past and present crashed in on her.

"Sonny," she said, walking towards him.

He said nothing as they hugged.

She sobbed into his chest. "They keep telling me he's gone. He's not. He's not!"

"Shhhhh," he said, patting her back.

"Please go bring Jake home like you did in Somalia. Please make these people believe this is all wrong. You can do it, Sonny." Her cries grew louder. She was losing control. Seeing Sonny was too much.

"C'mon, Mom," Johnny said, leading her away to a private room in the church.

Alex sat down on a couch, now crying hysterically. She'd been so composed and in control over the past several weeks, but Sonny had been the reason she and Jake were together. Seeing him made her remember the early years with Jake, the magical years of a young couple, dreaming of the life ahead.

Sonny had been there in the beginning, and now he was there at the end.

She finally looked up and dried her eyes. "What time is it?"

"9:50," Danielle answered.

"Okay, give me a few minutes alone, please." She sniffled. "I'll be out for the service."

The service started at 10 AM. The pastor performed a Catholic funeral. Alex remained oblivious for most it, her mind a million miles away. She shut out the priest's words, and held onto that small thread of hope.

The funeral moved to the gravesite, where the priest blessed the coffin and the ground.

Alex kept her head lowered the entire time, and as the casket dropped into the grave, she walked away.

Her leaving seemed to add profound sadness to the finality of the day. People cried loudly. Danielle fell to her knees.

As those sounds faded into the background, she felt as if a piece of her was in that coffin.

Johnny followed her, and put his arm around her. "Mom, are you okay?"

She looked at him with wide eyes and a slight smile. "Your dad is not dead. He promised me if he died before me, he would send me a sign, so I'd know he was still by my side. I don't feel him, Johnny. I don't feel him. He would never lie to me. I don't feel him. *I don't feel him.*"

She sobbed loudly again, fell to her knees, and pounded the ground. "Prove them wrong, Jake. Prove them wrong, baby."

CHAPTER 13
CRIES IN THE NIGHT

Officer Jimmy Red Cloud arrived first on the scene. A crowd stood on the berm of the road next to twisted guardrails, looking into the ravine below.

Desperate moaning echoed through the still night. "Oh, dear God, help me. Help me, please."

"Over here, Officer, please hurry," a frantic young woman pleaded, pointing over the guardrails.

Jimmy shined his spotlight into the darkness, illuminating a twisted vehicle resting at the bottom of the hundred-foot ravine.

"Help me, help me," an agonizing voice begged from the darkness below.

Two ambulances and a mountain rescue fire truck pulled to the scene.

"Jimmy, what do we have?" Captain Drake said.

"It looks like we have a single vehicle over the edge. I hear one person, but I don't know how many victims there are, Captain."

"I saw three men in the truck," the witness interjected. "They passed me before they went off the road."

The voice from the ravine cried out again, slower and more deliberate. "Help... me... God, please."

"Dear God, please help him," the witness said, pleading and crying.

Jimmy moved her from the guardrail. "We are, ma'am. The rescue team is getting their ropes ready now. Can you please have a seat in my cruiser? Officer Fields needs to get some information from you. Thank you."

"Jimmy, you ready to go down?" Captain Drake said.

"Yes sir."

As Jimmy, Captain Drake, and two of the rescue crew repelled into the ravine, the voice that had been crying for help stopped. They reached the bottom of the canyon and rushed to the wreckage. Jimmy shined his light into the upside-down truck to find one victim, his head twisted grotesquely, facing his back. The paramedic searched for a pulse out of protocol, and shook his head.

The crew shined their lights around the rest of the scene, looking for the other two men the witness reported.

"Over here," Captain Drake hollered.

The group rushed to another victim. His left arm had been torn from his shoulder, and massive head trauma exposed his brain. Again, the paramedic did the obligatory check for a pulse and shook his head.

"Obviously, these two were not still alive, so where the fuck is this other guy?" Jimmy said, looking at the crew.

"Help," a faint voice cried out.

Jimmy shined his light in the direction of the shallow voice, and spotted a man lying on a ledge halfway up the cliff, twenty yards from where the truck went off the road.

He pointed. "Up there, guys."

"Shit," Captain Drake said. "He must have been thrown from the truck went it hit the guardrail and went over."

"How the fuck are we getting up there?" Jimmy said.

One of the paramedics answered. "We aren't. We need to drop a basket over the edge."

Jimmy nodded. "Okay, based on the weakness of his voice, it sounds like we are running out of time."

"10- 4. I'll have Rescue Two send the basket over with a paramedic," Captain Drake said.

Gary, the head paramedic, traversed the rocky cliffs to the ledge and reached the injured man. The victim's eyes were wide, his mouth frozen in mid-sentence. Massive abdominal trauma had exposed his entrails. He reached down to check for a pulse, and then grabbed the radio. "Rescue Two to Captain Drake, over."

"Yes, Gary, what do you have? Over."

"He didn't make it. I'm loading him into the basket."

"10-4. Send him up."

The recovery crew retrieved the bodies from the ravine. They placed them in body bags, and then into the ambulances bound for the morgue.

"Not a good night for these boys," Captain Drake said.

"Nope," Jimmy said, pointing to two empty bottles of booze next to the truck.

Gary said, "That poor bastard on the ledge suffered for a while. The two down here looked like they went quick."

Captain Drake shook his head. "Booze and driving... people will never learn. Let's get out of here. We'll let the investigation crew do their thing at first light."

"Yeah," Jimmy said. "Head back to the station, do the paperwork, and contact the next of kin as soon as possible."

Jimmy sat at his desk and examined the driver's licenses of the three deceased men. All three were from Abilene, Texas.

Officer Fields walked over and placed a report on his desk. "Take a look at this."

"What do you have, Beth?"

"The witness said the vehicle was driving normally in front of her. Here's the strange thing. She said they slowed down to well below the speed limit, started weaving, and drove off the road. She saw no brake lights, and nothing in front of them that would cause them to swerve. Her words were, *They simply just drifted off the road.*"

Jimmy nodded. "Sounds like the driver fell asleep."

Officer Fields shrugged. "I guess, but it seems strange."

"We'll see what the autopsies and toxicology tell us."

Captain Drake approached his desk at that moment. "Hey Jimmy, what do you have?"

"The three victims are from Abilene, Texas. The boy's names are Richard Brett Dibella, the one we found on the ledge, Marcus John Dibella, the driver we found in the car—the truck is registered in his name—and Shane Rogers."

Captain Drake raised his eyebrows and rubbed his chin. "Dibella... I wonder if they're related to Vincent Dibella, as in Dibella Farms."

"Damn, Cap, I didn't think about that. I'll cross-reference Vincent's address and those of the the victims. Maybe we find next of kin quickly."

"Okay, let me know. I'm heading over to the morgue. They can remove the John Doe tags and give these bodies an identity."

At the morgue, Dr. Jessica Sanders stood over Richard Dibella's naked body.

Captain Drake walked over to her. "Hey, Doc, I have identities of the victims. That one is Richard Brett Dibella. The one with his head twisted backward is Marcus John Dibella. The third one is Shane Rogers. All three are from Abilene, Texas."

Dr. Sanders shook her head and looked back at the bodies. "They came a long way to die. It sounds like a family lost a couple of boys. What a shame."

"Anything out of the ordinary here, Doc?"

"No, Joe, their bodies are all pretty tore up, as you can see. All three had a blood alcohol above the limit. Cause of death will be trauma. The only thing strange about this one is his penis."

Dr. Sanders grabbed the bloody member. "It's bent and has trauma to it. A bit strange."

"We found him on a ledge. He was alive after the crash, crying for help. Unfortunately, we didn't get to him in time. We noticed his shorts were around his knees and figured the crash caused them to fall. We see that from time to time."

"Hmmm, it's possible the crash caused the trauma. If his shorts were down, it would make sense that whatever caught his shorts also caught his penis. He suffered, Joe. His wounds would have led to an agonizing death." She pulled the sheet over his head. "I'll have my report done by the morning. This is open and shut—alcohol-related crash, massive trauma as the cause of death."

"Thank you, Doc. Jimmy is working on next of kin. It's possible these boys are related to Vincent Dibella."

Jessica eyes widened. "As in Dibella Farms?"

"It's possible. We'll know shortly."

"All that money... what a future these boys had. Such as shame."

"Yep. Thanks again, Jessica."

"You're welcome, Joe."

Joe looked at his watch: 6:30 AM, half an hour before his shift ended. He hoped Jimmy had identified next of kin and he could shut down his side of the case.

Back at the office, he said to his officer, "What do you have?"

Jimmy looked up from his paperwork and leaned back in his chair. "They're Vincent Dibella's two boys and a nephew. Abilene police confirmed. The Captain on duty knows the family, and he personally notified them. Dibella is on his way in his private jet to claim the bodies. It's about a two hour flight."

"Damn, all that money and future these boys had," Joe echoed Dr. Sanders. "What a shame."

"I ran a report on each victim. It appears they were not exactly saints." Jimmy said.

"What turned up?"

"Possession, drunk and disorderly, and aggravated assault that was dismissed on all three of them."

Joe sighed. "Typical rich kid shit."

"Yep. Any surprises at the coroner's?"

"Nope, all three drunk, the cause of death massive trauma. The only thing she noticed was the boy we found on the ledge had a broken dick."

Jimmy laughed. "Doesn't surprise me she found that."

"Yeah, she's seen a few. You would know, Jimmy," Captain Drake teased. "Well, looks like our work is done on this one. Unless the crash team comes up with something out of the ordinary, I say case closed. The family arrives in about an hour to take the bodies home. That part always sucks. I can never get used to the family part."

"If you did, it would be time to retire," Jimmy said. "The cries in the night get me. I can hear them in my sleep."

CHAPTER 14
BONDS

The early morning sun shined into the cave above the ranch. Sonny opened his eyes, adjusted to the light, and panned his surroundings. The stone walls sprung to life, adorned with ancient drawings of buffalo, elk, and other animals. Depictions of hunts and battles captured the history of the tribes before the reservation.

He imagined Arapaho people had gathered here, perhaps to smoke ceremonial pipes. Elders may have told stories behind the paintings of great warriors doing battle, of hunts when the buffalo roamed freely — stories of a time before white men destroyed their culture.

A humbling experience.

He stretched, pulled his hair into a ponytail, and wrapped a bandana around his head. He winced in pain as he lifted his arms, opening up the knife wound. The butterfly stitches helped, but the cut really needed sutures.

From the cave opening, an unobstructed view of the Colonel's ranch unfolded. Every breathtaking aspect of western geography lay in front of him as he inhaled deeply, taking in the fresh morning air.

"Sonny," a voice came from below. Jim was looking up from his back deck.

Sonny wondered how long he'd been there, and if he'd been standing guard to make sure Sonny didn't escape. He shrugged it off and waved, gathered his gear, and traversed the rocky hill to Jim's deck.

"Good morning, Colonel."

"Please, I insist you call me Jim. Would you like some coffee?"

"Yes, sir, that would be great. Black, please."

"Have a seat. I will be right back."

Jim returned a minute later with the coffee and a warm biscuit.

"Thank you, sir. How is your granddaughter?"

"She is shaken up and does not want to report this to the police. Like you, she does not want her name dragged into this. Her grandmother and I disagree with her."

Sony paused for a second. "I understand her dilemma."

"I realize she does not want to start her life here with this publicity, but these men need justice. Her grandmother said they filmed her. They will identify her, as she is on a good deal of fitness magazine covers. They said they would be back to finish her. I cannot have her live with that fear."

"I destroyed the camera, Jim. It's in a deep ravine in small pieces, and will never be found. Her secret is safe."

The screen door opened and Dakota approached with a newspaper in her hand. She dropped the paper on the table. "*Our* secrets are safe," she said, calmly.

The headline on the front page set the stage:

Three Men Killed in Canyon Crash

The story included pictures and the names of the victims.

Sonny nodded and fought back a smile.

"It's all over the news," Dakota said. "Those pieces of shit were Vincent Dibella's only two sons and a nephew."

"Who's Vincent Dibella?" Sonny said.

Jim answered. "He is a wealthy, powerful rancher from Abilene. He supplies close to twenty percent of the beef to the grocery store chains west of the Mississippi."

Dakota stared at the pictures of the three men, and her body trembled as she began to cry. "I don't understand. With all that money, why would those men attack me? They filmed me and said they were sending the film to a client. They said there would be people bidding on me."

Anna must have heard Dakota from inside, as she walked out to comfort her with a hug. "It's okay, Honey, it's okay. These men can't hurt you anymore."

"Grandma, what they did will hurt for the rest of my life. They took from me the place I felt safest, the place I would run to in my mind when things got tough. They brought ugliness and sin into my Eden. They stole my paradise. If it were not for this man, they would have taken everything from me. I'm glad the Spirits cursed them. I hope they suffered to their last breath."

She turned and stormed away.

Jim, Anna, and Sonny remained silent for a few moments.

Jim finally broke the silence, his eyes fixed on the ground, his voice cracking. "They have taken our Lomasi's innocent spirit."

Anna nodded sadly. "Jim, should I call my father and tell him we cannot get him today?"

"I know Dakota is looking forward to seeing him, but probably does not want to see him until her wounds heal. I would ask her, just to be safe."

Anna left the deck to do so.

Jim turned back to Sonny. "Please sit down."

"Yes sir."

He looked Sonny squarely in his eyes. "First, I want to thank you for saving Dakota's life last night. I will be forever indebted to you. The men that did this have taken secrets to their grave. I need you to share your secret with me. Who are you, son? I know you are not Sonny Telesco. Sonny is a double amputee, as you probably know. Last night, I did some research. I don't believe I need to go into any more details."

Sonny—the false Sonny—looked down at the ground for a moment, and then raised his head. "Sonny was my best friend. We served together on three different tours. My name is Jake Michaels. You can look me up."

"That name sounds familiar. Wait... I remember now. You went missing a month ago over near Sulphur Springs. I remember my friend Jay Storm Walker talking about your case. They assumed you were dead and called off the search."

"I *am* dead, Jim, and *need* to stay that way."

"I don't understand. Have you done something so heinous to run from your life? I remember Jay telling me how difficult working your case was. Your family was here during the search. He said he was taken aback by how much your wife loved you. Your sons even helped in the search. Why would you do this to them?"

Jake's eyes welled, and his lip quivered. "I love my wife Alexi more than anything on this Earth, and our children are our lives. I did this for them. I did this to save them from a terrible future."

"What do you mean? What could be so terrible to cause this much pain to them?"

Jake fixed his eyes on Jim's. "I have a degenerative brain disease, and my future is bleak. I could not put Alexi through a future of taking care of me, watching me deteriorate. She would slowly die with me, but if I had a quick death, she would move on from it, as would the kids."

"So why are you here, Jake?"

"I'll find a place in the mountains and live out the time I have left. I will not be a burden to my Alexi. I will die with dignity."

Jim's eyes narrowed as he nodded his head, and paused before responding, making Jake nervous. "I do not know if I agree with you, but you saved the most important thing in my life. I will keep your secret. I also will provide you a safe haven to live out your life. Anna's father owns a piece of property in the mountains between here and Dubois. It is about a five-hour horse ride from the ranch, and is very remote. You can disappear there, never to be seen again, if that is what you choose."

Jake sighed in relief. "I am grateful, sir."

"You know," Jim said. "Your resistance to contact the police has my wife on edge. She will dig into this. I know her."

"If you need to, go ahead and tell her the truth."

The two men reached out and shook each other's hands, and just then Anna opened the screen door.

"Jim," she said. "Lomasi still wants Father to come. She said she would make up a story about her lip. She said Father could also stitch Sonny's shoulder."

Jim shook his head and smiled. "That girl... despite everything she has been through, she is worried about your shoulder. Lomasi's light still shines through the darkness."

"Honey, we will leave in about an hour," Anna said, before leaving the two men.

"Jim, I don't want to meet anyone else," Jake said.

"He is 89 years old. He may not remember you in two weeks."

"How can he stitch my arm?"

"He was a veterinarian for fifty years. I still have him stitch the horses. Some things he will never forget."

Jake peeled his sleeve back and looked at his shoulder. "Okay, thank you. This needs to be closed before it gets infected. Um... can I bother you with taking a shower?"

"Of course, Jake. Anna will show you to the guest bath."

Jake finished his shower, and shaved to keep any hint of his grey beard from showing. For now, he must stay in disguise — such as it was.

He found Anna, Jim, and Dakota sitting at the kitchen table, discussing plans to pick up Anna's father. Dakota didn't want to go into town with her wounds. Anna couldn't drive, but needed to be present to check her dad out of the nursing home. This left Jim to drive, meaning Dakota and Sonny would remain back alone.

Anna looked concern about leaving a stranger alone with Dakota, even despite his heroic events of last night, but had the good graces not to say anything in front of Jake.

"Sonny, do you feel better?" Anna said.

"Yes ma'am. I really needed that shower. Thank you."

"Sonny," Dakota blurted out. "You and I are on our own for a few hours while my grandparents pick up my greatgrandfather. Do you like to ride horses?"

Her grandparents looked at each other.

"Stubborn as a mule," Jim muttered under his breath.

Anna nodded in clear agreement, but Dakota just ignored it.

"Well," Jake said. "It's been a while, but yes, I do."

"Great, I can use a ride to clear my head. After last night, having company will make me feel better. Come, let's get the horses ready."

Jake and Dakota left for the corral.

Anna lowered her brow and shook her head, looking at Jim. "She will never stop trusting strays, will she? Even after last night?"

"Anna, trust me, he is fine. I looked him up last night after you went to bed. He is highly decorated. I know his commanding officer. I trust him."

"Why then does he not want to be involved with the Police?"

He knew this question would come up today, as Anna let nothing go unresolved, but he had to be careful with his answer. If it did not suit her, she would keep digging. She did research for the law firm, was very thorough, and had established strong connections over the past twenty years.

He would have to include some truth in his answer; she would know if he was lying.

He placed his hand on hers and looked her dead in the eyes. "Honey, I asked him the same thing. Sonny is terminal. He has a large amount of hospital debt and does not want to spend his remaining days watching all he worked for taken from him by collectors. He has decided to spend his remaining days in nature. He wishes to die in peace and with dignity, on his terms. He has no extended family and is alone in this world. He chooses not to die surrounded by hospital staff he does not know."

Anna shook her head, never losing eye contact with him. "So sad, after serving our country for years. He probably has saved more lives than just our Lomasi's. After all that selflessness, to die alone... it is heartbreaking."

"Like many Vets, Anna. Too many Vets."

Jim knew this was the right answer, that she would not dig deeper. Jake's secret would be safe.

Sonny and Dakota rode from the corral, silent for the first several minutes. Last night had created an intimate and awkward bond between these two strangers. They searched for words to start a conversation, but knew it would ultimately end with the attack. Sonny seemed hesitant, as if fearing Dakota didn't want to talk about it, but she wanted to know who this stranger was that had saved her life.

"Woooo," he said, almost losing his balance on the horse.

She chuckled at his awkwardness. "You're not going to fall off and break your neck, are you?"

"No, I'll be all right. It's nice to see you smile after everything. How are you doing?"

"I'm okay. I lay in bed last night trying to grasp what happened, trying to understand why me. I realized it could have ended much worse. Those men were organized. They had the lights and camera plugged into their vehicle and set up quickly. Clearly, they had done this many times. I ran into them before the attack, while I was jogging. They asked me for directions, and were quite charming. I let my guard down, telling them I live here. They must have seen my vehicle, and figured I would return to it. They had this planned out from the time they pulled away."

"I admire your strength, Dakota. Most women would have a more difficult time with this."

"Sonny, I was raised by an ex-military father, and my grandfather is retired military. I spent my whole life playing sports. The last five years, I did fitness modeling. That's a man's world. As a female, you must be tough to survive there. I just graduated from law school, and will be working with our tribal council and my grandfather, and believe me, Indian rights have always been challenging." She chuckled again. "Point is, nothing in my world allows weakness."

He remained silent, keeping his eyes fixed on the trail ahead.

She continued. "I will see those men and last night for the rest of my life. I know that. I also know the Spirits sent you. Eventually, my thoughts will focus on your bravery, not their vileness."

She stopped her horse and looked at him. "Do you believe in Destiny?"

He turned and locked his gaze on her. "I do, very much so."

She noticed the serious look in his eyes, but also saw a sparkle there.

She moved her horse forward, and refocused on the path, but a faint smile crossed her face. "So, Sonny, tell me about yourself. Why are you here? Be truthful. You know the internet has all kinds of information. I'll check up on your story."

He paused, knowing she was right. Her grandfather had found out the truth about him quickly. Besides, he felt compelled to tell her the truth, after seeing her in the most compromising position. Although naked, beaten, and vulnerable, the first thing she did after the attack was reach out to his bleeding shoulder. There was a unique spirit in her, and it did seem that Destiny had brought them together. He did not question Destiny.

He stopped his horse, and Dakota followed. He then reached up and pulled the long black wig from his head, and looked at her.

Her eyes widened in a fixed gaze.

"Don't be alarmed. My name is Jake Michaels. Sonny was my best friend in the Army. Your grandfather knows the truth. That's why he had no problem with you being alone with me. I will tell you my story."

Jake dismounted his horse, walked to the edge of the path, and looked out over the valley below.

Dakota walked up to join him.

"Beautiful, isn't it?" he said, staring forward.

Dakota watched silently as a tear trickled down his cheek, knowing instantly that the story to follow would not be easy to hear.

Jake told his story, and she didn't interrupt him. In fact, she was speechless, as her heart ached listening to him. He loved his wife, as Dakota dreamed of being loved one day. His story reinforced for her that, no matter how vile as those men who attacked her had been, there were still good men in the world—men like Jake.

Not once had he taken his eyes off the valley below as he told his story.

Dakota dried her eyes with the sleeve of her shirt, and then, with the same sleeve, reached up and wiped the tears on Jake's cheek.

Destiny had brought them together in suffering. Now, Destiny bound them with shared tears on the same fabric.

Chapter 15
On the Table

"Hey, Joe, you're here late," Lieutenant John Black Hawk said, approaching Captain Drake's desk.

"The family is flying in to claim the bodies of the boys killed last night. I want to be here to answer any questions they have. You know Vincent Dibella will want to talk to someone with a title."

"Nasty crash, Joe. It's a shame. Eight fatalities for summer already."

"Yep, and every one alcohol-related. Any surprises on the investigation, John?"

"No, sir, looks like they just veered off the road and over the cliff. There were no skid marks. I assume the driver fell asleep. It appears the truck made head on contact with a boulder after going over the edge, a significant front end impact. After that, the truck rolled several times, side over side, until it came to rest. They weren't wearing seat belts, not that it would have mattered. You saw the truck—looked like a crushed can."

"Well, that would explain how two of the victims were thrown from the truck. Looks like an open and shut case. Thanks, John."

"You bet, Captain. Good luck with the family. That's never easy. Call me if you need anything."

"Thanks. Enjoy your day off."

Joe's desk phone rang, and he reached out and snagged it.

"Captain, Mr. Dibella is here."

"Thank you, Joanne, I'll be right out." He took a deep breath and walked to the reception area.

A tall gray-haired man stood there, wearing a black suit and a black cowboy hat. He had an authoritative air about him, exactly what Joe had imagined a powerful Western billionaire would look like. Two men stood by his sides.

Joe reached out his hand. "Mr. Dibella, my name is Captain Joseph Drake."

The billionaire returned the greeting with a firm handshake. "Vincent Dibella, Captain. This is my pilot Kevin Smith, and my attorney Howard Sellman."

After the introductions, Captain Drake escorted the trio into his office. "Please, everyone, have a seat. Can I get you some coffee or water?"

"No, we're fine," Vincent said. "Please tell me what happened to my boys."

"They lost control of the vehicle. It subsequently went off the road and over a cliff. The truck rolled several times before coming to rest below in the ravine. They were all pronounced dead at the scene."

Vincent removed his hat and looked down at the ground. "Where they drinking?"

"There were empty alcohol bottles at the crash scene, and toxicology reports showed all three were well over the limit."

"Okay, Captain, please take me to them. Let me get 'em home."

The four men left the office for the short walk to the morgue, no one uttering a word. Joe led them to a viewing area. Although they'd made positive identification, protocol required a physical identification before the morgue could release the bodies.

"Mr. Dibella, do you want to identify them or have your attorney do it?" Joe said.

"Bring them to the window, Captain," Vincent said, in a steady voice.

"Yes sir. Please excuse me while I go back and talk with the coroner."

It took about two minutes to position the bodies, then Joe drew open the curtain to the morgue window, putting the three gurneys with body bags in view. He looked at Vincent, who nodded his head. One by one, he unzipped the body bags to chest hig, and one by one, Vincent nodded his head, showing no emotions whatsoever. The coroner closed the curtain, and Joe rejoined the three men outside.

"Are you okay, sir?" he said.

Vincent remained stoic. "Please bring me their belongings."

Joe nodded. "We've gathered up what was in the truck. We found a cabin key for Hangman's Bridge Campground, so two officers are there gathering the rest of their belongings as we speak."

"My attorney will take care of any paperwork, Captain. Do you have the means to take the bodies to my plane?"

"Yes, sir, we can arrange that. Let's walk back to the station, and I'll turn over the belongings. One question, sir: the young man that was not your son... has your attorney taken care of paperwork with the next of kin?"

"I am his next of kin, Captain. My sister and her husband are dead. I've raised him since he was nine."

"Yes sir. I'm sorry, but I had to ask that."

"I understand, Captain."

Vincent and his pilot followed Joe into his office, while Vincent's attorney stayed behind to take care of all the legal paperwork. Three boxes sat on the desk, each containing that victim's drivers license and belongings found on their bodies or in the truck, incuding their wallets.

Vincent picked up each wallet and looked at each boy's pictures, remaining emotionless.

Joe broke the momentary silence. "Mr. Dibella, the officers will be here with the rest of their belongings in a few minutes. They said there wasn't much in the cabin."

"They were only here for the weekend," Vincent said.

An awkward silence ensued, until a knock came at the office door. The two officers that gathered the belongings from the cabin had arrived, and Joe motioned them in. They set three packed travel bags down, and a plastic bag with some loose items.

"Is that everything, Captain?" Vincent said.

"Yes sir."

"Where is Richard's rifle?"

"Mr. Dibella, we found no guns at the scene, and if the officers had found it at the cabin, they would have brought it back."

"Richard goes nowhere without that gun. I saw it in his truck when he left. It's a very expensive, custom-made rifle, which I gave him on his eighteenth birthday. His initials are engraved on the receiver."

"Well, their truck rolled several times. I suppose it's possible the rifle was thrown from the vehicle. We recovered personal items in various locations at the scene, but saw no rifle. Where the truck landed is part of the Wind River trail system, so hopefully an honest person found it and will get around to returning it to us. I can't guarantee it."

"And the box of shells... I assume they were not found either?" Vincent said, sarcastically.

"No sir."

Vincent looked at his pilot as he stood up. "Kevin, give him your card." He then turned back to Joe. "Captain, if the rifle shows up, please call Kevin. Are we done here?"

"Yes, sir, we're done. The hearses will be at your airplane in one hour."

Vincent and his pilot turned and left abruptly.

Joe shut the door behind them and mumbled, "No thank you, or even a fuck you? Asshole! More worried about a gun than your dead boys."

He sat back in his chair, yawned, rubbed his eyes, and looked at his watch. It was already noon. There was a knock at his door.

"Come in."

Jimmy walked in and sat down. "Captain, your eyes look like two piss holes in the snow. Long night, huh?"

"I'm getting too old for these long days, and for assholes like Dibella. Fucking guy seemed more worried about a missing gun than his dead boys." He shook his head and sighed. "You know what has me puzzled, Jimmy? Why were those boy's bags packed, if they were staying for the entire weekend? Almost seems like they were prepared for a quick exit."

Jimmy shook his head and shrugged. "I don't know, Captain."

Joe traced his mustache and chin with his fingers. "I wonder what secrets lie on those morgue tables."

CHAPTER 16
SPIRIT WORLD

"Jake, we should get going," Dakota said. "My great grandfather will be here soon."

"Okay."

The two mounted their horses and started a slow ride for the ranch.

Jake said, "Your grandfather offered me a place to live. He said it's your great grandfather's property."

"That's awesome! It's beautiful, and very remote. There's a small creek with a waterfall, great for drinking water and trout fishing. The old hunting cabin needs some work, but if you're handy, it can provide warmth and shelter. And the hunting is fantastic! I haven't been there for years. It's a long horse ride from the ranch. If you leave from Dubois, it's about a four-hour hike one way, if you know the trail."

"I'm grateful for his offer."

"Jake, you saved my life. An old, abandoned hunting cabin is the least we can do to thank you. Is there anything I can do for you?"

Jake thought for a second. "When I was here on vacation a few months ago, we stopped at a gift shop in town. Alexi and I loved it. They invited us to be friends on Facebook to help advertise, and we agreed. I would love, somehow, to be able to see Alexi's Facebook page from time to time. I want to make sure she moves on with her life, and to know how my kids are doing. Do you know the folks at Totem Gift Shop?"

"The owner's daughter is one of my best friends, and I'm Facebook friends with Totem as well. We can set a date each month that I can meet you, and I can fill you in and print some pictures for you. I love riding out to the old cabin."

"That would be great. A time will come when I won't know them anymore, but if my memory can hold on long enough to see them move on with their lives, I would be happy."

The two rode for several minutes in silence.

"Dakota," Jake said at last. "I need to go to where the attack happened. I want to make sure there's nothing there that could ever come back to you. Can I use this horse to go there when we get back?"

She nodded. "There's a fork in the trail coming up, which connects to the trail we were on last night. I'll go with you before we get home."

"Are you sure you can handle being there so soon?"

"Yes, I wouldn't have suggested it if I wasn't. The surer I can be of that night staying just between us, the better I am."

The two continued their ride, making small talk. He told her happier details of his life, and she shared stories of the magical summers spent here. For that short time, the terrible events that had brought them together faded. They both smiled during the conversation, even laughed at times.

Dakota pointed. "The left up there will take us back to the trail. When I tried to escape, I wanted to get to this path. You probably didn't see that part."

The two made the turn, at which point the conversation ended. Last night played over in Jake's mind. He could see Dakota, naked, beaten, and crying. He could see the violence he'd inflicted on the men. He could see blood splattering and hear bones breaking.

Dakota must have been seeing it all over again, too, because she jumped off her horse, leaned over, and dry heaved.

Jake dismounted and rushed to her. "Hey, hey, are you okay?"

She shook her head, her eyes glassed over. "I'm sorry, Jake. I can't go back there yet."

He tried to comfort her, touching her shoulder. "Shhhh, Dakota, it's okay."

She pulled him towards her and hugged him tightly, crying into his chest.

He hesitated, and then puts his arms around her. "It's okay, it's okay. You don't have to go back there. I'll take you home and come back later."

She looked up at him. "Thank you so much for being there. Thank you." She gently pushed away from him as she calmed down. Wiping her eyes, she laughed lightly. "Well, so much for being tough, huh?"

"You went through a lot. You have the right to be upset."

"I was doing good, and then it was all there again. I could smell them, hear them, and feel them. I'm so glad those bastards are dead. I was lucky. I can't imagine how many women were less fortunate."

"Come, let's turn around," he said.

Dakota squinted her eyes, and her voice deepened as she said, "No, I will not run from ghosts. We're almost there."

They reached the spot and dismounted. Each meandered around the area, scouring every inch looking for remnants of last night.

Dakota found her running shorts and top in some tall grass.

Jake kicked dirt over blood drops and puddles. He picked up small pieces of the camera he'd destroyed and threw them into a crevice in the rocks.

Dakota said, "It's going to rain tonight. That will wash away their tire tracks and blood. Where's the camera and two light stands?"

He pointed to the deep crevice in the rocks. "Down there."

She looked over the edge. "Perfect! There's no way down except to repel there, and there's no reason for anyone to ever go down there. What about the phone that prick was filming with?"

He pointed. "I threw it into the river."

"Good. It runs deep in that ravine."

"Hold on, Dakota, stay with me. I feel a spell coming...."

"Jake, Jake, Jake...."

He heard her calling his name, her voice growing louder as he came out of his spell. He shook his head to clear the cobwebs. This marked the first time anyone had witnessed a spell from start to finish.

"Dakota, how long was I gone?"

"About thirty seconds."

"That's it? Did I say or do anything?"

"You looked at where they had me on my knees, and said, '*Sooner, sooner,*' about four times. I guess you wish you'd gotten here sooner."

"I guess. I don't remember anything." He opened his eyes wide and took a deep breath, clearing his thoughts.

Her concern seemed to ease a bit. "It looks like we have everything, Jake. Look, my grandparents are home." She pointed to the ranch house. "It's amazing how close I was to safety, isn't it?"

"Yes, it is."

The two mounted their horses, and Jake put his wig on.

She looked at him and laughed. "I thought you had really bad hair, but nope—just a really bad wig."

"Greatgrandfather," Dakota yelled, as she and Jake walked through the front door. She raced ahead, leaving Jake behind.

Jake looked at the older man, whose weathered skin covered strong features. Long gray hair flowed over his shoulders, and he had a wise look about him.

"Lomasi," the old man said. "What has happened to your lip?"

Dakota quickly moved to a kick boxing stance and threw some air punches. "Training, Greatgrandfather, a great warrior must prepare."

He shook his head and chuckled, then looked over and pointed at Jake. "And who is this?"

Jake walked up to him and extended his hand. "Sonny Telesco, sir."

"Samuel Red Hawk. Nice to meet you, Sonny."

Samuel's firm handshake impressed Jake, but he felt as if Samuel's eyes looked deep inside him, as the older man held the grip longer than normal.

He whispered something in Arapaho, nodded, and walked away.

Jim stepped in. "Sonny is an old Army buddy of mine. He is passing through to Jackson Hole."

"Come," Anna said. "Let's sit down and have a drink before dinner."

The group moved to the living room, where they reminisced about years gone by and debated current tribal issues. Jim and Jake — *Sonny* — spoke about common military acquaintances.

"Is everyone getting hungry?" Anna said.

"I could eat a buffalo," Samuel barked. "They feed me nothing at that place."

"Father, that is not true. The food is very healthy. I have seen the portions, and they are more than I can eat. Besides, we have asked you many times if you want to live here. You always say no, that you need to be near the council hall."

Samuel harrumphed. "You eat like a bird. My gifts take much energy. I need buffalo, elk, and trout, like our people *should* eat."

Anna rolled her eyes. "Well, Father, you are in luck. Tonight, we are eating elk roast."

Dakota winked at Jake and smiled.

He forced a smile, swallowing a lump in his throat. The banter reminded him of gatherings at his parents, and elicited memories of his family.

The group sat at the dinner table.

"Greatgrandfather, please say a prayer," Dakota said.

Samuel prayed in Arapaho.

Jake could not understand a word, except for the names of everyone at the table, including his—Sonny's.

"Now," Samuel said. "Let us eat before the Great Spirit takes me."

The group leaned back in their chairs, stuffed from dinner.

"Greatgrandfather, can you tell us a story about our ancestors?"

Jim intervened. "Lomasi, let's get Sonny's shoulder fixed first. Then we can relax."

"Oh, Sonny, I'm so sorry. I forgot about it," Dakota said.

"Honestly, I think it's fine. The butterflies are holding."

Samuel held up his hand. "Let me see, Sonny. Come over to the sink."

Jake rolled up his sleeve and saw that the butterflies were holding. There was no fresh blood on the dressing, but when Samuel pressed around the wound, blood started to ooze.

Samuel said, "We need to stitch it. This is a clean slice. How did you get it?"

"I was an idiot, sir, cleaning fish and drinking a few beers. When I got done, I reached up to wipe my blade on a towel draped over my shoulder, but had the wrong angle on the knife." He shrugged.

"Hmmm... Jim, grab me my kit from the barn."

Jim smiled and held it up. "Already have it, Doc."

Samuel pulled a needle from the bag, and filled it with a numbing agent. He then removed the butterflies, and started to stitch, his hands, surprisingly to Jake, steady as a rock. He closed the wound in no time at all.

Samuel looked at Jake and smirked. "There you go, Sonny. Be careful next time you clean fish."

"Story time," Dakota announced, with childlike excitement.

Jake saw a new side of her, the one Jim had feared was gone. She was pushing the attack further away, perhaps stronger than anyone thought, even her family. The strength of her ancestors shined through.

Samuel told a story of the Great White Elk and a warrior that hunted it. "The warrior cornered the Great White Elk, and drew his bow to kill the animal. The Great White Elk looked at the warrior and spoke. He told the warrior that sometimes, the hunt shows more skill than the kill. The Elk told the warrior that for many generations, his ancestors had hunted him, but he was the first warrior to corner him. He asked the warrior if he wanted to be known as a great hunter, or as a great slayer of beasts. The warrior thought, and lowered his bow. He allowed the Great White Elk to pass."

"Greatgrandfather, I don't understand. For generations, they hunted the Great White Elk. He would have been a legend to his people. Why did he not shoot?"

"Lomasi, searching for something is sometimes better than finding it," Samuel said, with great wisdom to his tone. "I am getting tired. It is time for this old man to visit the Spirit world."

Samuel walked to each person in the family and hugged them goodnight. When he approached Jake, he shook his hand again, and leaned in to whisper so only he could hear. "Thank you, Sonny. The Spirits showed me a great warrior last night."

CHAPTER 17
A NEW LIFE

Samuel walked to his bedroom, and Anna bid everyone goodnight and followed her father.

"Sonny," Jim said. "Tomorrow, I will take Samuel home early, and we will go to the property. It is a long ride. I will stay there for the night and help you get the old place in order."

"I want to go," Dakota chimed in.

"Lomasi, I think it is best you stay here and rest. You have been through a lot."

"Grandfather, it's been a while since I've been there. I need to refresh my memory. I've made a promise to Jake."

Jim's eyes broadened as he glanced a Jake.

Jake nodded. "She knows, Jim. I've told her everything."

Jim turned to his granddaughter. "What kind of promise did you make, Lomasi?"

"I told Jake I would monitor his family's Facebook pages. He wants to make sure they're moving on with their lives. He knows that one day he *will* forget them, but before he slips into that darkness, he wants to know they are okay. Once a month, we'll meet and I'll update him."

Jim paused as if considering their plan. "I understand."

Jake said, "Jim, Samuel said something strange to me. He thanked me, and told me the Spirits showed him a warrior last night. It took me by surprise."

"He is a Medicine Man. Sometimes he will say things about something I do not understand how he would know anything about. It makes me wonder if he truly can connect to the Spirit World. Most of our people have lost belief in the old ways, but Elders like him still hold on to them."

Dakota raised her hand. "I believe in Greatgrandfather's powers. He sees things."

Jake examined her expression and thought for a moment. "Well, I'm going to head up to the cave. I'm tired."

"Jake, we have a spare room. You're welcome to sleep here," Dakota offered.

"Thank you, but I enjoyed sleeping up there last night. There's something special about that cave. I want to experience it one more time." He said goodnight and excused himself.

"Woo Woo," Dakota said. "He has a sad story. He loved his family so much that he was willing to walk away from them at a time he would need them the most. I watched him have a spell, and it was like he was there, but in another world. It differs from Greatgrandfather's dementia. He spoke, but didn't remember what he said. His stare was strange, too, not blank but distant."

Jim thought about it for a moment, and said, "Lomasi, when Samuel was diagnosed, your grandmother and I did a lot of research on dementia and Alzheimer's. While most people have similar symptoms, individuals can exhibit different ones. No two brains are the same. We do not know what part of Jake's brain is degenerating."

"I wonder how long he has left, Woo Woo?"

"I do not know. It could be a year or two, or it could be twenty years, but I would think for Jake to walk away from his life, he probably feels there is not much time."

"What if he's wrong? What if he has decades left?"

"Then, Lomasi, he made the wrong decision. He stole something precious from his family and himself."

"Or the spirits guided him to me. They allowed *our* family to *keep* something precious."

Jim nodded. "Yes, they did."

"Well, we're leaving early. I'm heading to bed." His granddaughter kissed him on the cheek and retired to her room.

Jim sat in his chair and reflected on the events of the past twenty-four hours. He thought about Samuel's vision, and the odds that Jake would be on *that* trail last night to save Dakota. Perhaps the elders had been right the whole time. Perhaps the Spirits controlled everything, and humanity had turned their backs on them.

Jake sat at the entrance to the cave, looking out over the night sky bedazzled with the endless sea of brilliant stars. He lowered his head, wishing Alexi were by his side to share this. He would tell her everything looked in place in the solar system, and she would smile and say nothing. Then, they would slowly drift off to sleep under the majesty of the heavens. The last thing he would do would be to thank God for her, as he had every night since the first day they'd met.

He took a deep breath as a tear trickled down his cheek. He was tired of tears. He was tired of thinking about the tears that undoubtedly had flowed over Alexi's cheeks. Yet he knew that as long as his tears flowed, a piece of her would remain with him.

A light upstairs in the house caught his attention. He saw that Dakota had walked into her bedroom, and her shades were open. With nothing behind the house, she probably was not accustomed to closing them. She combed her long hair in the mirror, then walked to the closet, where she loosened the straps to her dress and let it fall to the floor. He turned away quickly, ashamed, but he found her beauty captivating. He struggled not to look back at the window, and lay down looking up at the darkness of the cave.

He thought about Dakota seeing him during his spell, and how she hadn't known what *'sooner'* meant, when he'd said it over and over. He knew, but she would never need to know. He would live with that guilt, and with the decisions that he'd made last night.

The early morning sun illuminated the cave. Jake woke up and walked to the entrance to revel in the sunrise, and looked down to see Samuel on the side of the house. The Medicine Man looked towards the sunrise, raising his arms to it, and Jake could faintly hear Samuel chanting. He nodded his head and walked back into the cave to gather his stuff.

He walked down the hill towards the house, and reflexively glanced up at Dakota's window. Her shades were closed.

"Sonny, good morning. The Spirits have blessed you with another day, as they have me."

"Good morning, Samuel. Yes they have, sir."

"Why did you sleep in the cave and not a bedroom?"

"There's something special about that cave, sir. I feel a connection up there."

Samuel walked over to him, put his hand on his head, closed his eyes, whispered something in Arapaho, and took his hand from Jake's head. "Sonny, there is a great battle in you. Like me, you cross into the Spirit World. I see great pain in your eyes. Do not question the Spirits. They have brought you here for a reason. I saw you and those evil men in my dreams. While the Spirits danced in the sky, you did battle like a great warrior. Let the Spirits guide you. Listen to them when you cross into their world."

He looked at Samuel, and realized Dakota had been right. "Samuel, I remember nothing when I have a spell. It's like my world goes dark."

"When you feel yourself crossing over, do not be afraid. It will take time to control your fear. Reach out your hand." Samuel placed a pouch, and a small wooden pipe with feathers hanging from it, in his hand. "When you are ready to learn the Spirit World, smoke this. It will allow you to see their world clearer. It will help you connect with your essence. You will learn not to be afraid when they call you. They will show you good and evil, and you will learn why you are here. I must go now. Jim is waiting out front. We will meet again, Cebisee Nohkuuhu Honi."

Samuel walked away.

Jake examined the leather pouch and pipe and put them in his backpack.

"Good morning, caveman," Dakota said, as she walked onto the back deck. "Would you like some coffee?"

"Yes, coffee would be great, thank you."

Dakota returned and sat at the patio table. "I saw you talking to Greatgrandfather. Did he have words of wisdom for you?"

"Nothing I understand. When he left, he called me something-or-other Honi."

She chuckled. "Honi is wolf. Maybe he thinks we will see wolves today? It's hard to tell with him. He's old and suffers from Alzheimer's. Sometimes he makes no sense."

Jake looked towards the mountains. "It looks like the weather is perfect for our trip today."

"Yeah, when you're ready, we'll go to the stables and saddle up the horses."

"I'm ready when you are. How long will it take for your grandfather to get back from town?"

"About an hour or so. He has his pack on the front porch. We can leave as soon as he returns."

"Okay, we can head to the stables when you're ready."

Dakota bounced up. "Let's go."

Jim, Anna, and Samuel drove toward the nursing home.

Anna said, "Father, you are quiet. Is everything all right?"

"Sonny goes into the Spirit World as I do."

"Yes, Father, he also has a brain disease."

Samuel stared out the window. "The Spirits guided him here. There is a storm coming to Wind River." His tone was prophetic.

Jim and Anna looked at each other. Samuel always talked about a battle coming to Wind River, and felt the Indian Nation would one day rise again, but they didn't respond to his comment.

"How long is he staying here?" Samuel asked.

"He has moved here," Jim answered.

"That is good. He is a warrior. He needs to stay close to Lomasi."

"Okay, Father, we are here," Anna announced.

Jim and Anna led Samuel into his assisted living home.

The Elder said, "Tell Lomasi to go to the Sacred Falls, clean the evil white men from her Spirit."

Jim and Anna looked at each other with raised brows.

Anna hugged him. "I love you, Father. We will tell Lomasi, and we will see you next weekend."

The couple walked to their car.

Once seated inside, Anna sighed. "How does he know? Did he really see something in his dreams?"

Jim shook his head. "I don't know. I honestly don't know."

Dakota and Jake finished readying the horses for the long ride to the old cabin.

"Perfect timing," she said. "Here come my grandparents."

Jim stopped the car at the corral.

"Woo Woo," Dakota shouted. "The horses are packed. We're ready."

"Very good, I will be down in a minute. I need to change my clothes."

"We'll walk the horses up to the house and meet you."

She was excited about the overnight trip. They hadn't done one together in four years.

Jim took the lead on the trip, while Dakota and Jake followed closely behind, grouped tight enough to have conversation.

The backcountry was even more beautiful than what Jake had seen on vacation, which he hadn't thought possible. He looked at Dakota, and pictured Alexi on the horse. She would have loved this.

"Jake, you've been quiet for the past couple miles," Dakota said, breaking conversation with her grandfather.

"The beauty here is beyond words. I'm just taking it in. Plus, I didn't want to interrupt Jim and you."

"Well," Jim said. "This is home to you now. Each day that passes, you will discover something new. Each season will bring its own majesty."

"I wish Alexi could be here with us. I wish we could have met under different circumstances. She would have loved both of you, and Anna and Samuel."

They all rode silent for a few seconds.

Jim said, "Yes, we would have loved to meet her. Sometimes the Spirits guide our lives in directions we do not understand."

"Yes sir. I stopped trying to figure out Destiny years ago."

"Speaking of Alexi," Dakota said solemnly. "I looked at her Facebook page before we left. There were no new posts. She has her profile picture as you, with a missing caption. It looks like the only update she's done for the past month has been increasing the days you've been gone."

He took a deep breath. "Thank you, Dakota. She's holding onto a thread of hope. Without my body, she'll believe there's a chance. Eventually, she will let go."

Jim added, "Jake, I know the officer and the tracker that worked on your case. They are some of the best in the business. What did you do so convincing to pull them off your tracks and declare you dead so quickly?"

Jake shook his head. "If they ever discover me, and somehow, they connect me back to your family.... Well, I believe the less you know, the better. If they ever find me, hopefully, my disease will have advanced enough that I won't remember any details. It will be another secret buried out here."

Jim nodded.

"Look," Dakota said, breaking the serious mood. She pointed to a clearing up ahead.

"A mother wolf and her pups," Jim said.

"Honi," Dakota and Jake said, simultaneously, then looked at each other and chuckled.

Jim smiled and looked back at them. "Jake, I see Dakota has taught you some Arapaho."

"Yes sir."

Dakota pulled her camera out and snapped several pictures.

"The cabin is about one mile ahead," Jim said. "We have made good time."

The group reached the boundary of Samuel's property, where old *"No Trespassing"* signs hung from trees. They reached a clearing. The old cabin stood in the middle.

"Well, it is in better shape than I thought," Jim said.

"Welcome home, Jake," Dakota added.

Jake dismounted his horse and walked around the small cabin. He saw three holes in the roof, and a few windows were busted out, but the logs appeared to be solid. He jiggled the front door knob, finding the cabin locked. "I can't believe no one has broken in here."

"No one comes out this far," Jim said. "For our people, sacred land surrounds most of the property. They will not cross over it, and the path from Dubois is very tricky. White folks will not come here in fear of getting lost. As promised, you are pretty much off the grid."

Jim tied his horse to the hitching post and opened the locked door. A table with four chairs, a wood cooking stove, and wash sink sat to the right side. Looking left, an Adirondack-style chair, draped with an old bearskin, sat next to a small hand-carved end table with a gas lamp. A stone fireplace positioned in the middle of the left wall commanded attention. Across from the Adirondack chair were three bunks placed side by side.

Dakota walked to the fireplace and ran her hand across the mantle. Her face lit up. "Isn't this cozy? I love this cabin."

Jake surveyed everything. "Wow, this will work. I'll patch the roof and fix the windows. It's perfect."

Jim nodded toward the rear of the cabin. "Out back is a small shed. Samuel kept basic tools and repair material out there. Let's see if there is anything you can patch the roof with."

They opened the shed door.

"Woooo, stand still, Jake." Jim pointed to a rafter. "Slowly back out." He reached for his sidearm, drew the weapon, and fired a single shot. A four- foot rattlesnake fell to the ground, its headless body writhing in a death dance.

"Nice shooting, Tex," Jake said.

Dakota heard the shot and ran back to them. "What happened?"

Jim walked out of the shed holding the rattlesnake's body. He raised it up. "Dinner tonight."

Dakota shook her head and returned to the cabin, where she'd been cleaning up, while Jake and Jim looked around the shed. They found wood and tar paper to fix the roof. All the basic tools Jake needed to survive were there.

This is just too perfect, almost as if I had planned it all out.

He shook his head and murmured, "Destiny," under his breath.

The men joined Dakota at the cabin, where she had the old mattresses outside airing out. The bearskin hung over the hitching post. She'd swept the floor, getting rid of all the leaves that had fallen through the holes in the roof, and the cabin was looking livable.

She motioned Jake towards her. "Come, let me show you the stream and waterfall. The fishing is great, and the water tastes so good. You can bathe in the summer here."

They took a short walk around a bend in the clearing and reached the stream, then followed it to the pool and waterfall. Jake saw trout darting through the chrystal clear water. The waterfall stood about six-foot high from the surface of the pool. It was narrow but had good flow.

Dakota said, "There are so many trout in this stream. No one fishes here, obviously. It will keep you full your whole life. Do you wanna swim?" She unbuttoned her denim shirt.

Jake quickly turned away.

"Silly, I have a bathing suit on." She laughed.

He looked back at her and held eye contact, not allowing his eyes to travel down her body as she removed her cut off denim shorts. "No, I'm fine."

"I love swimming here. The water is so refreshing on a hot day."

"Okay, well you enjoy your swim. I'm gonna look at the roof."

He rejoined Jim at the cabin, who had pulled boards from the shed and was measuring them to cover the broken windows.

"I assume Lomasi is swimming?"

"Yes sir."

"That water is so cold. I do not know how she does it." Jim shook his head, and returned to the task at hand. "There are only three broken panes, not bad after all these years. The boards will keep the weather out for now."

"One day," Jake said. "I'll go into Dubois and get some glass. I'm waiting till next spring. I wanna make sure I've faded from people's minds."

"That is a good idea. There are missing person posters of you from Dubois to Sulphur Springs. The picture does not look like you, though. It shows you with short gray hair and a beard."

Jake pulled his wig off. "How about now?"

Jim chuckled. "A dead ringer without the beard. Yes, you need to stay out of town right now."

Dakota rejoined the two men. "Hey, Jake, I seen you got a haircut."

"Lomasi, how was your swim?"

"Awesome, Woo Woo. You should have come."

Jim shook his head as he went back to measuring the boards.

Jake alternated between the two of them. "I have a question. What does Lomasi and Woo Woo mean? Is it granddaughter and grandfather?"

"Lomasi means Beautiful Blossom," Dakota said. "Woo Woo is short for Neibesiiwoo, which means grandfather. I couldn't pronounce it when I was young, and Woo Woo just stuck."

"Gotcha. Now I know three Arapaho words."

Jim said, "It is getting close to dinner time. Is anyone else hungry?"

"Starving," Jake said.

"Me too, but not for rattlesnake." Dakota wrinkled her nose.

Jim laughed and pointed to his horse. "I have burger in my cooler."

"I'll eat the rattler," Jake said. "I've had it several times, and like it."

"Better get used to it Nih'o'o' 3oo," Jim said.

Dakota looked at Jim, and both laughed.

Jake threw his hands up and smiled. "Okay, fourth word. What did you call me?"

Dakota smiled and winked. "White person."

The group went inside the cabin to prepare dinner.

After eating, they pulled chairs up around the fireplace. The log walls glowed warmly with the reflection of the dancing fire, and as the smell of dinner lingered, life had been breathed back into the abandoned cabin.

"Jim, how old is this cabin?"

"It is about seventy years old. Samuel's dad and his three brothers built it. This old place has a lot of history. I remember the first time they brought me hunting out here. Anna and I were still dating. We had a good day hunting, and all sat around the fireplace, like we are now. Samuel's dad told stories of days before the reservation, stories of when our people roamed free in these mountains. He was a great storyteller. I always looked forward to coming out here with them."

"When was the last time Samuel came out here? I'm sure this is a special place to him."

"It was ten years ago. He came out here to bury his last surviving brother. His brothers and father are all buried out here. Their graves are past the waterfall about a hundred yards. He claims he visits them here in the Spirit World. One day he will be buried next to them."

"Didn't his brothers have any family that wanted to carry on the tradition of hunting here?"

"Two of the brothers never married. One brother had a daughter that no one has heard from in twenty years. She married wealthy and never looked back on the Reservation. The fourth brother had a son that was killed in Vietnam."

Jake nodded, saying nothing.

"This cabin will give you shelter," Jim said, "but the winters here are brutal. They are unforgiving. Have you given thought to how you will survive?"

"I have a breakdown bow in my pack, and the gun and shells I picked up from those men helps a lot. I also have a telescoping fishing pole. Meat will not be a problem. I'll gather nuts and berries. In my pack is a ten-pound bag of cornmeal, and I have a year's supply of multivitamins. As you know, I'm trained to live off the land. The first winter will be tough. Next spring, I'll plant a garden. Things changed the other night. I planned on a solitary existence. Now, with Dakota and you.... Perhaps I can pay you to bring some canned vegetables out here before the snow flies?"

"I can bring canned goods next trip," Dakota quickly offered.

Jim still looked concerned. "Okay, food and shelter are handled. I know that pack you have does not have enough room for the clothing you will need out here."

"I have a three-layer jacket in there. It's rated for extreme conditions. I'll also tan pelts."

"It appears you have the basics covered. Tell me, how did the search party not realize you left with your pack? Hal Jones and Jay

Storm Walker are sharp men. After talking with your family, they would have known you were traveling across country. I remember Hal telling me they found your motorcycle in a ravine. When they saw it had no gear, red flags would have gone up. They would have never moved so quickly to declare you deceased in absentia."

Dakota watched as her grandfather softly interrogated Jake. His matter of fact tone would not alert Jake to his underlying intent. Woo Woo wanted to know how Jake faked his death. He needed to know how Jake could have tricked Jay Storm Walker, one of the best trackers in the country.

Jake looked at Jim and smiled. "I understand that you want to know the facts, but do you really want to carry the truth with you? Do you want Dakota to carry that burden also? Right now, I'm Sonny Telesco, just a guy trespassing on Samuel's property. No one knows you have brought me up here. Dakota's and my secret are buried with those three men. Jake Michaels is dead."

Dakota thought, *Damn, Jake is sharp.*

Woo Woo looked him in the eyes, and his tone turned serious. "Yes, Jake, I do. We are hiding dark secrets from the world. I do not want to hide any between us."

Jake took a deep breath, looked down at the ground for a moment, then back up at Jim and Dakota, and nodded.

"While I was riding, I searched for an access road to the Bighorn River. The river was running high and fast. I needed a road with a grade, so I could make it look as though I lost control of my bike while going down to the river. Just a few miles from Sulphur Springs, I found one. The river was too high to fish, so I knew no one would come down the road. I dropped my bike and tied a rope around it. I dragged it downhill for about twenty feet and pushed it off the edge into the ravine below. At the point of where I dropped the bike, I used a syringe to draw blood from my arm. I left a small puddle at what would have been the point my head made an impact with the ground. My helmet was attached to the bike. I left the syringe in my arm allowing blood to drip, making a trail to a small cliff. I walked around the cliff and down to the river, and left another puddle of blood at the river's edge. I cut a piece of cloth from the shirt I wore in the last picture I sent Alexi—I knew she would give that to the police—dripped some blood on it, and left it close to the river's edge. I threw that shirt and my dog tags into the river, knowing eventually they would send divers in once the water level dropped.

"I wanted them to locate my bike and the fake accident scene, so I stayed at that area for several minutes to establish a firm stopping point on GPS. My phone was in a floating fishing case. I threw it into the river knowing the current would carry the phone and the signal downstream. I knew Alexi would call the Police if she didn't hear from me that night, and that they'd wait until morning to ping the phone and start any search. This gave me a twenty-four-hour head start in the opposite direction of where the phone would have shown I traveled, as it floated downstream. I left all my belongings, including my wallet, on the bike. The pack out there with all my survival gear, I'd assembled during the trip. I paid cash for all of it. That's the whole story."

Woo Woo and Dakota had remained silent throughout, absorbing the details and analyzing Jake's plan.

"So," she finally said. "You made it look like you banged your head, wandered down to the river, and fell in. But the phone showed that did not happen. It made it look like you left the scene. Eventually the phone would get hung up on something or washed onto the bank. The ping would stay in that area until the battery died. They would find the phone and realize it must have fallen out of your pocket. This bought you even more time. They would then re-concentrate their search back in the crash area in the belief you fell into the water. Divers would find your shirt and dog tags, and you would be presumed drowned. The case is closed."

"That was my plan."

Woo Woo remained deep in thought.

Dakota said, "Would they not be hesitant to declare you dead so quickly without a body?"

Woo Woo finally jumped in. "It is a big river, and there are caves under the water. Parts that run through the canyons, where the rapids and waterfalls are, make it impossible to navigate, and animals would scavenge the body if it washed up on shore. It is not uncommon for bodies to not be found."

He paused, looked at Jake, and nodded. "Now we have no secrets."

The three spent the next few hours talking about the history of the cabin. Woo Woo retold stories Samuel had shared about great hunting trips here.

Dakota then lay in one of the bunks, listening to the two men talk, and drifted off to sleep knowing she was safe.

Jim and Jake retired to their bunks a short time later.

Jake's eyes panned the cabin. The log walls danced with reflections from the fireplace. He looked at Jim and Dakota as they slept peacefully. Tomorrow, they would be gone. Tomorrow, he would start his new life of solitude and loneliness.

CHAPTER 18
FIRST VISITS

Jake looked at the small calendar Dakota had left with him, and crossed off another day. Three weeks and four days had passed since Jim and Dakota brought him to the cabin. Dakota would return in three days for their first scheduled visit. He looked forward to seeing her, and having communication with another person.

His first month had gone by quicker than expected. He'd stayed busy with needed repairs to the cabin. He'd also built a small shed and root cellar to store food, and added a smokehouse and tanning rack. He had prepared himself for living out his life here.

The late morning sun warmed the mountain enough for his daily bath at the waterfall. A familiar feeling overtook him on his walk to it— his first spell since being at the cabin. Remembering what Samuel told him, he stayed calm, hoping to recall something from his *"visit to the Spirit World."*

The spell ended, and he regained his senses, but remembered nothing. He had no idea how long the spell lasted. He thought about the sack and pipe Samuel had given him, and decided that evening he would take his first *intentional* visit into the Spirit World, hoping Samuel was correct.

After returning to the cabin, he finished dinner, started the fireplace, and placed the bearskin on the floor in front of it. He opened the sack, pulled out a pinch of dried leaf, and filled the small bowl of the pipe. After some hesitation, he took a small puff of the harsh smoke, held it in, and exhaled. It tasted similiar to tobacco, but had a bitter tone he didn't recognize. His second hit from the pipe finished the small bowl and caused a wobbling head rush.

Several minutes passed as he stared into the fire, and a sensation moved through his body. He felt himself slipping away. The feeling reminded him of his tripping days with mescaline. The flames of the fire danced slowly, illuminated with glowing yellows and oranges.

The warm sun bathed his face as he stood in the field, ablaze with brilliant-colored wild flowers. He walked towards the waterfall.

A naked woman swam in the crystal clear pool. She stood up, facing away from him, and toned muscles moved as she pushed her long dark hair backwards, cascading over sun-kissed shoulders. Her ass was tight and well defined.

He removed his clothes and walked into the water. He moved behind her and caressed her shoulders. He let his hands drift around the front of her, and cupped her firm breasts as he pressed his dick against her.

She moaned softly with his touch, and her breathing quickened. She turned to face him.

He recoiled backwards, seeing Alexi's face on Dakota's body.

"What's wrong, Jake? Not who you expected? Have you forgotten about me, Jake?" The women's face aged, and her body morphed into an old woman.

Jake backed away.

The old hag pressed towards him. "Do you not find me attractive anymore? Fuck me, Jake. Fuck me."

He continued to retreat, and suddenly stopped as he bumped into something. Startled, he spun quickly to see a tall faceless Indian. A long ceremonial headdress framed a moving black abyss. A necklace made of snake skulls fell across his chest, and he held a spear with feathers covering the entire handle.

Jake's fears mounted. He wanted this to be over. He looked back for the woman, but she'd disappeared. He backed up from the Faceless Indian.

A deep, hollow voice came from the swirling abyss beneath the headdress. "Nih' o'o' 3oo, do not be afraid. This is your Spirit World. It is your past and present. You will learn to accept both. Your guilt will fade. You have been brought here for a reason. Do not question or fight the Great Spirit's plan for you."

Before Jake could respond, the Faceless Indian disappeared.

Jake stumbled from the water and raced towards the cabin, leaving his clothes behind. He wanted to get back to his body and end this vision. He made the turn around the bend into the clearing, and the cabin came into view.

The sky grew dark, and a biting cold wind whirled as snow began to fall. He quickened his pace to the cabin, but the harder he ran, the farther the cabin moved away. His red skin stung from head to toe.

Suddenly, four Indian men appeared in front of him. He attempted to flee, but his lower body was paralyzed. His fear grew as they approached, but even through the blizzard conditions, he recognized one of the four as they closed in on him.

"Samuel, what does this mean? Please make it stop," he pleaded, as he struggled to speak in the frigid air.

"Jake, these are my brothers. We are four to represent the four hills of life. Today, you see the Thunderbird of summer give way to the White Owl of winter. Like the seasons, the hills of your life change. You will soon be with the White Owl, as I am. Remember what you learned during the summer of your life. Accept what the winter brings."

Jake opened his eyes and saw the flames of the fire. He was back in the cabin, on the rug, fully dressed. He looked down at his watch: 10:30 PM. He had been in the Spirit World for an hour.

He took a deep breath, narrowed his eyes while staring into the flames. and nodded.

Dakota looked at the date circled on her calendar. She'd take her first trip to the cabin to see Jake in three days. She had gathered canned goods for him, as requested. She looked forward to seeing how he was handling living at the cabin.

She walked out on the front porch in her running gear.

Neiwoo sat on the porch swing sipping her morning coffee. "Where will you run today, Lomasi?"

"I'm running to the Sacred Falls as Greatgrandfather suggested. It's been almost a month since that night. It's time that I reclaim my life here."

"Do you have the gun your grandfather bought you?"

Dakota reached into her waist pack and pulled out a small derringer. "I do." She kissed her grandmother, stepped off the porch, and began her run.

The summer sun beat down on her, meaning the cool waters of the Sacred Falls would be invigorating. She weaved her way through the familiar canyons, all fear of being alone erased, as she felt the ancient warriors standing guard on the canyon tops. When she reached the turn for the falls and traversed the trail, the sounds of the waterfall sang through the forest. Her heartbeat quickened as she thought about the last time she was here.

She stood naked at the front of the pool, ready to wash the evil men from her, and dove into the cool waters. She swam to the falls, stood up, and allowed the water to cascade down her body. The feelings she'd enjoyed during the last visit were notably absent. The flowing water over her breasts and between her legs did not excite her.

Those men did not take my special gift, but did they take my desires?

A disturbance in the pool caught her attention. Strange reflections appeared, distorted by the ripples in the water, and she looked closely.

Terrified, she could not move a muscle as, from the depths of the pool, three bodies slowly rose towards her—the three men from that night. They were naked and erect, and their dicks were grotesquely large and dripping blood. Each body twisted with gruesome injuries, and their faces were pale, their eyes absent in their dark sockets.

They walked towards her, masturbating.

Blood spurted from their dicks, burning her as it hit her chest and stomach. She shielded her face and cried out in pain.

Demonic laughter echoed around the pool. "I told you, cunt, we would be back. Now we will rip you to shreds with our cocks," Hollywood growled.

The abominations reached out to grab her.

Suddenly, a loud splash behind them caught Dakota's eye. A beautiful Indian woman appeared from beneath the water. She raised her arms, and her eyes glowed like hot red embers. The water swirled around the three ghosts, and agonizing screams replaced their laughter as they were slowly sucked into the abyss of the whirlpool.

The water calmed, and the Indian woman's gaze softened. Her eyes now shined like emeralds. She walked forward and reached her hand out, palm up.

Dakota placed her hand on top of the Indian woman's, and a warm sensation rushed through her body.

The Oracle smiled, then backed up and slowly retreated beneath the water.

Dakota felt a dark spirit leave, and pureness return. She felt cleansed.

She moved to the flat rocks, and felt the warmth radiating from them. She closed her eyes and pictured a strong warrior standing in front of her. Her arms stayed at her side.

Jake awoke a little more anxious. Dakota would be here today.

After straightening up the cabin, he walked out to the smoke house and started a small fire. Tonight, they would dine on smoked trout, with fried cornbread mush and chokeberry sauce.

Dakota opened her eyes at first light. She walked downstairs to have coffee with her grandfather before leaving.

She leaned over and hugged him from behind. "Good morning, Woo Woo."

"Good morning, Lomasi, are you ready for your ride?"

"I'm looking forward to it. I love going out there."

"Are you sure you do not want me to go? I can put off work."

"Woo Woo, I'll be fine. It's an easy ride, as you know. It's just long. I thought about taking the ATV, but would rather just enjoy the quiet."

"I don't blame you."

Neiwoo joined Dakota and Jim at the table.

Dakota said, "Did we wake you?"

"No, Lomasi, I woke up when your grandfather got out of bed. He is so loud."

"I am not." Woo Woo smiled and winked.

Dakota finished her coffee with them, hugged them both, and headed to the front door.

"Tell Sonny we said hello," Neiwoo said.

"I will. See you all late tomorrow afternoon. Love you."

The trip was peaceful and uneventful, and Dakota could now see the cabin in the distance.

She rode into the clearing and saw Jake chopping wood. He was shirtless, and she could tell he'd lost weight—leaner and more muscular.

"Hey, mountain man," she yelled.

Jake turned and smiled as he put the ax down. He walked over to greet her. "How was your ride?"

"It was good." She dismounted and walked over to give Jake a hug. He stopped her. "I'm sweaty."

"I can see that. So am I."

He laughed and hugged her. "I guess there will be two of us at the waterfall bathing today."

She fanned herself. "I can't wait. It's hot today. We might as well enjoy it. Soon the winter will be here."

He walked forward, motioning her to follow. "Come, let me show you what I've done."

He showed her the new root cellar and smokehouse, and pointed out the repairs he'd made to the roof.

"Hey, I have a surprise for you," he said.

Her eyes widened and her voice rose. "I love surprises. Show me."

He led her past the waterfall and the graves of Samuel's brothers and father, and took her onto a path he'd cut through thick, head-high brush. The cover had grown together overhead, forming a tunnel.

"Jake, this is awesome! Where are you taking me?"

He pointed a few yards ahead to an opening. "It's dead ahead."

They emerged from the brush tunnel and Dakota gasped, looking down at a crystal-clear pool of bubbling water. "Oh my God, how did you find this?"

"I wounded a deer and had to track him back here."

"Have you been in it? How hot is the water?" She bent down to touch the spring.

"Many times, and the temperature is perfect. It will be great during the winter, when the waterfall is too cold."

Her eyes sparkled. "I want to go in it tonight. We can build a fire. It will be like sitting in a hot tub."

"Sounds like a plan."

The two spent the day talking about how Jake was getting along at the cabin. Dakota filled him in on Alexi's Facebook. Nothing had changed, just "days missing" updates, which he was upset to hear. She printed out the most recent pages from each of the kids. She knew he would love that. It appeared they were moving forward, looking at those posts—he was happy to see that.

They finished dinner. "Jake, that was delicious. I'm ready for the hot spring."

He blushed and looked down. "Okay, but Dakota, I don't have a swimsuit. I never thought about needing one."

"Silly, I'll turn around when you get in as long as you do the same for me. Not like you haven't already seen everything, though," she said, rolling her eyes.

"Okay, that's a deal. Let's go down there."

They walked to the spring.

He was still nervous about being naked in the spring with her.

"All right, I'll get in first," Dakota said. "Turn around."

He could hear her slip off her clothes and lower into the bubbling pool.

"Okay, I'm in and turned away."

He saw she was in and covered to the top of her breasts. He turned and removed his clothes, and quickly slipped into the pool.

"Well, now that we're in, we forgot one thing," she said.

"What?"

"The fire."

They both laughed, and agreed the full moon would be fine.

They spent an hour in the spring, engaged in lighthearted conversation. Dakota told Jake about starting her new job in a week, and they made plans for the next visit.

The setting intoxicated Jake, as did Dakota, who looked so beautiful in the moonlight. She moved from time to time to make herself comfortable, and there was just enough light to expose glimpses of her breasts. He struggled to keep his eyes focused on hers, or the starlit night above.

"Well, should we call it a night?" he said.

"I could sit here all night, but yeah, we should go. I'll get out first, shy boy."

A short time later, they lay in their bunks talking about how great the hot spring was. Their conversation slowed as the flames of the fire died down, darkening the cabin.

After a few minutes of silence, Dakota said softly. "That was a good first visit."

He turned his head towards her, and their eyes met. "Yes, it was. Thank you for coming out here."

She slowly blinked and smiled. "Goodnight."

CHAPTER 19
WOLF

Two weeks later, Jake stepped outside and into the chill of the September morning. The early leaves of fall painted the mountains with rich colors, even as dark clouds filled the sky. He grabbed his rifle and left for an area where he'd been successful on his first hunt at the cabin. He needed to harvest another deer and prep it for winter storage.

The hunting area sat about a quarter mile past the hot springs he and Dakota had enjoyed. As he passed it, a smile crossed his face. Visions of her naked in the moonlight lulled him into a daydream, but raindrops hitting him on the head snapped him back to reality.

The sky turned black as thunder echoed in the distant canyons. He picked up his pace to reach the hunting area, knowing the thick pines would provide cover if the storm reached him.

He settled into his spot, tucked behind the ground blind he'd built a few weeks ago. If the storm hit, the deer may not move. The thunder crept closer and the wind gusted, bending and breaking tree limbs overhead. He left the blind to tuck under the protection of the pine canopy.

Storm clouds swirled overhead and thunder crashed around him. Lightning brightened the dark sky like flashbulbs as a loud explosion shook the ground. He looked back towards his cabin, hoping it wasn't hit. Once the storm blew by, he would go back and check, postponing his hunt until late afternoon.

When the rain finally stopped, he left the pines and hurried to the cabin. He reached the clearing and saw everything was fine.

It was midday, and Jake piddled in the smokehouse. He stepped outside and saw smoke coming from a ridge close to where he'd hunted this morning. He grabbed his gear, deciding to investigate the smoke while hunting at the same time.

As he moved up the ridge, the smoke rising above the canopy grew thicker. He crested the hill and realized the fire was more extensive than he'd imagined. He estimated a 400-square-yard portion was burning, but the fire was young and affected mostly the ground cover. As he walked closer, a faint whine came to him, so he pulled his binoculars up and panned the area, but the crackling of the fire made it difficult to pinpoint where the whining came from.

Then a movement caught his eye, and after positioning himself to get a better view, he spotted a wolf puppy standing on a set of rocks surrounded by the smoldering underbrush. He grabbed his rifle, knowing the pup's mom would be somewhere close.

He crept as close to the wolf as the fire would allow, and panned the area for the mother, but saw no sign of her. The wind fanned the flames, whipping them to waist-high in spots. He *would not* hesitate to save this puppy, as he had that night with Dakota.

He removed his poncho, rolled it up, and plotted his course through the burning underbrush. He planned to sneak up on the pup, careful not to spook it. He circled the perimeter, all the while keeping a close eye out for the mother, moving quickly but silently, zigzagging around active flames. He reached the rocks, crouched down, and moved behind the pup.

Without a moment's hesitation, he threw his poncho over the wolf and scooped it up. The pup wiggled in his arms, yelping, and he worried his cries would alert the mother and bring her in closer. As he rushed through the smoldering ground cover to safe ground, he saw movement from the corner of his eye.

The mother wolf was here, but she couldn't save her pup. She was severely burned, and struggled with her last bit of life to run from Jake.

The scene upset him. He moved to a small knoll, and realized he faced a dilemma. He *could not* watch the mother suffer, but, if he put the puppy down to grab his gun, it would run off and surely die. So he pulled a drag rope from his hunting pack and tied it around the poncho and the puppy. Then he raised his rifle, took aim, and put the mother wolf out of her misery.

Jake sat in the middle of the cabin floor as he untied the poncho and set the wolf pup free.

Upon seeing him, it scurried away, looking for cover, and darted under one of the bunks.

"Okay, little one, I know you're scared. I bet you're thirsty and hungry too." He filled a small bowl with water and placed it next to the bed. "I'll call you Honi."

He left the cabin and walked down to the stream to catch a small trout, and returned to feed Honi. He found the water bowl knocked over and not a drop of the water left on the ground. He looked under the bunk, and Honi moved farther away from him, whimpering and shaking. The young wolf had likely never seen a human, so he placed the trout on the floor and left the cabin, so Honi would come out and eat.

He peeked through the front window. After several minutes, Honi cautiously moved towards the trout. The pup stalked his quarry, as he'd undoubtedly watched his mother do, then pounced on the dead fish and began eating it. After a few minutes, it was playtime. The pup rolled in the mangled fish, shook it and tossed it in the air, and fish blood and guts were strewn about.

Jake laughed and shook his head. "Okay, Honi, playtime is over." He opened the door.

The pup darted back under the bed.

Jake knew wolves were skittish, and that it would take time before Honi trusted him. Once the pup was big enough, he would set it free, but for now, he would need to keep him, to raise him to the point the pup could survive on his own. He decided to build a pen with chicken wire, in the shed that Samuel had used years ago for the old garden.

After several hours, the makeshift pen was finished. It stood eight feet long by three feet wide, and he'd strung the four foot-high chicken wire between wood posts. He'd also built a small, raised shelter area with three sides, a floor, and a roof.

He stepped back to admire the pen, stroking his beard, and turned to return to the cabin.

He chuckled and said, "This should be fun."

He opened the door and gagged. "Good God, wolf, what was your mother feeding you?"

He walked to the bunk, past the deposit Honi had left for him. "Okay, time for your new den."

His plan was to corner the pup, catch him with a makeshift lasso, and pull it from under the bed. He readied a blanket to throw over it, to avoid being bitten.

Surprisingly, the capture went rather smoothly, and he soon lifted the pup up over the chicken wire.

"Okay, Honi, here is your new home," he said, putting him down.

The pup panicked and ran into the makeshift doghouse.

Over the next several days, Honi gradually warmed up to Jake, because this strange human meant food to him. He didn't cower in the doghouse as much. Jake noticed the pup was letting his defenses down, and decided to try feeding Honi from his hand.

He approached the pen with a small trout cut into pieces, and bent down next to the pen.

Honi looked at him, cautious, but the smell of the trout was alluring.

"Come, boy. Here you go. I won't hurt you."

Honi crept closer, then sprung back. He repeated this several times.

Jake coaxed him in a calm voice. "Come on, baby, it's okay."

Honi edged closer to Jake's outlaid hand, crawling on his belly. He hesitated, grabbed the piece of trout, and ran with it. He then repeated that process with the next three pieces. On the fifth and last piece, the pup walked over to Jake's hand, looked at him, and took the fish without running.

Jake smiled. He'd started gaining the wolf's trust. The next step would be to pet Honi.

Three days passed, and Honi started greeting Jake when he saw him coming with food, wagging his tail and whining with excitement.

"Okay, Honi, next step." He stepped over the chicken wire.

Honi retreated to his doghouse, but Jake bent down to offer food. The pup crept towards him, and gobbled up several pieces without backing up.

"Good boy, Honi, good boy."

He held his hand out without food, and Honi smelled it. Jake gently touched his head, and the pup recoiled, but then stood up straight again. He looked Jake in the eyes and licked his hand, brushing his face against it.

When Jake sat down, Honi stepped back, but after a pause, he crept back and allowed Jake to pet his head. After several minutes, Honi allowed Jake to pet his back. Towards the end of the visit, Honi wagged his tail and played puppy games. He ran to and around Jake, wagging his tail the whole time. Jake rewarded Honi throughout the process with small pieces of dried trout.

When Jake stood up and left the pen, Honi watched him and whined. A bond had formed between two creatures that, under cruel circumstances, had united.

Jake woke up and looked at the calendar; Dakota would be here in four days. He couldn't wait to show her the new addition to the cabin. He grabbed a collar he made from tanned deer hide.

Honi had heard the cabin door open, and yelped, knowing it was food and playtime. Jake stepped into the pen and put the collar on the pup. At first, Honi thought this was something to play with, and rolled around trying to remove the collar.

Jake attached a rope to it, picked Honi up, and stepped over the cage to put the pup on the ground.

Honi was scared, and ran back to his pen and leaned against the chicken wire.

Jake walked away to the length of the ten-foot rope, and gently tugged on the line. The pup bit the leash, trying to free himself, but Jake threw a piece of fish to him. After a pause, the puppy walked towards the fish. Jake praised him in that tone of voice that Honi responded to, and walked a few more steps. Honi tugged, looking back at the safety of his pen, but Jake repeated the process until Honi was twenty feet from the pen, and the wolf started calming down.

Jake walked the pup around the clearing for nearly an hour, and Honi stopped many times to smell this new world. When Jake bent down, Honi ran towards him, recognizing Jake's position. It was playtime.

"You're a good boy, Honi. This was a big step for you. You did well."

The companionship in Jake's lonely world made him choke up.

They wrestled on the ground for a while.

"Okay, boy, time for me to get us some food."

Jake led Honi back to his pen, put the pup in, and walked away.

The wolf immediately started whining.

"It's okay, Honi. I'll be back soon."

Jake left for the woods to check his snare traps. He harvested two squirrels and returned to the cabin.

Honi saw him coming and yelped with excitement. Jake approached the pen, greeted his new friend, and dropped one squirrel on the ground. Honi ran to the squirrel and flipped the dead animal in the air, then pounced on it and flipped it backwards.

"That's dinner, silly, not a toy." Jake laughed as he walked into the cabin.

He finished his dinner and, at the clap of thunder in the distance, walked outside to find an angry sky. He looked over at Honi's pen, but didn't see him—strange, as the pup always came out of his doghouse when he heard the cabin door. He walked to the pen and called for Honi, but the wolf didn't respond. He quickened his pace towards the pen, calling Honi the entire time, but the wolf still did not appear.

Jake jumped into the pen, heard the pup whimpering in his doghouse, and realized Honi's fear. The last time the pup heard thunder, he was surrounded by fire, and his mother was taken from him.

"Come, Honi." Jake scooped up the shaking wolf and rushed him to the cabin.

That day, an unconditional love was forged.

CHAPTER 20
SPIRIT WORLD AGAIN

Since the night of the thunderstorm, Jake had allowed Honi to stay in the cabin with him. His quick domestication and intelligence were impressive, but sleeping was a bit challenging, as the pup wanted to play at odd hours. Jake had no schedule, so he was fine with it. He enjoyed the companionship.

"Honi, today you'll meet Dakota. She'll be surprised. Let's get the cabin straightened up."

Jake and Honi were down by the smokehouse when the wolf's ears perked up.

"What do you hear, Honi?"

Jake paused for a few seconds, concentrating his hearing in different directions. The faint sound of an engine echoed in the canyons. He figured Dakota was coming on the ATV, and took Honi to the cabin, worried the ATV would frighten the pup and he would run.

Jake then stood in the clearing to wait, and soon saw Dakota in the distance.

She pulled up and circled him playfully, then jumped off the ATV and hugged him. She flipped the salt and pepper hair on the side of his head, and looked at his beard. "You *are* starting to look like a mountain man, kind of rugged looking. I like it."

Jake smiled and ran his hand through his hair. "I don't have much choice. The barber shop has terrible hours, and I can't fit them in my schedule." He grabbed her hand and led her toward the cabin. "I have a surprise for you."

"It can't be better than that secluded hot spring. I've thought about that all month."

He said nothing. He just opened the door, and Honi bolted out.

When Honi saw Dakota, he stopped in his tracks and growled the best a puppy could.

"Honi, it's okay. Come here." Jake bent down, and Dakota mimicked him.

Honi sheepishly came to Jake, but his eyes never left Dakota.

"Put your hand out slowly," he directed a speechless Dakota.

Honi sniffed her hand, pushed it with his nose, smelled again, and then licked it. When Dakota slowly turned her hand over and started petting Honi gently, the pup responded with favor.

"Oh my God, Jake, where did you find him? He's beautiful. I hope he keeps his puppy coat. He'll be black, which is rare."

Jake told Dakota the story while Honi rolled on his back, letting Dakota play with him. The wolf had made a new human friend. His pack was growing.

They finished playing with Honi and unpacked the ATV. The pup followed Jake's every move.

Dakota beemed. "He is so cute. He won't let you out of his sight."

"Yeah, I think he thinks I'm his mom. He's still young, but his baby teeth are gone, so I figure somewhere around three months old or so. He knew how to eat raw meat."

"I wonder how much of his pack perished in the fire," Dakota said.

"Dunno. You know about his mom, and I would guess his brothers and sisters didn't make it either. The rest of the pack must have run from the flames. His mom stayed to try and save him, but her legs were badly burned."

"That's so sad. Oh my God, Jake, this must be what my greatgrandfather was talking about. He saw you with a wolf in his visions."

"I thought about that. Speaking of visions, I have a story for you."

Dakota raised her eyebrows and smirked. "What... are you having visions? Are you becoming a Medicine Man out here?"

Jake laughed. "No, I don't think so. I'll tell you the story after dinner."

"How about in the hot spring tonight?"

"Wow, you *have* been looking forward to that, haven't you?"

The couple went into the cabin and sat at the table, where Dakota opened her backpack. Jake looked at the supplies she'd brought: canned vegetables, fuel for the lanterns, dish soap, some natural bathing soap, and deodorant. She'd also brought a small grooming bag. He opened it to find a straight razor, a small set of scissors, and a mirror.

He held up the straight razor. "Are you trying to tell me something?"

"Actually, you look good in that long beard, but you never know when you'll want to cut it off." She reached across the table and handed him printed screenshots of his family's latest Facebook pages.

He looked at them and nodded his head. "I see Alexi updated her page. At least she has shrunk the 'missing' counter."

"It's been three months, Jake. I see she tagged a Sonny in the picture. Is that the same Sonny you pretended to be?"

"Yes, and his wife. I'm surprised to see all three of them together. We had drifted apart over the years—nothing bad, just life getting in the way. I hope she's not trying to hold onto the past through them."

"I saw Sonny in pictures from your memorial service. Of course, I didn't know who he was, because there were no tags on those pictures. Maybe they reconnected there. I didn't print them for you, though. I thought it might be morbid to look at your own funeral."

He chuckled and lifted his eyes from the picture. "How was the turnout?"

"You were a popular guy."

"This is a fucked-up conversation, huh?"

She chuckled. "Yeah, not one I thought I would ever have."

Dakota noticed a sense of peace about Jake. He wasn't as upset as last month when he saw the Facebook pictures. Perhaps having a companion in Honi had helped him. He didn't have to sit here alone, isolated, replaying his life over and over to the brink of madness in the solitude.

"How have your spells been?" she said, changing the subject.

"I haven't had one since the week before you came for the first visit. It's over a month now."

"Wow, Jake, that's good. Maybe being out here is helping you in some way."

"That's something we'll talk about tonight at the spring."

Dakota rolled her eyes. "Ugh, you're killing me with the suspense. Let's get dinner out of the way and get down there."

They finished dinner and headed for the spring, and Honi started yelping the moment they closed the door.

"Oh," she said, "I feel terrible leaving him behind."

"Well, considering we sit naked in the spring, and it's a crisp night, do you want to have to chase him if he runs off?"

"Good point."

A short time later, they settled into the spring one at a time, using the same method as the last time.

"It's so funny. I've been seen by millions of people, nearly naked in hundreds of fitness magazines, I stood naked in front of you during my most vulnerable time on that terrible night, and yet I slip into this spring like a bashful teenager."

"I've never been shy either. I've been to nude beaches, walked naked into parties on a dare. But, like you, I'm bashful. Maybe it's our age difference."

Dakota looked him in the eyes, the moonlight accenting her delicate features. Her long hair danced in the bubbles around her breasts. In a soft voice, she said, "No, Jake, age is not the reason."

He fidgeted, feeling movement in his dick that had been absent for the past several months.

She smiled in a strange way then, as if knowing she'd made him uncomfortable and thought it was cute, but he appreciated that she elected to say nothing.

He laughed awkwardly. "Well, maybe we don't want the animals seeing us?"

"All right, now that we're here, tell me what you've been keeping me on the edge of my seat for."

He told her about the sack and pipe Samuel had given him, and shared his visions in detail, excluding the part of Alexi's face on her body.

"That's wild. What did the three men with Greatgrandfather look like?"

Jake described them to the best of his memory.

Dakota remained still and silent for a moment, then said, "Jake, they were his brothers. You would have no way of knowing what they look like. I've heard of ancient potions the Medicine Men used for visions, but thought that medicine was lost in history. It appears Greatgrandfather still knows how to make it. Hmmm... maybe this is what helps his Dementia. He was diagnosed twelve years ago, but you can see he's still doing pretty well. He has bad days, but *he is* almost ninety. Maybe it will help you."

"It's possible. I haven't had a spell since I smoked that stuff. Would that not be ironic, after everything I've done?"

She hesitated. "What do you think the vision meant?"

Jake looked her in the eyes and kept his tone steady. "Do not question Destiny."

Dakota nodded, and her eyes narrowed as she again sat silent for several moments. Finally, she said, "We should smoke some of this together tonight."

Jake and Dakota sat on the bearskin rug facing the fireplace. He put a pinch in the bowl for her.

She said, "Is it like weed? I smoked some potent stuff in college."

"No, this is different. It takes you away and then it's over. It doesn't linger like weed. Are you sure you want to do this?"

"Yes, it's part of my heritage. I want to experience what my ancestors did."

He laughed. "You might see a few of them."

She took two hits from the pipe, and he quickly followed, so they would leave for the Spirit World together.

Dakota watched the fire dance, and a warm sensation came over her body as she looked at Jake. His eyes were fixed on the flames.

She felt herself drifting in and out of the physical world, and glanced at him again. He sat tall and proud, like the warrior that had saved her on that terrible night. She stood up and moved in front of him, and with the release of two buttons, her sundress fell to the ground. The light of the fire danced off the curves of her body. She stared into his eyes, and grabbed his hands to help him stand, then unbuttoned his denim shirt and ran her hands over his chest and down his stomach. She unzipped his pants and gently rubbed his erect dick, then dropped to her knees and took him in her mouth, never once losing eye contact. Jake's body tensed with each movement of her head. She paused and lay back on the bearskin rug, motioning him to join her.

"Are you sure, Dakota?"

She smiled, blinked her eyes slowly, and opened her legs for him. Tonight, she would give her special gift to a strong warrior. He entered her and paused, but she nodded, closed her eyes, and pulled him towards her, letting out a gasp. The pain of the first time quickly gave way to pleasure, as the drug heightened every sense in her. Their bodies glistened with sweat in the warmth of the fire as he moved quicker, harder, deeper inside her. She arched her back, clinching the bearskin rug. Her orgasms heightened, wave after wave, until she thought she would pass out. He arched his back at that moment, letting out a guttural moan, and she felt him explode inside her. Her eyes rolled back in her head as she drifted away to another world.

Jake opened the door and walked into the night air naked, with Honi by his side, and looked out across the field. The ground cover sparkled with rainbow colors.

The Faceless Indian stood at the edge of the clearing, motioning him over. Jake's fear eased, replaced by the desire to learn more from this strange being.

"Jake," the Faceless Indian said. "I see you walk with a wolf, just as Samuel said. The spirits have sent Honi to you. He will love you unconditionally, as Kelsey did."

The Faceless Indian pointed to another edge of the field, where Jake saw his beloved Kelsey standing. Tears ran down his face as he called her name and ran towards her. He bent down to hug his beloved Lab, but instantly, she disappeared.

Jake looked back at the Faceless Indian and yelled, "Why would you do that?"

"You must let go of the past. You cannot return to it."

The Faceless Indian pointed towards the cabin

Jake saw Alexi, naked and walking towards him, her beauty illuminated by the bright moonligh. He ran to her, anxious to tell her he may have found a cure. She held her arms out as he got closer, but suddenly the ground turned to a river, and Alexi was swept away. She screamed his name, and he tried to dive into the river, but could not move. He watched her disappear under the raging water, and then the river turned back into solid ground.

He fell to his knees and sobbed.

Jake wavered between worlds, and saw a flicker of the fire. He also saw a shimmer of Dakota lying on the bearskin rug, coming out of her visit to the Spirit World.

Dakota sat up and looked down to find she was fully dressed. Jake was, as well. She gathered her composure. "Wow, that was intense. How was your vision?"

He stared forward, not taking his eyes off the flames. "It made obvious to me the journey I'm on. I must not look back." He turned to her. "What did the spirit world show you?"

She hesitated, and said, "It showed me I need to listen to the Spirits and trust in the path they've provided. I'm glad we did that. We'll do that again next time I come. Do you have enough to last you, or should I ask Greatgrandfather for more?"

"I have enough for a few more times, but, after my first visit to the Spirit World, I believe Samuel knows everything. You may not have to ask him."

Chapter 21
The White Owl

Dakota glanced at her calendar. She had November 21st circled. In three days, she would be back at the cabin, and then into the Thanksgiving break. Her work schedule was hectic, and she looked forward to getting away from the daily grind and spending time with Jake and Honi.

Woo Woo walked into her office and sat down.

"Grandfather, I thought you left for the day?" She always called him Grandfather when at work, rather than her preferred Woo Woo.

"I was on my way out of the office when an old client called me. I want to hand his case over to you. I have told him you will take the lead. He will be here at 1 PM. How is your schedule?"

"I'm free from 1:00 to 2:30. What type of case is it?"

He slid a folder across the desk. "Embezzlement."

She examined handwritten notes Woo Woo had written during his initial interview. In the folder was also an old DUI case he'd handled. "Your notes say he's being charged with embezzling $900,000.00 from his own company. His partners are charging him. This is a little out of my wheelhouse, Grandfather."

"Lomasi, this is part of your learning curve. I will be right alongside you. The most important part of an embezzlement case is following the money. Our client claims he is innocent and being framed by his partners."

She rolled her eyes. "*Of course*, he's innocent. Aren't they all?"

Jim chuckled. "Occasionally, they really are."

"Okay, Grandfather, I'll get a quick workout and eat lunch, and meet you back here in one hour. Is that all right?"

Jim glanced at his watch. "Yes, that will be fine."

Dakota walked down the street to her gym.

"Hello, Dakota." Kathy greeted her, as she passed the front desk of the gym.

Kathy was the gym owner and Dakota's workout partner. She also made a living in the fitness world, though not as accomplished as Dakota. Her looks would afford her much more success in the industry, if she'd let it, but she refused to travel. Given her parents considerable wealth, money was not a driving factor in Kathy's life.

She walked from behind the desk. "What are we working today?"

Dakota sighed. "I just had a client dropped on me. We only have about twenty-five minutes, so let's do a quick leg workout."

"Squats and walking lunges, it is. We'll give the guys in the gym a treat." Kathy winked.

"Yeah, it will be good for their testosterone," Dakota joked.

The two women began their workout, and caught guys watching them in the mirrors as they did their squats. They didn't know Kathy preferred women, a lifestyle she kept quiet. They also didn't know Dakota had no sexual desires towards men since the attack. She found their gawking unsettling. Her sexual desires had shifted to the Spirit World.

Several guys in the gym had asked her out, but she politely told them she'd just left a long relationship through college, and wasn't ready to date yet. She accepted that her lack of desire was normal, after such an attack, but three months had passed.

After her visit to the Spirit World with Jake, she knew deep inside exactly where her desires lay.

The girls finished their workout and headed for the showers.

Dakota stood at the mirror in the locker room touching up her makeup. Kat walked out of the shower naked, and Dakota glanced at her in the mirror, admiring how beautiful her body was. Kat moved to the sink next to Dakota, still naked, and wrapped a towel around her hair. Dakota admired her muscle tone as she lifted her arms. Kat wrapped a second towel around her body.

"Damn, Kat, you look good. Those poor guys in there... if they only knew."

"Yeah, they'll be using their wrist muscles tonight after that little show we gave them."

The girls both made a mocking jerk-off motion and laughed.

"Same time tomorrow, Dakota?"

"Sounds good. Let me get to work on saving another *innocent* person."

Dakota met her grandfather on schedule in her office, and they discussed a few things about the client and his previous case.

"Dakota, Mr. Anderson is here to see you," an intercom on her phone announced.

"Thank you, Sally, please show him in."

Russ Anderson entered the office. He didn't look as Dakota pictured. His height, dark hair, and brooding good looks caught her off guard. His polo shirt accented an athletic body. He was forty-two years old, but looked much younger, just like Jake did, she thought.

He reached his hand out to her grandfather. "Jim, nice to see you again," he said, with a deep but soft voice.

"Russ, let me introduce you to your attorney, Dakota Reynolds, my granddaughter and future owner of this firm."

Russ extended his hand and looked her in the eyes. "My pleasure, Mrs. Reynolds."

"Ms., and please call me Dakota, Mr. Anderson."

"Okay, Dakota, if you'll call me Russ."

The two nodded in agreement and sat at Dakota's desk.

"So, Russ, please tell us what is going on," Jim said.

Russ told his side of the story.

Dakota listened to his deep, soft voice, and the more she looked at him, the more handsome he became. Before the attack, she would have been attracted to him. Now, she could admire his good looks, but they invoked no feelings past that.

"Russ," she said. "Can I see the ledger of money transfers, from the corporate account into the overseas accounts, which your partners claim you initialized?"

He handed it to her, and she examined the ledger, noting the transfers were sporadic. The denominations were small and irregular, spread over eighteen months.

"You said you contacted these banks, Russ. All their records show they transferred the monies to a corporation that is 100-percent owned by you in Freeport, but you claim you own no company in the Bahamas.Is that right?"

"Yes, that's correct."

"Your company is in the grain industry, correct?"

"Yes."

She lowered the ledger and look Russ in the eyes. "Is it not uncommon to have overseas accounts? How would your accounting department not see this early on?"

"Actually, we have several overseas clients, two in Mexico, one in Canada, three in the Western Caribbean. Accounting may not have given it a second look." Russ's veins throbbed in his neck as his cheeks flushed. "Jim and Dakota, I have a net worth in excess of twenty million dollars, and the company operates in the black every year. I need not steal from *anyone*. This makes little sense. *I am being framed.*"

Dakota said, "Is there any reason someone would want you removed from the company?"

"My daddy founded this company, and the partners all worked their way up. My family provided them with an income and future they would have never found elsewhere. I've known all of them since I was a kid, and look at them as part of my family. I can't understand why any of them would do this."

"How is the ownership divided?" Jim said.

"I'm the majority at 51%. The second and third partners own 24.5% each."

Jim paused and looked at him squarely. "Greed can do strange things to people, Russ."

Dakota leaned back in her chair and thought for a second. "We'll depose both of your partners. I'll work on that immediately."

Russ nodded his head.

Jim stood up. "I think that is all we need for now, Russ. We will call you after the depositions."

"How long before they are deposed?"

Dakota said, "I'll have the paperwork done after Thanksgiving, and I'm sure they'll contact their counsel. I would assume thirty days or so, maybe sooner."

"Thank you very much, Dakota." Russ stood and shook both of the attorney's hands before leaving the office.

"What do you think, Grandfather?"

"I think there is more to this story. Much more." He paused. "What time will you be home today, Lomasi?"

"I have a 3 PM DUI client, then I'm leaving."

"Okay, I will see you for dinner."

Dakota, Jim, and Anna sat at the dinner table.

"Lomasi," Anna said. "What day are you taking supplies to Sonny? They are calling for snow."

"I'm going up on Sunday, and will be back on Monday or Tuesday. Mom and Dad come in on Wednesday. I wish Sonny could join us for Thanksgiving. It's so sad to be alone on the holidays."

"Why do you not bring him down?" Jim said. "I will introduce him as an old Army buddy."

"He won't leave Honi alone. I asked him last visit. Besides, he doesn't want to be seen by anyone else."

Jim shook his head. "I still cannot believe he has a wolf. Are you sure he is not one of us?" he joked.

Dakota's eyes sparkled. "Actually, Woo Woo, his greatgrandmother was Cherokee!" She turned to Anna. "Neiwoo, I'll be back to help you with the dishes. I need to call a client at 6:00."

Anna waited until Dakota had left for Jim's office, and said, "I am concerned about Lomasi. She has dated no one since being here. Do you see how she glows when she talks about Sonny? I hope she does not have feelings for him. He can offer her nothing. That poor man is dying a slow, terrible death."

"I have noticed, but they share a very intimate bond, a bond we can never fully understand."

"I realize that. I know she is grateful he was there. We are *all* grateful. I think I should talk to her."

"That is not our place, Anna. She is a smart girl, and she will make the right decisions. She always has."

Anna took a deep breath and sighed. "I hope so. I hope so."

Jake woke and walked outside with his pup trailing behind him. He looked at the light blue sky painted with streaks of red/orange clouds. "Well, Honi, that is a winter sky. Snow is coming, boy. I hope Dakota gets here before it starts."

Honi's ears perked at the sound of Dakota's name.

"Thanksgiving is coming. Should we shoot us a turkey?"

The wolf jumped up and down excitedly, as if understanding every word, though Jake understood it was really more about tone of voice.

The two of them climbed to the top of a small bluff and sat silently. At the loud flutter of turkeys' wings as they dropped from the trees into the small ravine below, Jake drew up his rifle and panned the area through the scope. Movement caught his eye, and he watched a big gobbler strut into a small opening. He took a breath, held it a beat, and pulled the trigger. The load crack echoed through the still cold air.

He lowered his rifle and patted Honi, who'd remained still and quiet throughout. "Come on, boy, let's get Thanksgiving dinner."

Dakota heard the crack of the rifle, and smiled knowing Jake would cook something fresh for dinner. It amazed her how he used the bounty of the land to create meals that rivaled some of the best restaurants she'd eaten at. She thought about how lucky Alexi was — well, had been.

Jake and Honi walked into the clearing and heard Dakota's ATV in the distance. Honi's ears perked up as he looked at Jake.

"It's okay, boy, that's Dakota. You remember her, right?"

Jake took a step and felt a spell coming, his first in almost two months. He put his hand down to stop Honi. The wolf looked at him and whined, sensing something was wrong. Jake took a step and froze. Honi moved in front of his legs, placed his body across Jake's path, and leaned against him. His ears dropped as he looked up at Jake, who tried to take a step, but Honi prevented him from doing so.

Jake saw the Faceless Indian, pointing his feathered spear towards the path Dakota was coming up. The Indian said nothing.

Jake snapped out of the spell, remembering what he had seen for the first time. He felt Honi's weight against him, blocking his path. The young wolf starred up at his master and whined.

"It's okay, boy, I'm okay." He bent down to hug Honi.

The wolf calmed, his ears perked and his face relaxed, and he proceeded to lick Jake's cheek.

His brief visit to the Spirit World made clear what Samuel had told him. He questioned if his disease was truly a curse... or a blessing. Did he have dementia, or something much different?

Dakota pulled into sight on her ATV and beeped the horn.

Honi looked around for this new noise and looked up at Jake.

"It's okay, boy." He patted the pup's head.

Dakota parked the ATV as Jake and Honi walked across the field carrying the turkey. He lifted the bird, and she smiled and quickened her pace towards them.

Honi lifted his nose to the air, wagged his tail and whined. When the three met in the middle of the field, Dakota hugged Jake and immediately bent down to greet Honi.

"Oh my God," she said. "He has grown in a month, and he's keeping his black coat. Look at his eyes. They *are* staying blue. He's so beautiful, Jake."

"And smart. I'll tell you what just happened when we go inside."

Dakota looked down at the turkey. "I guess we're celebrating Thanksgiving early?"

"Yes ma'am."

"Well, great minds think alike. I have a turkey, stuffing mix, and fresh cranberries with me."

"That's perfect. I'll smoke this one, and we'll bake yours. I can't wait to taste how good it will be, cooking in the wood stove."

She beamed and clapped her hands "Yeah, it will taste like the turkeys our Ancestors shared with the pilgrims."

Jake smiled, finding her enthusiasm contagious.

They unloaded the ATV and sat at the kitchen table. "Would you like some fresh cowboy coffee?" he said.

"I will have a Mocha Latte, please, barista."

"Coming right up, ma'am."

"So, tell me why Honi is so smart, or are you going to make me wait till we're in the hot springs tonight? I think you keep these secrets just to get me naked." Dakota eyes sparkled, as she twirled her hair and smiled.

Jake laughed. "You have me figured out, counselor."

He told her the details of the spell and his glimpse of the Spirit World, and of how Honi stood in front of him to prevent him from moving.

"Jake, is it possible you have the same thing Greatgrandfather does? Could both of you be misdiagnosed? I know Greatgrandfather has his moments, but he honestly could have been living on his own up until two years ago. I think he just likes being waited on."

"Or looking at the young nurses?"

She rolled her eyes. "That too."

"I don't know, Dakota. Since I've been out of the stress of everyday life, my thinking is clearer. I do have my moments of forgetfulness, but they seem to be focused on older events. That's peculiar, based on what I've read on dementia. Whatever is causing the spells is still there, but... I don't know. I really don't know."

Dakota paused. She started to think Jake might not be terminal, after all.

Did the Spirits deliver him here for a higher purpose? Could this be a cruel irony that caused so much pain for another woman, but a blessing for me? Is he a blessing from the Spirit in the Sacred Falls?

She looked up and caught Jake staring at her.

"Hey," he said. "Are you having a spell, also?"

She shook her head and laughed. "No, just thinking about what you said."

"Dakota, did Samuel serve in the military?"

"Yes, he was in the Korean War. Why do you ask?"

"Hmmm... I'm just thinking. I remember reading something, after my diagnosis, about CTE and brain trauma to soldiers who served in wartime. The specialist never mentioned it, and my doctor dismissed it when I questioned him."

"There's no way to determine CTE until post-mortem," she said.

"I know, but there are treatments for suspected CTE. Maybe Samuel stumbled on something off the grid. Or maybe I'm just grasping at straws. I guess time will tell." He shook his head and sighed. "So, speaking of time, how has another month treated you?"

"I've been busy with a bunch of innocent people wrongly accused."

He chuckled. "They're all innocent, of course. How have things been in my old life?"

She reached into her backpack and slid screenshots across the table.

He looked at each picture, nodded, and smiled. "Looks like the kids are doing fine. Alexi still has the 'missing' counter up, but I see she's doing things with her friends. She looks a bit happier. When the counter comes down, I'll know she's let go of that last thread of hope and moved on with her life."

A tear rolled down his face.

Dakota welled up. She knew Jake loved Alexi, and hated seeing him upset. Selfishly, she wanted these visits to be about Jake and her. She knew that, one day, Jake would let go of that thread, just like Alexi. Dakota had to be patient and not rush the Spirit's plan.

Jake must have noticed she was upset, by the look of him. He reached across the table and laid his hand on hers. "Hey, these are *my* tears and pain. You don't have to share in them."

She smiled and paused for a moment, regaining her composure. "Well, mountain man, what surprises do you have this visit?"

"Nothing new. We'll let our visit to the Spirit World provide those."

Dakota flashed back to the last visit, subconsciously rearranging the hair on her shoulders and chest. "I look forward to that."

"What time are you leaving tomorrow?"

"It will depend on the snow. They're calling for two to four inches overnight. If it stops in the morning, I figured we could have Thanksgiving dinner around noon. I can leave afterwards and be home before dark. If they mess up the forecast, and we get more snow, or it lasts longer, I'll leave early the next morning. My mom and dad are coming on Wednesday, so I need to make sure I'm home by noon Wednesday."

"Won't Jim get upset if you don't return tomorrow?"

"He knows there's a storm coming. We talked about it."

Jake stood up from the table. "C'mon, I have an idea."

He grabbed the fishing pole from next to the door, walked out on the front porch, and picked up his hatchet.

"Isn't that a little overkill for cleaning fish?" Dakota joked.

"We're doing two things. I do have a small surprise now."

They walked off toward the hot spring with Honi in tow, this time.

"I knew you just wanted to get me naked."

"Nope. Since it's going to snow, we'll build a little roof over the spring."

She smiled. "That's an awesome idea."

They finished the roof, and on the way back to the cabin, they made a quick stop and caught four fish for dinner. The sun set in the pink/red sky as the first few snowflakes began to fall.

They finished dinner and relaxed at the table, drinking wine that Dakota had brought. Jake pulled out the pipe and cleaned it for their visit to the Spirit World.

She looked out the window. The snow started to cover the ground. "Should we go down to the spring before the snow gets too deep?"

"That's a good idea. Let's go."

They walked towards the spring again, and suddenly, Dakota ran ahead of him, laughing. He picked up his pace and reached the tunnel in the brush.

Her clothes already hung from the small trees, and she sat in the spring facing Jake. "I was thinking... you've seen me totally naked. I think it's only fair I see you," she said, playfully.

The wine had numbed both of their inhibitions, perhaps.

Jake shrugged his shoulders. "Fair enough." He took his jacket and shirt off, then unzipped his pants.

"Oh my God, you're doing it! I was just kidding." She put her hands over her eyes.

He laughed and said, "I called your bluff." He dropped his pants and walked towards the spring.

"No, you didn't." She'd dropped her hands and now looked at his dick.

He quickly covered up. "Hey, that's not fair. It's freezing out here."

"Well, mountain man, what I see is *just* fine."

They sat in the bubbling spring and the afterglow of the wine. The roof worked perfectly, and the snow fell around them, but not on them. When they weren't talking, the quiet of the night was broken by the soft sound of flakes hitting the fresh powder.

The wine and the serenity of the snow made Dakota's mind race. She purposely moved in the spring, exposing her breasts, several times. Tonight, for the first time since the attack, she felt a tingle between her legs. Her special gift had awoken.

She waited for Jake to make a move towards her, as the last vision she had in the Spirit World played over and over in her mind. She'd seen him naked now, so nothing was left to her imagination, and the bubbling of the spring between her legs had elevated her to a frantic state. She wanted to slide towards Jake and mount him, but she would not rush the Spirit's plan. When it was time, it would happen.

"The snow is piling up. We should get back to the cabin," he said.

"I know." She stood up and stepped from the spring.

She heard his sharp intake of breath behind her, and when he stood up to gather his clothes, she saw his dick had swelled.

She glanced down and widened her eyes. "You were right. It *was* cold earlier." She smiled and winked. "Race you to the cabin." She raced off, clothes in hand.

Jake gave chase until they reached the cabin and burst through the door into the warmth of the shelter.

"Oh my God," she said. "That was dumb. It's freezing." She laughed as she put her clothes on.

A couple hours later, the fire danced in front of Dakota's eyes as she slipped back into the physical world. She looked at Jake, who was still in the Spirit World. The drug lasted longer on him. She felt her crotch was soaked — the visions were so real, so intense.

Jake walked towards the Faceless Indian. He passed several white buffalo and a white elk. The world lay draped in snow, but he wasn't cold.

He watched as Dakota ran across the field naked. She stopped to spin in the snowflakes, looked up with her arms outstretched, and walked into the cabin.

Jake turned to face the Indian. "Why are we naked in this world? What does all the snow mean?"

"You are naked so the snow can cleanse both of you of your past. The White Owl is preparing you for the next hill of your life. It will be your final hill. Do not question what the Spirits put in front of you."

Everything shimmered again, and Jake returned, staring at the fire as he came back to the physical world. He felt a bit confused, unsure of place and time.

He looked at Dakota. "Should we go down to the hot spring now?"

She took a deep breath and smiled in a way that hit Jake right in the solar plexus.

"I was just there," she said.

CHAPTER 22
LONG COLD WINTER

The December winds howled outside the cabin. Winter had arrived with a vengeance, but Jake had prepared well. The woodpile would last several months, his cold cellar was filled with smoked fish and game, and he had plenty of canned vegetables and enough lamp oil to last until spring.

Dakota was scheduled to visit on the twenty-second. They'd left that date as tentative due to the uncertainty of weather. Besides her company, the only thing he needed was more medicine from Samuel. Dakota would see him at Thanksgiving and tell him Jake, aka Sonny, stopped in to see Jim at the beginning of November, and he mentioned how it helped with his symptoms. Jake ran out of the smoke last week. He had been spell-free, but didn't know how long the last dose would stay in his system.

"Well, boy," he said to his constant companion. "Do you think Dakota makes it up here this month? The snow pack is getting deeper. I'm not sure the trail will be passable."

Honi cocked his head back and forth as Jake spoke, and upon hearing Dakota's name, wagged his tail and ran to the door.

"No, boy, she's not here yet."

He turned on the small battery-powered radio Dakota had given him last month. It picked up only one AM channel, but that provided news and weather. It made him feel connected to the outside world. The weather forecast for Friday the twenty-second was good, so she should be fine.

He grabbed his shovel to clear each of the paths he kept open: to the waterfall, to the smokehouse, to the shed, to the woodpile, and to the hot spring. In some spots, the snow walls were four foot tall. If he shoveled every day, the work was manageable. When it snowed, he did it every hour. It was difficult, but he loved the workout. He hadn't been this lean since he was in his twenties. He felt good about taking his clothes off in front of Dakota now.

He made his way to the hot spring for his morning bath, settled into the hot bubbling water, and relaxed. Anxiety gripped him as he felt a spell coming on. He worried he might slip under the water, and quickly jumped up and into the cold snow before drifting away.

The Faceless Indian stood in the hot spring, fucking someone from behind.

Jake saw the woman had shoulder-length blonde hair. He heard a familiar moan, and crawled through the cold snow towards the spring.

The Indian and the woman turned to look at him.

"Noooo! Leave her alone, you bastard. Leave my Alexi alone," Jake screamed.

He clawed though the snow towards them, unable to stand, his skin stinging from the cold.

Alexi and the Indian laughed at him, fucking harder and harder, and her moans echoed in the still air.

Jake came out of the spell, shivering in the cold.

Honi lay across his body, whining.

He calmed the young wolf down and slipped back into the hot spring to warm up. The vision had angered him. He had no idea what it meant, and the duration was too short to understand.

The morning of the twenty-second had arrived. Cloudless blue skies hung overhead, and the forecast looked good for the next several days.

The sound of an engine rose in the distance, but it differed from the ATV. He listened more intently, and recognized the engine noise as a snowmobile.

Honi looked up at him.

"It's okay, boy, that's Dakota."

As she got closer, he saw the snowmobile had a red headlight versus the standard clear one, and that Dakota wore a Santa Claus hat.

She pulled into the clearing, slowly yelling, "*Ho, ho, ho...* the Ho is here." She parked the sled and jumped off to hug Jake. "Merry Christmas, mountain man."

"Merry Christmas, Ho." He smiled. "I like the Rudolph red nose light."

She'd packed the snowmobile with more supplies than usual. It looked like a Santa sled.

"Are you delivering toys in Dubois tonight or something?" He nodded towards the snowmobile.

"No, silly, I have some surprises for you. It's Christmas! *Ho, ho, ho.*"

They unloaded the snowmobile and sat at the kitchen table.

"So, Santa, how have you been?" Jake said.

"I've been busy with a strange case."

"Is it the embezzlement case you told me about last month?"

"Yes, it's taking a strange turn. It appears that my client's partners have a business connection to Dibella Industries. Considering they're in the grain industry, that in itself is not that strange. What *is strange*... is that the business connection is in overseas oil transportation. My client didn't know about this side business. I believe they want him out of the way for some reason."

Jake stroked his beard. "Hmmm, I know it's not unique for partners to have side ventures, but why would they want your client removed from their mutual business?"

"I don't know, but unless I can find a smoking gun, my client will lose this case. He claims he's being framed, but all evidence shows he embezzled the money."

"What do *you* think?"

"I think he's innocent, but ultimately we'll have to settle with restitution and his removal from controlling interest of his company." She sighed. "Okay, enough work! This is Christmas time. I have gifts for you."

"Dakota, you do enough for me. You didn't need to get me gifts."

She ignored him and pulled two wrapped packages from her supply bag, one large, the other small. Her eyes twinkled. "Open them up."

He opened the larger package to find a set of snowshoes. "Man, they will be so useful this winter. Thank you."

"They're the first part of that gift. Tonight, I'll show you the second."

Jake opened the next package. It was a medium-sized sack like the one Samuel gave him with the smoke. He smiled. "I see you didn't have a problem with your *"Sonny"* story?"

"I didn't have to say anything. At Thanksgiving, he pulled me aside and gave me this. He said it was different. He said the first stuff was to show you the path to take, and that this stuff will help you to remember things. It's what he uses. He said you should smoke one pipe a week."

"How did he know you've been visiting me?"

"I don't know Jake. I guess his powers are real."

"So, I guess our visits to the spirit world are over."

Dakota's gaze intensified. "I guess so, but I've seen what I needed to."

He nodded and looked her in the eyes. "Me too."

Their eyes fixed on each other for several seconds.

Dakota fidgeted and cleared her throat. "I have one more thing for you." She slid a folder across the table.

He opened the folder to find Facebook screenshots. He looked at each of them and smiled. He got to the last one and stared at it, then looked up at Dakota, then back down at the picture.

Alexi had removed the 'days missing' counter. There was a picture of her at a Christmas party. She stood with a group of co-workers, quite close to a man Jake didn't recognize.

He paused and looked back at Dakota, then nodded slightly and smiled. "Alexi has let go of the last thread."

"I don't know if she'll ever truly let go of you, but it appears she has accepted you are gone. There will always be a piece of you in her."

He recalled the last vision he had with the Faceless Indian banging Alexi, and now he understood what it meant. "Today, my life moved forward over the last hill, as the visions showed me."

Dakota paused, reflecting on her own visions. "Hold that thought." She reached into her pack, pulled out a bottle of high-end Bourbon and two shot glasses, and poured two shots. "To visions," she offered as a toast.

"To visions," he said, and they clinked glasses. "Okay, Santa, what's the second part of the gift you mentioned with the snowshoes? Are you turning the tables on me? Do I have to wait to get naked in the hot springs to find out?"

Dakota looked down at her watch, prompting Jake to do the same: 3 PM.

"No," she said. "Let's eat something quick, and I'll take you to the gift."

Jake tilted his head and glanced sideways. "Okay, Santa, how is smoked venison?"

"Perfect! We'll need protein for energy."

The two finished a quick dinner.

"Okay," she said. "Put on some warm clothes. It's time for your gift." She pulled clothes from her pack.

They added layers to their current clothing and started to leave the cabin.

"Grab your snowshoes," she said.

Outside, she grabbed her set from the snowmobile, started strapping them, and stood up. "Have you used snowshoes before?"

He fumbled with the bindings. "Yeah, it's been a while, but I'll be fine."

She led him behind the cabin.

Honi followed closely, snapping at the snow Jake's shoes kicked up, to which Jake and Dakota laughed.

"He's getting so big, but still has puppy in him," she said.

They traveled in a direction Jake had never been. The full moon glistened off the fresh snow, lighting their path beneath the sparse canopy.

They hiked for about two hours, at which point Dakota stopped and turned to Jake. "Now, close your eyes and take my hand."

He held her hand as she guided him forward and up a small incline.

"Okay, open your eyes."

In the valley below, Dubois sparkled with a sea of Christmas lights. The Milky Way painted the night sky above the dark silhouettes of the surrounding mountains.

Jake stood awestruck. "That is the most beautiful Christmas scene I have *ever* seen."

Dakota held her grip on his hand. She looked deep in his eyes, pulled him closer, and kissed him gently on the lips. "Merry Christmas."

Jake eased up and squeezed her hand softly. "Merry Christmas."

Their hands remained interlocked as they stared silently at the Christmas scene.

"Well, I don't know about you," she said, breaking the silence. "But after the hike back, I'll be ready to soak in the spring."

He panned the valley one last time. "I wish I could transport the spring here and stare at this all night."

They hiked back to the cabin and down to the hot spring.

Dakota set her pack down and looked at Jake as she removed her jacket.

Jake mirrored her.

Tonight, they bypassed the formalities of turning around as they undressed. Their eyes never lost contact with each other as each piece of clothing fell to the snow.

"Oh, one more surprise," she said. She reached into her pack and pulled out two glow sticks, one red and one green. She activated them and tossed them in the spring, illuminating the water in Christmas colors.

"Nice touch," he said.

They relaxed in the spring and made small talk.

Dakota changed the mood to a more serious tone. "Jake, the pass is getting tricky with the snow. I don't know if I'll make it up here in January or February. I'll try."

"Well, supply-wise, I'm fine. It's your company I'll miss, but I don't want you to risk your life to come out here."

She looked at him, stood up, and walked across the spring. The water covered her to just below the waist, and the glow sticks illuminated the rest of her below the water.

Jake felt himself get hard as she sat down next to him, and their shoulders touched.

"We'll enjoy tonight and hope the weather holds out for next month." She placed her hand on his thigh, and her forearm brushed against his growing dick.

He wanted to make a move on her, as his dick pulsated, feeling like it would split.

Dakota could see through the bubbling water that Jake was fully erect. Tonight, for the first time since the attack, she was aroused in the physical world. Her nipples grew hard and her insides quivered. She wanted her strong warrior to take her, and waited for a sign from him.

Their conversation grew awkward as the sexual tension mounted, but.... It was not time. The Spirits would guide them in their union, just as they'd brought them together.

After each realized it was not the time to act on their desires, the mood lightened. They spent about an hour in the spring, sitting next to each other, discussing the past and present, all the while avoiding the uncertain future.

"Well," he said. "Shall we head back to the cabin and that nice warm fire?"

Dakota sighed. "I could sit here forever, but yes. I do need to get some sleep eventually. I have to leave early to beat the storm coming."

She stood up and walked out of the spring, feeling Jake's gaze on her ass. He didn't seem to want to stand up, as if embarrased for her to see him hard.

She pulled her pants on and looked back at him. "Are you not coming?"

"I'll be there in a second."

"It's fine, Jake. I can see through the water. At least I know *that* part of Jake Michaels is not dead." She smiled and turned away.

The two sat on the bearskin watching the fire.

Jake held the pipe and new medicine Samuel had sent for him. "Should we see what effects this has?"

"Sure. I know we won't enter the Spirit World, but maybe it will have another type of buzz."

They each took two puffs from the pipe, and when Dakota felt her body relax, she lay back on the bearskin rug. Jake joined her, and they looked up at the ceiling. She felt no intense high, just a mellow feeling.

She sat up, moved to straddle Jake, and bent forward to kiss him. Then she pulled back and waited for a reaction.

He stared deep into her eyes and pulled her back to him. Their kisses were deep and passionate, until she leaned back and unbuttoned her denim shirt.

He reached up and grabbed her hand. "I have nothing to offer you."

She paused, bent over, kissed him, and guided one of his hands over her breasts and hard nipples. She felt him grow between her legs, and placed his hand on her heart, then leaned forward, laying on him. She knew it was not time, so she kissed his cheek, slid her head down onto his chest, and drifted off to sleep.

Jake stared at the ceiling, watching the shadows from the fire dance on the old paint. His eyes grew heavy.

Honi started whining, and Jake opened his eyes. The morning light shined through the cabin windows. He stood up and let Honi out.

Dakota had slept next to him, and the noise woke her. "Good morning," she said, smiling.

"Good morning. I'm making coffee. Are you ready for some?"

"I would love some."

He walked into the kitchen.

Dakota came up from behind and hugged him.

He turned to look at her. "About last night—"

Dakota stopped him mid-sentence by putting two fingers to his lips. "Shhhhh. Last night was beautiful."

He looked at her and smiled. "What time do you have to leave?"

She pouted. "In about an hour."

"Well, we have time for a Jake Michaels special omelet."

"That sounds perfect."

She kissed him on the cheek and left the kitchen area to start packing her bags for the trip home.

The Wyoming winter had unleashed its fury on the Wind River Range. The snow pack in the higher elevations had grown to over ten feet high. Jake thought about Dakota's planned January visit, just one day away. The weather forecast called for unseasonably warm weather tomorrow, but with that came the threat of an avalanche. Several of the canyons she would have to travel through had sharp peaks, and limited tree cover to protect the trail from snow slides.

He donned his snowshoes and headed out to check the conditions.

He traveled three miles to Grouse Pass, lifted his binoculars, and surveyed the steep mountains on both sides of the trail ahead. He saw clear evidence of snow slides, and moved to a higher point to get a better view of the path Dakota would travel. No evidence of the trail remained, only the upper halves of pine trees that bordered it. An earlier avalanche had closed it off.

"Well, boy, looks like we won't see Dakota for several more weeks. No telling what the rest of the trail looks like, so I guess it's you and me."

Honi looked at Jake as if knowing what he'd said. He wagged his tail at the sound of Dakota's name.

Jake smiled and patted his head. "C'mon, let's head home."

Jake sat at the cabin table looking at his calendar, specifically at the next date circled on it: February 15th, three weeks from today. It would be almost two months since Dakota's last visit.

He missed her, and often thought about their last visit, wondering if she was upset that he'd not made love to her. He wasn't ready for the emotional bond that would form between them, if that happened.

He looked at the picture of Alexi at her Christmas party, and rubbed his hand across it. As the months passed, he was forgetting her touch. It was being replaced by Dakota's.

Overwhelming guilt flooded him. Adding to it was the fact Samuel's medicine was helping him. He hadn't suffered a spell in three weeks. Now he questioned his decision to leave his family, despite the fact that memories of his past life continued to fade. Every day, he did exercises to hold onto them. He scribbled events and dates on a tablet, but as the days passed, he struggled to recall specific details. Simple facts, such as his kids' names, his anniversary date, and the day he met Alexi, remained vivid. Birthdates, graduation dates, and other important details of his life increasingly became a struggle.

Events since the day he'd left his motorcycle at the river, however, remained sharp and vivid. He could recount the smallest details since he'd met Dakota. One life was slowly being replaced by another. This is *exactly* what he'd imagined with his disease. *This* was why he'd left his family.

Eventually, Dakota and Honi will also fade from my memory. Or will they? Will Samuel's medicine keep me in the world, as it has Samuel? Do we have the same disease?

Jake's mind raced over scenarios every day, when he did his brain exercises. The unknown was the hardest part to deal with. He'd never expected to have a relationship with another person. He'd pictured his life as one of solitude, fading into a dark abyss and eventually passing away alone. He would burden no one with his disease. He would walk off into the woods like an old animal and die with dignity.

As it stood, however, an ironic twist of fate had ensconced him.

Should I have ignored Dakota that fateful night?

He'd been preparing to pitch camp when the truck pulled into the clearing that night. He'd watched them strip and beat her, and watched her run for her life. The verbal abuse still echoed in his brain. He'd seen the fear and despair on her face, but struggled with his decision, not wanting his plan jeopardized by interaction with anyone. He'd known that any involvement on his part would include confrontation and violence. Doing the right thing overpowered his selfishness, in the end, but he regretted having waited so long, causing Dakota to endure more than she would have, had he acted immediately.

Isolation in the long cold winter gave him time to reflect on his current life, and he thought deeper into the meaning of his visits to the Spirit World. Soon the snow would stop falling, and Dakota would be back. Spring would bring renewed life to this mountaintop.

He didn't yet know if he would tempt Destiny and ignore the Spirits—if he'd follow his basic human instincts, as he had the night he met Dakota.

Dakota listened to the weather report for tomorrow's trip to the cabin. They'd posted avalanche warnings for high mountain passes, so it would be too dangerous to travel the canyons. She could snowshoe the trail from Dubois, but that too carried its own risks. The trailhead sat in a visible area, and she was well known in town now, and didn't want to be seen going alone into the mountains this time of the year. It would raise suspicions.

Her work schedule offered little flexibility, so it was obvious she wouldn't see Jake this month. She'd have to wait until February, as Jake and she had discussed.

She stared out her bedroom window, looking in the direction of the cabin, thinking about him. She hoped her last visit hadn't scared him.

He had no idea she was a virgin, and that she'd chosen him as the recipient of her special gift. He *was* the strong warrior the Spirit of the Water had showed her that summer day at the Sacred Waterfall. He didn't know that, since the attack, she'd had no sexual feelings at all... except towards him.

She lay on her bed thinking about the last night they were in the hot spring, the look in his eyes and his hard dick as she stood up in front of him. Vivid memories of the bearskin rug and the fireplace played over in her mind—the kisses they shared and his touch on her breasts. She unbuttoned her shirt and ran her hands over her breats as he'd done, and her nipples grew hard and sensitive, sending shivers down her body. She closed her eyes and moved her hands between her legs. Her back arched as her fingers slid down the lips of her special gift.

She abruptly stopped and sat up. *No! I will save my passion for him.*

She looked again at the date circled on the calendar: February 15th, the day after Valentine's Day. She would adjust her schedule, and surprise Jake on Valentine's Day. She would tell him how she felt, and share her belief in the blessings of the Sacred Falls, and how the Spirits had delivered him to her that fateful night.

She believed the healing qualities of Samuel's medicine would overcome his disease. He was her strong warrior, promised to her by the stories of her peoples since she was a little girl.

She looked out the window again, at the light snow falling. The long cold winter could not end soon enough. She couldn't wait to share the miracles of spring with Jake.

CHAPTER 23
VALENTINE'S DAY

Dakota had set the alarm for 6 AM, but woke before it went off. Valentine's Day had arrived, and she lay in bed imagining the weekend to follow with Jake. That night, she would give him the gift she had saved her whole life. She would follow the vision the Spirit of the Waterfall had shown her.

She packed a feathered head bandana, a wide beaded turquoise necklace that fell over her breasts, and a deerskin loincloth, all of which she would wear when presenting herself to him. She could barely contain her anticipation and excitement. As soon as the darkness gave way to light, she would leave for the cabin. One last check on the weather and avalanche warnings showed both clear for the weekend.

When the sun rose over the mountains, she started the ride. As each mile passed, her excitement grew. She could almost feel Jake inside of her, and imagined this was how Indian Maidens felt the day of their wedding. She wished she could bathe one last time in the Sacred Waterfall, as they did, but the pass was closed off. She would say an ancient prayer in the hot spring before they united on the bearskin in front of the fire.

She glanced at the odometer for what felt like the hundreth time: two more miles. Her hands trembled with excitement. Jake would be expecting her tomorrow, and would be surprised to see her. She'd hug him upon arrival, and his strong embrace would make it difficult not to act on her desires. She hoped she could hold off making love to him until the evening. After inhaling deeply to calm herself, she laughed aloud.

One more mile... her heart raced. She found it difficult to concentrate on the path.

When she pulled up to the cabin, Jake and Honi were not there as she'd expected. Maybe Jake had gone to check his trap lines, which he did every morning. She walked into the cabin, and it was cold. She looked around and saw that Jake's belongings were gone.

Her heart sank.

On the table sat a letter propped up against a lantern. Her hands shook as she picked it up and read it. Tears soon rolled down her face. After reading it, she smiled and held the letter to her heart, then nodded and dried her eyes. She looked around the empty cabin, remembering the time they'd spent here, then folded the letter, put it in her pocket, and closed the door behind her.

As the letter had instructed, she looked up at the top of the butte to the right of the waterfall, and spotted Jake standing tall, his hair and beard blowing in the wind, with Honi by his side. He reminded her of the strong warriors she imagined watched over her in the canyons. Light snow sparkled in the sunshine as Jake put his right hand over his heart and raised it to say goodbye. Dakota wiped fresh tears from her cheeks, smiled, kissed her hand, and raised it to say goodbye.

They stood for a moment, looking at each other, and then Jake turned and walked away, disappearing from her sight.

Dakota fell to her knees and sobbed. The Spirits had delivered her a strong warrior, and now they had taken him away. She looked back at where Jake had stood, and a sun dog formed in the sky.

The Spirits continued to send signs.

She started the ride home, her heart broken, the excitement she'd experienced on the ride up now turned to profound sadness. She played over and over the words in Jake's letter, wishing she could have spoken to him. She understood his plight, but hoped he would eventually trust in the Spirits and stop questioning them—they didn't bring them together just to have it end like this.

Jim heard Dakota's snowmobile returning, and walked outside to greet her. "Lomasi, was the pass closed?"

Dakota pulled her helmet off. Her bloodshot eyes welled again as they met his. "No, Woo Woo. He is gone."

Jim placed his hand on her shoulder. "He is on a journey, Lomasi, one he must do alone. He must find his essence before he can live again."

Dakota walked into the house, her head hung low in sadness.

Jim looked out towards the cabin and nodded. He hoped Jake and he had made the right decision, for Dakota's sake. Hopefully, she would move past this and find a man that could give her a future, a man with whom she could spend many Valentine's Days.

Jake and Honi walked to their new camp, a cave that miners had built a small shanty onto. When Jim had secretly visited Jake a week earlier, he guided him to it. Dakota had never been here, and didn't even know it existed. This new camp was only about one mile from the cabin, and the same stream that fed the waterfall flowed nearby, offering plenty of trout and fresh water. The cave would serve as cold storage for his food, and the shanty had an old wood stove for heat and cooking.

He would spend the rest of the winter here in solitude. Eventually, he would move back to the cabin, once Dakota had moved on with her life. As agreed, Jim would meet him on May 1st, to assure him the cabin would once again be safe, and that Dakota would not travel out looking for him.

Jake stared at the fire burning in the woodstove, with Honi sitting by his side. "Well, boy, it's just you and me now. We'll make this journey alone. I miss her, but she deserves a future."

Jake thought about the visions, and about what the Faceless Indian had shown him, and knew he was tempting the Spirits and Destiny. He also knew one decision had already caused great pain to the family he loved, and he would not put another person through that.

The Spirits must understand that. They cannot be so cruel to Dakota.

CHAPTER 24
THE SPIRITS TEMPT

Winter had given way to spring in the Wind River valley. Wildflowers poked through the remaining spots of snow, and summer birds had returned, bringing the mountains alive with song.

Jake had met with Jim, who said Dakota was doing fine, dating one of the young lawyers from the office. This pleased Jake.

He'd made improvements to the old shanty, but looked forward to moving back to the cabin as soon as possible. His garden was showing the first signs of life, and he would have plenty of vegetables for the year.

His illness had progressed. Although the medicine Samuel had sent with Jim controlled his spells, his long-term memory continued to fade. Jake Michael's old life had grown smaller and smaller in the rearview mirror. Now late May, almost a year had passed since his vacation here, and details of that trip faded too.

Conversely, every event following the first sack of medicine Samuel had given him remained vivid. It felt to him as though the medicine had started erasing his past life, while magnifying his current life. He'd prepared for the memory loss—it was why he was here—but he *had not* prepared for the fact that his current state of mind was so... sharp.

Was I misdiagnosed? Was all of this in haste? Is it possible the correct medication could control my illness?

A combination of simple herbs from an old Medicine Man had kept him in this world, and he would have traded his old memories for new memories with Alexi. Maybe the old memories wouldn't have faded, had he gotten the correct treatment. Or maybe the modern world could offer him no medicine. Perhaps, if he stopped taking Samuel's medication, his current world would slip away too.

Jake would never know the answers to those questions, but he would not tempt that fate. All he could do is continue the journey that Destiny had designed for him.

"Well, boy, this is a big day for us. Are you ready to take our first trip into town?"

Honi cocked his head and, hearing the excitement in Jake's voice, wagged his tail and barked.

Jake had been making walking sticks, which he hoped to sell in Dubois. He had some money left, but it would soon run out, so he needed to establish a relationship with someone who would buy the sticks. Since Dakota had stopped coming, his supplies dwindled, and he didn't want to burden Jim with bringing anything except his medicine every three months.

They followed the trail Dakota had taken them on at Christmas time. It proved a challenging hike past the point they'd stopped that winter night. He discovered why most people would not attempt it. As the trail dropped in altitude, the melting snows made the path wet and slippery.

They reached a small butte about a quarter mile from town, and Jake surveyed the area. Cars moved up and down the street, and people walked from shop to shop. The tourist season had begun in Wind River, which made him nervous and anxious at the same time. This would be the first time in almost a year that he'd speak with anyone except Dakota's family.

He put a rope on Honi and tied it to a tree. "Okay, boy, you have to stay here. We don't need to attract any attention."

Honi whined as Jake walked away, and he looked back. "It's okay, Honi, I'll be back."

Honi walked as far as the rope allowed him and stood tall, not taking his eyes off his master.

Jake walked the busy street. People said hello to him, paying no attention to his mountain man appearance, having seen men with hair and beards longer than his. He blended in and could move about freely, his concerns erased.

He stopped at several gift shops trying to sell his walking sticks. Each time, the owner politely told him they had local carvers that supplied them, and suggested another store. After six shops, he became discouraged. The seventh shop he visited, a small one, appeared to be high end, based on the jewelry prices he saw in the window.

He shrugged his shoulders. *Why not?*

A distinguished-looking older Indian man greeted him at the door. "Good afternoon, can I help you?"

Jake's eyes panned the small shop for walking sticks. "Hello, sir, I'm looking for a shop that may be interested in buying my walking sticks."

"You can see my shop specializes in more upscale items. I am not sure I would have much success in selling them, especially given the fact almost every gift shop and gas station in town has them." The owner's voice was soft and polite.

Jake pulled one of the walking sticks out. "Can I at least show you my work? It's a bit different."

The man tilted his head and pressed his lips together, looking at the walking stick Jake handed him. It was straight, but had a unique feature in knobs scattered about the surface.

The owner examined the stick, not taking his eyes off of it. "Knobbled Pine, very rare around here. I have never seen walking sticks made from this. Where did you find the wood?"

Jake knew the wood was different but had no idea what it was. He thought for a second before answering. "While I was hiking on an old army buddy's property."

The shop owner looked up from the stick just enough to make eye contact with Jake. "Is the wood from around here?"

"Now, if I told you that, more people would look for it, and you and I would not have something unique to the town. Do we have a deal?" Jake smiled and reached his hand out.

The owner raised his eyebrows, chuckled, and shook Jake's hand. "Yes, we will give them a shot. How many do you have, and how much do you want for them?"

"I have ten, and based on the prices I saw in town for regular wood, I would like twenty dollars per stick."

"Let me see the rest of them, please."

The owner looked at Jake's work and nodded. "These are good. I will give you fifteen for the first ten. I need to polyurethane them. If they sell and you bring me more with a clear finish, I will give you twenty dollars."

Jake rubbed his beard and thought for several seconds. "Deal. I can supply you with five to seven every month, depending on my schedule."

"That is fine. What is your name or company name I should invoice these to?"

"My name is John Jacobs. We can keep this informal—cash-in/cash-out for both of us—if that's okay with you."

"That works for me. My name is William Black Feather. Pleased to meet you, John Jacobs."

The two men completed the deal, and Jake left the shop feeling good. It was nice to meet another person, and he'd established a business relationship that would allow him to purchase supplies, and maybe a treat or two, when in town.

He stopped by a store and purchased lantern oil, toiletries, a small bottle of Bourbon, and a real collar for Honi. He looked at a clock on the wall and realized Honi had been alone for almost two hours. It was time for him to leave, but he wanted to do one more thing while in town.

He'd seen Dakota's law office when he came down from the butte, and had ducked down a side street to avoid passing in front of it. Now, he stood one block away.

He struggled, longing to see her, but at the same time did not want her to rekindle feelings for him. He took a deep breath, remembering his agreement with Jim, then turned and walked the opposite direction, towards an alley.

The aroma from a small bakery caught his attention, and he stopped to look in the window. Displayed on a silver dish was his treat for this trip: cheesecake.

He reached the trailhead and looked up, and saw Honi standing on the butte. The wolf looked powerful, majestic, and dangerous. Jake smiled, and thought if people only knew what a loving animal he was....

He'd not taken more than a few steps when Honi's keen eyes and nose found him. The excited wolf started yipping, so Jake picked up his pace. He needed Honi to be quiet and not draw attention to them. Local people knew what wolves sounded like, but they didn't need to see one this close to town.

He reached Honi and bent down to hug him. "Well, boy, that was a good trip, and I have a treat for us tonight after dinner. Let's go home."

Dakota sat in her office going over the Anderson Embezzlement case. Her depositions of his business partners raised some questions, but produced nothing that would exonerate her client. She shook her head and tossed the folder on the desk. After months of continuances, the trial would come in two weeks, and she had nothing but his good reputation to build a defense around.

Another "innocent" client, she thought sarcastically.

Jim walked into Dakota's office, sat down, and nodded toward the Anderson file on her desk.

"What's wrong, Grandfather? You look troubled"

"You can stop worrying about the Anderson case."

She tilted her head and squinted. "Why, did they settle?"

"No, he is dead. They found his body at the bottom of a cliff in Utah. It appears he was doing some solo backcountry hiking and slipped."

"Oh no... he was such a nice guy. What a shame."

"Yes, he was. He had his issues when he was younger, but turned into a solid man. I guess his partners will be happy now. I still do not trust them, Lomasi, despite no hard evidence they did anything wrong. I dislike the fact they are connected to Vincent Dibella. There are bad spirits around this."

"I agree. What time are you leaving?"

"In about ten minutes. I am upset about Russ's death. I have known him almost fifteen years."

"I'm sorry. I have a four o'clock client, and then I'll be home. Maybe we can go for a ride?"

"We will see, Lomasi. I am tired."

Dakota watched her grandfather leave and looked down at her watch: 3:45.

She walked into the lobby to stretch, and spotted her receptionist and several of the female paralegals looking down at a phone, commenting and pointing at something.

"Sally, are you showing nude pictures of your boyfriend again?"

"No, Dakota, check out this guy. People in town are talking about him." Sally passed her the phone. "Folks are calling him the Wolf Man. Several people heard a wolf yelping around lunch, and when they looked up, they saw this guy bend down and hug the wolf. Then the two of them disappeared into the mountain. One of my friends had his camera out and snapped these pictures. Look at the close up of the next frame. For an older guy, he's hot. Look at those eyes and his ripped arms."

"He could do me wolf-style," Jennifer said.

All the girls laughed, and though Dakota fought to maintain her composure, she forced a laugh too.

"Well, I guess we have an eccentric hiker in town," she said, and walked back into her office.

She locked the door behind her and slumped at her desk. Her eyes glazed over as she stared into space. A rush of emotions paralyzed her, and her face burned just thinking about the girls talking about Jake in a sexual manner. Those pictures effectively destroyed months of healing, and her hands trembled.

"Dakota, your four o'clock is here," her intercom announced, snapping her back from deep thought.

"Give me a moment, Sally. Thank you." She walked to her bathroom to freshen her makeup and regain her composure, and returned to her desk and hit the intercom button. "Send Mr. Crane in, Sally. Thank you."

She greeted her client, and they discussed the drug charges against him. She searched for the strength to stay focused, but could only think about Jake and Honi. She convinced her client she was interested in his *innocence*, when in reality, she couldn't give a fuck less. The police had arrested him with almost an ounce of crystal meth, and he claimed the cops in Yellowstone planted it.

She drudged through the meeting, and finally said, "Thank you, Mr. Crane. I'll review what we spoke about and reschedule you for another appointment. Please see Sally on your way out. She'll collect your retainer fee."

Dakota shut the door behind him, blew out a deep breath, and walked over to her desk. She looked down at the notepad, full of scribbles of bits and pieces of their conversation. It also contained Jake's name, along with the words: visions, bear rug, Honi, hot spring, and fireplace. They almost covered the page. She hoped her client hadn't seen this.

Her phone rang, and it was Chris, the guy she'd been seeing for the past two months.

"Hey, you, how has your afternoon been?" he said.

"Busy. One of my clients died, and I just met with another innocent drug dealer."

"I'm sorry. Are you okay?"

"I'm fine, just worn out."

"Hey, did you hear about the crazy guy with the wolf today?"

Dakota put the phone to her waist, looked up at the ceiling, and took a deep breath. "Yes, the girls showed me pictures of him. Pretty wild, huh?"

"Yep. I wonder where he's hiking from and too."

She struggled with the conversation. Chris was an awesome guy, and she didn't want to seem short with him. After all, if she didn't know Jake, she'd be inquisitive about the situation too.

"I don't know," she forced out. "But it's pretty cool."

"Yeah, leave the corporate world, grow your hair and beard long, and hike to who-knows-where with your pet wolf and no cares in the world. Pretty fucking awesome, if you ask me!"

Each word he said about Jake cut Dakota's heart like a hot razor. She needed to change the subject, and answer him in a manner such that he wouldn't bring it back up.

"Honestly, I think it's kind of strange. He may be running from something, or he's a weirdo. The more I think about it, the more it creeps me out."

"Okay, we won't talk about it anymore. Are we still on for drinks tonight when I get back in town?"

"Honestly, I'm exhausted. Can we pass tonight?"

"Of course we can. Why don't you get a good night's sleep, and we'll do something tomorrow night. I'll talk to you in the office tomorrow."

"Thank you. I'll see you tomorrow. Bye bye."

She felt guilty. Chris was a great guy, and he'd lifted her up after Valentine's Day at the cabin. He also respected her choice to stay a virgin. She hated standing him up tonight, especially since he'd been out of town the past two nights on business. She knew he'd looked forward to seeing her, as she'd looked forward to seeing him. That was before she heard that Jake came into town.

She had to figure out how to handle this situation. The more Jake came into town, the more of a story he'd become. The rest of the town believed he was passing through, but she knew different.

Jake and Honi sat on the front porch of the shanty as gentle winds blew across the mountaintop. The sky was clear and bedazzled with stars as far the eye could see.

"Well, Honi, today was a good day. We have a new business, and we can go into town without anyone paying attention."

He broke off a small piece of the cheesecake. "Cheers," he said, and handed it to Honi.

Jake looked back at the sky, remembering the first time Dakota and he had sat in the hot spring. He marveled at the Milky Way as the arch of it fell behind the mountains, headed in the direction of Dakota. He imagined it as a bridge to her.

Dakota sat on the back deck thinking about today, looking up at the stars. The Milky Way arched behind the mountains towards the cabin. She wished she could walk across it to Jake.

CHAPTER 25
DEAD MAN'S TALE

The trout streams around Wind River crawled with fishermen this time of year, and Jim walked down to his entrance gate to pick up debris. Every summer, people parked near his gate to fish the stream that ran along the road, mostly locals, but a few tourists found their way out here, and they tended to leave trash behind.

He watched as a car pulled up and parked. A man and a boy, perhaps his young son, hopped out of the car.

"Is it okay if I park here, sir?" the man said.

Jim nodded. "Yes, that is fine."

The young boy walked to Jim and looked up at him. "You are tall, Mister. Are you ten feet?"

Jim laughed. "No, not that tall."

The boy's father joined them. "You have to excuse him, five years old and full of questions."

"It is fine. I remember when my kids and granddaughter were that young. They are fun years, so enjoy them. They disappear quickly."

"I want him to catch some trout, but the river is running high, and he's too young to be down there. I was hoping a smaller stream like this would be easier for him. Are there any fish here?"

"On the right-hand side where your car is parked, there is a path into the ravine. It is a little steep, but he will be fine. Go to the bottom of the path. There is a nice, deep, dark hole. He will catch fish there."

"Thank you, sir, I appreciate it."

As the two walked away, Jim smiled, remembering taking Dakota down there to catch her first trout. He had it mounted for her, and it still hung in her room, proudly displayed over her bed.

The young boy rushed to his father. "Daddy, Daddy, look what I found."

His father looked down at a cellphone in his son's hand. "Well, looks like someone lost their phone."

"Can I keep it, Daddy?"

"Son, that's an expensive phone. We'll plug it in when we get back to the car. Maybe we can figure out who it belongs to and give it back to them."

"That would be the good thing to do, right, Daddy?"

"That's right."

Joe Wilmer and son Freddie finished fishing, returned to the car, and Joe started it up. He plugged the phone into the charger, but it did nothing.

"Must be broke, Daddy."

"We'll give it a few minutes."

They drove towards their cabin.

Freddie was playing with the phone when suddenly they heard, "I want him to fuck me hard."

"Daddy, the lady in the video said a bad word, and the man's pee-pee is sticking up."

Joe pulled over and snatched the phone from his son. He turned down the volume and watched the video, and knew he needed to go to the police.

Joe pulled into the Fort Washakie Police Department.

"Yes, sir, can I help you?" Officer Jill Mendez greeted the man and the boy.

"Yes, Officer, my son and I were fishing, and he found this phone."

"Okay, I can put it in lost and found."

"Actually, I didn't bring it in for lost and found. It's what's in a video on the phone. I think you need to look at it. You'll need to be in an office, because the video is graphic."

The officer wrinkled her brow. "Graphic in what nature, sir?"

"Language, nudity, and assault."

"If you can please have a seat and fill out this paperwork, I'll be right back." Jill walked into Jimmy Red Cloud's office.

"Hey, Jill, what's up?"

"Jimmy, a man and his son found this phone. They say there's a video on here we need to see."

"A video?"

"He claims there's an assault on it?"

"An assault? Well, let's look at it?"

The video started with a brief side view of naked women on all fours, her face hidden by her hair. A naked man stood behind her as she said, "Fuck me hard." The man looked up from behind her, and the audio faded out. The video panned to a man in a poncho, his hood up and his head down. Audio returned, and the naked man asked the girl what she wanted to do with the stranger. She replied, "I want him to fuck me hard." Another voice said, "No one is fucking anyone tonight," and the camera turned back to the man in the ponco. He produced a walking stick and hit the naked man's erect penis, and the naked man fell to the ground in pain. The audio became garbled at that point, as the stranger moved quickly towards the person filming and raised the walking stick. The phone appeared to drop to the ground, and the audio faded in and out. In the sound that was clear, they could make out three distinct male voices. Each seemed to be in great pain. The video showed an arm and hand reach for the phone, and then the screen went dark.

The two officers looked at each other.

Jimmy said, "Where did he find this?"

Jill said, "I didn't ask. He's filling out a report now."

"Please send him in."

The man and his son walked into Jimmy's office, and Joe Wilmer introduced himself and his son Freddie, and they sat down.

"That is an interesting video, Mr. Wilmer. Where did you find the phone?"

"At the ten-foot-tall man's stream," Freddie chirped.

Jimmy and Joe chuckled.

"Freddie, let me answer the officer's questions, okay?" Mr. Wilmer turned to Jimmy. "It was about eight miles from here, towards Hangman's Bridge. We met a nice older gentleman off a side road, doing work on his gate. He told us where to fish."

"Was it a right turn off the main road?" Jimmy said.

"Yes, sir, do you know the stream?"

"I believe so. Would you mind taking a ride with me and show me exactly where you found the phone?"

"Of course, anything to help. That video didn't look too good for someone, did it?"

"No, Mr. Wilmer, it did not."

Jimmy, Officer Mendez, and the Wilmers drove to the area where they'd found the phone. Another cruiser followed, and they parked on the road and all walked down to the stream.

Freddie pointed. "It was right here, Officer Jimmy."

The phone had rested on a thick patch of creek moss. Jimmy looked around and then looked up. "Jill, I'll be right back. Please stay here. I'm going up to the top of the ravine."

Jimmy walked up the main road, and turned right on the dirt road leading to the Continental Divide trail. He positioned himself even with the group down below, pulled out the phone, and examined the video's brief glimpses of where the night sky met the canyons in the distance. The horizons were a direct match.

He walked over to the edge of the deep ravine. "Jill, come in. Over."

"Loud and clear, Jimmy. Over."

"Jill, look directly up. I'll move around. Let me know if you can see me. Over."

"10-4 Jimmy. Over."

He moved slowly from right to left, and the thick canopy prevented him from seeing the group below.

"Jimmy, shine your light down, and I'll do the same. Over."

The two officers turned their flashlights to strobe.

"I got you, Jill. Over."

"Same here, Jimmy. Over."

Jimmy looked at Jill's strobe. Despite the thick canopy, a phone could find its way to the spot where the boy found it. Jimmy figured the distance at about fifty yards out and down. It would take a person with some arm strength to make this throw. He stepped back and panned the area, trying to recreate the video.

He looked down at the phone. The date on the video was August 18, almost a year ago. He tried to move from video to the home screen, but the phone didn't respond.

The group returned to the station. After Jimmy dismissed the Wilmers, he met with the Captain to get directions on how to proceed.

"That is an interesting video," Captain Longbow said. "We need to find out who this phone belongs to. Based on the one injury we did see, I have to think he needed medical attention. Contact the local hospitals and see if there were any reports of three men checking in on or around August 18 of last year. A broken dick cannot be that common."

"One step ahead of you, sir. I spoke with Kimmie at the hospital, and she searched the emergency room records since that night. There are no records of three men coming in together, or of anyone with a broken dick. She's talking with hospitals in surrounding areas."

Captain Longbow smiled. "One day, you will take my place. You know what to do, Jimmy. Please keep me updated."

"Yes sir."

Jimmy left the Captain's office and took the phone to forensics. Once they could figure out the owner, this case would be easy.

"Hey, Skip, how are your phone skills these days?" Jimmy handed the phone to the Forensic Supervisor.

"I heard we have an interesting video," Skip said, and hit Play. He raised his eyebrows as he watched the video. "Jimmy, this almost looks scripted. Do you think it's real?"

"Honestly, I never thought about that."

Skip looked up and smirked. "Well, with all the porn I've watched connected to missing women investigations, you become a pro."

Jimmy thought for a moment. "But why would they throw the phone away?"

"Maybe they just lost it. I wonder who the girl is. From what I can see, she's put together."

"Most likely not from around here, just like the men in the video. The one guy we can make out doesn't look familiar."

Skip nodded. "Okay, let me see what I can do to identify the owner of the phone. I'll also start breaking this down frame by frame for more clues."

"Is there a way to burn a copy of this so I can examine it more closely, too?"

"Sure, I'll burn it right now and put it on a disk for you."

"Thanks, Skip, and let me know if you can identify the owner."

Skip raised an eyebrow. "*When* I find the owner."

Jimmy chuckled and left the lab.

For the next two hours, Jimmy watched the video over and over, stopping and starting, looking for any identifying marks on the people he could see. The video was clear but shot at a distance, with the closest shot that of the hand and arm that picked up the phone. Unfortunately, it was blurred. There were tattoos on the hooded man's arm, but no details were visible.

Captain Longbow and Skip walked into Jimmy's office and closed the door behind them. The Captain had a serious look on his face as he slid a folder across Jimmy's desk.

Jimmy opened the folder, labeled Dibella, and looked up puzzled. "What's this for, Captain? Is that asshole Vincent Dibella still crying about his son's missing gun?"

"No, Jimmy, the phone belonged to Marcus Dibella. Look at the coroner's report."

This was the first he saw of the coroner's report. Captain Drake had handled that part of the crash, and he retired a few months ago. The case was closed and filed away.

Jimmy read through each page. "A broken dick... son of a bitch! How did I forget that?" He slammed the folder on the desk.

"Your mind was concentrating on an injury to the living, not the dead," Captain Longbow said, and added, "Dr. Sanders is on her way over. I want her to see the video. I want to know if any of the injuries these men suffered in this assault could have contributed to their deaths."

Doctor Sanders entered the office. "Gentleman, I hear we're re-looking at the Dibella case. What do we have?"

Skip handed the phone to her and hit Play on the video.

She watched the video and put the phone down.

"Jessica," Jimmy said, "looking at this video, and at the injuries you noted on your reports, is it possible the assault could have led to the accident? Obviously, the only thing we can see is the blow to the one man's penis."

Dr. Sanders opened her reports to refresh her memory. "Who was driving, Jimmy?"

"Marcus Dibella, and he also shot this video. It's his phone."

"Do you know where the assault happened?"

"The trailhead by Jim White Feather's ranch," Captain Longbow interjected.

"The crash site was at Wolf Butte, about eight miles from Jim's place." Jessica paused and thought. "Marcus Dibella had a traumatic injury to his jaw. He definitely would have had a concussion. His blood alcohol content was the lowest of the three, but still over the limit."

Jimmy said, "The eyewitness reported they were not driving fast at the time they went over the edge. She said they were swerving a bit, and simply drifted over and off the road. We figured the driver fell asleep at the wheel. We couldn't figure out why the other passengers didn't try to correct the vehicle's path. They would have had time. Now I'm starting to get a picture of three wounded, bleeding victims."

"Gentleman, it's possible the driver lost consciousness due to his injuries. I didn't pay real close attention to his jaw wound, as his head was turned, facing his back. Cause of death was obviously a broken neck. I'll need to re-examine all the photos I took, and look for strike marks on each victim that matches that stick."

"So," Skip said. "It appears these boys had a girl with them. They partied, planned on a four-way, decided to shoot a video, and the hooded man took great exception to it."

"Jealous boyfriend?" Captain Longbow said.

Jimmy said, "Or maybe a religious psycho that just happened upon the group and took offense to what they were doing. But who and where is the girl?"

"And who is this hooded guy?" Skip asked.

Captain Longbow took a deep breath and paused. "Skip, break the video down frame by frame for any identifying marks on the girl and the attacker. Jimmy, contact Vincent Dibella and tell him there is a new development in his boys' deaths, and that we may need to talk with him again. Jessica, would exhuming the bodies help you at all?"

"Captain, they were marked for cremation on my report, per the family."

"Okay, dead men can tell no tales here. Looks like this video is all we have. Let's see what we can find." Captain Longbow stood up and dismissed the group.

CHAPTER 26
THE WOLF MAN

Jake walked out on the porch of the cabin and enjoyed the warm summer sun beating down on his face. The date was August 18th, one year to the day since his path crossed with Dakota's in the most heinous way. He took a deep breath and tried to erase the images of that night in his mind.

"Well, Honi, should we head into town and get more supplies?"

He gathered the eleven new walking sticks he'd carved for William Black Feather. He was excited to see how the first batch had sold.

They made the trek towards town and reached the butte overlooking the streets that bustled with tourists. Once again, he would be able to slip in and out with little attention. He'd trimmed his beard to neck length, and now pulled his hair into a ponytail to look a bit more presentable. Despite the fact that he'd felt safe walking around town the first time, he still wanted to alter his appearance on each visit.

"Okay, boy, stay here. I'll be right back."

Honi whined a bit then stood quietly. Each day that passed, the wolf became more domesticated, and his demeanor calmed.

Jake made his way into town and over to William's shop.

William was waiting on a customer when he looked up and saw Jake. He excused himself from the customer and walked over quickly. "Please tell me, John Jacobs, that you have a hundred sticks for me."

Jake smiled. "No, sir, but how will eleven do? I take it they sold well?"

"Yes, in the first week! I watched that door for the past six weeks, waiting for you to come through it. Let me finish with this customer, and we will take care of business."

Jake walked around the shop, admiring William's nice merchandise, the quality of which separated his store from the rest of town. He imagined some wealthy clientele were walking around with his sticks somewhere in the country.

William walked up to him with cash in his hand. "As we agreed, $20.00 per stick. I assume they have a clear finish and the quality is as good as the first batch?"

Jake opened the sack. "As we agreed, sir."

"John, I would love to spend some time with you, but as you can see, I am swamped. This is the last push for tourist season. Once school starts, they will be gone."

"I understand. I'll see you one last time before the snow starts flying."

Willam chuckled. "I wish you had said next week."

"I wish I could carve them that fast." Jake smiled and shook the shop owner's hand.

He walked out onto the busy street and meandered from shop window to shop window. In his past life, some of the material things he saw would have tempted him. Now, he had one priority: supplies for surviving the upcoming winter.

Sally knocked on Dakota's door.

"Come in, Sally."

"Dakota, he's back, The Wolf Man is in town. He was just seen down at William Black Feather's shop. He must be rich to be shopping in there. His Honi is up on the butte."

Dakota shot back, "How did you know his name is Honi?"

Sally winced at the sharp tone in her voice. "I don't. That is Wolf in our language."

"Oh, I'm sorry for snapping. I wasn't thinking. This DUI case has me flustered."

Shit, I need to be more careful.

"It's all right. Come check him out. He has his hair pulled back and trimmed his beard. He's sexy."

Dakota took a deep breath. "No, that's okay. I have work to do."

When Sally left the office, Dakota locked the door behind her and walked to the back window of her office, which faced the butte. She had looked up there every day since Jake came to town the first time. Today her workload hadn't allowed it. She pulled out a set of binoculars she'd kept in her drawer since his last visit, and zoomed in on Honi. He stood staunchly looking down on the town for Jake. He had grown since Dakota last saw him at Christmas.

A tear trickled down her cheek as she remembered the first time she saw him, the first time he allowed her to pet him, and the trust in the young wolf's eyes once he accepted her. A few minutes passed, and she saw Honi's tail wag. She panned down the hill to see Jake. He had taken his shirt off for the hike. His tanned muscles were toned from the hard living in the mountains. With his hair pulled in a ponytail, he looked from behind like a strong Indian Warrior.

Her heart sank when Jake reached Honi, untied him, and they disappeared into the woods.

She trembled, dropped to the ground, and wept. She wished she'd never found that letter on Valentine's Day. She questioned the Spirits, then cursed them. It had been eight months since she felt Jake's touch, and she thought she'd moved past him, but seeing him opened up the wounds. She crawled to her bathroom and gathered herself, reapplied her makeup, and returned to her desk. The case file in front of her meant nothing.

She stared at her intercom and daily planner. "Sally, please cancel the rest of my day. I'm not feeling well."

"Yes ma'am."

She exited from the back of the office, not wanting to hear the girls talk about the "Wolf Man." She did not want to hear them talk about the sex they would have with him.

He is not the "Wolf Man." His name is Jake Michaels, and the Spirits sent him to me.

CHAPTER 27
THE BLOOD SKULL

Skip walked into Jimmy Red Cloud's office. "Jimmy, I think I have something."

"What is it?"

Skip handed Jimmy an 8 x 11 photo of a tattoo he'd isolated from the video. The picture was fuzzy, but there was enough detail to see the image.

"I've never seen this before, Skip. Is it a gang tattoo?"

"No, I ran it through the database of known gang tattoos, and it came back negative. It's the exact opposite—a Special Forces tattoo that only a few men have. The flag is Somalian. The blood skull represents the troops lost. Our guy is ex-special forces—75th Ranger Regiment, to be exact."

Jimmy reclined back in his seat and thought for a moment. "Skip, can you tell how tall he is?"

"Based on knowing how tall Richard Dibella was, I would say around six foot-two, maybe a bit taller."

"Do you remember the guy that went missing about a year ago over near Sulphur Springs?"

"Barely. I didn't pay much attention to it. It was out of our jurisdiction."

"They searched hard for him. My cousin Jay worked on the case. I guess that's why I remember some details. I'm going to call over and talk to Hal Jones and Jay. Thanks, Skip, good work."

"Yes sir. Let me know how it goes with them."

Jimmy grabbed the phone and dialed. "Hal, Jimmy Red Cloud at Fort Washakie. How are you?"

"Hey, Jimmy, nice to hear from you. How is crime fighting going?"

"Tourist season. I don't have to go any further."

Both men laughed.

"Hal, remember the Dibella boys that died over here?"

"Sure, Jimmy, it was all over the news."

"Well, there's a twist. A couple of fishermen found a phone with a video on it. To make a long story short, it appears those boys were assaulted before the crash."

"Assaulted? How does that involve my department?"

"I don't want to go into details on the phone. Are you and my cousin Jay free later this afternoon?"

"Hold on. Let me call Jay."

Jimmy heard Hal speaking in the background to Jay.

"Your cousin said hello. He could be at the station around 1 p.m. He's questioning the same thing I am. How does this involve Sulphur Springs?"

"I'll be there in about an hour. We'll talk."

"Okay, Jimmy, see you then, and hurry up. You have me on fucking pins and needles." Hal chuckled and hung up.

Jimmy walked into the Sulphur Springs Police Department.

The receptionist at the front desk saw him, and leapt from behind her desk to hug him. "Jimmy Red Cloud, what are you doing here?"

"Hey, Millie, I didn't know you worked here."

"Yep, for the past six months." She batted her eyelashes and twirled her hair playfully. "How are you, Officer?

He laughed. "I'm good, just staying busy. Is Hal in?"

"He is. Let me call his office." She did, and followed with, "He said come on back. Oh, and Jimmy, I'm still waiting for that call you promised me six years ago after that night at Bluff Creek."

"Yeah, it seems I owe a few people calls from those days." He winked and walked away.

Hal greeted Jimmy in his office and the two men shook hands, after which Hal said, "Your cousin will be here in about five minutes. What do you have?"

Jimmy handed him a disk of the video.

Hal put it in his computer and watched intently. "Looks like their party got interrupted. Who's the guy in the poncho?"

"I don't know, but I have an idea." Jimmy slid the picture of the tattoo across the desk.

Hal looked at it and recognized it immediately. "When and where was the video shot, Jimmy?"

"August 18th of last year, near Hangman's Bridge on the Continental Divide Trailhead."

"Son of a bitch. Jake-fucking-Michaels survived the river after all. Then he showed up almost a month later, sixty miles away, and beats the shit out of a guy."

"Three guys, Hal. He messed them up pretty good. Our coroner believes it's possible the driver's injuries caused him to go off the road, ultimately killing all three passengers."

Hal took a deep breath. "Who's the girl?"

"Unknown, probably a tourist they picked up."

"Notonuk'oehib," a voice announced behind Jimmy.

Jimmy stood up and turned, smiled, and greeted Jay with a hug.

"Kooni'iini." Jay asked. *How are you?*

"Nii'iini." Jimmy answered. *I am good.*

Hal said, "Jay, you're not gonna fucking believe this. Come over to the computer, please."

Jay watched the video. "Okay, what am I looking at?"

Hal flipped over the picture of the tattoo.

Jay remained silent as he looked at it, then shook his head.

Hal said, "The video was shot one month after the disappearance, sixty miles from here."

"Do you think this is your missing person, Cousin?" Jimmy said.

Jay watched the video again. "He certainly moves as if he is trained."

Hal said, "He beat up three guys that night. They died in a car accident. It was the Dibella boys. The coroner thinks the injuries they received may have caused their death."

"Oh shit, this can not get more high profile," Jay said, with a cautious tone. "Does the reservation want this kind of press? Maybe this stays quiet until we find our guy, if he is still around?"

Jimmy shook his head. "Too late, Cousin. Vincent Dibella knows about the tape. He had instructed us to keep his lawyer informed of any findings, but right now, only the three of us know who this may be."

Hal said, "Jimmy, this is in your jurisdiction, and I can't tell Captain Longbow and you how to do your jobs, but I would keep this between us right now. If our boy is still around, the word could get out, and he jumps."

"He is not in town, if he did stay," Jay said. "He is in the mountains away from people. Remember, before the crash he was heading towards Yellowstone. No idea where his mind may have led him... if he has any of it left."

"What do you mean by that, Cousin?"

Hal answered for him. "Jake Michaels has a degenerative brain disease. On top of that, the crash scene indicated he had a head injury. The poor bastard may have no idea who he is." He muttered as he reached into the desk and pulled out the Michaels file. "Mother fucker, now what? Do I call Alex Michaels and tell her it appears her husband may have survived?"

Jay shook his head. "I would wait for a positive ID. That poor family is probably just getting back to normal."

Hal said, "Jay, how many people do you think are running around Wind River with that tattoo? And Jimmy, do we know how tall the attacker is?"

"Based on the deceased's height, we assume he is at least six foot two."

Hal raised his eyebrows and shot a glance at Jay.

Jay nodded without saying a word.

After a few seconds of silence, Jay looked Hal in the eyes and said in a solemn tone, "Let the dead stay buried for now."

Hal had worked with Jay for over twenty years, and knew he would quietly work this without prying eyes. He wouldn't even tell his cousin, Jimmy.

Hal nodded slightly at Jay and winked, as Jimmy looked down at the picture of Jake Michaels on the desk, signaling that he understood his plan.

Hal said, "Okay, I will not put the family through undue hell unless we find him. Jimmy, what are your thoughts?"

"Honestly, Hal, I think I'll keep this between us for now. I'm gonna poke around quietly in my area, and see if anyone noticed any strangers over the past year. It's hard with all the tourists, but as we know, once they leave, any outsiders that stay do stick out. I agree with Jay that he probably would not be living in town, but I would think he would need supplies from time to time."

"Not necessarily, Cousin," Jay said. "He is survival trained. It appears he moved like a ghost right out from under our noses during the search."

Jimmy nodded as if deep in thought. "So, he remembered all his training? Do you think he faked his death?"

Hal shrugged his shoulders. "He may have, but for what reason? He had a beautiful wife and family. Financial reports showed no issues. It appeared he had a dream life. I think he hit his head on the ground and has some sort of amnesia. If he's still alive, he's in survival mode. It could be similar to troops that are found years after the end of a war. They're oblivious to the real world, and think the war is still going on. He could be back in some battle he fought twenty years ago. Who knows?"

Hal just didn't know how to proceed on this one without causing real pain to *someone*. "Well, Jimmy, thanks for the information. Please keep us posted. Maybe our boy is still alive. I know his wife would be happy."

"I will, Hal. For the moment, Jake Michaels is still dead."

The three men shook hands and Jimmy left the office.

Hal and Jay exchanged a look, and Hal said, "Can you fucking believe this?"

Jay shook his head and looked down. "No."

"How the fuck did he disappear under our noses? Like some kind of ghost?"

"Maybe he is," Jay said, calmly.

"Jay Storm Walker, don't you start that Arapaho mumbo jumbo with me. I know you better."

Jay cocked his head and raised his eyebrow. "I can't explain how he did it, can you?"

Hal thought for a few seconds, replaying all the events in his mind. Then it hit him! "Diversion. Fucking diversion. The oldest trick in the book."

"What are you thinking, Hal?"

"He sent the phone downstream to divert us. It gave him time to move in the opposite direction, because he knew we would ping his phone. Everything indicated a missing person. We would have never looked at it differently at first—a loving wife, a grieving family... all a perfect smokescreen to buy time and disappear. Think about it. He had a fishing pole, which would indicate his need to keep his phone in a waterproof case. Again, a diversion, so we wouldn't question finding it in the case. He planned this, Jay. That cocksucker planned the whole thing."

"Do you think his wife is involved?"

"I don't think so, man. You saw her. No one is that good of an actress."

"Okay, Hal, do me a favor and burn a copy of that video. Did Jimmy say exactly where it was found?"

"C.D. Trailhead near Hangman's Bridge. Do you know that area?"

"Yes, that is right at Jim White Feather's place. I have hunted back there. Well, let me see what I can find."

On the drive back from Sulphur Springs, Jimmy thought about the meeting he'd just left. Jay believed that if this were Jake Michaels, he would not need supplies. Jimmy had the utmost respect for his cousin, but disagreed with him on this. Even if he didn't need everyday items, he would have to have basic tools to build a shelter. He would need a gun or archery equipment for food. He could not have carried all of that stuff for over sixty miles.

One of three things must have occurred: he kept moving and never held up in Wind River, he purchased supplies in a town close to where he is staying, or he had help.

He pulled over to look at a topographical map, and circled where they'd found the phone. From there, he drew an imaginary line in each direction. To the east lied campgrounds and lowlands, providing no places to stay hidden. To the west lied backcountry, but no towns nearby for supplies. To the south, which was heavily used by campers, fishermen, and hunters, he would eventually be seen. To the north lied massive backcountry and the town of Dubois. He knew the northern canyon area well. It would be a good area in which to disappear, and he could reach Dubois if he knew the trail into town. Jake Michaels would have had a year to learn that terrain.

Jimmy turned his vehicle around and headed to Dubois.

He parked in front of the Sheriff's Office and got out of his cruiser.

Sheriff Joe Kelly met him. "Hey, Jimmy, what brings you to town?"

"Joe, how have you been? How is that pitching arm of yours?"

"Same as your knee, old friend. We were close to making it, weren't we?"

"We sure were, man. How are Jane and the kids?"

"Everyone is good. Jane is working with Dakota now as her paralegal. Nice to see Dakota back in town, isn't it?"

"Sure is. I wish I could spend more time with her, but our shifts don't line up."

"You should stop by and see her and Jane while you're here."

Jimmy nodded. "That's a good idea. I think I'll do that when I get done here."

"Speaking of which... what brings you into town? Obviously, you're on the clock."

"Nothing pressing, just doing some follow-up on a drifter that caused a little ruckus over at Hangman's campground. When I questioned him, he said he was heading to Yellowstone. I figured he would have passed through here. Have you seen anyone out of the ordinary? I know it's tough with all the tourists. The last I saw him, he was wearing a western print poncho, and has long dark hair—white guy that stands about your height."

"Only thing out of the ordinary has been this guy they call the 'Wolf Man.'"

"The Wolf Man?"

"Yeah, some guy that comes down from the mountain. He has a pet wolf, most likely a hybrid. He comes into town every so often and visits William Black Feather when he's here. He walks around town, buys a few things, and heads up the butte. He grabs his wolf and goes out of sight. He minds his own business, so we haven't questioned him. We figure he's camping for the summer up there. He kind of fits your description, but this guy has salt and pepper hair, not dark."

Jimmy reflexively glanced up at the butte. "Hmmm, when was the last time he was in town?"

"Yesterday, actually. Should we talk to this guy next time we see him?"

"No, Joe, it may not even be my guy. If this guy minds his own business, let him go. My guy is traveling alone, no wolf."

"What do you want with the guy you're following up on?"

"Some campgrounds at Hangman's Bridge got robbed after I let him go. I want to question him about it." Jimmy smiled. "Well, Joe, I'm going to swing over to talk with William, just to make sure. Nice seeing you again, old friend."

"Yeah, Jimmy, and stop by to say hello to Jane if you have a chance."

"I will, man." The two men shook hands and parted ways.

A couple minutes later, Jimmy walked into William's shop.

"Jimmy Red Cloud, how are you, son?" William walked from behind his counter to shake Jimmy's hand.

"I'm good, sir, and how have you been?"

"Bored on Friday nights, since you stopped playing football."

"I hear that a lot. Hopefully, our team does better this year. It has been a while since we had a good team."

"Oh, these kids do not want to play sports anymore. They want to get high and play video games. It is a shame. Our ancestors weep for the future of our people."

Jimmy nodded. "It is sad."

"So, what brings you in here today?"

"What can you tell me about this man they call the 'Wolf Man'?"

William chuckled. "Oh, how this small town lets their imagination run wild. He comes in every six weeks or so. He sells me some of the nicest walking sticks I have seen. They are knobbled pine. They sell as soon as I get them. He was here yesterday, and today I have none left. He is well spoken, very polite, but I have not had much conversation with him. We do business, and he leaves. I cannot tell you much more."

"Has he told you his name?"

"Yes, of course. It is John Jacobs, a very nice man, Jimmy. Is he in trouble?"

"No, sir, he's not who I'm looking for. I just wanted to make sure. I see you have customers, so I'll let you go. See you this fall at the games?"

"Yes, you will. Are you coaching this year?"

"Yes, sir, I am."

"Good, these boys need someone like you in their lives. You are a good man, Jimmy Red Cloud. Nice seeing you again."

Jimmy smiled, shook William's hand, and left the shop.

He sat in his cruiser and called Sulphur Springs Police Department. "Hal, it's Jimmy. Is my cousin nearby?"

"Yeah, he just walked by. What's up?"

"Can you grab him, please? I want to update both of you on a lead."

"One second, Jimmy. Let me put you on hold." A couple of seconds passed, and he heard, "Okay, we're both here. What's up?"

"I'm in Dubois, just kicking the can around. It appears there's a man that kind of fits Jake Michael's description." He continued to tell them the information he had, and responded to a volley of questions.

Hal took it all in, and said, "Jimmy, let's meet Friday morning in Sulphur Springs at first light. That will give me two days to coordinate everything. I'll talk with Captain Daniels at the Dubois Sheriff's Department and take care of the jurisdiction issues. He's a good friend, and I'm sure he'll oblige us. Brief your captain and get his blessing. I know that won't be an issue. Oh, and good work, Jimmy."

Jimmy Red Cloud thanked him and hung up.

Hal looked at Jay. "He's a good cop."

"He has good genetics," Jay said, smiling.

"Well, what do you think? A fucking wolf? Could this be our guy?"

"Honestly, Hal, nothing about this case surprises me now. I guess we will find out soon."

CHAPTER 28
THE SPIRITS WILL DECIDE

Dakota had cleared her schedule for the remainder of the week after seeing Jake yesterday, which had been too much for her, causing her to lie sobbing on her office floor. She'd decided to ignore Jake's letter.

Now, it was first light. She could be at the cabin by noon.

Neiwoo saw her come downstairs. "Lomasi, how are you feeling?"

"I feel better, Neiwoo. I must have eaten something that didn't agree with me yesterday."

"Why are you up so early, dear?"

"I have a clear schedule, so I decided to get away and clear my head. It's been a while since I was at the Sacred Falls and the Red Canyon. I'm going to spend a few days camping while we have this beautiful weather. It won't be long before the White Owl returns."

Jim was reading the newspaper, and overheard the conversation, but he didn't pull it down as the two women talked. He knew Jake had been coming into town, and had asked Dakota how she felt after his first visit. Dakota has said she was okay, and that although she missed spending time with Jake, she understood that she had a future to worry about. She had added that Chris was a good guy.

Jim saw right through her, though, and he knew where she was really going. He hoped Jake would abide by their agreement and turn her away.

He peeked out over the paper. "Lomasi, do not forget your bear spray and gun. Red Canyon has a good amount of grizzlies. You know they have their cubs with them. The males are aggressive to mate right now."

"I have both, Woo Woo. I'll camp on the canyon rim where I have a good view."

She kissed her grandparents and left for the cabin.

Her mind raced the entire trip. She hoped she could find Jake's new camp, and prayed that when she did find him, he wouldn't stand by his words in the letter. She'd share what the Spirits had shown her—her visions were the opposite of Jake's. She would let the Spirits decide the outcome of this visit.

She neared the clearing at the cabin and saw a small wisp of smoke coming from the wood stove stack. She dismounted her horse and drew her gun.

Jake moved from the cabin. Is it possible someone else has taken it over? Or did Jake move back here?

She crept slowly towards the front porch. Her questions were answered by Jake's ax, leaned up against the hitching post, and his poncho draped over it. Her heart raced at the thought of opening the door and reuniting with him. She swung the cabin door open slowly, and walked inside.

Nobody home, but she saw Jake's fishing pole and rifle were both missing from the hooks next to the door, meaning he must be down at the falls fishing, or out hunting.

She walked back outside and headed towards the waterfall.

As she got close, she saw Jake wading in the pool, and Honi playing in the shallow water. Her heart beat quickly, pounding like a drum in her head. She stopped at the wood line to stay hidden, and took a deep breath to calm herself, but a million thoughts raced through her mind.

She stepped out from the cover of the trees and walked towards the stream.

Honi's ears perked up and he lifted his nose into the wind, then let out a small whine and started wagging his tail.

Jake turned to look at him, saw Dakota approaching, and froze.

She walked towards him while slipping off her clothes. Their eyes did not leave each other's, right to the moment they stood inches apart. Dakota pushed him gently back into the deeper water, and softly ran her hand down his face, and her eyes filled with tears. She wrapped her arms around his shoulders and her legs around his waist. She was deep enough in the pool to float gently. They kissed slowly at first, then more deeply.

Jake felt his excitement grow until his dick pressed against her stomach. She clearly felt it too, and looked into his eyes while positioning herself where he would enter her.

"Dakota, no, I can't."

She pressed her fingers to his lips. "Shhhhh."

Jake could feel her start to slide down on him. She was tight, and he couldn't resist at this point. When he felt resistance, he stopped and looked at her, realizing the gift she offered him.

"Dakota, no, I can't do that."

She ignored him and pulled him deeper inside her, let out a small moan, and arched backward.

He looked down at her body. Her every muscle tensed, and the veins on her arms looked ready to burst from her skin as she gripped his shoulders. A small stream of blood rose to the surface of the water, and he cupped her ass and drove himself deeper inside her. She dug her nails into his back and pulled herself tightly to him.

Dakota looked at the waterfall behind Jake, and to the sky. It had darkened quickly, and loud clasps of thunder erupted in the distance as lightning danced on the horizon. At that split second, she realized they had tempted the Spirits. The Thunderbird was angry.

She looked back at the waterfall and saw an image in it—the Lady of the water. The Spirit smiled even as the thunder and lightning moved closer and louder.

She rode him quicker, harder, deeper, her body tensing as waves of pleasure flooded her special gift. Exhausted, she paused for a second, then thrust her hips against him. She would not stop until she satisfied him. The storm grew more violent and angry as he drove his cock deeper and harder inside her, as if mocking the storm.

He grabbed the small of her back and tensed, breathing rapidly, and thrust himself forcefully several more times. Then he let out a long breath and his body relaxed.

They kissed softly at the end.

"Should we get out of the water before we get electrocuted?" He said, smiling.

"Look behind you."

Jake turned, then looked back at her and smiled. The sky had cleared, and rays of sunshine peeked through the remaining black clouds as they walked hand in hand from the water.

Honi ran to Dakota, and she bent down to greet him. The happy wolf licked her face.

She gave him a big hug. "I missed you too, Honi."

The couple spent the rest of the afternoon catching up. Jake showed her his second camp at the old mine, and they harvested some early bounties from the garden. Each of them purposely avoided any serious conversation. Today, they wanted the magic at the waterfall to continue. Though they would need to discuss the complications their reunion and passion had set in motion, this afternoon, they chose to avoid the inevitable... for a little while.

That night, they sat in the hot spring and enjoyed the crystal-clear evening as the stars shined brightly overhead. Dakota pointed out formations Jake taught her the first time they'd come here. She sat next to him with her head resting on his shoulder, her hand lying across his thigh, and the movement of the water caused the head of his dick to bounce off the back of her hand.

"Hey," she said with a wicked smile. "It feels like he's trying to get my attention." She took him in her hand and began stroking, then stood up, turned her back to him, and sat back down, straddling him as she guided him into her.

After they finished, she sat next to him. He was quiet.

"What's wrong, my warrior, did you not enjoy that?"

Jake kissed her cheek. "Of course, I did. I just feel like we're tempting fate and the visions I've seen."

"Your letter, and what the Spirits showed you, broke my heart. But I've also had visions, and the Spirits showed me something different."

She told him about her visions at the Sacred Falls before the night of the attack—how a strong warrior would come to her. She told him about seeing the Spirit of the Water while they made love at the waterfall, and how the Thunderbird was angry and conjured up the thunderstorm while she offered him her special gift, but how the Lady of the Water smiled.

"Jake, let the Spirits work this out. We *were not* brought together under such dire circumstances for nothing. *You* are meant to be here. *We* are meant to be here."

"I agree with you, but as I told you in the letter, I'm paying for sins of my past life. I don't know if my punishment is over. I wish I could revisit the Spirit World."

"Great Grandfather has never given me any more of the medicine. He said the last time I saw him that you had seen enough. Speaking of medicine, how are you feeling?"

"I'm good. I haven't had a spell in months. I'm losing memories of my past life, but current events are sharp. I try to recall things from then by looking at pictures, but it's becoming blurry. Sometimes I can't remember details about Alexi or the kids. Fortunately, I have them written down."

Dakota paused, stepped from the spring, and reached down into her backpack.

"More glow sticks?" he joked.

"No, silly, not tonight. I brought updates from Facebook for you. The kids are doing good. Alexi has posted pictures of her with the gentleman from the Christmas party. They appear to be spending time together."

He stared at Alexi's pictures and took a deep breath. "That's great. It's what I planned. I wish I could find more emotions, but details of that life are fleeing me. I feel guilty, but at the same time, I cherish my days with you. In the beginning, I had this tug of war going on inside me. My past life was vivid, but meeting you that night felt predestined, it felt right, despite the heinous events. I was *supposed* to be there, but I struggle everyday with my choice to leave Alexi. The last thing I want to do is burden another woman with this disease, especially one who is so young and with a bright future ahead of her."

"Jake, that is *my* choice. Besides, I'm not that young. I just turned 27. You're 49. You have years ahead of you. I believe you've been misdiagnosed. At least, I will take that chance."

"Dakota, say you're right. Obviously, Samuel's medicine is helping me stay sharp currently, but.... Will I one day forget you? How can I provide for you? What kind of life can we have hiding in the mountains?"

She smiled and leaned close to him. "Look around you. Is there anything else we need? One day, all of this will be mine. The practice will be mine. We'll never want for anything, financially. Eventually, we'll be able to get you to another doctor and get a second opinion. I'm an attorney. I can handle the legal ramifications of Jake Michaels coming back into the world. I've looked into the laws regarding Absentia. Trust in the Spirits. I do. They've given us each other."

CHAPTER 29
THUNDERBIRD

"Good morning, Dakota. I thought you were taking a long weekend?"

"Good morning, Sally. A couple of days off rejuvenated me, so I figured I'd get ahead of next week's schedule."

"Well, you look better. I was worried about you Wednesday. You looked worn out."

"Thank you, but nothing a few days in the mountains couldn't heal."

Dakota walked into her office, sat down at her desk, and looked at the file folders in front of her. She smiled and opened the first folder.

Her attitude had changed. She had a new fervor for her work. She had a means to an end now, and a clear goal: work hard, and eventually get Jake off the mountain and back into society by her side.

Jake walked out onto the cabin porch and looked up at the sun, allowing it to warm his face. He took a deep breath and smiled. The last two days with Dakota had been great, and her enthusiasm had breathed new life into him. Eventually, his guilt would pass, as memories of his old life faded, as time — and his disease — healed those wounds.

He cocked his head as if trying to listen to something.

A Police Search and Rescue Chopper flew overhead at a low level. It banked left and headed away towards the canyon.

Must be a missing person.

"Well, Honi, let's go check the trap lines."

Jay and Jimmy moved quickly towards the cabin, but stopped several hundred yards from the open field. They discussed their plans one last time, and separated.

Jay signaled Jimmy to move into position. Now they would wait for Jake to return.

Hal and the chopper sat two miles from the cabin waiting for direction to move in.

"Hal, we are in position. Over," Jimmy whispered into his radio.

"10 4. Be careful. We've seen what he's capable of. Over."

Jimmy and Jay double-clicked their mics.

Jake and Honi finished checking the trap lines, and stopped to cool off at the waterfall.

"Well, boy, no signs of the chopper for a couple of hours. Let's go eat."

Honi stopped and put his nose into the wind, and his tail fell between his legs.

"Honi, what is it, boy? What do you smell? It's okay, boy, come."

Honi stood still, refusing to move.

Jake shook his head and kept walking, knowing Honi would catch up to him.

He walked onto the front porch, looked back to see Honi cautiously moving forward, and opened the cabin door.

"Jake Michaels," a voice startled him from the corner.

He looked over and saw the police officer standing with his gun drawn. He put his hands up slowly and lowered his head—no need to deny who he was, or run, as the cabin was loaded with evidence. There was also proof of Dakota being here, if they dig deep enough, and he needed to protect her. He'd get them away from the cabin as quickly as possible.

Jimmy handcuffed Jake and read him his rights. He looked at the tattoo on his arm and advised him of the assault charges he was suspected of, then walked him out the door.

Jay came from the side of the cabin, and Jimmy introduced himself and Jay to Jake Michaels.

The three looked at the edge of the opening, where a wolf snarled and stood in attack mode.

"Honi, *no*," Jake said. "It's okay, boy. It's okay. Stay."

The wolf—Honi—reluctantly listened. He stood still amd lowered his snarling lips, though he still growled.

The sky turned black overhead, and the winds began to howl.

"Can I say goodbye to Honi?" Jake said, as tears filled his eyes. "He doesn't like storms. I want to bring him into the cabin."

Jay and Jimmy looked at each other and nodded.

"Please do nothing stupid, Mr. Michaels," Jimmy said. "We want no one hurt."

Jake nodded his head and walked to Honi. He bent down and nuzzled his face against the scared wolf's. "It will be okay, boy. Come, let's get you in the cabin."

Jake and Honi walked towards the cabin. As they passed Jimmy, Honi moved against the left side of Jake's legs, between Jake and Jimmy. When they moved past Jay standing on the opposite side, Honi moved to Jake's right side, again guarding him.

Jimmy and Jay watched this display, looked at each other, and each raised their eyebrows.

"Hal, suspect in custody. Move in. Over."

"Jimmy, we can't take off in this storm. Over."

"10 4. We can wait. Over."

"Negative. Radar has this thing blowing up. We may be here for a while. This was not forecasted. Over."

Jay looked up at the sky and shook his head. "The Thunderbird has been angered, Jimmy."

Jimmy looked at Jay and then up at the sky. "Hal, we can walk the suspect out. I know the trail. Over."

"10 4. We'll join you in town as soon as we can fly. Over."

Jimmy sighed and said, "Well, looks like we are walking. Mr. Michaels, please go into the cabin and get the proper gear for the walk. Jay and I will have guns drawn on you and the wolf. Again, please do nothing stupid, and no one will get hurt."

Jake said nothing as he gathered his shoes, socks, and a warmer shirt. The wolf sat in the corner, whining the whole time. Jake walked over to him, bent down, and whispered something to him. The wolf's ears perked up briefly, and he wagged his tail a couple of times.

Jake exited the cabin, and Jay watched as Jimmy helped the handcuffed prisoner put on his shoes and shirt. Jake grabbed his poncho from the hitching post as they left.

The trio had hiked about a hundred yards when the storm erupted.

Jay looked up at the black sky and sighed. Daylight had disappeared, and lightning danced from cloud to cloud and crashed to the ground, while thunder exploded around them. "We are on Sacred Grounds, Jimmy. The Thunderbird grows angrier."

Jimmy did not respond, and kept pushing forward.

Jay watched the darkness in the forest light up with the flashes of lightning. In those brief seconds, he could see the ancient ones lined up along the trail. They stood motionless with their heads lowered. Jay shook his head again.

The ancient ones are saddened. Something is not right.

Jake stopped for a second and looked back at Jimmy. "Officer, how did you know I was there?" A movement on the trail behind Jimmy caught Jake's attention.

It was Honi. Despite his fear of the storm, he followed Jake.

"Mr. Michaels, we will explain everything when we get to the station," Jimmy answered.

"Off the case, how did you train the Honi?" Jay said.

"I found him when he was a puppy. A storm like this caused a fire and killed his mother. He was stranded on a rock above the burning ground, and I rescued him. He's very intelligent. It was no different from raising a dog."

"Do you know he is following us?"

Jake looked at Jay and smiled. "You are very observant. Yes, I know."

Jake went over the arrest in his mind. The only way they would know he was at the cabin was if somebody had tipped them off. How did they know about the events of that night? How did they connect Jake and the Dibella boys? Only four people knew the truth, and none would expose Dakota like this. He was baffled.

The three men got closer to town. As they left the Sacred Grounds, the storm subsided.

Dakota looked out of her office, puzzled to see the girls had walked out onto the street. She opened the door and walked into the lobby. "Jenny, why is everyone going outside?"

Jenny yelled back as she rushed outside. "The police arrested the Wolf Man. They're bringing him down the butte now. Come, Dakota, let's watch."

Dakota felt her heart sink, and a rush of anxiety paralyzed her for a moment. She wobbled to a corner, bracing herself to regain composure. She took several deep breaths, feeling as though she would pass out... or at least throw up. Her knees shook, but she made it back to her office and into her bathroom, where she bent over the toilet... just in case.

She stood up, regained her composure, dried her eyes at the sink, and looked in the mirror. "Jake Michaels has rejoined the living. Are you ready, Dakota?"

She controlled her nerves, as she had done hundreds of time before walking on fitness stages, opened the door to her office, and walked with confidence onto the street. "Game time," she whispered.

She watched as they put Jake into the Sheriff's cruiser, and as the car passed by them.

Jake kept his head down.

She then saw many from the crowd pointing up at the butte. Honi was standing there.

She took a deep breath, keeping her cool, but the scene was heartbreaking. Honi was loyal to Jake, and he would stay on the hill waiting for him—morning, noon, and night. She worried Honi would perish up there.

I'll take care of everything, but one step at a time. First, I need to meet with Jake. Whatever the reason they arrested him, he'll need a lawyer. Then I'll get to Honi.

CHAPTER 30
RECKONING

Dakota walked into the Sheriff's office. The room buzzed with activity and faces she did not recognize. Officer Wade greeted her. "Dakota, how are you?"

"I'm great, Bill. What's all the commotion about? Why are officers from Sulphur Springs and Tribal here?"

"The Wolf Man, Dakota. It appears there's some confusion what jurisdiction has precedence."

Dakota played dumb. "Hmmm, what is he charged with? Has he lawyered up?"

"You know I can't talk about the charges until they're formal. But no, he doesn't have a lawyer. He's refused to talk until he has one. This may get some press. Maybe you should take his case."

Dakota lowered her voice. "Why press, Bill, is he famous or something?"

Bill looked around and leaned into Dakota. "I heard he's a missing person, presumed dead. That's why Sulphur Springs is here. I've said enough. See you at the gym tonight?"

"You bet, Bill. I'll be there. Thanks for the info." Dakota winked as she walked away.

She saw Jimmy across the room. "Jimmy," she yelled, waving her hand above the crowd.

Jimmy stopped and smiled, then motioned her over. "Hey, Dakota, how are you?"

"I'm good. This place is crazy over this Wolf Man guy, huh?"

"It is. We're trying to talk with him, but he refuses until he has a lawyer."

"Well, I'm a lawyer, and I'm here. Can I review his case before I interview him?"

"Short and sweet, Dakota, we arrested him on suspicion of assault and possibly manslaughter charges, on the Dibella boys, who died last year in that car accident. You remember that, correct?"

"Of course, it was all over the news for weeks."

"Now, there is a twist. It appears he's a missing person from North Carolina, declared dead last year. He has not formally admitted to it, but I believe after he has representation, he will. He's been very nice so far, but will not discuss anything legal."

"Well, Jimmy, *you have* piqued my interest. Give me a couple of minutes with him, and hopefully, he'll be represented."

"How can any man resist you, especially one that's been living in the mountains for over a year with a wolf?"

She smiled and punched him in the shoulder. "Funny, Jimmy Red Cloud. Lead me to him, please."

Jimmy opened the door to a secure room and led Dakota in.

"I'm Dakota Reynolds, an attorney." She reached her hand out.

Jake reached out his handcuffed hands to shake hers. "Pleased to meet you."

She turned back. "Thank you, Jimmy. I'll be out in a few minutes."

Jake looked at her, exhaling forcefully through his lips. "Ms. Reynolds, is it safe to talk in here?"

She took a deep breath, fighting back a tear. "Yes."

"They're charging me with assault on the Dibella boys. I have no idea how they know. They found me at the cabin. How did they know I was there?"

"I don't know. They will not share evidence with me until I agree to represent you. Of course, I will agree to it. I'll have more answers after I tell them I accepted the case."

"Honi followed me. He's probably on the butte. That's where he waits when I'm in town. I worry people will mess with him, or even shoot him."

"He is. I saw him up there. I'll figure something out. Let me look at the charges. Maybe I can get bail set. I'll be back as soon as I speak with the police."

"They know who I am, but I haven't admitted to it yet. What should I do?"

She didn't hesitate. "Bring Jake Michaels back to life. It's only a matter of time before they confirm it. I'll let them know when I meet with them. I'm not concerned about any charges stemming from an Absentia case. My concern is the assault."

She reached into her briefcase and slid several pieces of paper across the desk.

"These are attorney-client agreements. Sign them at the X, and we'll get started. I'm eager to see their evidence"

He quickly signed and passed the papers back to her.

"I'll be back. Don't leave." She smiled and winked.

Jake chuckled.

Dakota walked into a conference room, where Hal, Jimmy, Jay, Captain Longbow, Sheriff Miller, and Joe Ross from the DA's office in Fort Washakie, all waited.

"Dakota, are you taking the case?" Jimmy said.

She handed the signed agreement to Joe Ross. "Yes, I am."

Joe looked at the signature. "He signed as Jake Michaels."

All the men looked at each other and shook their heads.

"As we figured, I cannot wait to speak with him. I want to know *why*? His family was beautiful," Hal said.

Dakota knew this case would take her on an emotional roller coaster, and that the family would be notified and rush to Jake. She had to find the strength to hide her feelings.

"Can I see the charges against my client, Joe?"

"Of course, Dakota," Joe said, handing her a file.

She sat down at the conference table and read through each charge. "Gentlemen, I assume since the most serious charge of assault happened on the reservation, Tribal Law will take precedence?"

"Normally yes, Dakota, but if the charges push towards Manslaughter or Assault with a Deadly Weapon, the Feds will be called in," Joe answered.

"I see the police report mentions a video tape as the basis for identification of my client, and subsequent charges. I'll need to see that tape. I'll also need to see the coroner's report on each of the deceased victims. It's a big jump from Assault to Manslaughter, especially considering those men were killed in a vehicle accident, miles from the location of the alleged assault."

"I have no issues sharing this evidence with her, gentlemen," Joe directed the officers.

Jimmy walked over to Dakota, sat down, and pulled out the recovered phone. "Dakota, this is graphic. I just want to warn you."

She nodded, and Jimmy started the tape. She heard herself in the background, reliving the horror of that night, as she had done a thousand times, but it didn't move her one bit—she was callous to it now. She *was* thankful that the video didn't identify *her*, but it did put Jake at the scene.

She took a shallow breath. "Do we know who the girl is?"

Jimmy shook his head. "No idea, Dakota. No one has ever come forward, but would any woman do so, if they were having sex with three guys and knowingly being filmed? From listening to her, she was more than willing to have a fourth guy join in."

"How does this film prove the attacker is my client?"

Hal said, "Look at the picture of the tattoo in the police file. We isolated it from the video. It matches the one on your client's arm."

"There could be a million tattoos like this. That's a reach, gentlemen."

"Dakota, that tattoo is limited to a group of Special Forces that served in Somalia. Most of the group were killed in an ambush. Only twenty-two survived. Jake Michaels is one. We ran searches on the remaining twenty-one. Nine of them are amputees. The video shows all body parts are intact on the suspect. Six have passed away. The remaining nine do not fit the stature of the suspect. That's Jake Michaels," Jimmy said.

"Joe, can I get a copy of that tape, please? Also, of any other evidence the DA will share."

"Of course, Dakota, and by the way, the Dibellas are flying in their attorney. We would have liked to keep this low profile and avoid a media circus, but that probably isn't going to happen. The guy is a shmuck and loves the limelight. When he gets wind your client has risen from the grave, he'll alert the press. Be prepared."

Dakota took a deep breath and exhaled forcefully. "Great. Gentlemen, thank you for your time. When will arraignment be?"

"On Monday," Joe said.

Dakota rejoined Jake.

She sat silently at the table for a few moments, her eyes fixed on the table as she tapped her pen on a pad. She looked up at the ceiling, sniffling, and her eyes welled up. "They have a video."

"A video? What kind of fucking video? I destroyed the recorder."

Dakota's phone rang. "Yes, Grandfather, I'm with him now. I have taken the case. Yes, sir, I will fill you in when I get back to the office. It's getting late. I have a ton of paperwork to get done. I'll stay in town tonight, so don't worry that I'm not home. I love you, too."

"Grandfather is going to assist me on this."

"Good, now what kind of video, Dakota?"

"It was shot by one of the Dibellas on his cell phone. It does not show the full attack. It's from the time you approached until you hit that piece of shit across the face. It's very damning. You can hear me in the background asking to get fucked. It shows you in what looks like an unprovoked attack. They isolated your tattoo from the film. I didn't know how rare that skull is, but they ran a background check on the small group of you that have that tattoo. It's almost beyond a shadow of a doubt you're the person in the video."

Jake looked down at the ground. "Is there any way that they can isolate you in the video."

"No, the audio is faint. There's only a brief side view of me. My hair hides my face."

Jake shook his head. "I threw that phone into the river. It's over a year. How did it survive the fall and the water for that long?"

"I don't know, Jake. It was in a protective case. Maybe it landed in mud or on a bed of moss. Honestly, I don't know, but the fact is they have it, and I need to find a defense for you." She paused and took another deep breath. "Vincent Dibella is sending his attorney out here. The DA believes this will turn into a media circus. The fact that you've shown up alive, after a year of being presumed dead, will have the press all over this. I guess we're going to be famous for a while."

"That means Alexi and my family will be notified. How do I face them? How do I explain this? How do I interact with them? That part of my life is fading away. I have to look at pictures and notes to constantly keep details of each of them fresh in my mind."

She lowered her brow. "Jake, you *don't* remember them. You *don't* remember the attack. I'll get your medical records, and this will be our defense. It's the defense I was going to use one day to dismiss any charges from your absentia. Do you have your medicine?"

"No."

"Good, you need to regress. You need to look like the disease has ravaged your memory."

"We can't do that, Dakota. I have no idea how not taking it will affect me. I've already lost my grip on one life. I don't want to lose my grip on another."

"We have no choice. There will be psych and medical evaluations. You'll be questioned over and over. I'm sure they'll ask to put you on the stand, and millions of people could see your testimony, if the press covers this. They'll scrutinize every word. There's no way you or anyone could keep up an act through that."

"What happens if I forget *us*? What happens if I forget Honi? The two of you is what gave me the will to live."

"I don't know. We'll figure that out if it happens. Right now, we need to get these charges dropped."

Jake crossed his arms and sat back in his chair. "What's next?"

"They'll charge you on Monday, formally, and I'll ask for bail. I doubt they'll grant it, given the fact you have the skill set to disappear."

He shook his head and lowered his eyes. "Maybe I should have."

She reached across the table to touch his arm. "It's getting late. I need to get to my office and start a bunch of paperwork. I'll see you in the morning."

Dakota left the room. She informed the officer standing guard outside that she was done for the evening.

The officers in the conference room continued discussing the case.

Chief Long Bow stood up. "Well, gentlemen, it's getting late. I want to thank each of you for a job well done."

"I guess I need to call Alex Michaels," Hal said. "I don't even know how the *fuck* to start this conversation."

Jay laughed and said, "That is why they pay you the big bucks, Hal."

Hal shook his head. "Eight months from retirement, and now this."

The group exited the room and walked outside to their respective cars.

The silence of the night was broken by a mournful howl, long and echoing of distress. They all looked in the direction of the noise, which came from the butte.

Jay pulled out his binoculars. In the moonlight, he could see Honi standing on the edge of the rocks. The howl was unlike anything they'd ever heard.

Jay put his binoculars down slowly. "The Spirits cry in his howl. There is a firestorm coming to Wind River."

Jake sat in his cell listening to Honi. The wolf was scared, having never been seperated from Jake since the day they found each other. Jake's heart broke with each howl, and tears streamed down his face.

The Spirits did not show me this.

Dakota heard the mournful cries when she walked outside. She looked up at the butte, and her heart sank with each howl. She needed to find a way to care for Honi without raising suspicion, because otherwise, he would stay on the butte until he died. He had no idea how to hunt or care for himself in the wild.

Back at her office, she walked in and collapsed in her chair.

My visions did not show me this. Something has thrown my Destiny off course.

CHAPTER 31
A THIN THREAD

Alexi's phone rang.

"Who could that be, Alex?" Sam said.

She shrugged. "I don't know. It's ten o'clock. I hope everything is okay with the kids."

She jumped up from the couch and rushed into the office, where her phone was charging. Her hands started to shake when she saw the number.

"This is Alex."

"Alex, Hal Jones, sorry for calling you so late."

"No problem, Hal. What's going on? Did you recover Jake's body?"

"Alex, there is no body. I'm not sure how to say this." He paused. "Jake is alive. We've found him."

Her knees buckled and she fell into the office chair. Her immediate silence gave way to loud sobs.

"Alex, are you there?" Hal said. "Are you okay?"

Sam came into the office. "Alex, what is it?"

She sniffled, ignoring Sam for the moment as she struggled to get the words out. "Where is he, Hal?"

"He's in Dubois right now. We're holding him at the Sheriff's Department?"

"How is he, Hal? Does he know who he is?"

"Yes, Alex, he does. Something else you need to know. He's being charged with assault stemming from an attack shortly after he disappeared."

"Assault? What kind of assault?"

"Alex, he's being formally arraigned on Monday. I think it's best if you come out here and meet with his attorney. I cannot go into detail with you at this point."

"I understand. I'll be on the first flight in the morning."

She cut off the call and looked up at Sam. "Jake is alive."

He lowered his head, doing his best to mask his emotions, and looked up. "That's great, Alex. I'm happy for you and the kids."

She saw right through him and ran her hand over his cheek. "Hey, I want you with me."

He paused, and then shook his head. "No, I think this is something the kids and you need to do as a family. I need to go now. You need to call the kids, make flight arrangements, and get packed. Call me when you land out west so I know you made it safely."

He kissed her and left without another word.

She stood silent and watched him go through the front door, not knowing what to say.

She contacted each of the kids, and they all rushed to book morning flights. That done, she leaned back in Jakes's chair.

What will I find in Dubois? How far has the disease progressed? Will he remember me and the kids? What kind of assault was he involved in?

A million questions raced through her mind, accompanied by the rush of a million emotions.

She thought about how this would affect Sam. He'd been there for her, and she'd moved on with her life... without Jake.

Things instantly had gotten *very* complicated.

She looked at their wedding picture on the bookcase and thought about what Jake had told her when they were young: if he died before her, he would never leave her side; she would know he was with her; she would feel him.

Well, Alexi had never felt Jake after he disappeared. She'd held onto that, the finest of threads, and he'd proven he would never lie to her — hadn't lied to her.

CHAPTER 32
QUESTIONS

Dakota walked across the street to the Sheriff's Department to meet with Jake. Hal and Jimmy had already arrived.

"Dakota, good morning. You look like something the cat dragged in," Jimmy joked.

"Thanks, Jimmy, you're such a charmer. It was a long night. I stayed in the office looking at everything. I assume you'll want to interrogate him this morning?"

"If you do not object?" Hal said.

"Of course not. Just give me a couple of minutes to meet with him, please. Is there any coffee around here?"

Hal chuckled. "The best in Dubois! You know cops know how to brew coffee. Hell, there might even be some donuts around."

Hal returned with a cup of coffee for Dakota. "By the way, his family is en route. They should arrive around 2 p.m. today."

She raised her brow. "That should be interesting. Give me a few minutes, guys, and we'll be out."

She entered the safe room and pulled a chair up to the table directly across from Jake. Her eyes danced. "Good morning, I see they've given you some real coffee."

"Yeah, they've been quite nice, actually."

"Well, it's not like you're a mass murderer or something. Today they're going to question you. I'll be in the room. I'm sure Hal and Jay will want to know about your faked death and how you fooled them. How solid do you think your story will be regarding the way you set the scene up?"

"I thought about that. I think we tell the truth and the reason I did it. I know Alexi will be coming, and I don't want to lie to her. It will be hard enough when she realizes I'm forgetting our lives together. I'm sure that, as the medicine wears off, I'll rapidly decline. While I can still tell my story, I want her to know I did this because I loved her."

Dakota paused for a second. "I understand. Now, on the more serious charges, we must find a defense. I watched the video over and over, and there's simply nothing there that would show this was not unprovoked. It's really damning."

"Can we not tell the truth and say they were raping the girl and I stopped it? That the video only captured a brief scene, and the girl was saying what she said because she feared for her life?"

"I don't believe a jury will buy the rape defense. I'm having the police records of the three men pulled. Maybe we get lucky and find a history of sexual assault. Given the power Vincent Dibella has, I would assume we'll find nothing on his *little fucking angels*."

"How about I simply don't remember that night?"

"I thought about that, but if you're going to confess to faking your death and recalling those details, a jury will not believe you can't remember events a few weeks later."

He paused. "It *is* in my medical records that I have spells and have no recollection of what happens during them."

"Too convenient. The DA will rip that apart."

"How much jail time could we be talking about for assault with a deadly weapon?"

"It varies, could be one year to ten years. Since you have no priors, and it's clinically shown you have an illness, I would think it would be on the lower end."

He shook his head and breathed deeply. "Well, it appears I have a real problem."

She reached out and grabbed his hand. "*We* have a real problem. This complicates all my plans to eventually bring you off that mountain and have a life with you."

He nodded and smiled. "It certainly fast-tracked it."

"At mach speed."

"Did you hear Honi last night?"

"I did, and it was terrible. With each howl, my heart broke. I'll figure something out. I'll talk to my grandfather. Maybe we can take him to the ranch."

"Dakota, he will not leave there. It's the last place he saw me. He'll stay there until he dies. I am all he knows."

She looked towards the ceiling as her eyes filled with tears. The enormity of the whole situation was becoming clearer and clearer.

"I'll figure all this out, I promise. The Spirits did not bring us this far to abandon us." She regained her composure. "Are you ready to meet with the officers?"

"Yes, if you are?"

"When you're in there, only answer their questions with short, simple answers. If they ask you something you're uneasy answering, look at me. I'll interject."

"Very good, but what do we say regarding the attack?"

"I'll handle that. You say nothing. My grandfather is on his way, and will be in there with us. We need his experience. We'll come get you as soon as he arrives. I'll brief him on what we've discussed."

He smiled slightly. "See you in a bit, counselor. And hey, you look sexy in business attire."

She rolled her eyes and exited.

Jim entered the police station, and Dakota pulled her Woo Woo aside, briefing him on what Jake and she had discussed.

The guard opened the door to the safe room, and Jim and Dakota sat across from Jake.

Jim looked across the table with a serious glare. "Jake, your journey has taken a difficult turn. The current events can implicate all of us in this room, and Anna, if we are not careful. I have been back to the cabin and cleaned anything up that could connect Dakota and I to you. They will ask permission to search it for evidence—mainly, the walking stick that appears in the video. They will not find it. I am sure Dakota has briefed you on how to answer their questions."

"Yes, sir, she has."

"Very good. Let's go meet with them."

In the conference room were Jimmy, Hal, Joe Kelly, Jay, and the DA Joe Ross. Jim and Dakota exchanged greetings with them and sat down.

"Ladies and gentlemen," Joe Ross said. "Today will be formal questioning to determine what and if charges will be filed on Monday at the arraignment. I would like to start with the lesser of those charges being the absentia issue. That, I will direct to Hal Jones, who conducted the extensive search for Mr. Michaels. Is everyone in agreement?"

Everyone at the table agreed.

"Mr. Michaels," Hal said. "There are only two questions I have: why and how? I spent days with your family. They're beautiful people. What was your reasoning for faking your death?"

Jake swallowed hard and said, "Officer, I loved my wife and family more than any of you can believe possible, given the current events. The answer is complicated, yet simple. I was diagnosed with early onset of Dementia. I *did not* want to put any of them through watching me deteriorate. I didn't want to become a burden to them. I hid my symptoms for a while from them. Unfortunately, I couldn't anymore.

As we sit here today, my memories of them are drifting away. It rips me apart that what I tried to shield them from, they will now witness. I wanted them to remember me as a whole person, not a shell of myself." Tears trickled down his cheeks as he spoke.

The room fell silent.

Dakota gulped deeply trying to maintain her composure.

I cannot give any clues that I have anything but a legal relationship with Jake.

Hal looked at Jake, knowing the honesty in his voice was real. Alex had shared Jake's diagnosis with him during the search. Jake was telling the truth.

"Very well, Mr. Michaels," he said. "I will not burden all of us with the details of how you eluded us. I will ask that you provide a written statement with those details. I will need that for my report. One question I must ask, however: how did you provide the blood at the scene? Our experts were convinced, based on the pattern, that you were injured."

"I had a syringe, Officer. I stuck myself and let the blood squirt naturally."

Hal nodded and laughed. "Very clever, Mr. Michaels. Very clever. And I assume you sent the phone down the river in a floating case as a diversion?"

"Yes, sir, it was. It gave me time to go in the opposite direction."

Hal looked at Jay with an *I-told-you-so* look and smiled. "I have no further questions."

"Mr. Michaels, my name is Joe Ross. I'm with the DA office in Fort Washakie. I'll ask you a few questions about the more serious crime you're a suspect in, Assault with a Deadly Weapon. If your counsel does not object, I would like to proceed."

"No objections, Joe," Dakota said.

"Mr. Michaels, we have a video that appears to show an assault on three men on August 18th of last year. The attacker in the video matches your physical stature. We isolated a frame from that video that matches the tattoo on your right arm. We understand that tattoo is very rare, shared by a select few Special Forces. Our background research shows you were one of the brave men that survived a specific battle in Somalia. That battle led to each of you wearing this tattoo, in honor of your fallen comrades. Our background research also shows you were a model soldier and citizen, with not so much as a speeding ticket. What provoked you to attack these men?"

Jim answered before Jake could respond. "Joe, our client does not deny that is him in the video. However, he maintains he acted in self-defense."

"Self-defense, Jim? There is not a shred of evidence in that video substantiating that."

"We will let the courts decide that, Joe. At this time, we will not answer any more questions pertaining to this charge."

Joe smirked. "Okay, Jim. I do think you need to know we're waiting on a report from the coroner who examined the victims. It's very possible we will escalate the charges to Manslaughter at the arraignment."

"Fucking Manslaughter? On what basis?" Jim's voice escalated.

"Those boys died after the attack. Pending the coroner's report, it may be our position the injuries your client inflicted led to the fatal accident."

Jim laughed and reclined back in his chair. "Well, that is a reach. I guess it will be good for the press... and your political career, Joe."

"Fuck you, Jim," Joe fired back.

"Gentlemen, please, can level heads prevail?" Dakota interjected.

Jim stood up. "We are done here. I expect a copy of the coroner's report before the arraignment."

Jim, Dakota, and Jake left the room.

Joe Ross slammed his briefcase shut. "Gentlemen, I'm done. I will see each of you at the arraignment." He stormed from the room.

Hal looked at the rest of the men. "What was that all about between Jim and Joe?"

Jay said, "They have a past. Jim White Feather will make this case personal. Joe will have his hands full."

━━━━ ❦ ━━━━

Jake's team returned the safe room.

"Well, that escalated quickly. Assault to Manslaughter?" Jake exclaimed.

"They are grasping," Jim said. "I am sure Joe is already getting pressure from Vincent Dibella's attorney. He will want to turn this into a spectacle."

"Grandfather, I haven't seen you lose your cool like that yet alone ever curse."

"Dakota, that was planned. I wanted you to see how quickly Joe Ross can be rattled. He is a terrible lawyer. Money and favors got him his position. As for the curse, more theatrics. Now, the Manslaughter charge puts a twist on this. The FBI will be called in."

Jake sighed. "Jim, do you think they could make a case against me for that?"

"I will want to see the Coroner's report. We will want to retain our own Doctor if they push manslaughter. I have someone if needed."

Jake sighed. "What's next?"

Dakota said, "We need to wait for the arraignment and formal charges. We'll request bail, but it will be denied."

"If I don't get bail, what do we do about Honi?"

Jim shook his head and smiled. "Everything that is going on... and you are concerned about that wolf."

"Jim, that wolf is what kept me going day to day."

"Grandfather," Dakota said. "Do you think the court would allow Jake to introduce us to Honi so we can feed him? Obviously, Honi would have no problems with me going up to him, but we must make it look like we have no prior connection."

"It would be a unique request, but Judge Still Water is listed on the preliminary arraignment schedule. He is an animal lover. He may grant it."

Jake and Dakota looked at each other and smiled.

Jim stood up. "I am done for the day. Jake, I understand your family will be here this afternoon. They will have plenty of questions for you. Do not discuss the assault case with them, please."

"Yes sir. I don't believe their questions will be regarding that."

There was a moment of silence after Jim closed the door behind him.

Jake looked at Dakota, and took her hand. "Will you be able to handle Alexi being here?"

Her look softened. "I've been watching her for over a year on Facebook. I feel like I know her."

"I know, but this is different. I never planned to see her again. I don't know what emotions will take over. I also never planned on falling in love with you."

"Jake, the Spirits will answer all these questions. They will lead us *all* down the right path."

CHAPTER 33
GHOST

"Officer Jones, this is Alex Michaels."

"Hello, Mrs. Michaels, where are you at?"

"We're ten miles from Dubois. Will you be at the police station?"

"Yes, ma'am, I'll stand outside looking for you. What are you driving?"

"A silver Toyota Camry.

"Very good."

"Hal, how is he?"

"Besides looking like a mountain man, he seems fine."

"Okay, see you soon."

Alexi hung up and took a deep breath. "Well, kids, we'll soon find out how Dad is. Hal said he looks like a mountain man but seems to be fine."

When Alex pulled in, Hal walked to her car and greeted them. "Alex, it's nice to see you and your family again. I honestly did not think I ever would."

"Neither did we, Hal."

"Come in. Jake is with his attorney. I will let her know you're here."

"Come in," Dakota answered to the knock at the door.

"Dakota, Mr. Michael's family is here."

"Thank you, Hal. I'll be right out."

After Hal closed the door, Dakota looked at Jake. "Are you ready?"

He blinked slowly and half nodded. "Let me talk with Alexi first, before I meet with the kids."

"All right. I'll get her."

Dakota fought back anxiety as she walked down the hall to the reception area.

Hal was talking to the family, and he made the introductions. "Dakota, this is Mrs. Michaels, John, Robert, and Danielle Michaels."

Dakota reached her hand out to greet each of the Michaels family. "Dakota Reynolds. I'm Jake's attorney. It's nice to meet each of you."

"Ms. Reynolds, it's nice to meet you. When can we see Jake?" Alex said.

"Mrs. Michaels, please call me Dakota. Jake asked that I bring you back first, and then the kids."

"Please, call me Alex."

Dakota nodded, then led Alexi down the hall. She could see why Jake spent his life with her, an attractive woman who carried herself with grace and class.

They reached the door. "Dakota, wait for a second please." Alex looked at the ceiling. Her eyes teared as she took several deep breaths, and her hands shook.

Dakota touched her shoulder. "Alex, are you all right?"

Alex nodded, saying nothing.

"You can go in. After you and the kids meet with Jake, we'll sit down as a group, and I'll explain why I'm representing your husband."

"Thank you, Dakota."

Alex opened the door and walked into the room. Her eyes met Jake's as she sat down across from him.

They were silent, each searching for the right words.

"Hey you," Jake said, smiling.

Tears streamed down her cheeks. "When they told me you were gone, I didn't believe them. As time passed, I realized they might be right. I held on to the slightest thread of hope. I never felt you around me, like we talked about when we were young. You didn't lie to me."

His eyes welled.

"Jake, why did you leave me?"

He wiped his tears and sniffled. "Alexi, I didn't leave you. I left *us*. I *did* lie to you about one thing: my disease was further along than I let you know. I couldn't put you through watching me deteriorate. I would *not* be a burden to you. I wanted you to remember the good life we had, and not leave you with memories of me slowly slipping away — minute by minute, hour by hour, day by day, fading from this world in front of your eyes. I wanted more for you in your older years."

"Jake, that *was not* your decision! I would have taken care of you until you took your last breath on this Earth. I would have cherished every moment we had."

"I know, but I simply *could not* do that to you. I'm sorry for the pain I caused you. I'm sorry that you need to see me now. I grasp at pieces of our life that are being pulled away from me. As each day goes by, I lose more of us, more of you. I don't even remember the details of how we met anymore. I don't remember the kids being born. The worst part about this is that I *know* there's a rich history and a good life behind me, because I'm teased with those memories every second, but they're losing context. It's like looking at a picture and not remembering the reason why you took it."

She paused and reflected on what he said, then reached out and puts her hands over his. "Several months before we went on vacation to Yellowstone, you said something odd to me. I didn't pay much attention, as you always said off-the-wall stuff, but this one stuck with me. We were lifting and talking about a story you saw regarding a baseball coach who was diagnosed with Alzheimer's. You looked at me and said if that ever happened to you, you wanted me to drop you off in the woods and let you crawl away like an old bear, to die with dignity. Do you remember that?"

"Yes, I do."

"Did you start planning to leave me then?"

"No, I started after seeing the pain you were in after the doctor's visits."

The conversation paused.

She stared at him and cracked a small smile. "Well, you do look like an old bear." She could feel the tension in the room ease.

"I have a pet wolf," he said.

"That does not surprise me. Did you name it Kelsey?"

He seemd puzzled. "Kelsey... that's a strange name for a wolf. Is that a name I should recognize?"

She tilted her head and sighed softly. "She was our dog. You loved her."

Jake thought hard for a second, and then lit up a little. "That's right. Now I remember. No, his name is Honi. It's Arapaho for wolf."

Alexi could see Jake had slipped. For him to have forgotten Kelsey... it tore through her heart like a hot razor. Just that small picture of what her life would be with him made her understand why he thought he'd done the right thing. In his mind, she would have been reminding him of things for the rest of his life, and he'd been unable to bear that.

"I know the kids are anxious to see you, as I know you are to see them. Do you want me to get them?"

"Of course, but... please tell them that I may not remember certain things."

"I will. I'll be right back."

Alex left the office, leaned up against the wall, and sunk to the ground. She sobbed quietly so the kids couldn't hear her.

Dakota looked down the hall in her direction, and saw her. She walked over and bent down next to her. "Mrs. Michaels, are you okay?"

"That's a ghost of Jake Michaels," she said between her cries.

CHAPTER 34
PREPARE FOR BATTLE

Alex and the kids sat silently in a conference room after their meetings with Jake, waiting for Dakota to come in and brief them on the legal issues.

"Mom, Dad did not remember surprising me with a car on my sixteenth birthday," Danielle said, fighting back tears.

"He didn't remember my first deer we shot together," Johnny said.

"He forgot about me being in the service, and how proud he was when I graduated Special Forces training," Robert said.

Alex stared down at the table. She heard the pain in her kids' voices, and felt her own pain at the realization that their life with Jake was fading away for him. She was angry with him, but realized why he had done what he did. In her mind, it was selfish, but she knew that in Jake's mind, it was an act of compassion. Throughout their life together, she often failed to understand why he made certain decisions, yet ultimately, most of those decisions had proven to be correct. He could look past current issues and analyze the long-term cause and effect of situations. Still, it didn't erase the pain of this decision and the circumstances it had created.

She didn't know the extent of his legal issues, and anxiously waited for Dakota to explain.

Dakota entered the conference room and sat at the head of the oblong table. "Is everyone all right?" She kept her voice soft and compassionate. "I know that had to be very difficult. I cannot begin to imagine the emotions all of you are going through." She looked at each member of the family.

"Thank you, Ms. Reynolds," Johnny said. "Please tell us what we need to do to get our dad home?"

Those words cut through Dakota's soul, but she had prepared for that question.

"Your dad has several charges pending. Pseudocide, or faking one's death, is inherently not illegal, but any *gain* from faking one's death constitutes fraud. For example, collecting insurance monies, skipping out on taxes or debts, etc, would justify charges. Based on Jake's living arrangements, I would assume he had no financial gain from his actions. Mrs. Michaels, any life insurance benefits you received, you'll most likely be required to pay back. The insurance company will probably investigate you as an accomplice."

"Ms. Reynolds, I never filed on Jake's life insurance. I paid all of his debts off with our savings. I always held out a small hope that he was not dead. I decided until a body was found, I would not accept any monies from his insurance."

Dakota raised her eyebrows. "Well, I can see no criminal charges that can be substantiated by his pseudocide. The police department may pursue civil actions for expenses for the search. I don't know if they will or not. That hasn't been discussed up to this point. We'll see how that plays out."

"What else is he facing?" Robert said.

"I must warn each of you that what we discuss in here needs to be treated with the utmost confidentiality. You cannot discuss anything until formal charges are filed. After that, I urge that you continue to be very guarded on what you discuss." Dakota looked at each member of the family, and they all nodded agreement in turn.

"Jake is most likely going to be charged with Assault with a Deadly Weapon. They may escalate charges to Manslaughter."

"Manslaughter? Did he kill someone?" Alex's voice rose in pitch and anxiety.

"Not directly. He came upon a group of men that were having sex with a woman. He maintains that they were raping her, and he stopped them. Our stance is that he acted in self-defense."

"What did the woman say?" Danielle said.

"She never came forward. The police don't know who she is."

"Well, how do they know it was my dad? Did he beat them to death? I'm confused." Johnny said.

"There's a video on a phone from one of the deceased. It only shows part of the attack. Unfortunately, what it shows is very compelling and benefits the prosecution. The three men he attacked died shortly after in an auto accident. The coroner may conclude the accident resulted from injuries sustained in the attack. What makes this worse is that the deceased are the sons and nephew of Vincent Dibella."

Alex's eyes widened. "As in Dibella Farms?"

"Yes, so you can imagine the coverage this will get. The Dibellas have sent their lead attorney here. They'll pressure the DA into throwing the book at Jake."

"How will you prove self-defense?" Johnny said.

"Your dad suffered a knife wound. He has a scar on his shoulder. Our medical expert will testify it's not an old wound. I'll maintain that the video doesn't show the entire altercation, and that Jake walked into the situation, felt the woman was in danger, and a fight ensued."

"Will that hold up without the woman coming forward? It will be Jake's word against the video. He's the only witness, and he's the one accused. Does he stand a chance? Can we see the video?" Alex rapid-fired the questions.

"Ms. Michaels, not having a witness is difficult. I cannot show the video until it's accepted as evidence and formal proceedings start."

Danielle said, "Can we say my dad simply doesn't remember, and hope for a lesser sentence if things start going against him?"

"The truth is, if the trial lasts a long time, your dad may not remember all the facts of that night. I don't know how the courts would rule on that. I also know he suffers from seizures. I thought about using that as a defense, stating he was not in his right mind at the time of the attack, but that would complicate the self-defense angle. It truly is a tough situation. All of you will understand more clearly once you see the tape."

"Ms. Reynolds, this *does not* sound good for Jake," Alex said.

"My dad will help me with this case. We *will* find something, Alex."

Alex nodded. "I know the arraignment is in two days and you have a lot of work. Have you discussed your fees with Jake? I'll need to know so I can arrange payment."

"Mrs. Michaels, before I knew the whole story, I was taking this case for free. I knew nothing about him or the faked death. All I knew was that he came into town and had a pet wolf, which polarized everyone here. They affectionately called him the Wolf Man. He was becoming something of a folk hero, and people were creating all kinds of stories about his identity. I figured it would be beneficial to my career to represent him. Once I met with him and learned the whole story, I stayed committed to working for free."

"Thank you, Ms. Reynolds, that is very kind of you," Alex said.

"I will request one thing from all of you: please call me Dakota. We'll all be speaking with each other a lot. Can we be less formal?"

The Michaels family all smiled and agreed to Dakota's request, and the meeting ended.

Joe Ross sat in his office preparing for the arraignment.

A voice came over the intercom. "Mr. Ross, Mr. Sellman is here to see you."

"Thank you, Liz, please send him in."

Joe leaned back in his chair and took a deep breath. Howard Sellman was a high-profile attorney, brash and relentless. He'd be a pain in the ass to Joe and the entire DA staff.

The two men made the perfunctory introductions and sat down across the desk from each other.

"Mr. Ross," Sellman said with unabashed arrogance. "As you know, Mr. Dibella has sent me to represent his sons and nephew in this case. I would assume that the DA's office takes no exception to co-counsel?"

"Mr. Sellman, I welcome your assistance in this case. In advance, I have prepared the necessary paperwork for you to sign."

Joe slid a folder across the desk to Sellman.

He glanced at each document and executed them. "Very well, now that the formalities are over, what evidence do you have to share with me?"

Joe handed a file to him along with a video player. "I assume you knew the victims. I warn you the video is a bit disturbing."

"Yes, I've known them since they were born. I'll be fine, I assure you."

As Sellman watched the video, his facial expressions did not change one bit. He reacted as if the Dibella boys were strangers.

His lack of empathy surprised Joe.

"Okay, what do we know about the attacker?" he said.

"He's ex-Special Forces and committed Pseudocide—no priors, a model soldier and citizen his whole life. He has medical evidence of early Dementia. He left his family to spare them the pain of watching him deteriorate."

Sellman shook his head and dropped his pen on his pad. "Fucking great, the jury will love this guy. Who's representing him?"

"A young female attorney from Dubois and her father, Dakota Reynolds and Jim White Feather."

"Oh boy, Native fucking Americans. Let me guess: she's attractive?"

"Yes, very attractive, and a well-known fitness model. She's been on hundreds of magazines."

Sellman took a deep breath. "Well, the jury and the press will love them. I guess this'll be fucking Cowboys versus Indians. We know how that ended. This will not be Little Bighorn for them. I can assure you."

Joe had spent his whole life living alongside American Indians. His best friends were Arapaho and Shoshone. "Mr. Sellman, I grew up here, and I dislike your references. We can work together, but I will not tolerate your racial epithets. Is that clear?"

Sellman paused, and the veins in his temple flared. "I really don't give a shit what you like, but I admire your conviction. You have some fight in you. That's good."

"Shall we move on?" Joe said.

Sellman nodded. "What charges are you bringing against him on Monday?"

"Assault with a Deadly Weapon and possibly Manslaughter. I'm waiting for a statement from our coroner. She texted me about twenty minutes ago and said it would be here within the half hour."

"Mr. Ross, Dr. Sanders to see you," the intercom announced.

"Right on time," Joe said. "Please send her in, Liz, thank you." He stood to welcome Jessica and introduce her to Sellman.

"Mr. Sellman," she said. "Nice see you again."

Joe said, "Jessica, you've met Mr. Sellman?"

"We met briefly after the accident," Selman interjected. "Nice to see you again, Doctor."

"What do you have Jessica?" Joe said.

"I reexamined the wounds in the pictures I took, and matched them with what the tape shows. The size of the marks on the victims appears to coincide with the diameter of the stick he used. Because the bodies suffered much graver injuries, I didn't pay much attention to those marks when I first examined them. Each wound, on its own, would not have been fatal. They would have required medical attention, but recovery would have been full. The blow to the penis of the one victim may have had long-term consequences, but again, not fatal."

"So, Doctor," Sellman said. "You're stating that these wounds did not cause their deaths?"

"Not so fast, Mr. Sellman. I will testify that they were not fatal wounds, *but...* the injury to the driver would have definitely caused a concussion. In the pictures, you can see a large amount of swelling around his right eye. It's very possible that he lost consciousness as the brain swelling continued, or at least visual distortion and depth perception."

Joe said, "Jessica, in your opinion, did those injuries cause the driver to swerve off the road?"

"I would like to re-examine his body to see the extent of brain trauma, but I understand they were cremated. Is that true, Mr. Sellman?"

"Yes, they're dust," Sellman said.

Jessica remembered how indifferent he'd been after the accident. She darted a glance at Joe, who raised his eyebrow.

"In my report," she said, "I stated that the injuries could definitely have contributed to the accident."

"Doctor, please," Sellman barked. "Answer the question with a simple fucking yes or no. Spare us the conjecture."

"Mr. Sellman, without being able to re-examine the body, conjecture is all I have. So I guess you'll have to do your job and get a jury to decide on a *simple fucking yes or no.*" Jessica sarcastically added air quotes at the end. "Gentlemen, if there's nothing else, I have work to do."

"Thank you, Jessica, we have nothing else," Joe said.

Jessica closed the door hard behind her.

Joe looked at Sellman and smirked. "I must say you're a real fucking charmer."

"Charm is for getting laid, not for court battles. Unless she was going to drop to her knees right here and blow me, I could give two shits less if she likes me. We'll hold the Manslaughter charges for the preliminary hearing, not the arraignment. The less time we give Pocahontas and Sitting Bull to prepare, the better we are. I'll examine what you gave me, and see you at the courthouse an hour before the arraignment on Monday."

Sellman closed his briefcase and left Joe's office.

Joe sat down at his desk and shook his head. "What an asshole."

His text alert sounded.

> Jessica: *What a douche bag! Do you have to work with him?*
> Joe: *Unfortunately, yes. I thought you were gonna kick him in the balls. LOL.*

Jessica: *I thought about it. Regarding balls, Mr. DA, why don't you bring yours over tonight? I think we both need some stress relief. [Happy Face Emoji.]*

Joe: *We will be there at 8. [69 Emoji, Wink Emoji.]*

Jim and Dakota sat in the office at the ranch. Jim poured them both a snifter of Jack Daniels.

Dakota settled into the high-back leather chair. "I remember when I was young... I would sit in this chair watching you work. You'd pull book after book from the shelves as you did your research. I visualized one day being in here with you, working on a case together." She smiled as she reminisced.

"Lomasi, I loved it. I would look at the case in front of me and the ugliness of humanity, and then I would look at you. You gave me hope that not all was lost in this world."

"I would ask you a million questions, and not once did you ever ask me to be quiet."

Jim took a sip of his whiskey. "They were simpler times."

"Woo Woo, Jake is in trouble, isn't he? I can't see how we can defend that tape without telling the whole story."

"Dakota, you *cannot* tell the whole story of that night. You must stay distanced from him. His family is here now. Jake Michaels is alive. He needs to return to his life. It is only right. You must concentrate on your future here."

She wanted to argue with her grandfather, to tell him what the Spirits had shown Jake and her, and that she loved Jake. But she knew this was not the time or place. "I know, Woo Woo. Our job is to get Jake out of this. Do you think there is any chance for bail? I can't watch Honi die up there alone."

"No, I do not believe the Judge will grant bail. He is very tough. I do believe he will make some concession for Honi. I know of no precedent, so it will be a first."

"Do we maintain self-defense? Do we use his disease? I just don't know where to go with this."

"We will wait until the arraignment in Superior Court. At this point, we simply sit back and prepare for battle."

CHAPTER 35
ARRAIGNMENT

Dakota and Jim walked into the safe room.

"Good morning, Jake," Jim said.

"Good morning, Jim, Dakota."

Jim smiled. "How are you holding up? I know it must be tough going from the mountain into here."

"Actually, I'm doing better than I thought. Besides hearing Honi crying all night, I'm making it all right. I don't want to spend much more time in here. Hopefully, we can move all this along quickly."

"After arraignment today," Dakota said, "the courts have ten days to hold the preliminary hearing. If the judge decides there is adequate evidence to support the charges, an arraignment in Superior Court will happen within two weeks. From there, it is usually within sixty days to trial."

Jake ran his hands down his face. "That's three months. I can't make it three months in here. Honi can't make it three months on that mountain."

"That is if we are lucky," Jim said. "And the prosecutor does not request waiving a quick trial."

Jake sighed. "We all know I'm innocent. I can't rot away in here. Everything I have done to my family was to avoid being held hostage by a disease. I can't be hostage now to false charges. You two must find a way out of this without implicating Dakota. That, I cannot allow. If it comes down to her life or mine, I will choose hers, just as I chose Alexi's. You must find a way to defend me on the merits of just the evidence."

Jim stared at Jake, hearing his commitment to Dakota, and for the first time, he understood what she meant to him. Jake would sacrifice his freedom for hers. Jim knew now that he must draw on every bit of experience he had to defend Jake.

Dakota turned away from Jake and Woo Woo, her eyes welling despite her resolve not to let that happen.

Jake is every bit the warrior I knew he was. He would give everything of himself for me. I must find a way to free him. I must find a way for us to be together as the Spirits showed. I must find a way to convince the Michaels family that this is where Jake needs to stay.

Woo Woo interrupted her thoughts. "Jake, we will get you out of here. We just need to be patient. Let us see where the prosecution goes with this. Today, I will ask for bail and concessions for Honi. Depending on how the judge acts, we will have some indication of how the rest of this will go. Okay?"

"Okay, Jim, when do we leave?"

"Dakota and I will go over there now. They will take you over fifteen minutes before we start."

"Will they allow my family in there?"

"Yes, it is public."

Jake nodded his head. "Good, see you all soon."

Jim and Dakota entered the back door of the courthouse.

Joe Ross came around the corner and greeted them.

Jim said to him, "I saw on court documents that you have a co-counsel."

"That's correct, Vincent Dibella's attorney Howard Sellman. He'll be here shortly. I'll introduce both of you to him. In fact, here he comes now."

Jim and Dakota looked down the hall and saw Sellman. A tall, silver-haired man, he walked with a confidence that bordered on arrogance.

Joe motioned him over.

"Damn, Joe, I didn't know there was a back way into here. That would have been nice to know. The courtroom is a fucking madhouse. I've never seen so many people at an arraignment. You must not have much excitement out here." Sellman rambled, paying no attention to Jim and Dakota standing behind Joe.

Joe turned his back to Sellman, faced Dakota and Jim, and stepped aside. "Howard, I would like you to meet the defense team, Dakota Reynolds, and Jim White Feather."

"Ms. Reynolds, Mr. White Cloud, nice to meet you." Sellman reached out to shake their hands.

Jim reached out and grabbed Sellman's hand with an unordinarily hard grip, and stared him in the eyes. "White Feather."

Sellman stared back, clearly not intimidated by Jim's icy glare. "My apologies, Mr. White Feather."

He broke the grip with Jim and looked at Dakota without reaching out to shake her hand. "Ms. Reynolds, nice to meet you." He turned back to Joe. "I need to speak with you before going in there." He walked away, not waiting for Joe to respond.

"What an asshole," Dakota said.

Joe raised his eyebrows. "The best asshole money can buy." He spun quickly and caught up to Sellman.

"Joe, the courthouse is a fucking circus. There are tree-hugging motherfuckers everywhere with wolf posters that read, *"Free the Wolf Man."* Indians everywhere. This does not bode well for us. This is only the fucking arraignment. What is the trial going to be like? I don't like this."

"Did your camp release any press on this?" Joe said.

"No, not a fucking peep. We were waiting till the Superior Court hearing."

The prosecution and the defense took their positions as guards escorted Jake into the courtroom. It erupted with the chant *"Honi, Honi, Honi."*

The support moved him to smile and lip the words "thank you" as he took his position. He looked at Alexi and his family, raising his eyebrows.

Alexi looked at him, shrugged, and raised her hands palm out as if to ask, *"What is all this?"*

Jake leaned over to talk to Dakota. The crowd noise made it hard for him to talk in a low voice. "What the hell is going on?"

She looked at him and smiled. "Word travels fast in a small town, especially if it gets to the right people."

Jake looked at Jim, who winked at him and nodded quickly.

"All rise for Judge Still Water," the court bailiff shouted over the crowd noise.

Jake shook his head and stood at attention, as if he were in a military tribunal.

The courtroom quieted.

"Please be seated," the judge said. "Case number 1465, State vs. Jake Michaels. Are all parties present?"

The defense and the DA acknowledged their presence.

"Mr. Michaels, please state your full name and birthdate."

"Yes sir, Your Honor. Jake Michaels, May 1st, 1965."

"Mr. Michaels, you are being charged with Felony Fraud and Assault with a Deadly Weapon. I see you have obtained counsel, so I do not have to advise you of your Constitutional Rights to representation and a fair trial. I see that you have entered a plea of not guilty. Based on the circumstance around your faked death, I am denying bail. The preliminary hearing will be set for one week from today. Each member of the legal teams is advised to have all documents submitted to the court before that hearing. Do either counsels have any questions?"

"Prosecution has no questions, Your Honor."

Jim looked at Dakota.

She took a deep breath and said, "Your honor, counsel recognizes the denial of bail, but we have a unique request. My client, as you know, has a pet wolf that is sitting on the butte outside town. The wolf was raised by my client, and without proper care, he will die on that butte. We would request that my client can pay several visits to the butte with a caregiver to establish trust, so that caregiver can feed the wolf."

The courtroom erupted with the *"Honi"* chant again, and people raised the wolf posters.

Judge Still Water slammed his gavel. "Order, order in the court, please. Order in the court, please."

The courtroom quieted.

"Ms. Reynolds, I am familiar with your client's unique pet. In fact, like everyone in town, I have heard his mournful howls all night. I sympathize with your request, but cannot allow taxpayer dollars to be spent escorting your client up and down the butte until his wolf trusts another human being. I will, however, allow your client to introduce a caregiver to the wolf, if your client will cover any expenses to the sheriff's department."

"Objection, Your Honor," Sellman barked. "The court is showing partial treatment to the defendant."

The courtroom exploded with boos and wolf howls. "Fuck you, asshole," someone yelled.

"Order, order in the court," the judge commanded.

Jim looked down, clearly trying not to let anyone see him chuckling.

"Mr. Sellman, Jake Michaels is being charged, not his wolf. Overruled. This arraignment is adjourned."

"Thank you, Your Honor." Dakota rubbed Jake's shoulder.

Jake nodded. *Dakota and Jim did it.*

Sellman stormed out of the courtroom with Joe in tow, using the back entrance to avoid the crowd. They jumped in a limo in the back parking lot.

"Fuck, fuck, fuck! Those fucking Indians planned this! They've already endeared the people around here to Jake Michaels. He'll become some kind of martyr to those tree-hugging cocksuckers."

Sellman's face was fire engine red. He whipped his file folder against the opposite seat.

Joe found amusement in the scene. He felt a burning temptation to remind Sellman of Little Big Horn, but fought back the urge. After all, they were on the same side, and this case could be significant to Joe's career. Still, he couldn't help gloating over Sellman being so humbled.

"Back to my office please, driver," Joe requested.

"Yes sir."

Jake, Jim, and Dakota returned to the Police Station and sat down in the safe room.

Jake's face beamed. "You did it. You guys did it. When can we see Honi?"

"I've talked to Sheriff Kelly," Jim said. "He will give us an off-duty police officer at 4:15 p.m. every day. We will pay his overtime rate for two hours per day, until Honi is comfortable with whoever goes up there."

"I'll go up every day," Dakota said. "Honi knows me. He'll feel comfortable."

"Dakota, there will be watchful eyes on you. If Honi runs right to you, it will raise suspicion," Jim warned.

Jake said, "Jim, do you know who the officer will be?"

"Yes, Chris Cooper, a young guy right out of the academy."

"Does he speak Arapaho?"

Jim laughed. "I doubt it, Jake, why?"

"I taught Honi commands in Arapaho. I can make it look like he's hesitant of Dakota at first."

Jim put his hands behind his head and leaned back in the chair. "Well, it will be showtime in four hours. I will be watching along with the whole town, and Channel 5 from Cheyenne."

Jake shook his head. "What made Dakota and you decide to turn this into a circus? Why didn't you tell me?"

Dakota jumped in. "We knew the defense would eventually go public and make this high profile. We wanted to beat them to the punch and establish our story first. After Cheyenne broadcasts the story of "The Wolf Man" feeding Honi, a national station will pick up on it. It will go viral in minutes on social media. We spin our side first, and then the defense has to counter. We didn't tell you, so you would look surprised when you walked in."

Jake raised an imaginary drink. "Cheers! That was brilliant."

"Oh," Jim said, "this old man still has a fight or two left in him. I do not like the DA, and I dislike his co-counsel even more. They have a good case, and they will be tough, especially Sellman. But we have more to fight for than power, greed, and fame. Don't we?"

Jim smiled at Dakota and Jake as he got up to leave the room.

Dakota glanced sideways at Jake. "Is that a sparkle I see in your eye, mister?"

"Today, as I entered the courtroom, a calm came over me. I realized I no longer have to hide. Actually, I will go from recluse to famous in the matter of a few hours. A strange twist of fate, isn't it?"

She placed her hand on his. "The Spirits know what they are doing. We just have to *not* question them."

"Do you think they will take care of Alexi and my family?"

"I think they will, Jake."

CHAPTER 36
SHOWTIME

Jake, Dakota, and Officer Cooper walked out of the Police station to an eruption of applause. Multiple news station vans lined the street, and reporters attempted to interview Jake and Dakota, which they politely declined. The trio made their way to the base of the butte, where the Police had roped off the area. Several more newspeople and multiple photographers with telescoping lens had taken up position to capture the scene with Honi.

As they made their way up the butte and out of the pandemonium below, Jake moved closer to Dakota. "I cannot believe how quickly Jim and you assembled this much press. The DA has to be furious."

"We beat Sellman at his own game," she whispered, assuring the officer could not hear anything to report back to his superiors.

Jake looked up the butte at Honi. The wolf's keen eyesight spotted him, and Honi yelped with excitement.

When they got to within twenty-five yards of Honi, he saw the officer and started pacing.

"Officer," Jake said, "I'll need to go forward from here by myself. Once I get Honi calmed down, Dakota and you can move forward."

The officer hesitated only a moment. "Mr. Michaels, I'll allow that, but please do not do anything stupid. Snipers are watching you and the wolf."

Jake smiled and looked down. "I don't think I'm moving anywhere quickly in these leg irons."

Jake moved closer to Honi and dropped to his knees. Honi ran forward and jumped up on him, knocking him down. The wolf's tail wagged frantically as he licked Jake's face. Jake laughed and hugged Honi. "Hello, boy, I missed you too. You look hungry. Are you hungry?"

Honi understood the word hungry. He backed off of Jake and started spinning in circles out of excitement.

"I know you are. Dakota has food for you."

His ears perked when he heard Dakota's name. He looked down at her and wagged his tail.

"Okay, Honi, we have to play a game as Dakota and the officer come up here. Do you want to play?"

Honi knew "play" meant games Jake and he had enjoyed since he was a puppy.

Jake looked back at Dakota and Officer Cooper, and signaled them to come forward slowly.

"Honi, oxoohowut," Jake whispered.

Honi lifted his lips and growled.

"Honi, Nonoonowuuni."

Honi started to back up.

Dakota and Officer Cooper stopped when Honi growled. Dakota and Jake had choreographed this in the safe room. She acted scared, while the Officer had his hand on his gun.

"Dakota," Jake said. "Walk very slowly towards me, and bend down behind me. Officer Cooper, please keep your distance."

Dakota walked hesitantly towards Jake, pausing every time Honi growled.

Jake *very* quietly continued to give Honi growl commands.

Dakota bent down behind Jake and whispered, "This must look great to the people on the ground."

Jake whispered back, "Watch this." He looked at the wolf. "Honi, coowo oxoohowut."

Honi got down on his belly and slowly crawled to Jake, continuing to growl.

Dakota said, "Jake, look at his eyes. He wants to play with me."

"I know. I'll end this soon. I don't know how long he'll hold out."

Honi reached Jake, and whined as he looked up at Dakota.

"Good boy, Honi," Jake said louder, for the benefit of the officer. "Reach out your hand, Dakota, and let him smell you." He then said, "Stay, Honi, no jump."

Honi smelled Dakota's hand, and applause and shouts erupted from the street below.

"We pulled this one off so far," Jake whispered to her, then said louder, "Start feeding him."

Dakota pulled out pieces of elk meat and tossed it to Honi. The wolf devoured it as fast as it hit the ground. "Jake, he's so hungry."

"I know. Thanks to the judge, he'll be fine now," he said loud enough for the officer to hear. Then he whispered to Dakota, "Okay, next trick. This will be the hardest part. I hope he doesn't jump on you and lick your face." He raised his voice and said, "Come to my side. We'll do the introduction."

He held out his hand and said, "Honi, down."

The wolf dropped to his belly, and Dakota reached out to pet him.

"Honi, nonoonowuuni," Jake whispered.

Honi started to back up.

"Honi," he said louder. "It's okay. Come."

Honi stood up and walked forward, and Jake held Dakota's hand as he guided it over Honi's head.

Another burst of applause lifted from the streets below.

"Honi, good boy, no jump," Dakota whispered.

Jake and Dakota put on the petting show for a couple of minutes. Then Jake commanded Honi to lie down and roll over, and Dakota rubbed his chest and belly.

"I think that's enough for today," Jake whispered.

"I agree. Honi, you're a good boy," Dakota whispered.

The young wolf, clearly feeling he was in a safe place, fell asleep.

"Look at him," Dakota said loudly. "He probably hasn't slept soundly since he's been up here. Let's stay with him for a bit more."

Jake whispered again. "Let's give everyone a show. You back up, and I'll lie next to him." He added more loudly, "That's fine, if you can convince Officer Cooper to give us a few minutes."

Dakota stood up, and Honi opened his eyes as she moved away.

"It's okay, Honi. I'm here. Sleep boy." Jake lay down and wrapped his arm around Honi, and the wolf drifted back to sleep.

"Officer Cooper," Dakota said. "The wolf has not slept for days. Can we stay for a bit, so he feels safe and sleeps?"

"Ms. Reynolds, that was the most amazing thing I have *ever seen*."

Cooper had said with more than a little enthusiasm, which caused Jake to smile.

"I'm an animal lover," Cooper said. "That's why I volunteered for this. We can stay here as long as you like, and I don't even want to be paid."

"Thank you, Officer Cooper, but we must pay you. My client will be more than happy to do so."

Jim sat in his office watching various social media sites blow up with streaming videos. He knew the evening news would be abuzz with this story, and could only imagine what Sellman and the DA were thinking. He settled back in his office chair and lifted a snifter of brandy to the screen. "Fuck you, Sellman." He smiled broadly.

Howard and Joe Ross watched the streaming video on the local news website.

"I have underestimated our opposition," Howard said calmly. "They are beating me at my own game."

His phone rang, and he looked down to see it was Vincent Dibella.

"Howard, I assume you're watching what I am," Vincent said.

"Yes, sir, I am."

"Please explain to me how you have allowed this to happen. How the fuck is a man that killed my sons all over social media like some kind of rock star? How the fuck is some two-bit attorney beating you at your own spin game?"

"I underestimated them, sir."

"Under-fucking-estimated them? *No, Sellman*, you paid *no fucking attention to them*. Now, you find a way to eliminate this distraction and get this case back on track. *Do you understand me?*" Vincent cut the line.

Howard calmly placed his phone on the desk. "We need something to counter this. We need to vilify Michaels."

"What do you have in mind? This guy doesn't even have a parking ticket, and he's a war hero. On top of that, he has a disease. Hell, the National Alzheimer's Group is raising money for his defense already. Jim and Dakota had this all thought out. I have no idea how we will even get a non-sympathetic jury," Joe said.

Sellman lifted his snifter of scotch, giving it a swirl. "We wait for the preliminary hearing, file as many Felony charges as possible, and request that the trial be moved to the Reservation where the crimes occurred. That will bring the Feds in."

"You want to go into the heart of Indian country against local Indian attorneys that are well known and respected there? And you want to bring the Feds in *to finger-fuck everything? I understand none of this thinking.*" Ross's jaw clenched.

Howard narrowed his eyes and stared into his drink. "Sometimes, you have to go into the belly of the beast to defeat it. *My showtime* has not started yet."

CHAPTER 37
DREAMS

Alexi and the kids watched from the street as the scene unfolded on the butte.

"Oh my God," Danielle exclaimed. "Dad is all over social media. This is streaming."

"I know," Robert said. "My friends are blowing up my phone."

"Mine too. Dad is famous," Johnny added.

Alex did not share the same excitement as the kids. As she watched Jake and Dakota on top of the mountain, she felt it should be her up there with her husband. She couldn't stay for the duration of the trial, and it would be difficult to acclimate the wolf to her, but it would have been nice for Jake to at least ask. The *old* Jake would have never ignored her—he'd have found a way to include her—but that was *not* the old Jake on the hilltop. He'd lost the sparkle in his eyes when he looked at her. A part of him had died. The meetings they'd had since she'd been in town had lacked feeling, as if Jake *wanted* to be there for her, but just couldn't remember their history. She questioned which was more heartbreaking: him being dead, or their life dying before her eyes. It became clearer by the day why Jake had done what he did.

"Mom, Mom, can you hear us?" Danielle said.

Alex snapped out of deep thought. "I'm sorry, Danni. Yes, I hear you. Dad is famous."

Her phone rang.

It was Sam. "Hey, you, Jake is all over social media."

"I know, it's a circus here, Sam."

"How are you doing with everything?"

"It's difficult, to say the least. Jake is here, and then he's not."

"The disease?"

"Yeah, it's tough on the kids. They want their dad back, but I'm afraid that will not happen, at least a hundred percent."

"How do *you* feel about it?"

"Torn. The more I see here, the more I realize this is where he needs to be. I'm going to talk to him after he comes down from the mountain. The police have been gracious, allowing us to visit with him."

"Hang in there. Remember, I'm here for you."

"I know, and thank you. I'll be home soon."

She hung up and watched as Jake and Dakota stepped from the butte, and reporters rushed to interview them.

Dakota stopped for the news station from Cheyenne. "I know everyone has a lot of questions, and as soon as I can discuss this case, I will. I apologize for not being able to say more now. Thank you."

Reporters shouted questions as they moved away.

Jake turned and saw Alexi and the kids, and he walked in their direction.

"Dad, you're all over the internet," Danielle shouted over the crowd. "You're like a rock star." She held her phone up to show him.

Jake hugged her. "Now you'll be famous too, Danielle."

He looked at Alex and grabbed her hands. "How are you holding up to all of this? Are the reporters stalking you?"

She forced a slight smile. "They've been very respectful. They're more interested in the Wolf Man than they are me."

A crowd closed in on Jake and her.

Dakota touched his arm. "Jake, we need to keep moving."

He turned back to Alex. "I'll talk to you later."

"Okay," she said, fighting back tears.

Jake's eyes were emotionless, as if he'd felt *compelled* to stop and talk to her, to try to show he cared, but didn't have the feelings or conviction she hoped for. The past year had changed him. It had stolen him from her.

Jake and Dakota sat in the safe room.

"Well, Mr. Michaels, that went well." Dakota took his hand.

"Yes it did, counselor. Honi was so good, wasn't he?"

"He was amazing. I can't wait until we can run free with him on the mountain again." She smiled and winked. "When this is over, we're going to the cabin, take our clothes off, and not put them back on for a whole weekend."

"Counselor, is that not a conflict of interest? And a bit unfair painting that picture in my mind right now?"

She moved her foot between his legs and rubbed his dick.

"Counselor, that is *definately* a conflict of interest."

There was a knock at the door, and Dakota quickly pulled her foot down.

"Come in," she said.

"Ms. Reynolds, Mr. Michael's family is here for visitation."

"Thank you, Officer. I'll be right out. We're almost done."

She chuckled, looking towards Jake's crotch. "Are you okay down there, or do you need a moment?"

He took a deep breath. "Give me a moment."

She stood up, slowly stretched, and rubbed her hands across her breasts. "Have a good visit."

"I want a new attorney! About sixty years old and a hundred pounds overweight," he said.

She smiled back from the door handle, then closed the door behind her and walked down the hall.

That may have been a bit unfair to Jake, but I know he'll think about me as Alex sits in front of him.

"Alex," she said. "Sorry I had to pull Jake away from you and the kids out there, but the press has a million questions that we simply cannot answer at this point. We need them on our side. I don't want to piss them off by losing my cool and snapping at them as they ask the same questions over and over."

Alex nodded. "We understand, and we trust in your judgment on this. Are you finished with Jake? Can we see him?"

"Yes, I'm done. He's waiting for you."

"Thank you, Dakota, have a good evening."

Alex looked at her kids. "I'm going to talk to Dad for a couple of minutes. I'll be right out."

"Okay, Mom, don't hog all the time. We want to show him all the videos," Danielle said, half-jokingly.

"I know you all want to see him. Give me ten minutes."

She walked into the safe room and sat down.

"Hey you," Jake said with a smile. "What did you think about that craziness this afternoon?"

She shook her head. "I never expected any of this in my wildest dreams. It's so much for me to take in."

"I know, and I'm sorry our journey has taken these turns. I know this has to be hard."

She looked up, shaking her head. A tear fell down her cheek to the table. "Hard is an understatement, Jake. This trial is going to take weeks, if not months. The kids and I want to support you through it, but I know you realize we have to work. We have lives to go back to."

He nodded. "Alexi, I understand that."

The conversation paused.

He looked down, then into her eyes. "How is your life without me?"

She shook her head slightly, and tears filled her eyes again. She looked away for a moment before making eye contact with him again.

"When they called me, and presumed you had drowned, a piece of me was ripped from my soul. I didn't know if I could carry on. You'd been my life since I was twenty years old. Quitting was not an option. The kids needed me. Over time, as the hurt subsided, I worked my way out of the shell I'd built around myself. I started to hear the birds sing in the morning again. I looked up at the stars again, and imagined you looking down on me. It gave me some peace, but I always held onto a fine thread. You always said that if you died before me, you would never leave my side, but I never felt you. After a while, I realized that even Jake Michaels couldn't break the finality of death. I pressed forward and was doing okay, Jake. Now, I don't know how I'm doing. It breaks my heart you're forgetting what we had. It kills me looking across the table at a shell of Jake Michaels. The spark you had in your eyes when you looked at me... is gone. *I know* that you are trying to recall our lives, but I also realize there's probably nothing we can do to bring Jake and Alexi back. There's no cure for your illness. I realize now the pain you tried to protect us from. Unfortunately, Destiny had other plans for us."

Jake looked at her, and a tear rolled down his cheek. He knew that she had a man in her life now, but he also remembered how compassionate she was, and that she'd never say anything about it here.

"Alexi, I have no words to express how sorry I am for all of this. It didn't happen as I planned. I've lived my whole life knowing you *cannot* change Destiny, and I went against that anyway. It backfired, but maybe all of this will prove to be what was supposed to happen. As cruel as it may seem, perhaps there will be some greater good to come from it."

Her face softened and she laid her hand on his. "You have always been the dreamer, the optimist. It's what I loved about you. Despite how bad a situation was, you always had a plan. You always made it work. I don't know what kind of plan you have now, but I'm sure you'll make it work. What I ask of you is simple: make that plan about *yourself* first. You have a terrible disease. You're facing serious charges. I don't know exactly what happened that night, but I do know you had your reasons. I believe, once this is all over, so many questions will be answered. The Jake Michaels I know would not have it any other way."

He tilted his head and smiled. "When are you leaving?"

"Tomorrow. We'll be back out for the trial if there is one. I'm sure that every move you make from here on out will be all over the news and internet. The kids and I will see it over and over, and Dakota and I will be in contact every step of the way. Now, the kids are excited to see you. They want to show their dad what a star he is."

She got up from the table and walked over to him, and he stood up. They looked at each other and hugged tightly. Tears met on their cheeks.

She smiled and wiped the tears from his cheek. "Keep dreaming, Jake Michaels, for both of us." She pulled away, keeping eye contact, and held his hand until she was out of reach. "I love you," she whispered, before closing the door.

Jake sat down at the table and quickly gathered himself.

The kids came in excited, as Alexi had said they would. They showed him video after video, and as he watched, he remembered small bits and pieces of when they were young on Christmas mornings, when they'd had the same kind of excitement.

They all laughed, and they all cried.

Jake knew this was hard on them, but they were young, and this would pass. They'd move on with their lives. Once he was gone, they'd have memories and videos of this troubling time. Once the hurt passed, fondness and love would prevail in their memories and dreams.

CHAPTER 38
RETURN TO THE SPIRIT WORLD

Jake sat in the safe room and stared at the table, reflecting on his family's visit as a battle raged inside him. The past, which was already foggy, demanded he abandon a future that was crystal-clear.

Do I chase ghosts or follow Spirits?

He knocked on the door. The guard opened the door, then accompanaied him down the hall towards the lobby.

Dakota, his family, and several officers had gathered and were talking. Their mood seemed light. The group saw him and moved toward him. Visitation was over, but the officers would allow them say goodbye.

Suddenly, a familiar but recently absent feeling came over him. It had been months since his last spell, but he'd been three weeks without his medication. He signaled the officer to stop.

His body tensed as he moved into the Spirit World. The Faceless Indian waved Jake over to a burning fissure in the ground. Jake looked down and saw the tormented faces of Dakota and Alexi dancing in flames.

The Faceless Indian spoke. "You must decide. One must carry pain on a journey. Choose correctly and end the suffering. The Spirits will do battle at Wind River."

He responded in a deep guttural voice. "Niihentoo neene'ee hesowowu3oo niiwoo3heihiit heeneyeixohei bebiisiihi beet hessoxuuhetiit cei3wooo boo3etiit heteiniicie."

"Jake, Jake, are you okay?"

"Jake, can you hear me?"

"Mr. Michaels, Mr. Michaels."

Jake heard Dakota, Alexi, and the officer as he came out of the spell. He shook his head, regaining his thoughts as beads of sweat dripped from his brow.

This spell was different.

The group stood watching Jake.

"I'm sorry, officer," he said. "How long was I gone for?"

"About a minute. Do you need to sit down?"

"No, I'm fine. Let me say goodbye to my family and attorney, please."

Jake walked over to Alexi and the kids.

Danielle said, "Are you okay, Dad?"

"Yeah, I'll be fine. They come and go."

"What language were you speaking?"

"I don't remember saying anything, Dani." He glanced at Dakota.

"It was Arapaho," Dakota said.

"Well, I guess a year studying it at the cabin sunk in, huh?" He joked and winked at Dani, then walked over to Alexi and hugged her. "Have a safe trip. I'll see you at the trial, okay?"

"Jake, you need to see a doctor," Alexi urged. "That was nothing like you had before you left."

"I will. Dakota and Jim have arranged an examination. I'll make sure she updates you and the kids. Don't worry, I'm in good hands here."

Alexi's eyes narrowed as she looked over at Dakota and half smiled. "I know you are."

"Mr. Michaels, it's time to go."

"Yes, officer." Jake kissed each of the kids and left the lobby.

The Michaels family walked over to Dakota.

"Please keep us up to date," Alex said

Dakta nodded. "I will. I promise."

"Do you know what he said?" John asked.

"My Arapaho is not very good. I only caught a few words. It sounded like he was talking about Wind River. I don't know."

"We have an early flight," Alex said. "Thank you for everything, Dakota. Make sure they treat him well in here, please."

"Alex, he's like a folk hero around here now. He'll be fine. I promise."

After the Michaels family left, Dakota sat down on a bench, worn out from the day. Jake's spell had upset her. He'd not had one for months. She feared the medicine was wearing off, and that he'd go downhill quickly. She understood a few more words than she'd let on with the Michaels family, but the context confused her.

Jay Storm Walker had stood in the corner of the lobby during Jake's spell. Now he walked over and sat down next to Dakota. "Hello, kiddo, you look tired."

"I'm exhausted, Jay."

"That was some spell your client had."

"Yes, it was. He told us about them, but that's the first one I've seen. I have no idea where he learned our language. I couldn't make out very much. Do you know what he said?"

"Yes, I do. He spoke of making decisions, a journey filled with pain. He must choose wisely to end the suffering, and... the Spirits will battle at Wind River."

"I don't understand what any of that means, Jay."

"When we captured him, a violent storm came from nowhere. The Thunderbird was angry. As we escorted him through the Sacred Grounds, I saw the Ancient Ones in the shadows. They lined his path. There is more to his story than we know, perhaps more than he knows. I have heard that voice he spoke in before. It was through a Medicine Man many years ago while he was in the Spirit World."

"Jay, I'm so confused. What does this all mean? You're much more in touch with the old ways than me." Dakota played dumb, though she had an idea what it all meant.

"Dakota, I do not have the sight like your Greatgrandfather. You should speak with him."

She paused and put her hand over his. "I have known you since I was a child. I trust your words. I will speak with Greatgrandfather. By the way, and you don't have to answer this, but how did you find him? What made you look at the cabin?"

"It was luck. We were searching for the two missing hikers. The infrared on the helo picked up the wolf's and Jake's heat signature. That is between you and me."

"Jay, I would never compromise you. You and Grandfather have been friends since childhood. You're part of the family. Thank you for sitting with me."

"Dakota, be careful. The Spirits have a hand in this. Talk with Samuel."

She watched Jay leave, and remained on the bench for a few more minutes thinking about everything. Jake's spell concerned her. She worried he might say something incriminating next time. She needed to talk with Samuel, as Jay advised. She would visit him tomorrow.

Dakota drove to Samuel's assisted care home.

He was outside fussing with his rose bush. "Lomasi, how are you, young one?"

She hugged him. "I'm good, Greatgrandfather. How are you?"

"I would be better if I could get this rose bush to stop leaning in the wrong direction. The earth is battling me." He chuckled.

"You will figure it out Greatgrandfather. You always figure things out."

"Your eyes tell me you are confused, Lomasi. Come inside. Let's have some tea and talk."

Inside the home, Samuel prepared two glasses of tea and sat with Dakota. "Let me see your hands, Lomasi."

He held both of her hands, closed his eyes, and whispered several sentences that she didn't understand. His head drifted side to side, and then up. The veins in his temples flared as his grip tightened. He sat motionless for several moments, slowly loosened his grip, and opened his eyes.

He nodded. "You have been to the Spirit World with him. You have seen things that have sent you on a journey. There will be a battle ahead for you. The Spirits will test both of you. Stay true to the path that the Lady of the Water has cleared for you."

"Greatgrandfather, he spoke fluently in our language while he had a spell. How did he do that?"

"The Faceless One spoke through him."

"But how? Who is the Faceless One? Why in front of everyone?"

"Lomasi, I will not tell you that. You have the gift, as I do. You must learn on your own, as I did, and as many did before me. It is part of your discovery."

"Greatgrandfather, I'm scared he will say something incriminating. He hasn't been able to take the medicine that keeps him in this world. I thought it would be best for his defense. Should I give him some?"

"No, the Faceless One will not block your path. You made the right decision. He must go back into the Spirit world more often now. Listen carefully to the words of the Faceless One if he speaks again."

"I worry that he will forget his current life, like he's forgetting his past life, and that I'll lose him as his wife has lost him."

"Lomasi, trust in your skills to free him from the bondage of the white man. Jim will be there for you. When it is time, I will be there for you, in the Spirit world."

"Thank you. I'll see you at the house on Tuesday, right?"

"Yes, I will be out on vacation."

Dakota laughed. "You've been on vacation for twenty years."

"Young one, you have no idea how busy I am here. It is difficult advising these young doctors and keeping these nurses off of me. I need a break."

She hugged him. "Okay, see you on vacation. I love you, and thank you."

Samuel watched her leave. He hoped she would be prepared for what lay ahead. The Faceless One had warned her of pain on this journey. She would have to be stronger than she ever thought.

CHAPTER 39
THE LETTER D

"Good afternoon, Wolf Man," Dakota said.

"Good afternoon, counselor. I thought I asked for a replacement yesterday after you sexually harassed me."

"Sorry, but no one would take your case."

"Okay, I guess I'm stuck with you."

"Yes, you are."

"Jake, being serious, we need to discuss the spell you had yesterday. That's the first time I've heard you speak during a spell. Do you remember anything?"

Jake paused, and she couldn't help but suspect he was trying to hide something. "No, I remember little, just the Faceless Indian saying something about the Spirits and a battle. I assumed he was talking about the court case."

Dakota hesitated and decided not to give him the full translation. "I recognized a few words, Spirits and Wind River. I guess you're right. It was probably about the case. I saw Greatgrandfather, and asked if we should put you back on the medication. He said no, that you need to spend time in the Spirit World. They'll guide us through this. Hopefully, you can remember more during the next spell... and not say anything incriminating about us if you speak again."

"Well, perhaps with all the police witnesses, this can help our case somehow?"

"It's possible. Your medical and psych exams were approved by the judge. Grandfather had scheduled them for tomorrow. He wants the report before we go to the preliminary hearing. Given the attention this case has garnered, the judge has accelerated the court process. He set the preliminary hearing in three days."

"That's good, right?"

"Yes, it is. We'll learn exactly what the prosecution's intent is. I assume they'll try to throw the book at you. We're prepared."

"Good, the faster we get this bullshit over, the faster I can get out of here. I'm starting to get a little stir crazy now."

"I know, and I want you out of here more than you can imagine. While this seems overwhelming, the bright side is that you no longer have to hide. *We* will soon not have to hide." She smiled and reached across the table to hold his hands.

"That will be nice," he said in a subdued tone.

Dakota tilted her head and squeezed his hands. "Are you all right?"

"Yeah, I'm fine. It's been confusing having my family here. It just didn't fit into what I planned. Meeting you didn't fit into what I planned. Everything has changed, and it has my head spinning. I question my path."

She knew his emotions would be challenged, and had prepared for this. "The Spirits placed you on the trail that night, and you saved my life. I will forever be grateful. I never planned to fall in love with you, but it happened. I also knew that, one day, if we were going to bring you off that mountain, you and I would have to face your family. I know that I cannot replace Alex. You spent your whole life with her. I would never ask you to walk away from your kids. What I will ask you to do is let the Spirits guide us through this. If you are meant to be with me, it will happen."

He looked deeply into her eyes. "I died. You and Honi have resurrected me. *I too* am grateful." He paused for a moment, looked down, shook his head, and wrote the letter *D*. "How ironic is this situation, that the one word defines it. It separates my old life and new. Loved versus love, lived versus live."

She picked up the pen and finished the word *Destiny*.

He smiled, and his eyes sparkled when he looked back at her. "Very good, counselor."

"Let's concentrate on getting you out of here. We'll let the rest unfold. As of now, none of us has a future with a jailbird." Dakota said it in a light-hearted tone.

Jake chuckled. "Deal."

Sellman stormed into Joe's office. "Joe, I have another coroner looking at the autopsy reports, a heavy hitter from Dallas. I've used him successfully in other cases. Based on my initial conversation with him, he believes he will have *no problem* definitively linking the auto accident with the injuries. We can't risk that local yocal, half-assed coroner leaving any fucking doubt in the juror's mind. The only thing she has going for her is a nice ass and a set of tits. That wouldn't win us shit unless we were auctioning her off for blowjobs in the judge's chamber."

Joe bit his tongue. He and Jessica were keeping quiet about their relationship until his divorce was final. He also didn't want any thoughts of collusion introduced in the trial by the defense.

"Sellman, nice to see you're your charming self this afternoon," Joe forced out with a smile.

"We have the preliminary hearing in three days, and all I hear about is that fucking wolf and his fucking owner. Everyone is forgetting that cocksucker is charged with a crime. I can't wait to see Poke-a-hot-ass's and Chief Bull Shit's face when we bring up Manslaughter charges. Then we request the trial be moved. Fuck them."

"I assume you saw they're having a Med and Psych eval done tomorrow?"

"Yes, but I don't see what golden ring they're reaching for there. Whatever. It's their dime, not mine. Make sure we get the results ASAP, just in case they try to pull another publicity stunt. I have a tall glass of Scotch calling my name. Have a good night." Sellman turned and left, slamming Joe's door.

"Yes, masta, can I shine your shoes? Fucking asshole!" Joe flipping his middle finger in Sellman's direction, then picked up his phone and texted Jessica.

Joe: *What time do you get off tonight?*
Jessica: *Whenever you get here. [Smiley Emoji.]*
Joe: *LOL. I need a drink. See you at six at the cabin?*
Jessica: *OK. Luv you.*
Joe: *[Heart Emoji.]*

Joe put his phone down, leaned back in his chair, inhaled deeply, and closed his eyes. He wanted to beat the shit out of Sellman when he talked about Jessica the way he did, but soon this trial would pass, Sellman would leave, and things would be back to normal.

Jay and Hal sat in a boat on Jenny Lake.

"Well my friend, the fish are not hitting today," Hal said.

"You are bad luck, Hal. Every time I fish here with you, we get skunked. The Lake does not like white men," Jay joked.

"Or maybe it doesn't like you," Hal rebutted.

The men laughed, and let their lines back out. The boat gently rocked on the warm late summer day, and they relaxed in the tranquility.

Jay said, "It is nice to see the tourists have left. Too bad we do not get more time out here before the White Owl comes."

Hal nodded. "Yeah, looking up at the Tetons, it looks like winter is trying to settle in early this year. I'm not sure I want to work another winter. I'm ready to retire. How about you?"

Jay rubbed his shoulder. "I have been thinking about it. I think this will be my last winter. The cold is starting to make these old bones hurt."

"What do you make of the Michaels case?"

Jay paused to consider his words. "There is something more to all of this. I have seen things."

"Like what?"

"I watched Jake Michaels have a spell. He spoke fluent Ancient Arapaho. His words were foreboding."

"I did hear about that. I figured he'd been up on that mountain with nothing to do, had an Arapaho dictionary, and taught himself the language."

"It is possible, but the dictionary would teach him the modern language. This was the language of the Ancient Ones."

"Well, you know I don't believe in the supernatural as you do, but given the way this is playing out, maybe I should start. Now, why don't you use some of your magic and make the fish bite."

"I told you, the lake does not like white men." Jay smiled, pulled his hat down, closed his eyes, and reclined back.

Jake, Jim, Dakota, and a sheriff's deputy entered the Lander Medical Center.

"Yes, may I help you?" The receptionist said.

"Yes, ma'am," Jim said. "We are here to see a visiting physician, Dr. Harold Taylor."

"Yes, sir, he's in room 214. Security has been waiting for you. They will take you there."

Hospital security escorted the group to the exam room.

The doctor approached when they entered. "Jim, nice to see you, my old friend. How have you been?"

"Not bad for an old man, Harold," Jim said, as the two shook hands.

"Shit, you don't look much older than when we served together forty years ago. This clean living out here is keeping you young."

"Or the hard living, keeping up with the ranch, Doc."

"There *is* something to say for that. I assume this is your granddaughter?"

Dakota reached out her hand and introduced herself. "Dakota Reynolds, nice to meet you, sir."

"I've heard a lot about you, Dakota. You are the jewel of your grandfather's eyes."

She smiled and put her arm around Jim. "He's pretty important to me too."

"Harold, this is Jake Michaels," Jim said.

"Mr. Michaels, it's nice to meet you. Jim has told me about your situation. I was able to contact your old doctor and have your records sent to me. I've reviewed them, and would like to repeat a couple of cognitive tests, and I've arranged for an MRI."

Jake smiled. "It's nice to meet you, Dr. Taylor. Thank you for coming out here. Did anything jump out at you in my records?"

"Officers, if you can excuse us now." Dr. Taylor motioned toward the door, requesting the deputy and security officer leave, and waited until they did so. "Jake, I specialize in working with Vets who've seen battle. I know you've been in several war zones. We'll talk about that a bit. PTSD can occur years after your military service. There's also a link between soldiers who suffer Traumatic Brain Injury from repeated concussive blasts, and CTE. The results can mimic Alzheimer's and Dementia symptoms."

"Doctor, are you saying it's possible I don't have Alzheimer's or another degenerative brain disease?"

"It's possible Alzheimer's could be ruled out, but CTE is a degenerative disease. However, it can be treated to some degree. We can get more into that after the exam."

Dakota and Jake shot a glance at each other.

The doctor turned to Jim and Dakota. "If you two will excuse us, I'd like to get started. I'll be about an hour or so."

"Sure thing, Harold, we will be outside," Jim said.

Dr. Taylor did a quick physical exam and had Jake do a few cognitive tests.

Afterwards, he said, "Jake, everything looks good physically. You're in great shape for your age. The cognitive tests are better than the ones you took a little over a year ago. In fact, they were perfect. Now, let's talk about your combat activity, and then your memory loss and spells. After that, we'll do the MRI. Okay?"

"Yes, Doctor."

Jake and Dr. Taylor finished their exam and the MRI.

Dr. Taylor let Dakota and Jim back into the room, and they waited with Jake while the doctor met with the radiologists.

"Jake, what did he say?" Dakota said.

"Not much. He wanted to review the MRI first. He asked a ton of questions and made notes. He did say my cognitive tests have improved. In fact, they were perfect."

Her face lit up. "That's awesome."

"Maybe for Jake's health, but not our case," Jim said, breaking the happy mood.

Jake and Dakota looked at each other without a response.

The door opened, and Dr. Taylor returned with the MRI results. "Jake, is it okay that I speak in front of your attorneys?"

"Of course, Doctor."

"Your cognitive tests show no decline. When I spoke with you about specific past events, you showed an alarming loss of episodic memory. I cannot easily diagnose the impact of concussive blasts or possible CTE, due to the fact you can't remember exact details from your combat experiences. I will need to access your military medical records for that. Even then, if you reported no injuries, I cannot determine the number of blasts you endured."

"Okay, Doc, what do you think the memory loss and spells are from?"

"The MRI showed a tiny mass in the front of the hippocampus. I compared the results with the past MRI your doctor did. There was nothing visible at that point, but that doesn't mean it was not there. Given the fact that it wasn't detectable, and it's very small now, I would conclude that it's not aggressive or malignant. However, it may be large enough to disrupt the recall of episodic memory. There are many debates about where long-term memory is stored, but we do know that damage to this area does result in amnesia. The spells... I'm still confused by those. They could be seizures caused by the mass, or they could be from CTE, or PTSD. Since you told me you were using a holistic approach to your symptoms, which seemed to control those spells, I will assume CTE/PTSD."

"What's the bottom line?"

"I believe you have damage to the hippocampus. I don't think it's life-threatening, and I think further damage may be averted by treatment of the mass. I believe you suffer from mild CTE. At this stage, you should be able to treat and live with it."

"So, no Alzheimer's?" Dakota said.

"If Jake had Alzheimer's, he would have issues with learning new things. That appears not to be the case. I would have cognitive tests done annually, and watch for symptoms other than what he reports now."

"If I treat the mass, will I regain my old memories?"

"The brain is tricky. Honestly, Jake, I can't answer that with certainty, but I would say no. If the mass is the cause, the damage in that area will not heal itself. The treatment of the mass can also increase the damage, depending on what treatment is used. I suggest that you have an MRI done every six months to monitor the growth."

"So, Harold," Jim said. "In your opinion, is there anything that you could testify would cause sudden or unexplained violent behavior?" Jim said.

"PTSD certainly could, but Jake indicated to me that he's relatively calm unless provoked. With his training, any physical altercation can lead to injury to the other party. The PTSD could certainly trigger an overactive response during that altercation."

"Very good, my old friend. Can I count on you if needed for his trial?"

"Only if you promise to take me Elk hunting this fall." Harold smiled and reached out to shake Jim's hand.

"That is a deal, first-class airline tickets and everything on me," Jim said.

"Jim and Dakota, I will forward you my reports later today. Jim, I wish I could spend more time with you on this trip, but I need to get back to L.A."

"I would have enjoyed that. We will be talking, and we will set the hunt up after the trial. I believe we will be done by November."

Harold reached out and shook Jake's hand. "Good luck with everything, Jake. You are in good legal hands. Medically, I think that with the right treatment, you should be fine. You'll have to learn to deal with the loss of your memory, and that part of your life, but support groups can help you."

"Thank you, Doctor."

"Jake, Dakota, and Jim sat in the safe room back at the police station.

Jim opened the conversation. "Well, Jake, it appears that your doctors may have missed something. I know you must be happy with what you heard today, as it would appear your long-term diagnosis is not as grave as you originally thought."

Jake didn't know *how* to feel. "Obviously, a tumor is never good to hear. I know my past life will be a constant blur, and may fade all the way out before I can get this treated, but yes, it would appear I have a future. Hopefully, I won't spend too much more of it in this jail. How do you think the diagnosis will impact my case?"

"I don't know. Dakota and I need to see what the prosecution has in store. We will find out in two days, how and if we use Harold. I also have a coroner in the wings, should we need her for expert testimony." Jim stood up and stretched. "I am calling it a day. Dakota, I will see you at home. Jake, have as good a day as you can in here."

"Thanks, Jim, actually I will be up on the butte with Honi today. The officer reported that Honi was not friendly yesterday, and requested I go back up with Dakota and him. It's amazing what one command in Arapaho can do." Jake winked at him.

"You two are lucky they did not send an Arapaho Sheriff up there with you." Jim smiled and closed the door behind him.

Dakota looked at Jake, then leaned back in her chair and twirled her hair provocatively. "Well, I can tell you what I would do to you to celebrate the doctor's assessment today, if we were out of here. But, I don't want to be accused of sexual harassment."

"Hmmm, would you make me dinner?"

"Nope, but I *would* tell you that part of *you* would be *my dinner*."

"Counselor, I don't understand. What do you mean?"

"Mr. Michaels, you'll have plenty of time tonight when they close your cell door to think about that. *I will be*, in my bedroom. We can compare notes tomorrow. The letter *D* is your hint."

Jake shook his head and pursed his lips. "I am still confused."

She sat up and laid her hands on his. "Okay, on a serious note, how did you feel about what the doctor said? Can you see the Spirits have their hands on this?"

"Obviously, my physician and the specialist missed this one."

"How does it make you feel, regarding your decision to leave your old life?"

"The course of action the doctors were going to take treating Alzheimer's would have missed the tumor. They would have never connected my military service to CTE. My spells would have gotten worse and worse without Samuel's medicine. My quality of life would have declined. My family's quality of life would have declined."

"As I said, Jake, we need to trust in the path set by the Spirits."

CHAPTER 40
PRELIMINARY PROCESS

"All rise for the Honorable Judge Still Water. This Court is now in session," the clerk announced.

"Be seated, please," the judge said. "Let the records read this is the preliminary hearing for Case Number 1465, The State of Wyoming vs. Jake Michaels. Are all parties present?"

The prosecution and defense each acknowledged.

"These proceedings will be held *not* to determine guilt, but *probable cause* to move this case forward. I will hear arguments from both sides. The State will open."

Joe Ross stood up. "Thank you, Your Honor. Based on the evidence, the State charges the defendant Jake Michaels with Manslaughter, Assault with a Deadly Weapon, and Fraud. The evidence submitted to the court supports these charges. We will also request that the trial is moved into the jurisdiction where the criminal activities occurred, the Wind River Reservation. I give the floor to the defense, thank you."

"This comes as no surprise," Jim whispered to Dakota. "You know what to do."

Dakota faced the judge. "Your Honor, the defense maintains the defendant acted in self-defense. On the charges of Fraud, let it be known that neither Jake Michaels nor any member of his family benefitted financially from his Pseudocide. Thus, we request that the Fraud charges be dismissed. All documents submitted to the court prove our position. We take no exception to the trial being moved to Wind River. The one thing we do request is that the defendant remains in Dubois until the trial, for the benefit of his Counsel and his wolf. We again petition for bail. That is all. Thank you, Your Honor."

"What are they doing," Howard mumbled to Joe Ross. "No counter argument, just a weak-ass self-defense plea and worrying about that fucking wolf?"

The judge looked at the defense, puzzled. "Ms. Reynolds, these are serious charges. Do you have no further arguments to support your client?"

"Not at this time, Your Honor," Dakota said with a confident tone.

Howard and Ross looked over at the defense to see Jim and Dakota relaxing in their chairs and closing their briefcases.

"Very well, based on the tape that I've seen and the coroner's statement, I find probable cause for Manslaughter and Assault with a Deadly Weapon, both felony charges. Regarding the Fraud charge, I agree there was no intent for financial gain. The records show no gain was realized by any parties. Pseudocide is not a crime. I will dismiss the Fraud charge. Regarding the request to move the trial to Wind River, I will agree with that. I support sufficient evidence for criminal charges in that jurisdiction. I will allow the defendant to remain in Dubois until the trail. Request for bail is denied. I request that the State moves quickly in filing the necessary information in Superior Court for arraignment. This court is adjourned."

Judge Still Water banged his gavel.

"All rise," the clerk announced as the judge left the bench.

Howard walked over to Dakota and Jim. "I don't know what fucking games you two are playing, but this is *my world*. I *do not lose*. You have no case, and I will not support a plea bargain, if that is your intent."

"Mr. Sellman, you have something grossly wrong. Your world is not in Indian Country. Have a nice day." Dakota smiled and walked away.

Howard stood motionless, his face burning hot and no doubt red. He normally kept his cool, but there was something about Jim, Dakota, and this case that rattled him. He couldn't put his finger on it.

Back in the safe room, Jim, Dakota, and Jake regrouped.

"What's next, Dakota?" Jake said.

"The formal arraignment. They'll file criminal charges, we'll enter a not guilty plea, and the case will move to a jury trial."

"Yes, there will be no plea bargain, obviously," Jim said, laughing.

"Boy, was he hot!" Dakota said.

Jim nodded. "It is his weakness. We will focus on bringing that out in the trial. The jury will hate his arrogance."

"How has he been so successful?" Jake said.

"He is accustomed to battling high-end attorneys like himself. They go to the same country clubs, eat at the same restaurants. They belong to the good-old-boy network in Texas. It is just a game and a money grab for them, something to feed their egos. He does not know how to deal with us. He does not understand the human side of the judicial process."

"So how do we counter the tape once the jury sees it? It doesn't make me look too good."

Jim waved it off. "We will wait until the jury is selected. I want to see the demographics. I am hoping there is at least fifty percent female and at least forty percent American Indian. That will determine what evidence and witness selection we use."

Jake sighed. "What kind of time frame are we looking at for all of this? Winter will be here before we know it. Honi will freeze up there."

"I believe that the DA will push this along quickly. The election is in six weeks, and he would like this victory on his resume. Sellman does not want to be here for any longer than he needs to. He probably does not want to fly back and forth, disrupting his life in Texas either. I would not be surprised if arraignment happens next week, and we go to trial shortly afterward."

"At the arraignment," Dakota added. "We will do the same as today, plead not guilty and avoid showing any of our hand. We'll do everything possible to expedite all of this, Jake."

The arraignment hearing took place three days after the preliminary hearing. Jake pled not guilty on the formal charges.

The court date was announced for October 1st, three weeks from the arraignment, and the jury selection concluded. It consisted of six men and six women, and six of of the twelve were American Indians.

Dakota and Jim had their game plan set, and all the necessary evidence and witnesses lined up. They even built a dog house on the butte for Honi, becuase they needed Jake concentrating on the trial and not to be distracted worrying about his wolf.

Dakota contacted Alex and the family with the court date.

She knew from "discovery" exchanges that Sellman and Joe had their case in order, too, and were confident it would be over quickly.

We'll see.

The FBI assigned a young, overzealous agent to the case, named Charli Evels. The FBI had believed the evidence in the case was pretty straight forward, and saw no need to place a seasoned agent on it. Evels conducted her investigation looking for more evidence that simply did not exist, and her persistence was a distraction to the police at first. As the weeks passed, however, she saw there was nothing else she could add of relevance.

Jake's condition regressed, and he had spells on a weekly basis. Fortunately, he remained silent during them. Whatever the spirit world showed him, he elected not to share with Dakota. She couldn't shake the feeling that he was making plans without her — again.

CHAPTER 41
LET THE GAMES BEGIN

The atmosphere outside the courthouse was electric. Local and national news stations surrounded the building, as all attention turned to the *"Wolf Man with Alzheimer's, charged with beating the billionaire's sons."*

Dakota and her grandfather sat in the prep room watching interviews on TV.

Dakota said, "It looks like half of the people are on our side, Woo Woo, while the other half believes he needs to be convicted despite his illness. The funny part is they don't even know all the facts. They're forming their opinions on emotions."

"That is good, Lomasi. Hopefully, the jurors use emotion. It is what this case is all about. Emotion is what started Jake on his journey. Emotion is what will allow him to continue as a free man."

"I'm nervous. There's so much riding on this."

"Lomasi, I cannot begin to tell you how proud I am of you. Today is a dream come true for me. Since you were little, I have looked forward to fighting alongside you in the courtroom. I know that the outcome of this trial has immense implications for you personally, but in there, you must separate yourself from that. Just be a lawyer. Connect with the human side of the jurors. Impress upon their emotions. That is where you beat Sellman. He will be a tough adversary, one with years of experience. You worry about the jurors. I will worry about him."

There was a knock at the door.

"Come in, please," Jim said.

"Your client is here. Shall I bring him in?" the court officer said.

"Yes, please have him come in. Thank you, Officer," Jim said.

Jake walked into the room dressed in a perfectly fitted suit, with his hair pulled back in a ponytail and his beard groomed.

Dakota looked him up and down, raising her brow. "Wow, Jake, I must say the women will love this new look."

Jim nodded. "You clean up well," he said in a serious tone. "You look ten years younger. I am not sure we want you looking this healthy."

"Grandfather, what are you thinking?"

Jim paused, looking at Jake. "Never mind. We will introduce Jake looking like this. As the trial moves forward, we will roughen him up a bit. We will make it look like it is worsening his mental state. I am going to leave you two alone for a few minutes. I need some breakfast. Do either of you want anything? We have about a half hour."

"I would love a cup of coffee, Grandfather."

Jake said, "A bottle of water would be great, Jim, thank you."

After Jim left, Jake turned his attention to Dakota.

Her eyes sparkled. "You look so handsome. I can't take my eyes off of you."

He smiled. "Counselor, you are twirling your hair. Not sure you want to do that in there."

"Ohhh, sorry, good catch. Yes, that would not be good. Hopefully, you can get the female jurors doing that." Dakota winked. "How do you feel?"

"I'm ready to get this over and move on with my life. I feel Jim and you have this handled, and I'm just a spectator."

"I *am sure* you will be asked to take the stand. Remember the jurors are the ones who decide your fate, not the judge, not Jim and I, and not the DA. When you speak, you speak to them. Okay?"

"Yes. How was Honi yesterday?"

"He wanted to play all day. He's so spoiled. He has even made friends with the officer."

"Good, all I have to worry about is in that courtroom right now. How do you feel?"

"I'm nervous. I can't fail. Your future—*our* future—depends on it. No pressure, right?" She chuckled nervously.

"You'll be fine. You will say and do the right things. I'm not nervous one bit, and you shouldn't be either."

Jim walked back into the room. "Well, we are fifteen minutes till game time. Is everyone ready?"

"Yes, Coach," Dakota said.

"All rise for the Honorable Judge Still Water," the bailiff announced. The packed courthouse quieted.

"Please be seated." The judge went through the formalities of starting the trail, and called on the prosecution to open the case.

Joe Ross presented the opening statement. "Your Honor, ladies and gentlemen of the jury, thank you. The case we are about to try has garnered much attention. There are legal questions, moral questions, and ethical questions. We *must* concentrate on the legal questions. I am not asking you to make an immoral or unethical decision. I only ask that you focus on the evidence that will be provided.

"The Defendant is being charged with Manslaughter and Assault with a Deadly Weapon. Both are serious felony charges. The evidence will clearly show beyond reasonable doubt that the brutal actions of the defendant led to the death of three young men."

Dakota sprang to her feet. "Objection, Your Honor, that is conjecture."

"Sustained. Mr. Ross, please stick to the facts."

"Yes, Your Honor. I will rephrase that. The actions of the defendant may have contributed to injuries that led to the fatal accident in which three men perished.

"The evidence will show that the defendant, unprovoked, attacked those men. The defendant is a highly trained Military Special Forces soldier. The three unarmed men stood no chance to defend themselves."

Dakota started to stand up, but Jim grabbed her arm and whispered, "Let him lay out his case. We will have our chance."

Joe continued. "The Defense will maintain he acted in self-defense. They will talk about his mental state. The evidence will clearly show their arguments will be unfounded. Again, I must ask you: *please* focus on the facts and evidence presented, and *not* on the emotions that surround this case. Thank you." Joe smiled at the jury as he sat down.

Dakota stood up, walked over to the jury, and faced them. "Ladies and gentlemen of the jury, thank you for taking time out of your lives to hear this case." She made eye contact with each and every juror.

"The prosecution asks you to make your decision based only on the facts. I too will ask you to do the same. However, there *will be* moral and ethical questions that will arise in this case. They are undeniable. Moral and ethical decisions are what led my client to his actions the night of the attack. Evidence that we will present will prove that. Thank you."

Judge Still Water banged his gavel. "Let the court show opening statements are complete. The prosecution may now present their case."

Joe mimicked Dakota's approach to the jury and walked over to them. "Ladies and gentlemen of the jury, the first piece of evidence is graphic in nature. It is violent and shows nudity. I urge that you do not look away so you can fully understand the brutality of this attack. If the bailiff can please darken the room, I will direct the court's attention to the screen."

The video of the attack played. Several female jurors were visibly disturbed by the content.

Dakota watched each juror closely as the frames played. She noticed the females showed more reaction to the sexual nature and graphic language than the men did. The men grimaced as the walking stick struck Hollywood's penis. That did not surprise her. Overall, the male jurors did not seem as affected by the video as the women did. This is what she wanted.

The lights in the courtroom came back up.

Joe paused purposely and looked at each juror without saying a word for several moments. "Pretty horrific isn't it? At no moment do you see the men provoke the defendant. In fact, they offer to allow him to participate in the consensual sexual encounter they were having. I emphasize, consensual."

Dakota's stomach turned as she heard the DA describe the sexual encounter as consensual.

Jake's face reddened with anger.

Jim looked away. Beneath the table, his hands trembled.

Joe continued. "Those young men sustained excruciating, disfiguring injuries. The coroner's report details the extent of the injuries suffered by each victim. Richard Dibella suffered blunt force trauma to his penis. Photos show that his penis was bent in half. Because he was erect at the time, the stick opened up a gaping wound. That injury resulted in a fair amount of blood loss. It is clear that he was rendered incapable of protecting himself. Marcus Dibella suffered a broken jaw, a laceration to his face, had several teeth knocked out, and it is presumed he suffered a concussion. Remember, he was driving the vehicle when it crashed. *It is crucial that you remember that.* Shane Rogers suffered a fractured arm, a fractured leg, and a fractured knee cap. Ladies and gentlemen, these boys suffered. Given the vulnerable, compromising position they were in, they stood no chance to defend themselves. The video shows how quickly and diligently the defendant attacked. He is highly trained in close-quarters combat. Even in different circumstances, these men had little to no chance to protect themselves."

Joe walked away from the Juror's box. "At this time, Your Honor, I would like to turn the floor over to Mr. Sellman, Co-Counsel in this case."

Sellman stood up, walked to the center of the courtroom, lowered his head and shook it. He looked up at the jury and pointed in the direction of Vincent Dibella and his wife. "How difficult this must be for the parents of these young men to watch. They are present in the courtroom. How difficult this is for *any of us* to watch who are parents, to know that a vicious, unprovoked attack led to the deaths of three young men."

Dakota interjected, "Objection, Your Honor, counsel is leading the jurors."

"Sustained. Counsel, please state the facts."

Sellman ignored the judge and said, "At this time, I would like to call Dr. Jessica Sanders to the stand."

Jessica took the stand.

"Please state your name and title."

"Dr. Jessica Sanders, Chief Coroner of Fort Washakie."

"Dr. Sanders, you performed the autopsies of the three victims, correct?"

"That is correct."

"Your original exam focused on injuries due to a vehicle accident, correct?"

"That is correct."

"Because of the multiple traumas caused by the crash, you did not pay much attention to the more acute injuries they suffered from the attack. Is that correct?"

"Yes, that is correct."

"Once it was determined that these victims suffered injuries prior to the accident, what did you do?"

"I reexamined my original injury notes and photographs, then compared them to the video."

"What did you find once you made that comparison?"

"I found bruises and wounds that would match the strike pattern of the stick seen in the video."

"Doctor, in your opinion, is it possible that those injuries caused the death of the three young men?"

"In my opinion, none of those injuries would be life-threatening."

Dakota and Jim looked at each other, puzzled. Dakota wondered why Sellman would call her to the witness stand.

The jurors looked at each other, as did people in the courtroom.

"Doctor, are you stating that they could not have contributed to the victim's death?"

"No, I'm stating that, on their own, they were not life-threatening injuries. Given the fact that the driver, Marcus Dibella, did suffer head trauma, it is possible that his judgment was impaired. His vision could have been compromised by that trauma, or he could have passed out."

Several gasps erupted in the courtroom.

"Thank you, Doctor, no further questions."

The judge said, "Ms. Reynolds, your witness."

"Thank you, Your Honor." She looked first at the jurors, then at the doctor. "Dr. Sanders, what was the blood alcohol content of Marcus Dibella?"

"0.10"

"0.10... is that not considered legally intoxicated, Doctor?"

"Yes, it is."

"Dr. Sanders, is it possible alcohol could have played a significant part in the accident?"

"Yes."

"No further questions, Your Honor."

The judge said, "Dr. Sanders, you may step down. Prosecution, your next witness...."

"Your Honor," Sellman said. "I would like to call Dr. Evelyn Wells to the stand."

A scholarly woman took the stand.

"Please state your name and position, Doctor."

"Dr. Evelyn Wells, Chief Forensic Pathologist for Dallas, Texas."

"Dr. Wells, in your long tenure, how many cases would you say that you've worked on?"

"Close to ten thousand over the past forty years."

Sellman spun and faced the jury. "*Ten thousand cases!* That, in my opinion, would make you very qualified."

"Just a tad," Wells scoffed.

"Dr. Wells, have you had a chance to review the tape and Dr. Sanders' reports?"

"I have, in great detail."

"Based on your wealth of experience, do you see a connection between the injuries suffered in the attack and the fatal car accident?"

She nodded. "I started paying closer attention to the attack on the driver, Marcus Dibella. I looked at his injuries post-mortem, and something caught my eye. Based on the location of the blow and the bruising caused, I believe the strike moved his head past a healthy axis. When I examined the post-mortem photos, I noticed his neck had snapped, placing his head in an unnatural position. I have seen this in high impact trauma many times, but, based on the police report, the vehicle was not traveling at high speeds."

Sellman interjected, "Doctor, you may be losing some of us. Are you saying that Marcus Dibella also suffered a neck injury in the attack?"

"It is my opinion that he indeed suffered a neck injury that would have weakened the muscles and possibly the vertebrae in his neck. The secondary impact of the accident caused just enough movement to an already compromised neck, allowing it to break."

Murmurs moved through courtroom.

"What a reach that is," Jim whispered to Dakota.

"Good old boy network at its finest," she said.

Sellman panned the courthouse after hearing the reaction. "No further questions, Your Honor."

The judge turned to Dakota. "Ms. Reynolds, your witness."

"Dr. Wells, do you agree with Dr. Sanders that each injury on their own was not life-threatening?"

"Yes, with medical treatment, they were not life-threatening."

"Dr. Wells, in *all* of the cases you worked over your illustrious career, I would assume you've seen many alcohol-related fatalities. Could a BOC of 0.10 create enough impairment to cause the fatal crash?"

"It is possible, but without knowing the deceased's tolerance, it is hard to say one hundred percent."

"Could it at the *very* least have contributed to the crash?"

"Yes."

"No further questions, Your Honor."

"Prosecution, your next witness."

Sellman said, "At this time, Your Honor, I'm turning the floor back over to the DA, thank you."

Joe moved to the center of the court. "Your Honor, before I call my next witness, I would like to call the court's attention to Exhibit B. This is an eyewitness statement of the crash. In her own words, the eyewitness stated that the Dibella vehicle passed her and was moving at a slow speed. The vehicle drifted off the road and over the cliff. At that point, Marcus Dibella had driven six-point-eight miles through winding canyon roads, roads much more treacherous than the slight bend he failed to navigate. Based on her statement, it did not appear he was driving erratic at the time of the crash. I want the jury to please note this as they consider his blood alcohol content. At this time, I would like to call Officer James Red Cloud to the stand."

Jimmy looked at Jim and Dakota as he took the stand.

"Officer, please state your name and title."

"James Red Cloud, Police Officer, Fort Washakie."

"Officer Red Cloud, in a cooperative effort between Sulphur Springs Police Department, Dubois Sheriff Department, and your police department, you successfully apprehended the defendant. You are the arresting officer on the report. Is all of this correct?"

"Yes, sir, it is all correct."

"The report reads that you made initial contact with the defendant and proceeded to handcuff him and read him his rights. How did the defendant act?"

"He was very cordial. He did not resist. He did not attempt to flee. He was more concerned about his wolf than anything, it seemed."

This brought a murmur from the courtroom.

"How would say his mental state was?"

Dakota barked, "Objection, Officer Red Cloud is not trained to make that assessment."

The judge turned to Joe. "Sustained. Mr. Ross, please rephrase that."

Joe said, "Officer Red Cloud, you and Special Investigator Jay Storm Walker escorted the defendant out of the mountains. It is roughly five miles from where you apprehended him to Dubois. In those five miles, did the defendant give you any indication that he did not understand what was happening?"

"No."

"During your interrogation, did the defendant ever deny an altercation with the deceased?"

"No."

"Again, through that process, did the defendant understand the situation?"

"Yes, he was clear."

"Officer Red Cloud, have you ever seen the defendant exhibit any form of incoherent behavior?"

"No, I personally have not."

"So, in your opinion, the defendant knew exactly what he did that night and understood the charges that he faced?"

Dakota started to stand, but Jim held her arm and whispered, "Let him go. The DA is beating a dead horse."

"Yes," Jimmy said. "In my opinion, he did."

"Thank you, Officer, no further questions."

The judge said, "Ms. Reynolds, your witness."

"No questions, Your Honor."

"It's noon," the judge announced. "We will recess for lunch for one hour."

Jim, Dakota, and Jake regrouped in a holding area.

"Well, what do you all think?" Jake said.

Jim said, "The tape is very damning, as we know. The Texas doctor's testimony does not help."

Dakota said, "Grandfather, do you not think the blood alcohol content will help us?"

"It is hard to tell. The eyewitness stated they were not driving erraticly. Joe brings up a good point in the fact that they did navigate much more difficult canyon roads before the crash. The jury is all local, and they know the route those men traveled. They will agree with the prosecution on the road conditions. There certainly are much more hazardous areas that a drunk driver would have had a better chance of crashing on."

Jake jumped in. "Do you think they will buy into self-defense? Remember, I do have their gun. I can say I disarmed one of the men."

"Dakota and I thought about introducing it as late evidence that you did not disclose. The only problem is getting a jury to believe that you took out two men before the third could fire a shot. The tape shows there would have been more than enough time for the third man to shoot."

"What if I say that I took the gun from the truck before confronting them?"

"Then the prosecution could say that you had time to react to the situation you came upon. It could lean the jury towards premeditation, and not an instinctive action, as we will contend in our closing arguments. And, if you did have a gun, the prosecution will ask why you did not use it to deter the rape, versus beating them. We need to leave the gun out of it," Jim concluded.

"Well, Jim, I do have the knife wound on my shoulder."

"Yes, with no knife to prove that the cut came from the attack over a year ago. We will still bring that up. If anything, it will cause the jurors to think about it."

Dakota threw a file on the desk. "Those pieces of shit are starting to look like poor helpless angels."

Jake held up his hands. "I know this is a dumb question, but did we run a background on them?"

Dakota nodded. "Yes, and we got nothing other than some minor stuff. Vincent Dibella would have never let anything serious hit their records and tarnish his name."

Jim paused and looked down, tapping his pen on the desk. "We will stay on track with our defense. I believe the medical and military angle will help us."

"Jake," Dakota said. "The prosecution wants to call you to the stand after lunch. You do not have to agree to their request. Are you sure you want to take the stand, and are you prepared?"

Jake pushed out his chest and narrowed his eyes. "Yes, let the games begin."

CHAPTER 42
THE GAMES CONTINUE

"All rise, this court is in session," the bailiff announced.

"Please be seated," Judge Still Water ordered. "The prosecution may call its next witness."

Sellman stood up. "Thank you, Your Honor, we would like to call the defendant to the stand."

Jake took the stand.

The judge turned to him. "Mr. Michaels, by law you do not have to testify. Do you understand this and agree to proceed?"

"Yes, Your Honor."

The judge nodded. "Very well, Mr. Sellman, you may proceed."

Jake glanced over the crowded courtroom. He smiled at Alexi and the kids, and looked at Dakota and Jim, both of whom nodded.

Sellman stood before Jake as if ready to do physical battle. "Mr. Michaels, in your own words, can you tell the court why you attacked the three men on that fateful night?"

Jake paused for a few moments. "Mr. Sellman, first and foremost, I will not agree to your terminology — to your use of the word *attack*."

Just as Jim and Dakota had said would happen, Sellman quickly became angry. The veins in his temples flared "Mr. Michaels, this is not a vocabulary debate. I have asked you a question. Please answer it."

"Rephrase the question, and I will be happy to."

A slight chuckle bounced around the courtroom.

Sellman smirked, easing his tone. "Okay, Mr. Michaels, please tell the court what happened the night shown in the video."

"I was hiking on the Continental Divide Trail. I came up to a clearing and saw lights in a field. I pulled up my binoculars, and saw three men pushing a female around. I watched one man cut off her clothes and throw her to the ground. At that point, I moved swiftly towards the field. The three men removed their clothes. I could hear the female crying as I got closer, and watched as the one man grabbed her hair and forced his penis to her mouth. At that time, I was close enough to survey the position of each man. I approached the first man as he began to rape the female, and hit him across the penis. The second man, who was shooting the video, was close enough for me to disable. The third man, not seen on the video, rushed at me with a knife. He slashed me before I could defend myself."

Jake pulled up his sleeve, showing the wound on his shoulder. "I ordered the three men to leave, standing between them and the girl. The men gathered themselves and drove off. I then escorted the woman to her car, and she drove off."

Whispers moved through the courtroom.

Sellman looked down, shook his head, and chuckled. "Mr. Michaels, this is a very convenient story, given there are no witnesses to collaborate it. In the video, the woman clearly states that she wants you to join the other men. What did the deceased say to you before you said, "No one is fucking anyone tonight?"

Jake squinted and shook his head. "I don't remember." He glanced at Dakota.

"You don't remember?" Sellman barked.

"No, I don't."

"Mr. Michaels, at any time, did any of the men threaten you before you assaulted them?"

Jake stared at the ceiling, again shaking his head. "I know they said something to me, but I don't remember."

Sellman turned to the jury. "You don't remember. This is becoming too convenient, Mr. Michaels." He paused and sauntered to the jury box. "It is tough for the jury to trust the words of a man who faked his death, left his family behind, moved to a mountaintop, lives with a wolf, and now has selective memory."

"Objection, Your Honor," Dakota shouted. "That is irrelevant."

"Sustained. Mr. Sellman, refrain from expressing your personal beliefs."

Jake looked at the jury. "It's fine, Your Honor. He's right. My words should be scrutinized. I don't hide from the fact that I faked my death. I don't hide from my illness. My secrets are out now. I have no reason to lie about anything."

Sellman stalked towards him again. "Then, Mr. Michaels, tell us why you attacked these three men. If this was rape, as you contend, *why* did the woman not go to the police? I would think with *all* the press covering this, she would come to your aid now, as you claim to have done for her. Your story just does not add up, sir."

Jake looked at Jim, Dakota, Alexi, and the full courtroom. He straightened his back, paused, and glared at Sellman. "Mr. Sellman, perhaps, like many sexual assault victims, she chose not to report this. Maybe she realizes that crimes against American Indian women go mostly unpunished. Think about it, Mr. Sellman. Would that women stand any chance of success accusing your client's sons, given their stature? I think you know that answer, don't you?"

Sellman looked at Jake for several moments, then smiled and clapped his hands slowly. He turned to the jury and then the Court Room. "Bravo, Mr. Michaels, bravo! Obviously, you have spent some time covering all bases. On questions you chose not to answer, you simply claim you don't remember."

Sellman moved towards the stand. He exaggerated a laugh and head shake. "So, let me get this correct, Mr. Michaels. You show up in the middle of nowhere, happen to walk upon a rape, you save the women, she drives away, you continue your hike, and both of you go about your life as if nothing happened. Mr. Michaels, do you not find it a bit peculiar that the woman had a vehicle at the scene? *Is it possible*, Mr. Michaels, that the woman drove to the area to meet up with these men? *Is it possible*, Mr. Michaels, that you just simply took offense to the sexual act that you came upon, taking some moral stand against what you saw?"

"Mr. Sellman, I agree that the video and circumstances paint a different picture. As I said earlier, I have no reason to lie about this. That woman was being attacked, and I defended her."

"Mr. Michaels, how did the cellphone get to the bottom of the ravine?"

"I threw it."

'So, you knew they were filming their sexual encounter. After you attacked them, you threw the evidence of your attack into the ravine, hoping it would never be seen. Is that correct?"

"I threw it out of disgust, and to destroy their trophy of the heinous acts they were doing to that woman."

Sellman's tone turned angry, and he leaned on the bench rail, staring Jake in the eyes. "Bottom line is, Mr. Michaels, you are alive, and those three young men are *dead* because of your actions." He straightened up and turned back toward his seat. "No further questions, Your Honor."

The judge said, "Defense, your witness."

Dakota approached the jury box. "Mr. Michaels, have you ever been arrested or charged with a crime in your life?"

"No."

"Mr. Michaels, how long have you been married?"

"Thirty years."

"What is your anniversary date?"

Jake struggled with the answer. He looked at Alexi, and after a long pause, said, "I don't remember."

"Mr. Michaels, what are the middle names of your three children?"

Jake looked down and shook his head. Tears fell down his cheeks as he lifted his head and looked at his family. "John's is Michael, Danielle's is Marie, and... I cannot remember Robert's."

The jury's eyes fixed on the Michaels family. Alexi and Danielle dabbed tears from their eyes. John and Robert lowered their heads.

"Mr. Michaels, what is your wife's maiden name?"

Jake wiped tears from his eyes as he looked at Alexi. "I am sorry, but I can't remember. Please, for the sake of my family, can we stop these questions? *This* is why I left them, to spare them this pain."

Danielle stood up and raced from the courtroom, her sobs breaking the dead silence that had fallen over the chamber. Robert followed after her.

Dakota paused and composed herself. Jake understood that she knew this was causing him and his family pain. He also understood that it had to hurt her to put them through this.

"Mr. Michael's," she said. "When you came upon the attack, what was your first thought?"

"I needed to save this woman."

"So, despite the fact that you were trying to disappear from society, you unselfishly risked your life, your *secret*, to come to her aid?"

Jake sighed. "Yes."

"You must have had an overwhelming concern for her safety?"

He nodded. "I did. The video simply does not show the whole truth."

"So, let me put this in context. You created an elaborate plan to fake your death. You walked away from a family that you loved, to spare them from watching your mental decline. You put them through the heartache of believing you were dead. You did all of that, but... when you came upon a stranger in distress, you were willing to risk not just exposing your secret, but possibly your life?"

"Of course."

"No further questions, Your Honor."

Low murmers whispered through the courtroom.

Jim smiled and lipped, *"Good job,"* to Dakota as she returned to her seat.

"Prosecution, your next witness," Judge Still Water directed.

Joe approached the bench. "Thank you, Your Honor. We call Ms. Lauren Nicoles." After she took the stand, he continued. "Ms. Nicoles, you were the first person on the scene the night of the accident. Can you describe what you saw please?"

She nodded. "Yes, sir, I had just pulled onto Red Canyon Road. The truck the men were driving passed me. They were driving normal, and then suddenly started weaving, and drove off the cliff. I pulled up to where they went off, and could hear one of the men crying for help. His voice echoed in the night from the ravine below. It was horrible. I will never get that out of my mind. I called 911. The police arrived pretty fast, but it seemed like an eternity. That poor man just kept crying for help."

"Ms. Nicoles, when the men passed you, were they speeding?"

"No, sir, like I said, I had just pulled onto the road, and was probably only going 25 miles an hour. They passed like normal. There was no oncoming traffic. They had time."

"So, they were not driving erratic, aggressively, or in a manner that one would consider a drunk driver would behave?"

"No, sir, just right before they went off the road. They weaved a bit, like they were trying to avoid something, but I didn't see anything in front of us."

"Thank you, Ms. Nicoles, no further questions."

Th judge said, "Your witness, Ms. Reynolds."

"Thank you, Your Honor. Ms. Nicoles, where were you coming from that evening?"

"I had just left work at the Cowboy Saloon."

"Did you leave work immediately?"

"No, ma'am, I stayed for about an hour afterward."

"Did you have any drinks during that time?"

Joe jumed up. "Objection, Your Honor, the witness is not on trial."

Dakota said, "Your Honor, I want to make sure that Ms. Nicole's perception was clear."

The judge said, "Overruled. Ms. Nicoles, please answer the question."

"Yes," she said sheepishly. "I did have a couple of drinks."

"A couple being one or two, three or four, five or six?"

"I had three beers, Ms. Reynolds."

Dakota glanced at the jury. "You're a small woman. Could three beers in an hour, after a long day, have impaired your judgment a bit?"

"*Objection, Your Honor*, conjecture," Joe interjected again.

"Sustained."

Dakota said, "No further questions, Your Honor."

"Prosecution, please call your next witness."

"Prosecution has no more witnesses, Your Honor."

The judge looked at his watch. "The Court will adjourn until 9 a.m. tomorrow."

"All rise," the bailiff announced.

Dakota, Jim, and Jake regrouped in the safe room back in Dubois.

Jake's nerves were firing on all cyclinders. "Well, what are you two thinking?"

"Honestly, Jake, I don't know," Dakota said. "The fact that my car was there is damning. It would seem like I did meet those pieces of shit. The fact that you threw the phone is a compelling argument for the prosecution. That damn tape plays like it was edited to convict you. If I did not trust Jimmy and the officers who had it, I would have my suspicions. Grandfather, what are your thoughts?"

Jim said, "Our only shot is to stay committed to appealing to the human and medical element of this. We will call our witnesses tomorrow. There will be plenty of news tonight covering the first day of the trial. I am interested in seeing the tone of the legal analysts. They may give us some insight into how the jurors perceived today. I am going home. Dakota, I will see you tonight. Jake, I will see you tomorrow."

"Goodnight, Jim, and thank you."

Jim nodded as he left the room.

Jake turned back to Dakota. "What do you think, counselor?"

"I'm worried about you forgetting details from that night and your past life. I think you need your medicine."

"I remember every detail of that night. The past life answers were honest."

"Jake, I just don't know if we're going to be successful. I don't know what I would do without you. I can't have you sitting in jail for years. I must find a smoking gun."

"Is it too late to cop a plea for a lesser charge?"

"Sellman would never go for it. He can taste blood right now. He wants victory on the national stage." She looked him in the eyes. "I want to call Alex to the stand tomorrow. I believe we need to build your character to the point that the jury will at least ponder the possibility that you're telling the truth."

He lowered his eyes and shook his head. "No, Dakota, can we please keep them out of this as much as possible? I've put them through enough."

She placed her hands on his. "Jake, listen to me. If we do not get you off of these charges, or at least convince the jury to find you not guilty of Manslaughter, you're facing up to forty years in prison. Neither your family nor I could bear that. You will die in there."

He looked at the ceiling. "How could this get so turned around? Where are the Spirits now, Dakota? Am I, or we, being punished for our actions?"

Dakota half-smiled and her voice softened. "No, we're being tested."

"I don't see how putting Alexi on the stand will help us."

"Can you talk with her during visitation? And trust me on this, please?"

He inhaled deeply. "Okay, I will ask her."

Dakota stood up and leaned across the table to kiss Jake. "Soon, we will be past this, I promise. Have faith." She exited to get Alexi and the family.

"Alex, I'm sorry I had to ask Jake those questions and cause you and the children pain."

"Dakota, I understand. It's not looking too good right now for him, is it?"

Dakota paused. Her eyes welled. "No, it's not. Hopefully, our witnesses will help tomorrow. Jake is waiting for you."

Dakota walked away, mad at herself for allowing her emotions to show in front of Alex.

Alexi was taken back by the emotion Dakota showed, which seemed a bit much for an attorney-client relationship. On the last visit to Dubois, she'd noted how Jake looked at Dakota, and dismissed it as normal. After all, Dakota was strikingly beautiful, and Jake had been on a mountain, isolated, for over a year. Besides, he always did have a wandering eye.

Still, her intuition told her there was more to this, but she couldn't put her finger on it.

She entered the safe room, and Jake stood up and hugged her.

She playfully grabbed his ponytail. "You look handsome. Maybe I should have let you grow one of these years ago."

"No, I had a hard enough time beating the women off," he joked, then grew somber. "I'm sorry that you and the kids had to watch me not being able to answer those questions. I know Dakota told you about the tumor. It's only going to get worse, Alexi. You see now what I wanted to protect you from."

"Jake, you can't apologize for something you can't control. You owe me no apologies for anything. I was mad at you when I left here a few weeks ago. I felt betrayed. But when I thought about how you devoted your life to me, and how you always had my best interest in mind, I forgave you. Now, all I want for you is to be out of this jail. I want you to live the remainder of your life in peace. You earned it. You've been the most unselfish man I've ever known. As the tumor grows, I will fade from your memory, but you will not fade from mine. So please don't apologize anymore. Okay?"

She dried the tears falling down her cheeks.

He dabbed a tear she missed. "Thank you, Alexi. I don't know what the outcome of all this will be, but, knowing that you understand will allow me to live my remaining days in peace."

They held hands, and he smiled warmly at her. She noticed the sparkle in his eyes was still dead, though. The disease had taken that forever.

"Jake, this trial is not looking good for you. You can't spend the rest of your days in jail. I know you. It will kill you quickly. I know there's more to the story of that night. I know you would never attack those men for no reason. Is there nothing your attorneys can find or do?"

"No, but you're right, Alexi, there is a great deal more to this story to unfold. I've told all I can tell, all I can remember. Dakota and Jim feel our only defense now is to allow the jury to see who the real Jake Michaels is, or was. Perhaps it will put enough doubt in their minds to not convict me. Dakota wants to put you on the stand tomorrow. You're the best character witness, and can paint a picture of Jake Michaels better than anyone. I told her no, that I would not allow you to endure any more pain."

She looked crossly at him. "Listen here, you've made *enough* decisions for me in all this. I will take the stand tomorrow if it gives you a chance to leave this jail, a chance to at least have a part in your kids' lives while you can remember them."

"What about your life, Alexi?"

"Jake, you and I both know this is where you need to spend the final chapter of your life. You probably don't remember, but those were your exact words when we came on vacation out here. My life is back home. If you want me to stay here as the disease kills off Jake and Alexi, I will, but if that were truly what you wanted, you would not have faked your death."

He smiled. "I do remember saying that, but this is not how I intended it to happen. Thank you."

"It's getting late, and the kids want to see you. I'll tell Dakota that I'll take the stand tomorrow. Get some sleep. Tomorrow is a big day." As she knocked on the door to be let out, Honi's nightly howls started. "My God, he sounds so sad. He needs you back on that mountain."

Jake nodded and smiled sadly. "When I get out of here, I'll take you and the kids to meet him. He's a big baby."

"That sounds good, Jake. Goodnight."

She told the kids it was their turn, and they rushed in to see their dad.

Alex looked across the lobby to Dakota, who sat by herself on a bench, her head down as she reviewed notes.

"Dakota, may I sit down?"

"Of course, Alex."

"I will testify tomorrow if it helps Jake. What do you think his chances are? You don't know him. He hates being cooped up. If he has to spend any significant time in prison, it will kill him. I want my kids to spend time with their father before this disease erases them from his memory."

Alex's selfless commitment to her kids pulled at Dakota's heart. Jake had told her many times about "The Momma Bear." One day, she hoped she would have children of her own to devote herself to.

She took a deep breath, so as not to show any emotion—like earlier. "I'm watching the news and reading legal blogs. The majority of the people recognize that Jake has an illness, but they can't see how it would cause him to attack those men. Many of the pundits believe that, despite the illness, he still must be held accountable for his actions. There's a minority that believes the tape only shows a small picture of that night, and they believe Jake. In many cases, the feedback from the media is a good barometer of what the jury believes. If this is the case, his chances are not good."

"How many years is he facing?"

"Up to forty on Manslaughter, ten on Assault." Dakota's tone was solemn.

"That's a life sentence, given his age," Alex said.

Dakota breathed deeply. "Yes, it is."

Jim and Anna sat on the couch watching the coverage of the trial.

Jim shook his head. "Anna, we made a terrible mistake. An innocent man is going to go to jail because of our actions. Our Lomasi is going to be heartbroken. She will not recover from this. She will stay dedicated to him in prison until he is gone. Her life will stop. His family must now endure more pain. We should have never tipped off the police. We did not understand the bond Dakota and Jake had formed that night. We should not have tried to alter Destiny."

Anna held his hand. "We thought his disease would provide a defense, and that he would be committed to a hospital back home where his family could care for him. We did not do this on purpose. In our hearts, we were doing what was best for Lomasi, Jake, and his family."

"I understand that, but we miscalculated. Now more suffering is coming."

"What about a plea, Jim? Joe Ross is an idiot, but he is fair."

"Joe is not the problem. Sellman is circling like a shark, and he can smell blood. He will never agree to a plea on a national stage."

Anna paused for a moment. "You don't think Dakota would tell the truth to save Jake, do you? That would expose all of us?"

"She would face the same scrutiny by the court. We have no proof to counter that tape. You should have seen the jurors' faces as they watched it. The case was all but over for several of them. Dakota coming forward would just add to the spectacle. Sellman would have a field day. The press would devour it."

"So, what can you do?"

Jim sighed. "Let's see how tomorrow goes. Alex Michaels has agreed to take the stand. At this point, all we can do is take it one day at a time, and pray for a miracle."

CHAPTER 43
DAY TWO

"All rise for the Honorable Judge Still Water," the bailiff announced.

The judge said, "Thank you, and please be seated. Today the defense will call their witnesses. Ms. Reynolds, please proceed."

"Thank you, Your Honor. Defense calls Dr. Harold Taylor." After he took the stand, she said, "Please state your name and title, Doctor."

"Dr. Harold Taylor, Chief of Neurology for the Department of Veteran Services."

"Dr. Taylor, you have examined Jake Michaels. You supplied the court with a report that is very detailed with medical language. Briefly, in layman's terms, can you describe your findings, please?"

"Certainly. Mr. Michaels has a 2mm growth in the hippocampus of the brain. The hippocampus is believed to be one of the areas of the brain that long-term memory, or episodic memory, is stored for recall. I believe that growth impedes Mr. Michael's ability to remember things from his past, as we have witnessed."

"Doctor, is the damage this growth is causing reversible?"

"Unfortunately, the position of the growth makes it inoperable. The damage that has occurred cannot be reversed."

"Doctor, you also noted in your report that Mr. Michaels served in eleven battle zones. You theorize that the multiple concussive blasts that he endured may have caused CTE, or Chronic Traumatic Encephalopathy. How many concussive blasts are needed for CTE?"

"In autopsies, we have seen as little as one concussive blast cause damage."

"One blast? And how many has Mr. Michaels endured?"

"I cannot put an accurate number on it, but based on knowledge of the battle zones Mr. Michaels served in, I would estimate sixty to seventy, maybe more."

Dakota looked at the jury, raising her eyebrows. "Sixty to seventy... that is significant." She returned her attention to the witness stand. "Doctor, if a person had CTE, what would his symptoms be?"

"Many patients show signs of memory loss and confusion. Impulsive control issues, aggression, and depression are common. Parkinson-like symptoms can occur, and eventually severe dementia. Not every person will show the same symptoms. The brain is difficult to predict."

"Doctor, you also note that Mr. Michael's could have PTSD. You stated that PTSD could cause a person to react with more than necessary force in altercations. Can you explain this, please?"

"We have seen cases were PTSD patients under great duress will revert to their formal training, and react in a manner similar to battle."

"Is it possible, in your opinion, the night that Jake Michaels confronted the three men, that CTE, PTSD, or his tumor, or any combination of those, could have clouded his judgment? Could he have come upon a consensual sexual encounter and seen it as an attack?"

"No, all tests that I conducted show that Mr. Michaels' reasoning skills are fine."

"So, you would say that Jake Michaels knew exactly what he witnessed, and acted accordingly?"

"Yes."

"Is it also possible that Mr. Michaels' "selective memory," as the prosecution called it, is very much *not* selective, but uncontrollable?"

"Yes, without a doubt."

"Thank you, Doctor, no further questions."

The judge said, "Prosecution, your witness."

"Thank you, Your Honor." Joe stood up as Sellman passed him some notes. "Dr. Taylor, you state that the defendant's reasoning skills are intact. Is it reasonable to preclude no medical conditions would have caused him to attack these men?"

"Yes."

"So, Doctor, please tell us what medical condition you have identified, which the defendant suffers from, and which would have caused him to use excessive deadly force on three unarmed men?"

"There is no medical condition. I believe he *did* act in defense of the young women. Given the fact that he was outnumbered, I believe he used appropriate force. Jake Michaels is highly trained. If he wanted to use *deadly* force, as you call it, counselor, these men would have never left that field."

"Objection, Your Honor," Sellman barked. "The witness is not trained to make the assumptions of reasonable force. That is conjecture."

"Sustained."

Joe said, "No further questions, Your Honor."

"Defense, please call your next witness."

Dakota said, "We call Dr. Jason Weston."

A stately, older gentleman approached the stand.

"Dr. Weston, please state your name and title."

"Dr. Jason Weston, Deputy Coroner of Luzerne County, Pa."

"Dr. Weston, you've had an opportunity to review the tape and the attending coroner's report, correct?"

"Yes, in detail, Ms. Reynolds."

"The prosecution maintains that the injuries sustained by the individuals ultimately caused their deaths. What is your opinion?"

"I believe that, while possible, it's a huge stretch without a more detailed examination of the bodies."

"How many autopsies have you performed?"

"Over the past twenty-five years, 5,860."

"Is there anything in the autopsies of those men that would lead you to believe they suffered life-threatening injuries before the accident?"

"Based on the severe trauma that the bodies sustained, I would not have given much thought to several welts."

"What is your opinion regarding the possible concussion and neck injury the prosecution claims caused the driver to swerve off the road?"

"Is it possible to pull the video back up? I would like to point something out."

Dakota looked at Judge Still Water, who directed the bailiff to do so.

Once ready, the doctor said, "Please fast forward to the very end and slow down if possible."

The technician did as requested.

"That's perfect," the doctor said at the important point. "Now, please watch the attack angle. This man is struck from left to right. The neck injury that the victim suffered was in the opposite direction. It is my opinion, first, that the blow could not cause traumatic neck damage from the limited rotation of the head, as we see here. Second, even if it could, the blow moved the head in exactly the opposite direction of the fatal injury."

The courtroom sprung to life with chatter.

Sellman sprung up, barking, "Objection, Your Honor, that is speculation."

"Overruled, Mr. Sellman. It is no more speculative than what your expert witness testified to."

Dakota nodded and said, "Thank you, Dr. Weston, no further questions."

The judge said, "Prosecution, your witness."

Joe began to stand, but Sellman pulled him down, whispered something, and sprung up. "Dr. Weston, in your own words, you admitted that it is possible that the injuries could have led to the fatal accident, correct?"

"Possible, but highly improbable."

"I did not ask for opinion, Doctor, only a simple yes or no answer. Is it possible?"

"Yes."

"No further questions, Your Honor."

"Call your next witness, Ms. Reynolds," the judge directed.

"The defense calls Colonel David Johns."

A confident-looking, well-built, middle-aged man approached the stand.

"Please state your name and position, Colonel."

"Yes ma'am. Colonel David Johns, US Army Retired."

"Thank you, Colonel. What was your position with the US Army?"

"I was Jake Michaels' commanding officer on two separate occasions. I also served as commanding officer of Personal Combat Training School."

"Colonel, what type of soldier was Jake Michaels?"

"He was one of my most trusted covert ops soldiers. He was smart, decisive, and cared about his men."

"Colonel, you expressed some concern over the interpretation of the video. Can you go into more detail for the court?"

"Certainly. Can we please replay it?"

The judge nodded to the bailiff.

As it played, the colonel said, "I want to call everyone's attention to the very beginning. As Jake moves into view, notice his stance is neutral. The stick is at his side. The first victim says something that we cannot understand. At that point, Jake makes his comment that we can hear. Can we put this in slow motion, please? Now, and this is very important... watch Jake's head look slightly to the right. Immediately, he moves into a defensive stance. He glances quickly to his right again, then back in front of him. The first man moves forward. Watch his head as he connects to the man's penis. It turns to the right. He knows there's danger coming from that direction. He spins and incapacitates the man filming. At that point, we lose video. If Jake were attacking these men, it would have been from behind. They would have never known what hit them. Jake is *confronting* these men, *not attacking* them. Whatever the first man in front of Jake said, it moved him into a self-defense position. He knew danger was imminent."

The lights came up in the courtroom, and Dakota purposely paused to let the moment sink in. Colonel Johns' testimony was compelling, and she could see by the look in several of the jurors' eyes that it had moved them.

"Colonel, thank you. No further questions."

Colonel Johns looked at Jake, who tilted his head slightly and smiled. He lipped, *"Thank you."*

The judge said, "Prosecution, your witness."

Sellman paused, looked at Joe Ross, and shook his head. "No questions, Your Honor."

"Defense, please call your next witness."

"Your Honor, the defense calls Alex Michaels to the stand." Once Alex sat down, Dakota said, "Mrs. Michaels, please state your full name and relationship to the defendant."

"Alexandra Lorraine Michaels. I'm his wife."

"Mrs. Michaels, everyone in this courthouse realizes how difficult this is for you, given the emotional rollercoaster you've been on for the past year and a half. I want to thank you for taking the stand today. In your own words, please tell the court what kind of man Jake Michaels is."

"I met Jake over thirty years ago. He's the most compassionate, unselfish, caring man I've ever met. He's been a perfect husband, and a great father to our three children."

"Mrs. Michaels, have you ever seen Jake use physical force unless first provoked?"

"No."

"As someone who knows Jake Michaels better than anyone, do you believe he would, without good cause, attack these men?"

"No, there is not a chance in the world."

"Thank you, Mrs. Michaels, no further questions."

"Prosecution, your witness."

Sellman approached the stand. "Mrs. Michaels, is the Jake Michaels that sits in this courtroom the same Jake Michaels that you knew for the past thirty years?"

"Mr. Sellman, I think we all know that answer. Jake's memory is fleeing him. Our life together is moving into the rearview mirror for him."

"Mrs. Michaels, how many years were you with Jake as he served our country?" ·

"Twelve years."

"When Jake would come back from deployments, did he ever confide in you what he was doing?"

"No, I was not allowed to know, and honestly, I didn't want to know."

"Mrs. Michaels, I would have to assume you knew your husband killed people in the course of duty. Correct?"

"Of course, I knew. That's a stupid fucking question."

The courtroom erupted in laughter and applauds, as if they'd been waiting for someone to put Sellman in his place for two days.

The judge slammed his gavel. "Order! Order in the court!"

Sellman's face turned crimson red. He spun and said, "No further questions, Your Honor."

Alex left the stand, and Dakota nodded at her, noting that Jake looked at her and winked.

The judge said, "Defense, please call your next witness."

Dakota leaned over to Jim and whispered, "Should we call Jay to talk about the spell he witnessed?"

"No, we have established Jake's illness. Besides, I am scared Jay might punch Sellman." Jim chuckled.

Dakota turned back to the judge and said, "We have no more witnesses, Your Honor."

The judge nodded and said, "Does the prosecution or defense wish to recall any witnesses?"

"No, Your Honor," both parties said, in turn.

"This Court is adjourned until 9 a.m. tomorrow morning. Both counsels will present their closing arguments."

"All rise." The bailiff announced.

Dakota, Jim, and Jake sat in the safe room.

"Well," Jake said. "How would you say our witnesses did today?"

"I think the colonel's testimony was very compelling," Jim said. "Dr. Taylor's testimony could cause the jury some confusion. If anything, it painted a picture of your character, and your service to this country that has caused long-term medical issues for you. The pity factor may help. As for Alex's testimony, it also painted a picture of your character. I just do not know if any of it will be enough to overturn how the jury sees the video."

"Tomorrow," Dakota said, "Sellman will argue that your character is not on trial, but your actions are. There was nothing in our testimony today that showed you were incapacitated by your illness when you confronted these men. That worries me."

Jim nodded. "I believe we have done a good job introducing Jake Michaels to the jury. We painted a picture of a good man, but good men are found guilty every day." His tone was a bit less than positive.

"So, is it time to look for a plea?" Jake said.

Jim sighed. "Jake, it is a shame that an innocent man must admit guilt. If the prosecution would agree to a plea, which I highly doubt, you would still face jail time. Their weakest charge is Manslaughter, which they may drop. Assault with a Deadly Weapon can carry up to ten years, and they would want the maximum sentence."

Jake looked at Dakota. "What will your argument be tomorrow?"

"I don't know yet, Jake. I want to see what the feedback is in the media tonight. I'm interested in how they look at the colonel's statement. I can drive home the notion that alcohol led to the crash, not their injuries, but... I just don't know. Our case is built around opinions. Their case is built around hard evidence—the video—whether it's complete or not."

Jim stood up. "I will leave you two alone. I am going to review everything and start working on language for the closing argument. I will see both of you in the morning."

Jake looked into Dakota's eyes and smiled loosely. "Well, Counselor, it appears we have quite the quandary here."

"Yes, we do. We surely do."

"So, what's our plan?"

"All we can do is try to figure out how the jury will look at today's testimony, and play on that. Grandfather and I will present a compelling closing argument." She stood. "I need to go and start working on this. I'm going to clear my head and hike to the butte to see Honi. I'll send your family in. Have faith, Jake. This will work out. The Spirits will not let us fall from their grace." She kissed him on the forehead and left.

Alexi walked in. "How are you doing?"

"Nervous. Oh, by the way, your drunken sailor mouth could not have come at a better time." He laughed.

"That guy is a flaming asshole. What kind of question was that to ask the wife of a Special Forces soldier who served in multiple war zones?"

"He was probably heading in a path that showed I led a secret life away from you. He probably will still do that tomorrow, to paint a picture that you really didn't know me. He *is* an asshole."

"Dakota was very quiet when she told me to come in. Normally, she'll talk with me. She looked concerned."

"She is. Our case is built on opinion. They have compelling hard evidence. Were you watching the news in the lobby while you were waiting to come in?"

"Yes, it seems to echo what you just said. There are some who bought into the colonel's testimony, but many feel the attack was unprovoked. Jake, where is this girl? She can free you."

"I don't know, Alexi. She chose not to report it from the very beginning. From what I can recall, they never penetrated her. Perhaps she feels that it wasn't worth pursuing charges against a bunch of rich kids. Perhaps she simply didn't want to go through the scrutiny that sexual assault victims do."

"Jake, I know you're innocent. I know if these three boys were not high profile, the cops probably would not have put much effort into this. The constant craving of today's social media for stories they can debate is feeding this. You're a victim of everything you hated about today's society. You use to tell me, if you could, you would move to a mountaintop and throw away all connection to the outside world. You would be perfectly fine living untethered from society. The irony is, you did it. Ultimately, though, you couldn't escape the tentacles of social media."

He chuckled lightly and looked down at the table, reflecting on the conversation. "You know, for over a year I had no contact with the outside world. I lived as our ancestors did. It's hard living. Once you learn that food, shelter, and companionship is all we need as humans, you understand how far off track we've gone as a species. Laziness drove modernization. Modernization drove greed. As the two fed off each other, basic human needs and principles were lost. The human race *was* lost."

She looked at him and smiled. At that moment, no doubt remained: Jake Michaels would never return to the world from which he walked away. She thought about him spinning in the field on their vacation in Yellowstone. His eyes had sparkled when he said he was *'reconnecting with the land.'* At that moment, Jake already knew where his journey would take him.

"Hopefully," she said, "Dakota and Jim can free you, so you can find peace in this world."

She stood up, kissed him on the cheek, and left.

There was a knock at Joe Ross's door as Sellman and Joe were reviewing their closing arguments.

Sellman snarled, "Who the fuck could that be? I thought your staff had left."

Joe shrugged his shoulders. "Come in."

Jim walked into the office and took the seat offered by Joe. "Gentlemen, let's talk."

Sellman laughed. "Counselor, what can we possibly talk about?"

"Your future, Mr. Sellman. Joe, may I have a word alone with him, please?"

"No, Joe, you can stay," Sellman said. "This fucking guy has been hitting the peace pipe or something."

Joe looked at Jim, and could see a fire in his eyes as Jim's fists clenched. "Sellman, that was unnecessary," Joe said.

Jim ignored them both. "Mr. Sellman, a while back I had a client named Russ Anderson. Do you know him?"

Sellman took a sip of his scotch. "No, Counselor, never heard of him."

"Well, Mr. Anderson was being charged with embezzlement by his partners. He met an untimely death."

"Chief, I don't see where this is going. Don't you have a closing argument to write for that cowardice-piece-of-shit client of yours?"

"This was in my mailbox today, with no postmark on it." Jim threw a file on the table in front of Sellman, marked *Anonymous*.

Sellman took a brief look at it.

"Well, Mr. Sellman, Mr. Anderson's partners were connected to Dibella industries—mainly, the Dibella boys. Someone did a little digging and discovered that Richard Dibella, Marcus Dibella, and one of my client's partners were charged with sexual assault and intent to deliver pornography in Belize. Is any of this ringing a bell, Mr. Sellman?"

Sellman swirled his scotch. "Those charges were dropped. The whore came forward and admitted she was trying to make money off of the Dibellas."

"Of course, they were dropped. I am sure that "whore" is living very comfortably somewhere. If she *is* living."

Sellman's face turned blood red. "Listen here, you backwoods fuck. I don't know what angle you're trying to use here, but it will not save your client. If you came here to try and blackmail me into a plea, you and your half-breed granddaughter can go fuck yourselves. You know that evidence will be inadmissible."

Jim leaned forward and looked Sellman in the eyes. "There are three things, Mr. Sellman. First, I will take my chances on a continuance tomorrow based on new evidence. I am sure the jury will like to know that two of your clients have had prior sexual assault charges. They will also be interested to know about the pornography charges, given the fact that they were filming this encounter. The second thing, Mr. Sellman, is that even if I cannot get it into court, I can get it into the press. I am sure the Dibella family will like that. And the third thing, Mr. Sellman, is that I will remember your comments. You will have to find your way off the reservation. I will wait for you. Good day."

Jim stood up and walked out.

Joe looked at Sellman.

"Fuck him," Sellman growled. "He knows that will be inadmissible. Those charges were dropped. Our clients are not on trial."

"Howard, do you want to take that chance? Maybe we offer a plea and make this circus go away? Would Mr. Dibella want his dead son's names tarnished like this?"

"Fuck Vincent Dibella! He's a pussy! I *am* his muscle. This is about *me*. I don't lose cases, especially to a pair of half-assed, half-breed Indians. The one thing nobody understands is that I could give two shits less about those boys. They were pieces of rich dog shit. I spent too much time keeping them out of trouble, and keeping the Dibella name clean. We go for the juggler tomorrow."

CHAPTER 44
THE FINAL DAY

WooWoo took a sip of his bourbon, paused, and set the glass down. He and Dakota sat in the home office, exhausted from the day.

Dakota settled into the high-backed leather chair, looking into her glass of bourbon as she swirled it. "Woo Woo, we're in trouble, aren't we?"

"I went to see Sellman after court today. I thought threatening him with what we found would move him to at least talk about a plea, but he does not care about the Dibella family. I believe we could get the evidence admitted, but it will probably just prolong the inevitable. The fact that victim admitted she was trying to blackmail the family does not bode well. Heck, social media and the news is bombarded every day with charges against wealthy people. Society is numb to it. Yes, Lomasi we are in trouble."

"One good thing," she said. "All the polls that the media is putting up show most of the results are 50/50. It would appear our witnesses helped."

"The problem is, Lomasi, those people have not seen the video, only written descriptions. They have not seen the autopsy photos showing the bruises and the trauma to the bodies. This is going to be close. I believe Jake and you need to be prepared for some jail time out of this."

"Woo Woo, I still believe the Spirits will intervene." She sighed long and deep. "I'm worn out. I'm gonna get a good night's sleep, wake up, go for a run, clear my head, and finalize our closing arguments. Goodnight. I love you."

Dakota lay in bed and, more than ever, welcomed the hug this room always gave her. She stared at the ceiling and drifted off.

She walked naked through the field in front of the cabin, the warmth of the summer sun kissing her skin. She continued to the waterfall looking for Jake, who was fishing. She moved towards him, and suddenly the ground shook and split in front of her. She yelled for him, and he looked up and ran to her, but the opening was too wide for him to cross.

A glow came from deep inside the earth. Dakota and Jake watched as the light slowly ascended from the depths. As it got closer, they could make out a figure. As the entity reached the top of the opening, the glow was blinding.

They both turned away.

"Open your eyes," a deep but non-threatening voice commanded.

Jake knew the voice, and told Dakota it was the Faceless Indian.

They looked into the glow as it dimmed, and could now see the black abyss had been replaced by a face. It was chiseled but had soft continence. His eyes were steel grey.

"Hurit and Mingan, for thousands of years your souls have traveled the earth apart because of your past indiscretions. You have searched for each other through hundreds of mortal lives, each of those lives ending in great pain and loneliness. It was the curse we put on you, your punishment. For almost ten millennia, you both continued to control your human vessels, to feed your desires. Lust, greed, and selfishness always prevailed.

"Mingan, in this body of Jake Michaels, you learned. You witnessed great selflessness and sacrifice, to spare the ones Jake loved. You did not influence him. The compassion you were created with, which you lost so long ago, has returned. It is time to end your suffering. Hurit stands across the split in this earth, ready to reunite with you for eternity. She must make decisions to end her punishment."

"Who are you?" Jake yelled, defiantly. "Who are Mingan and Hurit?"

"I am the one that Humanity has tempted since the beginning. I am cursed and prayed to. I am feared by Gods and Mortals. I have many names. You know me as Destiny. Mingan and Hurit are two of the First Ones. They fell from our grace and were dammed for thousands of years. They are the second part of your essence, your soul."

"What decisions, what decisions?" Dakota screamed, as the Oracle disappeared.

Jake smiled at her, and then he and Honi walked back to the waterfall.

"Jake, come back! Come back! What decisions do I have to make?"

Dakota sprung up in bed soaked in sweat. Her heart raced in her confusion, as she didn't understand what the Spirit had meant. She covered her eyes and cried as she fell back. The Spirit world had provided her the answer, but she didn't understand. What could she offer so selfless that it would end her punishment?

It can't be to testify that it was me in that video. I can't prove it!

She stared at the ceiling, thinking until it exhausted her.

The alarm rang, and Dakota reached over and hit the off button: 6:00 a.m. Her first thoughts moved right to the dream, which still confused her. She decided to go for a run and try to make sense out of it with a clear head. She had four hours to finish her closing statement and report to the courthouse, so she had time.

She ran down past the barn and into the canyon. As the sun started to rise, she looked up at the sky and prayed for guidance today. As she ran, she thought about every second she'd spent with Jake, searching for some clue as to what her dream meant.

Suddenly, she stopped dead in her tracks.

"Oh my God, the letter! The fucking letter!" She looked around to make sure no one was nearby to hear her, and recited a line from the letter: "Behind the visions of fire the truth lies."

She'd always thought Jake was talking about their visits to the Spirit World in front of the fireplace, but....

"There must be something at the cabin."

She raced to the barn and hopped on a dirtbike. She could make it to the cabin in one and a half hours if she went all out.

Jim and Anna heard the bike rip wide open past the house and up the canyon trail.

"Where is she going, Jim?" Anna said with concern.

"I don't know. Maybe there is something at the cabin that can help Jake."

"She will never make it back in time."

"She is a good rider. She can get there and back in three hours or so. If she hurries, she will make it by court time."

Dakota ripped down the trail with reckless abandon, using every skill she possessed to stay on the path at high speeds. She passed areas where even the slightest mistake would send her into the ravines below, but she didn't care. If she couldn't get Jake off, her life was over anyway. If she couldn't end her punishment, she would live another lifetime searching for him. She trusted the Spirits would deliver her safely to the cabin.

She glanced at her watch when the cabin was a mile ahead.

There's still time.

She roared into the clearing by the cabin, jumped off the dirtbike, and ran up to the door. It was locked, and she'd come without the keys.

"Fuck, fuck, fuck!" she yelled.

She walked around the cabin looking for a window to break, but Jake had boarded them up for the oncoming winter. She stopped, regained her composure, and thought.

The tool shed! Shit! Jake always left a key in there for me.

After grabbing the hidden key, she opened the front door, grabbed a flashlight Jake kept in the kitchen area, and looked at the fireplace. Nothing sat on the mantle or hung from it, so she got down on her hands and knees and looked up inside the chimney.

Nothing.

She sat down on Jake's cot and stared at the fireplace. Despair started to set in as she decided she must have been wrong. She wiped the tears from her eyes, stood up, and looked around the cabin, remembering her time here. It seemed the plans she and Jake had made for their future were dead.

She walked to the door, turned for one last look, and caught a twinkle of light from the corner of the fireplace where it attached to the wall. She walked up to it and, upon seeing a sliver of daylight, shook the loose stone. Puzzled, she pulled it out to find a small pouch, similar to the ones Samuel had used to send medicine to Jake. She opened the sack.

"Oh... my... God!"

She raced from the cabin and jumped on the bike, and took a quick glance at her watch: 8:15 a.m.

Jake walked into the safe room to find Jim sitting there by himself. "Good morning, Jim. Is Dakota getting something to eat?"

Jim looked worried. "No, Jake, she is not here."

"What do you mean? Is she running late?"

"She got on a dirtbike at dawn, and headed towards the cabin like a bat out of hell."

"The cabin? What's in the cabin?"

"I don't know, Jake."

"What happens if she doesn't make it by 10:00?"

"I will start for us. The prosecution will give their closing arguments first, and that windbag Sellman will take forever. She will be here."

Jake shrugged. "Okay, I guess she had her reasons."

"You look worn out today. Are you all right?"

"Yeah, I just had a rough night. I had some crazy dreams."

"Well, that is to be expected."

"What do *you* think, Jim?"

"I do not know. The media polls show anywhere from a hung jury to slightly in the prosecution's favor. I think you need to prepare for the worst. I do not think the judge will impose a maximum sentence when the time comes—he is pretty compassionate—but you will face some time."

Jake shook his head and could only chuckle. "It's a shame, isn't it? Do the right thing and get punished anyway."

"This is our world now. There is no more room for the right thing, if it is boring or unsensational. I am glad I am in my final chapters here."

"It's funny, Jim, but when I was living on that mountaintop, I didn't miss any of this. Granted, I was lonely at times, but all this shit.... I would trade solitude for having none of it, any day."

Jim looked at his watch. "I need to get seated. I will see you in there."

Dakota glanced at her watch as she reached the blacktop outside the ranch: 10:00 a.m. The courthouse was fifteen minutes away.

"All rise, the Honorable Judge Still Water is in Court."

"Be seated, please," the judge said. "Today we will hear closing arguments from both sides. Mr. White Feather, where is Ms. Reynolds?"

"She will be here, Your Honor. She was working on something last minute." Jim looked over at Sellman, raised an eyebrow, and smiled.

Sellman glared at him.

"Very well," the judge said. "The prosecution may proceed."

Sellman walked slowly to the bench, and turned dramatically to face the court.

Just as he started to speak, Dakota busted in wearing running gear, her legs caked with mud and her hair pulled back in a ponytail.

Everyone in the courthouse started talking.

The judge tapped his gavel. "Order please! Ms. Reynolds, I am glad to see you could join us, and dress for the occasion."

"Please excuse me, Your Honor," Dakota said between breaths. "I had engine problems this morning."

The judge shook his head. "Mr. Sellman, please continue."

Sellman looked at Dakota and Jim with puzzlement.

Jim scratched his cheek with his middle finger.

Sellman's face turned red, but he cleared his throat and regained his composure. "Ladies and gentlemen of the jury, today you will hear the closing arguments of a difficult case...."

Jake whispered to Dakota, "Why did you go to the cabin?"

"To end my punishment."

Jake looked at her, astonished. "You had the *same dream*?"

She nodded her head.

"...the defense will maintain that the defendant acted in defense of a young lady and himself," Sellman droned on. "They will point out that Mr. Michaels is a man of good character, that he is a hero to this country. I do not dispute those facts. Mr. Michaels was married nearly thirty years. He served bravely, fighting for this country, and is now medically challenged due to his heroic service. Please remember, the *character* of Jake Michaels is *not* on trial. *The actions* of Jake Michaels are on trial. Please remember, that you *must* make your decisions based on facts and evidence, not opinions and theories. Onus Pobandi, the burden of proof, is the backbone of our judicial system. We have provided that burden of proof. It is clear and evident that Mr. Michaels assaulted those three young men. The Defense *has not* shifted that burden of proof. They have *not* given this court *any* tangible evidence to prove their stance of self-defense. Normally, when I deliver a closing argument, I'm much more verbose. Normally, I have numerous points that I need to counter from the defense. But honestly, I don't have much to say. All I ask is that you make your decision on Jake Michaels' actions, and not his good character. *Good people* sometimes make *bad decisions*. Thank you very much for the time you took out of your life to hear this case. God bless you."

"What a two-faced fuck he is," Jake whispered to Dakota.

"Ms. Reynolds, will you be delivering the defense's closing statement, or will your grandfather?"

Dakota said, "I will be, Your Honor."

"Very well, please proceed."

Dakota stood up and walked over to the table of evidence. She lifted up the flash drive the video was on and held it in front of her. "Ladies and gentlemen of the jury, in my hand is all the hard evidence the prosecution has provided. It is an incomplete tape. I want you to watch this one more time, please. If we may play this again, Your Honor?"

"That's fine," the judge said. "Bailiff, please dim the lights and play the video."

The video started.

"Take off your clothes," echoed over the loud speaker.

"Fuck you," the female snarled.

The camera zoomed in on Dakota as Richard Dibella ran a knife down her cheek.

"If you scream, I will slice that pretty little face of yours, understand...."

"No, Dakota!" Jake yelled. *"Don't!"*

Sellman jumped up and yelled, *"Objection, Your Honor! Objection!"*

The courtroom errupted in disarray, and the judge ordered the bailiff to turn the video off.

Dakota held her back. *"Let it play!"* she screamed over the chaos, as tears poured down her face. "Let everyone see what those pieces of shit did to me. Let them see that Jake Michaels saved my life."

The video continued to play, and the Court watched in horror the assault on Dakota.

Police officers rushed in and restrained her. They turned the video off right as Jake approached the screen.

"Order! Order in the court!" The judge slammed his gavel over and over.

Police officers pulled Dakota from the courtroom.

Jim buried his head in his hands.

Jake starred forward as a surreal quiet blanketed the chaos.

Jim's sobbing echoed through the still courtroom.

Jay walked over and helped him from the table.

Dakota's yells were heard in the hall, sobbing, crying out, *"Let them see what those pieces of shit did to me!"*

Judge Still Water looked at the prosecution. He then looked at the jury, and over the stunned courtroom. "This court is in recess until further notice. Jurors, please return to sequester until I can sort this out. Prosecution, please come to my chambers. Bailiff, please bring me that tape."

The judge, Sellman, and Joe watched the tape from start to finish, and the mood in the room was somber.

Joe shook his head. "Why would they not bring this forward in the beginning? Why would Jake Michaels risk his freedom?"

"Joe, I think these are questions for Mr. Michaels," the judge said.

"Let's bring him in along with his counsel," Joe suggested.

"Which one?" Sellman chuckled. "The one hysterical in the holding cell, or the one crying like a baby in the hallway?"

Joe looked at him. "You're a fucking asshole."

Sellman shrugged his shoulders. "So I've been told."

The judge turned to the court officer. "Bring Jim in, when he is ready, with Mr. Michaels."

"Yes, Judge."

The court officer approached Jay and Jim. "Mr. White Feather, the judge would like to see Mr. Michaels and you in his office, when you are ready, sir."

Jim nodded without saying a word.

"He will be right there," Jay said.

"Jay, I want you in there," Jim said. "I want you to keep me from killing Sellman."

Jay chuckled. "Who will stop *me*?"

They looked at each other and laughed lightly, both finding some levity in the moment.

Jim sat down. Jay stood off to his side, behind Sellman, as a guard escorted Jake into the room.

The judge looked at Jim. "Are you okay, Jim?"

"I am fine, Sam."

"Jim, this is a unique change of events. I want to ask your client a few questions, as does the DA. Is that okay?"

"Of course, Sam."

Joe said, "Mr. Michaels, why did you and your counsel not bring this tape forward in the beginning?"

Jake stood ramrod-straight. "Since the night of the attack, we didn't want to drag Dakota through this. When those boys died, we figured this secret was buried. She didn't know about the tape. I threw the camera they used off the cliffs, but not before I grabbed it. I 've kept it hidden."

The judge said, "Mr. Michaels, do you understand that you were most likely going to lose your freedom over the charges? And all along, you had the proof to exonerate yourself?"

"Yes, Your Honor."

The judge shook his head and leaned back in his chair. "From a legal standpoint, this is difficult. The evidence is inadmissible due to improper procedures to enter it into the courts. In itself, it clearly shows the defendant is innocent. I could declare a mistrial, and the DA could opt not to retry the case. I think if everyone is in agreement, that is the way we will end this."

"The DA agrees, Your Honor," Joe said.

"The defense agrees," Jim said.

"Mr. Sellman, you have not said much," the Judge said.

"Your Honor, I get paid to talk. When my talking does not generate income, I will reserve it for people I find pleasure in speaking with. There is no one in this room—hell, in this state—that I wish to have a pleasurable conversation with."

"Very well, Mr. Sellman, you can leave my office... and this state." The judge looked at Jake and smiled. "Mr. Michaels, you are a free man. Please take that wolf off the butte, so we can all get some sleep in town."

"Thank you, Your Honor. I will gladly do that."

Joe said, "Mr. Michaels, will you go back to North Carolina with your family?"

"No, Mr. Ross, I am going to finish the journey I started." Jake turned to the judge. "Your Honor, is Dakota in trouble?"

"Mr. Michaels, honestly, I have not even given any thought to that. In my opinion, her having to watch that tape over and over during the trial, all the while knowing the truth—it was *her* in that tape, and she was *reliving* it each time—should be enough punishment for anyone. Nonetheless, the BAR will have to decide, not me."

CHAPTER 45
A NEW BEGINNING

The early morning sun shined through the curtains in Jake's hotel room. He walked out on the balcony and looked down the quiet streets of Dubois. The press had left, and the public works department worked dilligiantly to clean up the garbage the crowds had left behind. The chaos of the trial had moved out as fast as it moved in, and Dubois returned to its quiet slumber as winter approached.

He looked up at the butte where Honi still waited for him. Soon, he would reunite with his wolf and head back to the solitude of the cabin.

It was a new beginning.

He was free from the bondage of the legal system, free from the chains of secrecy that had bound him for the past year. He would start a new life with his family. They would stay in touch him from afar, but understand how and why he chose the path he did.

Dakota opened her eyes and looked around at the walls in her bedroom. She stretched and smiled.

It was a new beginning. Now she would be free to move about with Jake.

She walked over to the window and opened the shades, letting the early morning sun shine on her face, and looked towards the cabin. Tomorrow she would join Jake for several days of rest. Her indiscretions in the courtroom would be dealt with. She knew the BAR would investigate and most likely impose some punishment, but for the next couple days, she would block that out of her mind.

Her new life with Jake was all she cared about.

Alexi woke up and looked around her hotel room, at the walls adorned with American Indian decorations. She smiled, thinking about how much Jake had loved walking around the gift shops when they were here on vacation.

It was a new beginning for her.

She would meet with the kids and Jake to hike to the cabin. He'd show them where he lived, where the kids could visit him anytime in the future. Today, she would say goodbye to Jake Michaels. He would move on with the life he was meant to live, and she would move on knowing he was happy, and that she was blessed to have had him in her life. Today would be a proper goodbye to Jake and Alexi.

Jim and Anna sat across the table from each other drinking their morning coffee. Today was a new beginning for them. There are no more secrets to hide except the one that started the legal proceedings. That secret they will keep buried. Ironically, their decision actually worked out best for Lomasi and Jake. They will welcome Jake into the family. He had proven to be a good person. He is a good man for their beloved Lomasi, to take her journey with.

Joe Ross woke up next to Jessica, and reflected on the trial. He'd seen a sharp contrast between a good man and a terrible man. His life fell somewhere in the middle—in between Jake's and Sellman's. He would do some soul searching and decide how he wanted his life to finish, how he wanted to be remembered. Was the fame, power, and money worth turning his back on the values he was raised with in Wind River?

Howard Sellman and Vincent Dibella boarded the private jet. Today they would return to their life of privilege, leaving behind the poverty and strife of the Reservation.

Howard would do damage control for the Dibella family, knowing that Vincent would deal with the truths that had been exposed. Wealth would spin this in a direction relieving Vincent of any responsibility for his boy's actions. His group of friends would feel for him. They, too, had skeletons in their closets.

Jake met with Alexi and the kids in front of the hotel. The kids were excited to be with their dad. They couldn't wait to meet Honi and see where their dad would be living.

Alexi looked happy to see their excitement.

Danielle ran up to Jake and hugged him. "Good morning, Dad. I didn't think I was ever going to be able to do this again."

"Good morning, Sunshine."

"You remembered calling me that when I was young?" Danielle beamed.

"I haven't forgotten *everything*. When we get to the cabin, I'll show you all something."

Jake walked over to John and Robert and hugged both of them. He then walked up to Alexi and hugged her. "Thank you for doing this."

She smiled and nodded.

Jake looked at his family. "Okay, troops, let's head up the mountain."

As they approached the top of the butte, Honi looked down and saw Jake, and put his nose up in the wind. Then he wagged his tail wildly, yelped with excitement, jumped in the air and ran in circles.

Jake looked up at him. "What a big goof he is. Look at him! When we get to the top, let me greet him, and then I'll introduce each of you one at a time, okay?"

Everyone agreed.

When Jake reached the top of the butte, Honi ran at him and jumped up, knocking him down. He licked Jake's face repeatedly.

Jake laughed and tried to calm him down. "Okay, boy, good wolf. Let me up. We have people for you to meet."

Jake looked down to see Alexi wiping tears from her eyes. He thought he should probably know why, perhaps something about the dog he apparently had, but he just couldn't remember.

"John," he said. "Come over slowly."

John walked forward, and Honi put his tail between his legs and started to back up.

Jake said, "Honi, it's okay. John, bend down and hold your hand out."

Honi crept forward and sniffed John's hand.

"Good boy, Honi," Jake said.

Honi looked in Johns' eyes, and must have seen something familiar. He gently pushed John's hand with his nose.

John pet Honi's head gingerly as he calmed.

Danielle and Robert repeated the same exercise.

Afterwards, Jake said, "Alexi, come on over."

"Mom, he's so sweet," Danielle said.

Alexi walked over and crouched down, and Honi looked into her eyes and licked her hand. "You are beautiful," she said, and petted him.

Jake stood up. "Honi, are you ready to go home?"

Honi recognized the word home, which he'd not heard for a while. He wagged his tail and ran up the trail, but stopped to look back at Jake to make sure he was following.

The group started the hike, and Jake pointed out landmarks as they walked. He stopped at a fork in the path. "Follow me. I want to show you all something."

They walked down a short path and came out on a cliff's edge. Below them lay the town, and a view of the mountains as far as the eye could see. The fall foliage painted a landscape only Mother Nature could create.

He smiled. "How beautiful is this?"

His family looked out over the majesty of fall splendor.

Alexi smiled. "How fitting you would be freed during the fall, your favorite time of year. You always said if you could create your own Heaven, it would be fall for eternity."

"This is a beautiful place, Dad," John said. "I wondered what it would be like during the fall. Remember... we talked about it during our vacation?"

"I remember, Son." Jake put his hand on John's shoulder. "Okay, let's get back on the trail. We have about two more miles."

They passed through the Ancient Burial Ground, and Jake told them the story of Arapaho Spirits that guarded it against unwelcome visitors. Ahead, he could see the chimney of the cabin. He was home.

He opened the door of the cabin, and the cold air inside greeted him. "Well, this has been, and will be, my home. It's not very big, but I'll add onto it for when you guys visit."

"It's awesome," John said.

"It's so cute, Dad," Danielle said.

Robert said, "How is the hunting and fishing, Dad?"

"It's fantastic! I'll show you the smokehouse I built, and the trout stream."

Alexi chuckled. "Jake, you always said you wanted a log cabin in the middle of nowhere."

Jake smiled. "Not quite the way I envisioned. Come, let me show you all something." He reached up on the shelf above the wood stove and pulled out a tablet. "In this tablet, I have written everything that I can remember about each of you since I've been here. This is the life that I've forgotten pieces of, the life that I will forget if I don't read this every day."

"Dad, why can't you just bring this home with you?" Danielle said. "We'll help you remember."

"Sunshine, it's more than that. Just because I read this every day, it will not restore my memory. It keeps me familiar with all of you, but the day will come when this will not help me. I'll only remember new events. I know it's hard for you to understand, for all of you to understand, but we'll make the best of it. For me, I need to stay here. This is a simple life. It helps me. I only have to concentrate on basic needs."

After a pause, he stood up and motioned to his family. "Come, let me show you the waterfall and my hot tub."

"Your hot tub?" Robert said.

Jake laughed. "Follow me."

He showed his family the property, and when they got back, he built a fire. The kids went to the waterfall to catch trout for dinner, and while they were out, Jake and Alexi configured the small cabin to allow everyone a place to sleep.

She looked at him. Her eyes welled as a smile crossed her lips. "This reminds me of when the kids were young and we were pressed for money. We would get the smallest rooms possible, but we always made it work. We never missed a vacation."

Jake squeezed her hand. "I remember some of those days."

The family spent the night reminiscing I front of the cozy warmth of the fire. Johnny, Robert, and Danielle talked about moving to Jackson Hole so they could be close to their dad. There was laughter and some tears as the night grew late. One by one, Jake's family fell asleep.

He looked at each of them, grasping for splintered memories. Tonight, with the help of Samuel's medicine, he would form new memories.

He looked at Alexi as shadows from the fire danced off her face. She was as beautiful as the first day they met. Even the disease could not erase that memory. He started to whistle the haunting melody from one of their favorite songs, Winds of Change.

Alexi heard it and opened her eyes. She looked at him, and a tear fell down her cheek.

Deep inside him, a piece of them still existed. They looked into each other's eyes, and she smiled and drifted back to sleep.

When the early morning songbirds woke up Jake, he started the coffee.

Alexi joined him shortly thereafter. "Cowboy coffee?"

"Hell yeah. This will wake everyone up for the hike back to town."

She smiled, nodded, and turned to leave the kitchen. "Let me get the kids up."

Jake watched her, knowing she was fighting a deep sadness, all the while finding ways to accept everything.

After breakfast, Jake led his family to the butte above town. The mood was somber, and he took a deep breath, trying to hold back his emotions as he turned to look at them.

Alexi's and Jake's tear-filled eyes met. They each knew what the future held for their story.

The kids looked away when they saw their dad's tears. Danielle began to sob, while John and Robert looked up, trying to be strong and maintain their composure.

Jake walked to each one of them, but did not say a word. He hugged them, holding each one tightly as they cried.

Honi looked up at Jake, sensing Jake was upset. He whined and licked Jake's hand.

Jake bent down and asked Honi if *he was leaving too*, chuckling between his tears.

The levity broke the gut-wrenching goodbye, helping each member of the family as they wiped the tears from their cheeks and regained their composure.

"You all better get going," Jake said, "or you'll miss your flights. As we planned last night, we'll talk every week online. I'll go to Dakota's office at six o'clock every Friday. You each have her cell number in case of an emergency. She'll get a message to me."

Jake hugged each of the kids a final time and told them he loved them.

He walked up to Alexi. "I know this is not how we pictured our final chapter, but know I loved you more than anything on this Earth. Thank you for being part of my life. I know I will forget us, so I wanted you to hear these words while they still mean something to me. These are the words I wanted to say to you the day I left on the motorcycle, the day I tempted Destiny."

She looked at him, pushed back the long hair framing his face, stared into his eyes and smiled. "Jake Michaels, you have been my life. I could have never asked for a better man to be by my side. I love you and always will, till the day I take my last breath on this Earth. When I do, I know that we'll reunite, and run through this *"piece of Heaven on Earth, for eternity."*

They hugged, then kissed tenderly, holding each other's hands as they pulled apart.

Jake watched his family walk back down to town. They looked back at him occasionally, and he stood tall on the butte with his wolf by his side, his long hair blowing in the wind. They waved one last time to each other, then he turned and headed back to his mountain.

CHAPTER 46
IN THIS LIFE...

Jake and Honi arrived back at the cabin to prepare for Dakota, who would be there around 3:00 p.m. He couldn't wait to see her. Saying goodbye to his family had been difficult, but paled in comparison to the finality of his Pseudocide.

He sat on the cabin porch in the old rocker, looking out at the fall landscape, reflecting on the decisions he'd made over the past year and a half. Choosing Dakota over his family was difficult. When he looked at Alexi last night, flashes of their life passed before him, eliciting a certain degree of guilt. On the outside, it would appear he followed the path of many middle-age men, but the outside didn't know the whole story. They didn't know the forces that had intervened to bring Dakota and him together. The outside didn't understand the Spirits.

He thought about the Spirits' plan. At times, he'd wondered if the drug-fueled visions and lust for a young, beautiful woman weren't the underlying cause of his decisions. He wondered if the loneliness of the mountain, and her vulnerability, hadn't opened the door for them to fall in love, *rather than* the intervention by greater forces.

He reflected on a statement his mom once said. "The definition of insanity is complete freedom." Was his decision to walk away and live without the boundaries of society... insanity? Was the complete freedom of this mountain a manifestation of insanity, one his disease had brought on? He shook off the negative thoughts that clouded him. He would trust the path the Spirits had sent him on.

In the distance, the sound of the ATV came into focus, and Honi's ears perked up.

"It's Dakota, boy. She's staying with us for a while."

Honi ran into the clearing and stood waiting for her.

Jake walked off the porch to greet her.

She pulled into the opening and abruptly stopped the ATV. She jumped off and ran to him, leaping into his arms.

Honi ran to their side.

They hugged and kissed passionately, after which she pulled away and ripped her clothes off.

Jake followed suit.

"Remember what I said?" she said. "When this was over, we were going to spend the weekend naked. I also told you I would have you for dinner." She dropped to her knees and took him into her mouth.

He looked down, and she looked up, not taking her eyes off of his. He tensed with each movement of her head.

Suddenly, she stopped, stood up, and ran towards the waterfall. "If you catch me, I will finish," she yelled back at him.

"Counselor, that is unethical behavior," he shouted as he gave chase.

When he caught her, they fell to the ground and made love.

They lay quietly afterward, enjoying the moment.

"That is just the beginning, Mr. Michaels." She sat up and kissed him. "I cannot believe how warm it is today for this time of the year. The Spirits knew we were going to walk through our Garden of Eden like Adam and Eve this weekend. Let's go down to the waterfall for a swim."

They strolled hand in hand through the meadow, Honi by their side.

Jake said, "So, Dakota, tell me. How did you know about the video? And how did you switch it up at trial?"

"In your letter, you talked about that night and said the truth was in the fire. I was grasping for something to exonerate you, so I trusted my gut and rushed to the cabin. I saw a small glimmer of sunlight peek around one of the stones at the fireplace. I pulled it out and found the tape. The video in the courtroom was on a common flash drive. I went back to my house and transferred the full video to an identical flash drive. When I picked up the court video, I simply switched the two in my hand."

"And there are so many people that do not believe in Divine Intervention," Jake said, shaking his head.

"Jake, you had the truth the whole time. Why did you not tell me?"

"I think you know the answer to that."

They reached the stream at the bottom of the pool.

"Dear God, that water is cold," Jake said. "Shrinkage on the way."

Dakota rolled her eyes. "Not like I haven't seen him before when it's cold. Don't be a baby."

She rushed forward without hesitation and dove through the layer of bright fall leaves that floated on the cold pool. She came up gasping for breath and laughing. "That *is* cold. This will be our last swim of the year."

Jake ran forward and dove into the pool. "Oh my God, forget shrinkage! This will be disappearance!"

They splashed each other a few times and laughed, and Honi jumped at the flying water.

When they'd had enough, they walked hand-in-hand to the shore and sat down in the warm fall sun.

"Jake, I don't ever want to go back to town. I could stay here forever. This is paradise up here, especially when you're with me. We'll figure a way to make the best of both worlds. We have time now, and we don't have to hide."

Jake took her hand as they lay basking in the warmth of the sun, enjoying the peace of their new life.

Dakota broke the silence. "It's getting hot. Let's take one more dip, and head back to the cabin." She jumped up and tugged Jake's hand.

"You are a glutton for punishment," he said. "Okay, last time."

They dove into the cold water, and Dakota swam to the small waterfall and stood up. As the gentle cascade flowed over her, she tilted her head back and pushed her hair into the flow of the waterfall.

Jake couldn't take his eyes off her. She looked so sensual, so exotic. Bright-colored leaves hit the water around her. Despite the cold water, he felt his dick start to rise.

He backed up to bring it out of the water. "Hey, my Indian maiden, I have something for you."

She looked at him, raising her eyebrows. "I thought he was cold?" She walked slowly forward, teasing him as she ran her hands across her hard nipples.

THE BEGINNING...

WATCH FOR BOOK TWO IN THIS "CALL OF DESTINY" SERIES TO RELEASE IN 2020.

Acknowledgements

Many thanks to my wife Lorri, who supported me for the past two years while I developed *The Temptation of Destiny*. Her selflessness and understanding made it possible for me to live in another world for hours each day.

Thank you to Dave Lane (aka Lane Diamond) and Evolved Publishing. Dave saw the potential in a project where others did not, or which others were just not willing to work at developing. He took a chance on a new author with a big, ambitious story.

Another thank you to Dave Lane (aka Lane Diamond), who did a brilliant job of editing. I know I tested his patience at times, but he stood the course and delivered, while teaching me how to be a better writer.

Thank you for the rich culture, the reverence for the world around us, and ancient mythology of the true founders of this country. Indian Nation, your heritage breathed life into some unforgettable characters in this book.

Thank you to the men and women of the Park Services that keep Yellowstone, Grand Teton, and our other National Parks pristine despite the millions of visitors each year.

Thank you to Headwaters Campground at Flagg Ranch, which made my stay at Yellowstone and Grand Teton Parks memorable. Sunrise walks along the Snake River uncluttered my mind.

Thank you to my brother-in-law Harold Drake, who piloted an RV across country and drove for a week in Yellowstone. You allowed me to concentrate on the countryside and develop my storyline.

Many thanks to the beta readers of my first draft of *The Temptation of Destiny*. Your encouraging words propelled me to move this book forward.

To Joe Perkovich and Cody Gibson, many thanks for your honest input on content and cover art.

Thank you to Sam Keiser. Your artwork was spot on.

Last but not least, I thank the Grand Architect of the dreamlike landscapes of the American West. It was the true inspiration of *The Temptation of Destiny*.

ABOUT THE AUTHOR

Like many new authors, I said for years I wanted to write a book. Life, careers, and other necessary evils seemed to always derail that goal. Then, last year, on a road trip out west, I found the spark that ignited *The Temptation of Destiny*.

My journey began in Hazleton, Pennsylvania. After high school, I joined the U.S. Coast Guard, spending the better part of eight years busting holes in the sky on C-130s. After the military, my career path meandered through the financial services industry, auto industry, bar industry, and construction management.

I am excited to start my next adventure with a move out west, and begin work on my second book. New Mexico, The Land of Enchantment, will provide the rich Native American mythology to take readers on another roller coaster ride (as *The Temptation of Destiny* does).

In my downtime, I enjoy hiking and other outdoor adventures with my wife. Hunting, fishing, and doing everything possible to stay from falling into the "status quo," fuels me.

When it's time to wind down this adventure we call life, I hope to be sitting in a cabin high in the alpine forests of the Rockies, spending the days with my wife, children, family, and friends, reminiscing about the blessings this life afforded us all.

D.M. Earley

For more, please visit me online at:
Website: www.DMEarleyAuthor.com
Goodreads: D.M. Earley
Facebook: DM Earley
Twitter: @DMEarleyAuthor

What's Next?

D.M. Earley is already well into the second book in this "Call of Destiny" series, which we expect to release in the spring of 2020. Please stay tuned to his page at our website for updates.

www.EvolvedPub.com/DMEarley

In fact, to make sure you don't miss out on any important announcements, please subscribe to our newsletter below. We do not share your email address or information with anyone, and we never spam you. Indeed, we don't send out that many newsletters each year, but when we do, they always have important information and/or special offers.

www.EvolvedPub.com/Newsletter

MORE FROM EVOLVED PUBLISHING

We offer great books across multiple genres, featuring high-quality editing (which we believe is second-to-none) and fantastic covers.

As a hybrid small press, your support as loyal readers is so important to us, and we have strived, with tireless dedication and sheer determination, to deliver on the promise of our motto:
QUALITY IS PRIORITY #1!

Please check out all of our great books,
which you can find at this link:

www.EvolvedPub.com/Catalog

Thank you!

CPSIA information can be obtained
at www.ICGtesting.com
Printed in the USA
LVHW090805100619
620692LV00012B/749/P